About

Liz Fielding was born ~~~~ Zambia before her twent~~~~ her own special hero an~~~~ way, lived in Botswana, ~~~~ her titles have been nomi~~~~ and she has won the Best Tradi~~~~ Romance in 2000, the British Romance Prize in 2005 and the Best Short Contemporary Romance in 2006.

Scarlet Wilson wrote her first story aged eight and has never stopped. She's worked in the health service for twenty years, trained as a nurse and a health visitor. Scarlet now works in public health and lives on the West Coast of Scotland with her fiancé and their two sons. Writing medical romances and contemporary romances is a dream come true for her.

Born and raised just outside of Toronto, Ontario, **Amy Ruttan** fled the big city to settle down with the country boy of her dreams. After the birth of her second child, Amy was lucky enough to realise her lifelong dream of becoming a romance author. When she's not furiously typing away at her computer, she's a mum to three wonderful children who use her as a personal taxi and chef.

A Christmas Fairytale

LIZ FIELDING

SCARLET WILSON

AMY RUTTAN

MILLS & BOON

First Published in Great Britain 2020
By Mills & Boon, an imprint of HarperCollins*Publishers*
1 London Bridge Street, London, SE1 9GF

A FAIRYTALE CHRISTMAS © 2020 Harlequin Books S.A.

Mistletoe and the Lost Stiletto © 2010 Liz Fielding
A Royal Baby for Christmas © 2016 Harlequin Books S.A.
Unwrapped by the Duke © 2016 Amy Ruttan

Special thanks and acknowledgement are given to Scarlet Wilson for her contribution to the *Christmas Miracles in Maternity* series.

ISBN: 978-0-263-29840-6

MIX
Paper from
responsible sources
FSC™ C007454

FSC
www.fsc.org

This book is produced from independently certified FSC™ paper to ensure responsible forest management.

For more information visit: www.harpercollins.co.uk/green

Printed and bound in Spain
by CPI, Barcelona

MISTLETOE AND
THE LOST STILETTO

LIZ FIELDING

PROLOGUE

Wednesday, 1st December
Appointments for Miss Lucy Bright
09:30 Beauty salon
12:30 Lunch with Marji Hayes, editor, Celebrity magazine
14:30 Celebrity photoshoot (with my mum!)
16:00 Serafina March, Wedding Designer.
20:00 Dinner at Ritz, guest list attached

Lucy Bright diary entry, 1st December:
Wish I could be at press conference for the unveiling of the Lucy B fashion chain this afternoon but, according to Rupert's dragon of a secretary, it's for the financial rather than the gossip pages. Which put me in my place. I can't even appeal to Rupert since he won't be flying in until lunchtime. And how come he gets out of the meeting with the über scary Serafina March? It's his wedding, too.

Stupid question. He's too busy for 'girl' stuff. He's been out of the country more than he's been in it for the last month and at this rate I'll be walking up the aisle on my own.

The celebration dinner tonight is, as I'm constantly reminded, my moment in the sun and, obviously, a morning being pampered, a luscious lunch with the editor of Celebrity and then a meeting with the wedding designer to the stars meets all the criteria for the fairy tale. I am Lucy Bright. It's my name— Lucy B—that's going to be above the doors of a hundred High Street shops come the spring. So why do I feel as if I'm on the outside looking in?

RUBBING at the base of her engagement ring with her thumb so that the huge diamond sparkled, Lucy Bright made an effort to shake off the feeling that things weren't quite as fairy tale as media coverage of her romance with Rupert Henshawe would suggest. Determined to shake off the feeling, she logged into Twitter to update her followers on what she'd be doing for the rest of the day.

Morning, tweeps! Off to have the curls flattened. Again. I swear everyone hides when I turn up at the salon! #Cinderella
LucyB, Wed 1 Dec 08:22

Hair straight for the moment. Fab lunch at Ivy. Lots of celebs. Off to meet Mum for photoshoot. Will update blog later. #Cinderella
LucyB, Wed 1 Dec 14:16

PS Don't miss Rupert's Lucy B press launch live on website feed today, tweeps! 4 p.m. It's going to be so exciting. #Cinderella.
LucyB, Wed 1 Dec 14:18

'Is that the time?' Lucy squeaked.

'We are running a little late, miss.' Rupert's chauffeur

held the umbrella aloft as she ran from the photoshoot to the car.

Little was an understatement. The photographer had been relentless in pursuit of the perfect photograph and she had less than twenty minutes to make the meeting with the wedding planner—sorry, make that wedding *designer*—to discuss a theme for the big day. While it was acceptable, even necessary, for the bride to arrive late at her wedding, Serafina March did not allow the same latitude where appointments with her were concerned.

'There's no time to go home for the wedding file, Gordon. We'll have to stop by the office.' Rupert's deadly efficient PA maintained a duplicate in the office. She could borrow that.

CHAPTER ONE

'LIAR!'

The only sound in the room was the clatter of motor drives as tycoon, Rupert—just-call-me-Prince-Charming—Henshawe's press conference was hijacked by his fiancée, Lucy—I-feel-like-Cinderella—Bright as she tugged off her engagement ring and flung it at him.

'Cheat!'

Every lens in the room zoomed in on the bright splash of blood where the huge diamond found its mark on Henshawe's cheek.

The gathered press pack—city newsmen, financial pundits, television news teams—held their collective breath.

They'd been summoned to a full dress press conference by the Henshawe Corporation. Whatever Henshawe did was news. Good news if you were one of his shareholders. Bad news if you happened to be on the receiving end of one of his corporate raids. At least until recently.

The news now was all about how he'd changed. How, having met his 'Cinderella', he had been redeemed by love and was no longer Mr Nasty, but had been transformed into Prince Charming.

Boring.

This was much more like it.

'Why?' Lucy demanded, ignoring the cameras, the

mikes, dangled overhead, pushed towards her face. The larger than life-sized images of herself, wearing her own custom-made originals of the Lucy B fashions, being flashed across a screen. All she could see was the man on the podium. 'Why did you do it?'

Stupid question. It was all there in the file she'd found. The one she was never meant to see. All laid out in black and white.

'Lucy! Darling…' Rupert's voice was deceptively soft as, using the power of the microphone in front of him, he drowned out her demand to know *why her?* 'These are busy people and they've got deadlines to meet. They've come to listen to the plans I've been making, *we've* been making, for the future of the company,' he stressed. 'Not a domestic tiff.'

His smile was tender, all concern for her. It was familiar, reassuring and even now it would be so easy to be sucked in…

'I don't know what's upset you but it's obvious that you're tired. Let Gordon take you home and we'll talk about it later, hmm?'

She had to fight the almost hypnotic softness of his voice. Her own weakness. Her longing for the fairy tale that had overtaken her life, transformed her into a celebrity, to be true.

She had a Lucy B fan page on Facebook, half a million people following her every word on Twitter. She was a modern day Cinderella, whisked from the hearth to a palace, her rags replaced with silken gowns. But Prince Charming's 'bride ball' had been a palace-generated crowd-pleaser, too. There was nothing like a royal wedding to keep the masses happy.

It was exactly the kind of stunt to appeal to some super-smart PR woman with a name to make for herself.

'Talk!' she hurled back as someone obligingly stuck a microphone in front of her, giving her equal voice power. 'I don't want to talk to you, Rupert Henshawe! I never even want to see you again.' She held up the file for him to see. So that he would know that there was no point in denying it. 'I know what you've done. I know *everything!*'

Even as the words left her mouth, Lucy sensed the mood in the room change. No one was looking at the podium now. Or Rupert. She'd stolen his limelight. She'd stormed into this plush hotel, her head exploding with the discovery that her new and exciting life, their engagement, the whole shooting match, was nothing more than a brilliantly executed marketing plan. The focus was now on her as she put an end to a sham smoke-and-mirrors engagement that was as false as his 'new man' change of heart.

Rupert Henshawe had no heart.

But, as the attention of the room shifted to her, it belatedly occurred to Lucy that this might not have been her best move.

In the months following her whirlwind romance with her billionaire boss she had become used to the press, but this was different. Until now she'd been supported every step of the way, whether the interviews had been personal or about her new role as the face, and name, on his re-branded chain of fashion stores.

When she'd gate-crashed this press conference, she hadn't had a thought in her but to confront the man who had so shamelessly used her.

Now the focus point of every lens, every eye in the room, she suddenly felt alone, vulnerable and all she wanted to do was escape. Escape from the lies, the cameras, the microphones. Disappear. But, as she stepped back, attempting to distance herself from Rupert, from everyone, she stumbled over someone's foot.

She put out a hand to stop herself from falling, grabbing at someone's lapel. There was the ominous sound of cloth ripping and, as she turned, instinctively, to apologise, she discovered that her retreat was blocked by a wall of bodies.

And the man whose lapel she was clinging to was now hanging onto her, pulling her towards him, shouting something into her ear as she was jostled, pushed by other newsmen trying to get closer, photographers shouting to attract her attention.

She forgot all about apologising, instead yanking her arm free. Someone tried to grab the file she was carrying. She used it to beat him off, swinging the tote bag she was carrying to clear a space, provoking a blinding series of flashes as the photographers caught the action.

Another hand made a grab for her in the scrum, catching the back of her coat. One of the buttons flew off and she nearly went down again, but the sight of two of Rupert's bodyguards elbowing aside journalists and cameramen alike as they made their way towards her sent a shot of adrenalin surging through her veins.

Until now she'd only seen the gentle side of Rupert Henshawe, had believed that he was truly her Prince Charming. But she was carrying proof of just how ruthless the man could be in pursuit of his ends and he wasn't going to let her leave with that.

Of course they would make it look as if they were rescuing her from the press scrum, but denouncing him in public, on camera, had put her on the other side.

She'd seen his eyes, the truth behind the soft words, the smile, and she knew that he'd do whatever it took to keep her quiet.

Swinging her tote again in an attempt to batter her way through the enclosing wall of bodies, she managed to make a little headway but then someone grabbed her wrist, a camera lens caught her a sharp blow on the temple and, head spinning, she staggered back.

There was a yelp loud enough to be heard over the bedlam as her stiletto heel encountered something soft and yielding.

As the man behind her backed off, swearing creatively, an apology was the furthest thing from her mind. A gap opened up and she didn't hesitate. She dived through it.

Christmas.

'Twas the season to make money.

Nathaniel Hart paused at the brushed stainless steel rail of the department store founded two hundred years earlier by another Nathaniel Hart, looking back down into the swirling mayhem of spend, spend, spend.

It was a scene being replicated in Hastings & Hart stores in major cities throughout the country as money was poured out on those small luxury items that made such easy and portable gifts. Scent, jewellery, silk scarves, all perfectly placed on the ground floor to be within easy reach for the desperate shop-and-run male.

Women, fortunately, were prepared to put real effort into shopping. They thronged the glass escalators that rose into the atrium as if ascending to the sky. An architectural illusion created by light, glass, mirrors.

He knew it was an illusion because he'd created it, just as he knew it to be a cage. One he was trapped inside.

Lucy's shoulder hurt where she'd charged the emergency exit, setting off a barrage of alarms that lent wind to her heels as she raced down the narrow, darkening streets behind the hotel.

She had no idea where she was heading, only that there

were men on her heels, all of them wanting her, all of them with their own agendas. But she was done with being used.

'Aaargh!' She let out a wail of fury as her heel caught and snapped in a grating, bringing her up with a painful jerk. Someone yelled behind her, closing fast, and she paused only long enough to kick her foot free of the grating, leaving the shoe behind, and race on, casting around desperately for a cruising cab. But there was never one when you were desperate!

Idiot, idiot, idiot…

The words hammered in her head in time to the jarring of her feet on the freezing wet pavement as she ran, dot-and-carry-one lopsidedly on one heel.

She'd just made the biggest mistake of her life. Make that the second biggest. She'd made the first when she'd fallen into the fairy tale trap.

In retrospect, she could see that calling her erstwhile Prince Charming a liar and cheat in front of the nation's assembled press pack had not been her brightest move. But what was a girl to do when her magic castle-in-the-air had just turned into one of those blow-up bouncy things they had at kids' parties?

Stop and think?

Stand back, line up her allies before firing her ammunition from a safe distance? Hardly the action of the girl Rupert had proclaimed to love for her spontaneity, her passion.

That was the difference between them.

The woman who'd appeared on the cover of *Celebrity* wasn't some figment of a PR man's imagination. She was real. Capable of feeling not just joy but pain. Which was why she'd leapt in with both feet, puncturing the fake castle with the four-inch heels of her Louboutins, letting out the hot air and bringing it down around her.

Idiot was right but who, having just discovered that she was the victim of the most cynical, manipulative, emotional fraud imaginable, would be thinking *rationally?*

As for allies, there was no one she could turn to. The press had already bought everyone who'd known her since she was a baby—anyone who had a photograph or a story to tell. Every moment of her life was now public property and what they didn't know they'd made up.

And Rupert owned the rest.

All those people who had fawned over her, pretended to be her friend, there wasn't one she could trust or be sure was genuine rather than someone on his PR company's payroll.

As for her mother...

She had no one and, run as hard as she might, nowhere to go. Her legs were buckling beneath her, lungs straining as she headed instinctively for the sparkle of Christmas lights and crowds of shoppers in which to lose herself, but she couldn't stop.

In moments her pursuers would be on her and she didn't need the dropping temperature, the huge white flakes that had begun to swirl from a leaden sky, to send a shiver up her spine. Then, as she rounded a corner seeking the safety of the crowds of Christmas shoppers, she saw the soaring asymmetrical glass pyramid of Hastings & Hart lighting up the winter gloom like a beacon.

She'd been in the store just the day before on a mission from Rupert to choose luscious Christmas gifts for his staff. Giving the gossip mag photographers who followed her everywhere their photo opportunities. It was all there in the files.

The plan to keep her fully occupied. Too busy to think.

The store seemed to mock her now and yet inside were nine warm and welcoming floors, each offering a hundred places to hide. Within its walls she would be off the street, safe for a while, and she flew across the street, dodging through the snarled-up traffic, heading towards the main entrance, slithering to a halt as she saw the doorman guarding the entrance.

Only yesterday he'd tipped his top hat to her in deference to her chauffeur-driven status.

He wouldn't be so impressed by her arrival today but, dishevelled and limping, he would certainly remember her and, pulling her coat tidily around her and shouldering her bag, she teetered precariously on her bare toe as she slowed down to saunter past him, doing her best to look as if she was out for a little shopping.

'You'll find footwear on the ground floor, ma'am,' he said, face absolutely straight, as he opened the door. And tipped his hat.

Scanning the ground floor from his bird's-eye view, Nat's attention was caught by two burly men in dark suits who'd paused in the entrance. They were looking about them, but not in the baffled, slightly desperate way of men trying to decide what gift would make their Christmas a memorable one.

Men didn't shop in pairs and he could tell at a glance that these two weren't here to pick out scents for the women in their life.

He'd seen the type often enough to recognise them as either close protection officers or bodyguards.

The doorman, well used to welcoming anyone from a royal to a pop star, would have alerted the store's security staff to the arrival of a celebrity, but curiosity held him for the moment, interested to see who would follow them through the doors.

No one.

At least no one requiring a bodyguard, just the usual stream of visitors to the store, excited or harassed, who broke around the pair and joined the throng in the main hall.

Frowning now, he remained where he was, watching as the two men exchanged a word, then split up and began to work their way around the glittering counters, eyes everywhere, clearly looking for someone.

Make that a charge who had given her bodyguards the slip.

In the main hall, mobbed in the run-up to Christmas as shoppers desperately tried to tick names off their gift lists and stocked up on exotic, once-a-year luxuries, Lucy had hoped that no one would notice her. That once she was inside the store she'd be safe.

She'd been fooling herself.

She did her best to style it out, but she hadn't fooled the doorman and several people turned to look as she tried—and failed—to keep herself on an even keel. And then looked again, trying to think where they'd seen her before.

The answer was everywhere.

Rupert was *Celebrity* magazine's new best friend and his and her—mostly her—faces had been plastered over it for weeks. Their romance was news and cameras had followed her every move.

Everything she'd done, everywhere she'd been was a story and, as she tried to ease through the crowd, eyes down, she knew she was being stared at.

Then, from somewhere at the bottom of her bag, her phone began to belt out her *I'm In Love With a Wonderful Guy* ringtone.

Could anything be any less appropriate?

Or loud.

She might as well put a great big sign over her head, lit up and flashing 'Dumb blonde here!'

Hampered by the file, she hunted for the wretched thing but, by the time she'd dug it out of the bottom of the bag, it had gone to voicemail. Not for the first time.

There had been half a dozen missed calls while she'd been making her escape and, as she looked at it, it beeped at her, warning that she now had a text, adding to her sense of being hunted.

She had to get off the ground floor and out of sight—now—and, giving up on the attempt to look casual, she kicked off her remaining shoe—after all, if she was four inches shorter she'd be less noticeable—and stuffed it, along with the file, in her bag.

As far as she could recall, the nearest powder room was on the third floor. If she made that without being discovered, she could hole up there for a while, lock herself in a cubicle and think. Something she should have done before barging into that press conference.

Avoiding the glass lifts and escalators—her red coat was too bright, too noticeable and the people following her had been close enough, smart enough to have figured out where she'd gone to earth—she hurried towards the stairs.

It was a good plan. The only problem with it was that by the time she'd reached the first floor she had a stitch in her side, her legs felt like jelly and her head was swimming from the crack on the temple.

For a moment she bent double as she tried to ease the pain.

'Are you all right?' A sweet lady was looking at her with concern.

'Fine,' she lied. 'Just a stitch.' But the minute the woman was out of sight she slithered behind a floor-to-ceiling arrangement of silver and white snowflakes that had been constructed in the corner where the stairs turned. Safely out of sight, she sank down onto the floor and used her free hand to massage her ankles, which were aching from the strain. She pulled a face as she saw the state of her foot. Her shredded tights. But there was nothing she could do about that now.

Instead, she leaned back against the wall to catch her breath, regarding the state-of-the-art all-singing, all-dancing phone that had so quickly become a part of her new life with uncertainty.

It held all her contacts, appointments. She dictated her thoughts into it. Her private diary. The elation, the disbelief, the occasional doubt. And it was her connection to a world that seemed endlessly fascinated by her.

Her Facebook page, the YouTube videos, her Twitter account.

Rupert's PR people hadn't been happy when they'd discovered that she'd signed up to Twitter all by herself. Actually, it had been her hairdresser who'd told her that she was being tweeted about and showed her how to set up her own account while waiting for her highlights to take.

That had been the first warning that she wasn't supposed to have a mind of her own, but keep to the script.

Once they'd realised how well it was working, though, they'd encouraged her to tweet her every thought, every action, using the Cinderella hashtag, to her hundreds of thousands of followers. Keep them up to date with her transformation from Cinderella into Rupert's fairy tale princess.

Innocently selling the illusion. Doing their dirty work for them.

But it was a two-way thing.

Right now her in-box was filling up with messages from followers who had watched the web feed, seen the ruckus and, despite everything, she smiled as she read them.

> @LucyB Nice bag work, Cinders! What's occurring? #Cinderella
> WelshWitch, [+] Wed 1 Dec 16:08

> @LucyB What's the b*****d done, sweetie? #Cinderella
> jenpb, [+] Wed 1 Dec 16:09

> @LucyB DM me a contact number. You're going to need help. #Cinderella
> prguru, [+] Wed 1 Dec 16:12

Too true, she thought, the smile fading. But not from 'prguru', aka Mr Public Relations, the man famous for selling grubby secrets to grubby newspapers and gossip mags. It didn't matter to him if you were a model in rehab, a politician having an affair with his PA or the victim of some terrible tragedy. He'd sell your story for hard cash and turn you into a celebrity overnight.

Nor any of the other public relations types lining up to jump in and feed off her story. As if she'd trust anyone in the PR business ever again.

She wasn't sure how long the phone would function—Rupert would surely pull the plug the minute he thought of it—so she quickly thumbed in a message to her followers while she had the chance.

And maybe she should update her diary, too. Just in case

anything happened to her. Something else her hairdresser had clued her up on. That she could set up a private web document, record her thoughts on her phone and then send it to be stored on her own private Internet space.

'Think of it as your pension, princess,' he'd said.

She'd thought him cynical, but she had started keeping a diary, mostly because there were some things she hadn't been able to confide to anyone else.

Diary update: *Day hit the skids after the photoshoot when I realised I'd forgotten the wedding file and went to the office to borrow R's copy. His dragon of a personal assistant had gone with him to the Lucy B press launch and her assistant is on holiday so there was a temp holding the fort or I would never have been handed the key to his private filing cabinet.*

I had my hand on the wedding file when I spotted the one next to it. The one labelled 'The Cinderella Project'.

Well, of course I opened it. Wouldn't you?

Now meeting with wedding planner off. Celebration off. Dinner at Ritz most definitely off. As for wedding... Off, off, off.

Time to Tweet the good news.

Thanks for concern, tweeps. Fairy tale fractured— kissed prince, got frog. HEA cancelled. End of story. #Cinderella
LucyB, [+] Wed 1 Dec 16:41

The phone belted out the ghastly ringtone again just as she clicked 'send' and made her jump nearly out of her skin. It was a sharp reminder of the need to keep her head down and she switched it to silent, unable to cut herself off entirely.

There had to be someone she could ring. Someone she could trust. But not from here.

This was no haven.

She had to move before someone spotted her, but first she had to do something to change her appearance.

She'd felt so utterly Christmassy when she'd set off in her bright red coat that morning. Utterly full of the joys of a season that had never before felt so exciting, so full of promise.

Now she felt as conspicuous as Santa in a snowdrift.

She would have liked to abandon it. Abandon everything. Strip off, change back into who she was. Her real self, not this manufactured 'princess'.

Easier said than done.

This morning she'd had everything a woman could possibly want. This afternoon she had nothing in the world except what she stood up in and it was going to be freezing tonight.

But she could manage without the coat for now and, easing it off in the cramped space, she folded it inside out so that only the black lining showed. Better, although she could have done with a hat to cover her head.

She didn't even have a scarf. Why would she? Until half an hour ago she was being chauffeured everywhere, an umbrella held over her head at the slightest suggestion of anything damp descending from the sky whenever she stepped onto a pavement. Cosseted. Precious.

Very precious. A lot of time and money had been invested in her. And Rupert—not the fantasy figure of her dreams, but the real one—would expect, demand a profit for all that effort, cost.

Legs still a little shaky, she shouldered her bag, tucked

her coat over her arm and, still clutching her phone in her hand, peered cautiously around the display.

No sign of any big scary men, or journalists, hunting her down, just shoppers preoccupied with what to wear at a Christmas party or buying gifts for their loved ones. Taking a deep breath and doing her best to look as if it was the most normal thing in the world, she eased herself back into the flow.

It took all her nerve to take one ladylike step after the other, matching her pace to those around her and trying to look as if walking barefoot through the poshest store in London in December was absolutely normal, when what she really wanted to do was take off, race up the stairs two at a time and get out of sight.

She kept her eyes straight ahead instead of looking about her to check for anything suspicious, doing absolutely nothing that might draw attention to herself.

Nat called down to his head of security to brief him on the fact that they might have a 'situation'; something to keep an eye on. That done, he continued his afternoon walk through the store, conscientiously looking in on each department before heading for the stairs to the next floor.

Even at the height of the Christmas buying frenzy the H&H reputation for perfection had to be maintained. He might not want to be here, but no one would ever be able to accuse him of letting standards slip and he was alert for anything that jarred on the eye, anything out of place.

Why, for instance, had the woman ahead of him taken off her coat? Was the store too warm? It was essential that shoppers had both hands free, but it was a delicate balancing act keeping the store comfortable for both staff and customers who were dressed for outdoors.

Not that he was complaining about the view.

She had pale blonde hair cut in soft, corn silk layers that seemed to float around her head, stirring a thousand memories. Despite the fact that they were in the middle of the busiest shopping season of the year, he wanted to slow the world down, call out her name so that she'd turn to him with an unguarded smile...

He slammed the door on the thought but, even while his brain was urging him to pass her, move on, the rest of him refused to listen, hanging back so that he could hold on to the illusion for a moment longer.

Foolish.

She was nothing like the fragile woman whose memory she'd evoked. On the contrary, the black cashmere sweater-dress she was wearing clung enticingly to a figure that curved rather more than was fashionable. No snow queen, this. Inches shorter, she was an altogether earthier armful. Not the kind of woman you worshipped from afar, but the kind built for long, dark winter nights in front of an open fire.

Then, as his gaze followed the pleasing curve of her hip to the hem of her short skirt and he found himself enjoying the fact that her legs lived up to the rest of the package, he realised that she wasn't wearing any shoes.

She might have taken them off for a moment's relief. It wouldn't be the first time he'd seen a woman walking barefoot through the store carrying shoes that were pinching after a hard day's shopping. But she wasn't laden with glossy carriers. The only bag she was carrying was a soft leather tote clutched close to her side beneath the coat, heavy, but with the weight of a protruding file rather than parcels, gift-wrapped by his staff.

But what really jarred, jolting him out of the firelight fantasy, was the fact that one foot of the ultra-fine black tights she was wearing had all but disintegrated. That her slender ankles had been splashed with dirt thrown up from the wet pavements.

As if sensing him staring, she turned, still moving, and almost in slow motion he saw her foot miss the step and she flung out her arm, grabbing for him as she stumbled backwards.

He caught her before she hit the stairs and for a moment they seemed to hang there, suspended above them, his hand beneath her as she peered up at him with startled kitten eyes, her arm flung around his neck.

His head filled with the jarringly familiar scent of warm skin overlaid with some subtle, expensive perfume that jumped to his senses, intensified colour, sound, touch...the softness of the cashmere, the curve of her back, her weight against his palm as he supported her, kissing close to full, soft lips, slightly parted as she caught her breath.

His world was reduced to the pounding of his heart, her breath against his cheek, her gold-green eyes peering up at him over a voluptuous cowl collar that was sliding, seductively, off one shoulder.

She smelled like a summer garden, of apples and spice and, as he held her, a rare, forgotten warmth rippled through him.

CHAPTER TWO

LUCY was drowning in raw sensation. Lying in the arms of a total stranger, drowning in the quicksilver heat of his eyes, his touch, parting her lips to gasp in air, struggling to breathe as she went under for the third time.

What was she thinking? What was she doing?

For a moment her brain, its buffer overloaded with more information, more emotion, more of just about everything than a body was built to handle, had backed up, was refusing to compute.

On some distant level she knew she had to move, run, but here, now, only the most primitive sensations were getting through. Touch, warmth, confusion...

'The bedroom department is on the fifth floor,' someone said with a chuckle as she passed and Nat felt, rather than saw the sudden realisation hit her.

The sheer madness of it. But her reaction was not the same dazed feeling that had him staring at her like an idiot. Not even an embarrassed laugh.

Instead she emitted a little squeak of alarm and squirmed away from him, using her hands and feet to scrabble backwards up the steps before she got far enough away to turn, push herself to her feet and run.

'No!'

It wasn't a command, it was the cry of a man bereft.

'Stop!'

But the urgency of his words spurred her on, giving her feet wings as she bolted, dodging through slower moving shoppers, taking the stairs two at a time, fear driving her escape.

Leaving him shaking, frozen to the spot while visitors to the store flowed around him. Not surprise, or pleasure, or even amusement at an unexpectedly close encounter with a stranger. Raw fear that dredged up the memory of another woman who'd run from his arms. Who, just for a moment, he'd forgotten.

Fear, and the bruise darkening her temple.

Someone tutted irritably at him for blocking the stairs and he forced himself to move, pick up the shoe that had tumbled, unnoticed, from her bag.

He turned it in his hand.

It bore an expensive high-end designer label at odds with the damp edge around the platform sole, splashes of pavement dirt on the slender and very high stiletto heel. This was not a shoe for walking in the rain. It had been made to ride in limousines, walk along red carpets, to be worn by the consort of a very rich man. The kind who employed bodyguards.

Could she be the one the two men on the ground floor were seeking? That might explain her fear, because she hadn't run from his touch. On the contrary, she'd been equally lost, wrapped up in a sizzling moment of discovery until a crass comment had jolted her back to reality.

He didn't know who she was or why they were looking for her, only that she was afraid, running perhaps for her life, and the last thing he wanted was to draw more attention to her. No one hunted a frightened woman in his store, not even him, and he clamped down on the swamping need to race after her, reassure her, know her.

Not that there was any need to hunt.

If she was looking for a hiding place, common sense suggested that she was heading for the nearest Ladies cloakroom, looking for somewhere to clean up, hide out for a while.

But why?

His jaw tightened as he continued up the stairs with rather more speed, fighting to hold back the memories of another frightened woman. Vowing to himself that, who-ever she was, she'd find sanctuary within his walls. That history wouldn't repeat itself.

He'd ask one of the senior floor managers to check on her, return her shoe, offer whatever assistance she felt appropriate. A new pair of tights with the compliments of the store. A discreet exit. A car, if necessary, to take her wherever she needed to go.

But his hand was shaking as he called Security again, wanting to know where the two men were now.

Before he could speak, he was practically knocked off his feet by one of them, racing up the stairs, heedless of the safety of the women and children in his way, running through, rather than around them, scattering bags, toys.

His first reaction was to go after him, toss him bodily out of the store, but a child was crying and he had no choice but to stop and ensure that no one was hurt, pick up scat-tered belongings and summon one of his staff to offer the courtesy of afternoon tea in the Garden Restaurant. Deal with the complaints before they were voiced. It was a point of honour that no one left Hastings & Hart unhappy.

But, all the time he was doing that, the questions were pounding at his brain.

Whose bodyguards? Who was her husband, lover? More to the point, who was she?

And why was she so scared?

While her face—what had been visible over the big, enveloping collar—had seemed vaguely familiar, she wasn't some instantly recognizable celebrity or minor royal. If she had been, her bodyguards wouldn't have wasted time scouring the store for her but would have gone straight to his security staff to enlist their help using CCTV. Keeping it low-key. No drama.

There was something very wrong about this and, moving with considerably more urgency now, he ordered Security to find and remove the two men from the store. He didn't care who they worked for, or who they'd lost, they had worn out their welcome.

'Hold the lift!' Lucy, trembling more now than when she'd run from the press conference, heart pounding beyond anything she'd ever experienced, sprinted for the closing doors. 'Thanks,' she gasped as someone held them and she dived in, squeezing into a corner, her back to the door where she wouldn't be instantly visible when they opened again. Her brain working logically on one level, while everything else was saying, no... Go back...

'Doors closing. Going down...'

She snapped out of the mental dream state in which she was floating above the stairs, her whole world contained in a stranger's eyes.

Nooooo! Up, up...

The recorded announcement listed the departments as, despairing, she was carried back down to the ground floor. *'Perfumery, accessories, leather goods, stationery. Ground floor. Doors opening.'*

As the doors slid open, she risked a glance, then froze as she caught sight of one of Rupert's bodyguards scanning the surge of passengers making a beeline for the exit.

She pressed herself back into the corner of the lift,

keeping her head down, drawing a curious glance from a child who looked up at her as the lift rapidly filled. Holding her breath until the doors finally closed, aware that it wasn't just the people she recognized who would be searching for her.

She'd got used to the front page—she'd been booked for a photoshoot this afternoon just to show off her new haircut, for heaven's sake—but this was different.

She'd announced to the world that she had the goods on Rupert Henshawe and it wouldn't be just the gossip magazines who'd want to know where she was.

Within hours there would be a press-orchestrated manhunt. It was probably already underway. And there was the risk that any minute now someone was going to say Excuse me, but aren't you, Lucy B?

It had happened before when she'd been shopping and the result tended to be mayhem. It was as if everyone wanted to touch her, capture a little of the magic.

Rupert's marketing men had got that right, but it was the last thing she wanted now so she kept her head tucked well down, desperate not to catch anyone's eye.

Not all eyes were over five feet from the ground, however, and she found herself being scrutinised by the little girl, who continued to stare at her as the recorded announcement said, '*Going down... Sporting goods, gardening and recreation, electrical. And...*' there was a pause. '*...The North Pole...*'

The rest was drowned out by whoops of excitement.

'Are you going to see Santa?' the child asked her as the doors closed.

Santa?

Well, that explained why the North Pole had been relocated to a department store basement.

'We're going on a sleigh ride to see him at the North Pole,' she confided.

'Well, golly... What a treat.'

Right now a sleigh ride to the North Pole was exactly what she could do with. She'd planned to clean herself up, certain she'd be safe for a while in the Ladies. She didn't know what had made her look back. Just a feeling, a prickle on the back of her neck...

The man following her hadn't been a bodyguard. She knew them all and that wasn't a face she would have forgotten.

Eyes grey as granite, with just a spark of silver to lighten an overall sense of darkness; a reflection from the store's silver and white decorations, no doubt. That moment of magic was all in her imagination. It had to be. Whoever he was, he'd oozed the kind of power and arrogance she'd come to associate with Rupert's most intimate circle.

He was a power broker, the kind of man who took orders rather than giving them. She'd learned to recognise the type. Mostly they ignored her and she was happy about that, but there had been an intensity in his look as he'd caught her, held her, that had turned her bones to putty. And not with fear.

A déjà vu moment if ever there was one, the difference being that whatever Rupert had been feeling on the day he'd picked her up, dusted her off, all concern and charm, her heart rate hadn't gone through the roof. The air hadn't crackled, sizzled, fried her brains. He'd taken his time, wooed her so gently, so...so damn *sweetly* that she'd fallen for every scummy lie. Hook, link and sinker.

She'd thought he was the genuine article, a real Prince Charming, when the truth was he hadn't actually fancied her enough to jump her bones.

The grey-eyed stranger, on the other hand, had made

her forget everything with a look. It was as if his touch had
fired up some deep, untapped sexual charge and she felt
her skin flush with heat from head to toe at the memory,
the promise of the kiss that she'd been waiting for all her
life. The real thing.

Maybe.

She shivered. Shook her head. She'd been drawn into a
web of lies and deceit and she would never be able to trust
anyone ever again. Never be able to take anyone at face
value.

Mortified as she'd been at being discovered as good as
kissing a total stranger on the stairs, that remark had jolted
her back to reality. Common sense and self-preservation
had kicked in and she'd run because there were some mis-
takes a smart woman didn't make twice.

Some she didn't make once.

She'd thought the Ladies room would provide a safe
haven but, even as she'd bolted, she'd realised her mistake.
It would be obvious to anyone with half a brain cell that
was where she'd take cover and in the nick of time she'd
seen the trap. That it was a dead end with only one exit.

It was several hours until the store closed, but Rupert
was a patient man. He'd wait, call up female reinforce-
ments to keep an eye on her until she had no choice but to
emerge.

He had enough of them.

All those women in his office who'd collaborated with
him in the make-believe.

What she needed was somewhere to hide, a bolt-hole
where no one would ever think of looking for her while
she considered her options. Easier said than done.

All she possessed in the world was what she currently
wore. She'd been too shocked to plan anything. To even
think of going back to the little apartment at the top of

Rupert's London house. Packing the gorgeous wardrobe that was all part of the fantasy. Always supposing she'd got out with a suitcase.

No doubt someone would have delayed her while the alarm was raised and Rupert was warned that the game was up.

And she'd bet the farm that the platinum credit cards Rupert had showered on her would go *uh-uh* if she attempted to use them.

Or maybe not. Could he use them to track her movements? Or was that just something they did in TV thrillers?

Either way, they were useless. Not that she wanted anything from him. Right now she wished she could rip off the clothes she was wearing and toss them in the nearest bin.

Since she was trying not to draw attention to herself, that probably wasn't her best option.

Not that she'd done such a good job of keeping a low profile, she thought, still aware of the tingling imprint of a stranger's kiss.

'Do you think there'll be room on the sleigh for me?' she asked the little girl.

She lifted her shoulders in a don't-know shrug, then said, 'Do you believe in Santa Claus?'

Tough question. Right now, she was having trouble believing that the sky was blue.

'My big sister said there's no such person,' she added, then stuck her thumb in her mouth, clearly afraid that it might be true.

Okay, not that tough.

In her years working in the day-care nursery, she'd come across this one plenty of times. Big sisters could be the pits, although right now she wished she had one. A really cynical, know-it-all big sister who would have ripped away the rose-tinted spectacles, shattered her naivety, said, *Prince Charming? Are you kidding? What are the odds?*

She wasn't about to let that happen for this little girl, though. Not yet.

'Your sister only told you that because she thinks that if you don't write to Santa she'll get more presents.'

The thumb popped out. 'Really?'

Before she could reply, the lift came to a halt and the doors opened, sending her heart racing up into her mouth. Under cover of the mothers, dads, children pouring out, she risked a glance.

There were no dark-eyed men lying in wait for her, only more parents with hyped-up children, clutching gifts from Santa, waiting in a magical snowy landscape to be whisked back up to the real world. Which was where she'd go if she didn't make a move and get out of the lift. And that was not an appealing place right now.

Nowhere near as attractive as the North Pole, which the finger-post sticking out at an angle from a designer snowdrift suggested was somewhere to her right. As if to confirm that fact, an ornate sleigh was waiting in a glittering ice cave, ready to whisk the children away.

They stampeded towards it, climbing aboard while their mothers dealt with the more mundane matter of checking in with the elf in charge of the departure gate. Trips to the North Pole did not, after all, come cheap.

She barely hesitated.

She could do with a little magic herself right now and Santa's Grotto had to be just about the last place anyone would think of looking for her.

As she stood in the queue she nervously checked her phone—it was as good a way to keep her head down as any.

There were half a dozen texts, voicemail messages and the twittersphere had apparently gone mad. *WelshWitch* had started it with—

Where is Cinderella? What have you done to her? Tell the truth, Your Frogginess! RT@LucyB Kissed prince, got frog. #Cinderella
WelshWitch, [+] Wed 1 Dec 17:01

It had already been replied to by dozens of people. Rupert was going to be furious, but since this—unlike all her other social media stuff set up by his PR team—was her personal account, there wasn't a thing His Frogginess could do about it. At least not while she managed to stay out of his way.

What he might do if he caught up with her was something else. She shivered involuntarily as she continued to scroll through the tweets.

There was another one from Jen.

@LucyB If you need a bolt-hole, DM me. #Cinderella
jenpb, [+] Wed 1 Dec 17:03

In a moment of weakness she almost did send her a direct message. But then she came to her senses and shut the phone.

That was what was so horrible about this. It wasn't just Rupert she couldn't trust.

She'd chatted daily on Twitter. She had nearly half a million 'followers', an army of fans on Facebook, all apparently fascinated by her story, her amazing new life. But who were they really?

Jen had seemed like a genuine friend, one of a few

people who, like WelshWitch, she constantly tweeted with, but suppose she was just another of Rupert's people? Someone the PR company had delegated to stay close. Be her 'friend', guide her tweets, distract her if necessary, steer her away from anything controversial? She was well aware that not everyone in the Twittersphere was who or what they seemed. Logging into her appointments, she scrolled down and, under the crossed-through entry for *Dinner at Ritz*, she added another entry—

Rest of life: up the creek.

And then her thoughts shifted back to the man on the stairs. His face forever imprinted on her memory. The strong jaw, high cheekbones, the sensuous curve of his lower lip...

'Can I help?'

She jumped, looked up to discover that everyone else had moved off and she was being regarded by a young elf.

'Oh...um...one adult to the North Pole, please,' she said, closing her phone and reaching for her purse, wondering belatedly how much it would cost. She didn't have that much cash. With a fistful of credit and charge cards, she hadn't needed it. 'A single will do,' she said. 'I'm in no hurry. I can walk back.'

He grinned appreciatively but said, 'Sorry. This flight has closed.'

'Oh.' It hadn't occurred to her that there wouldn't be any room. 'How long until the next one?'

'Forty minutes, but you have to have a pre-booked ticket to see Santa,' he explained.

'You have to book in advance?' Forty minutes! She

couldn't wait that long. 'Where's the magic in that?' she demanded.

'There's not much magical about dozens of disappointed kids screaming their heads off,' he pointed out.

'True…' She had enough experience with screaming children not to argue. 'Look, I don't actually want to have a one-to-one with the man himself. I just need to get to the North Pole,' she pressed as the doors to the ice cave began to close. 'It's really urgent…'

It occurred to her that she must sound totally crazy. That, shoeless and apparently raving, she was going to be escorted from the premises.

It didn't happen. Apparently, someone who could cite 'elf' as his day job took crazy in his stride because, instead of summoning Security, he said, 'Oh, *right*. I was told to look out for you.'

What…? *Nooooo!*

'You're from Garlands, right? Pam's been going crazy,' he added before the frantic message from her brain to flee could reach her feet. 'She expected you ages ago.'

'Garlands…'

What the heck was that? The department responsible for store decorations? Did a snowflake need straightening? A tree trimming?

Whatever.

She was up for it, just as long as she was out of sight of the lift.

'You've got me,' she said, neither confirming nor denying it. 'So, *now* do I get a ride on the sleigh?'

'Sorry,' he said, grinning. 'The sleigh is for paying customers only. Staff have to put on their snow shoes and walk. Both ways,' he added with relish. Clearly this was a young man who enjoyed his job. 'Don't look so worried.

I'm kidding about the snow shoes.' He looked at her feet and, for a moment, lost the thread.

'It's a long story,' she said.

'Er...right. Well, you're in luck. There's a short cut.' He opened a door, hidden in the side of a snow bank and tucked behind the kind of huge Christmas tree that you only ever saw in story books. Smothered with striped candy canes, toys, beautiful vintage decorations. 'Turn left, ask for Pam Wootton. She'll sort you out.'

'Left...Pam... Got it. Thanks.'

Better and better. She'd be much safer behind the scenes in the staff area.

Forget Pam whatever-her-name-was. She'd keep her head down until closing time and then leave through the staff entrance with everyone else. By then, she might even have worked out where she could go.

'She's not in there, Mr Hart.'

'Are you sure? She hasn't locked herself in one of the cubicles?'

'All checked. That's what took me so long.'

'Well, thanks for looking,' he said, outwardly calm.

'No problem.' She hesitated, then said, 'The lifts are right opposite the stairs. If she got lucky with the timing, she might have doubled straight back down to the ground floor and left the store.'

'It's possible,' Nat agreed, although he doubted it. He had her shoe and no one with a lick of sense would choose to go barefoot from the warmth of the store into the street. She was still in the store; he was certain of it. And, with nine sales floors, she had plenty of places to hide.

In her shoes—or, rather, lack of them—where would he go? What would he do?

If it was serious—and her fear suggested that this wasn't

just some rich woman wanting a little time out—changing her appearance had to be the first priority. Not a problem when she had a store full of clothes and accessories to help her, except that would mean exposing herself while she stood in line to pay for them.

Maybe.

Just how desperate was she?

Desperate enough to grab something from a rail, switch clothes in one of the changing rooms? When they were this busy it wouldn't be that difficult and she could rip out the security tags without a second thought. It wouldn't matter to her if the clothes were damaged, only that they didn't set off the alarms when she walked out of the store.

'I'll put the shoe in Lost Property, shall I?'

'No!' Realising that he'd overreacted, that she was looking at him at little oddly, he said, taking the shoe from her, 'I'll do it. I've already wasted enough of your time. Thanks for your help.'

'No problem, Mr Hart. I'll keep my eyes open.'

He nodded, but doubted she'd see her and, more in hope than expectation of finding some clue, he retraced his steps back down to the first floor, where he stopped to take another look out over the busy ground floor.

As the afternoon had shifted into evening and offices had emptied, it had become even more frantic, but he would have spotted that black dress amid the madness, the pale blonde swish of hair. That was a real giveaway, one that she should cover up as quickly as possible.

She'd need a scarf, he thought. Or a hat. A hat would be better. It would not only cover her hair, but throw a shadow over her face where a scarf would only draw attention to it.

And once she'd changed her appearance she could risk the shoe department. He'd wait there.

As he started down the stairs, he noticed a display slightly out of alignment, stopped to adjust it and saw a lace-trimmed handkerchief lying on the floor.

He bent to pick it up and caught again that faint, subtle scent that hadn't come out of any bottle.

Had she dashed in from the street to take cover, bolted up the stairs, paused here for a moment to catch her breath, get her bearings?

Where was she now?

Famous last thoughts.

The minute Lucy opened the door to the staff area she was leapt upon by a flushed and harassed-looking woman wearing a security badge proclaiming her to be Pam Wootton, Human Resources.

'At last! The agency said you'd be here an hour ago. I'd just about given up hope.'

Agency? Oh, good grief, the elf hadn't been talking about Christmas garlands but the Garland Agency. The suppliers of the crème de la crème of secretarial staff. She'd had an interview with them when she was looking for a job but she didn't have the kind of experience it took to be a 'Garland Girl'.

There was a certain irony in being mistaken for one now, but she wasn't going to let that stop her from grabbing the opportunity with both hands.

'I'm soooo sorry. The Underground…' She didn't have to say another word. It was the excuse that just gave and gave. 'And it's started to snow,' she threw in for good measure.

'Snow! Oh, great,' Pam said. 'That's all I need. Getting home tonight is going to be a nightmare.' And she pressed her hand to her forehead as if trying to keep her brain in.

'Are you all right?' Lucy asked, forgetting her own wor-

ries for a moment. The woman looked flushed and not at
all well.

'Ask me again in February,' she replied with a slightly
hysterical laugh. 'When the January sales are over.' Then,
pulling herself together, 'It's just a bit of a headache. I'll
take something for it when I get back to the office. Come
on, there's no time to waste. Let's get you changed.'

'Changed?'

'Into your costume,' she said, opening a cupboard and
revealing a rail of short green tunics. Then, glancing back
at her, 'Didn't they tell you anything...' she looked at her
clipboard '...I don't seem to have your name.'

'Lu...' *Noooooo!*

Pam looked up. 'Lou? As in Louise?'

Gulp.

'Yes! Louise.' Whew. Pam was still waiting. 'Louise...
Braithwaite.' It was the first name that came into her
head.

'And you *have* got a CRB Certificate, Louise?' Pam
asked, pen poised to tick boxes, going through the
motions.

'A CRB Certificate?'

She sighed. 'You can't work in the grotto without a crim-
inal records check. I did explain the situation to Garlands.
If you haven't got one...'

Grotto?

The penny dropped.

Pam had mistaken her for an elf.

Out of the fairy tale frying pan, into the...um...fairy
tale fire...

CHAPTER THREE

'DIDN'T Garlands explain?' Pam asked.

'It was a bad connection…' so bad it was non-existent '…I must have missed that bit. But I have been CRB checked,' she said. 'I worked in a day-care nursery before… Well, until recently.'

Oh, boy, Lucy Bright. The ability to look someone in the eye and tell a big fat lie had to be catching. His Frogginess would be proud of her.

Not that she'd lied about having a CRB Certificate. It wasn't under the name Louise Braithwaite, of course, but it was the real deal. She'd had to have one for the day job at the nursery while she'd been studying at night school. She'd worked as a waitress in the local pizza parlour on her free evenings and at the weekends to earn the money to pay for her course.

Much good it had done her.

She'd applied for hundreds of jobs before she'd got an interview for a clerical assistant post at the Henshawe Corporation. The fact that there had been an interview panel for such a junior position had thrown her, but it had been very informal. They'd been incredibly impressed at how hard she'd worked and encouraged her to talk about her ambitions.

She still remembered the stunned silence when she'd

finished telling them passionately that she wanted to prove herself. Make something of herself, be someone. And then they'd applauded her.

When, the following day, they had called her to offer her a job, she'd thought herself the luckiest woman in the world.

'I realise that Garlands know what they're doing, but I still have to ask,' Pam muttered. 'It's been so difficult since the new laws about working with children were introduced. We normally get in drama students at Christmas but not too many of them have had the foresight to get a CRBC. I don't suppose they see themselves doing a Christmas gig as one of Santa's Little Helpers when they get a place at RADA. That's why I called Garlands.'

'They supply elves?' she asked, which got her an odd look.

'They place temporary nannies.'

'Just kidding.' *Whew...*

Pam stared down at her feet. 'What happened to your shoes?'

'I broke a heel in a grating.' The truth, the whole truth and almost nothing but the truth...

'Oh, bad luck.' They shared a moment of silent mourning, then, pressing on, 'You're a bit buxom for an elf,' she said, looking at her doubtfully, 'but beggars can't be choosers. There should be something that fits.' She held one of the tunics up against her, then thrust it at her, piling the rest of the costume on top. 'You've got small feet. These should do.' She put a pair of soft felt bootees on top of the pile and then took a small plastic pouch out of a box and added that to the pile. 'The elf make-up pack. Rouge for your cheeks, a pencil for freckles—you'll find a picture of what's required inside. And there's a pad to remove your nail polish. You can change down here,' she said, leading the way down a short flight of steps. 'Find a spare locker for your clothes and be as quick as you can.'

She opened a door and Lucy found herself confronted on one side by a vast locker room that seemed to stretch to infinity and on the other by a room providing not only loos and basins, but showers, too.

She quickly crammed her coat and bag into an empty locker, stripped off her dress, tossed the shredded tights in a bin. There was no time for a shower so she dunked her feet, one at a time, in a basin of warm water to wash off the street dirt, half expecting Pam to burst in with the real elf at any minute.

She didn't but, until she did, she was grateful for being in the warm and, more importantly, in a very neat disguise.

She dabbed circles of rouge on her cheeks, scattered a few freckles across her nose, then a few more, before removing the nail polish that had been applied at great expense just hours ago. A shame, but clearly elves didn't have bright red nails.

Finally, she donned the costume, tucking her hair out of sight under the pointy felt hat and regarded herself in a handily placed mirror.

It wasn't a good look.

The green and white striped tights made her legs look fat and the tunic was doing her bum no favours. Right now, she didn't care.

Diary update: *The day has gone from bad to surreal. I've been mistaken for an elf. Not an entirely bad thing since I'm off the streets and I've been supplied, free of charge, with a neat disguise. It's just temporary, of course, like the new name. What I'm going to do when Hastings & Hart closes at eight o'clock is my next problem. But with luck I've got three hours breathing space to work on a plan, always assuming the real elf doesn't turn up in the meantime.*

Three hours to get my breath back after a very close encounter with Mr Tall, Dark and Dangerous.

Lucy ran her tongue over her lips to cool them, then shook her head and stuffed her phone and her locker key into the little leather pouch on her belt before presenting herself for inspection.

Pam sighed, adjusted the hat so that a little more of her hair showed. 'You've been a little heavy-handed with the freckles.' Then, frowning, 'Is that a bruise?'

'It's nothing,' she said. 'Someone caught me with a bag,' she said.

'The Underground just gets worse… Never mind.' She took a small camera from her pocket. 'I'll just take a picture for your ID. Say cheese…'

'Cheese.'

'Great. I'll log you into the system later. Sort you out a swipe card.'

'Swipe card?'

'It's how we keep track of staff. How we know who is working, how long they've worked and that they've left the premises at the end of the day. You'll need it to get out and, hopefully, get in again tomorrow.'

'Oh, right. Absolutely.'

'Come on. I'll take you to meet Frank Alyson, Deputy Manager of the toy department and Chief Elf, and then you can get started.'

She passed her over to a tall lugubrious man wearing a long green tunic. She sort of sympathised with him. It couldn't be much fun being a middle-aged man with his dignity in shreds, but walking around Santa's grotto in a suit and tie would undoubtedly compromise the illusion.

'Louise Braithwaite,' Pam said, her voice fading to nothing as she introduced her. She cleared her throat, gathered herself. 'Be nice to this one. Elves don't grow on trees, you know.'

'Don't they? You surprise me. Most of them appear to have sawdust for brains.' He gave her a look that suggested he had no hopes that she had anything but wood pulp between the ears before turning back to Pam. 'You look ghastly. Go home. You'll be no use to anyone if you're ill.'

'And ho, ho, ho to you, too,' she said as she walked away.

'You could have handled that better,' Lucy said without thinking. She was good at that. Saying the first thing that came into her head. According to her file—the one she wasn't supposed to ever see—it had been her most usable asset. That and her passion. People would, apparently, "...*instantly warm to her enthusiasm, her natural openness and lack of guile...*"

They'd nailed that one.

It was saying the first thing that came into her head without thinking that had got her into this mess in the first place and now Frank was staring at her, clearly unused to criticism. Or maybe he was wondering where he'd seen her before.

'So, what happened to the last elf?' she said to distract him.

'She asked too many questions and I fed her to a troll,' he replied.

Sheesh...

'Anything else you'd like to know?'

She pressed her lips together and shook her head.

'Fast learner,' he replied with satisfaction. 'Keep it up and we'll get on.'

'Great.' She couldn't wait.

'So, Louise Braithwaite, what can you do?'

Do?

Wasn't standing about in a pointy hat and stripy tights enough?

Obviously not. Through a small window in his office, she could see an army of elves busily 'constructing' toys in Santa's workshop. They were dressing teddies and dolls, test-driving remote-controlled cars and encouraging children to join in and help them while they waited their turn to see Santa.

Otherwise known, if you happened to have a cynical turn of mind—and she'd just had a crash course in cynicism from a world master—as try-before-you-buy.

'Have you any experience?'

'Of being an elf?' Was he kidding? 'No,' she admitted quickly, 'but I am used to working with children. They tend to throw up when they get over-excited. Just tell me where the bucket and mop are kept and I'll cope.'

That earned her something that might have been a smile. 'Well, I have to admit that you're less of a fool than the last girl Pam brought me. She couldn't see past her mascara.'

Lucy resisted the urge to bat her expensively dyed eyelashes at him, but it was harder to keep the smile from breaking out. And why not? She was safe.

Without a pre-booked ticket, no one, not even Rupert's bodyguards, would be able to get beyond the entrance. More to the point, they'd realise that she couldn't either and wouldn't even bother. For the moment, at least, she could relax.

And what about grey eyes?

The thought popped, unbidden, into her head. The

thought of those eyes, a mouth that gave her goosebumps just thinking about it.

For heaven's sake, Lu...Louise Braithwaite, get a grip!

What would a man on his own be doing in Santa's grotto? And why would she care? He was the last person on earth she wanted to see.

Not that he'd recognize her dressed like this.

Even if, beneath the rouge and abundant freckles, someone spotted a passing resemblance to the face that had been on the front cover of *Celebrity* magazine a dozen or more times in the last few months, they would dismiss it. Why, after all, would Lucy B, aka Cinderella, be working as an elf in a department store?

'You can start by tidying up, straightening shelves while you find your way around. When you've done that you can take the empty space on the bench, dressing dolls and teddies. You'll have to fit in a break with the rest of the staff.'

'Right. Thanks.'

She stood in the doorway for a moment, taking a look around, familiarising herself with the layout before launching herself into the mix of elves, children and parents.

This was all new to her. Shunted around the care system all her life, she'd never been taken to see 'Santa' when she was a child. Even if she had got lucky, it would never have been like this.

The grotto had been designed to give children the illusion that they were in Santa's North Pole workshop and there was a touch of magic about it that only a high-end designer—and a great deal of money—could have achieved. She didn't know about the kids, but it certainly worked for her.

She was still taking it all in when there was a tug on the

hem of her tunic and she turned to find herself looking at the child from the lift.

'You're not an elf,' she declared loudly. 'I saw you out there—' she pointed dramatically '—in the real world.'

Oh... fairy lights!

Having done her best to restore a little girl's faith in Santa, she'd immediately shattered it.

Maybe that was the message. There are no such things as fairy tales. On the other hand, if she'd had a moment or two of fantasy as a child, she might not have grabbed so desperately for it as an adult.

But this was not about her and, putting her finger to her lips in a quick, 'Shh!' she folded herself up so that she was on the same level as the child. 'What's your name?'

'Dido.'

'Can you keep a secret, Dido?'

The child, thumb stuck firmly back in her mouth, nodded once.

'Well, that's great because this is a really huge secret,' she said. 'You're absolutely right. You did see me in the lift, but the reason I was up there in the real world was because I was on a special mission from Santa.'

She hadn't worked as an assistant in a day-care nursery for years without learning how to spin a story. The pity of it was that she hadn't learned to spot one when it was being spun at her.

'What's a mishun?'

'A very special task. The toughest. I shouldn't be telling you this, but the thing is that Rudolph—'

'Rudolph?' Eyes wide, Dido abandoned the comfort of the thumb.

'Rudolph,' she repeated, 'had run out of his favourite snack. I had to disguise myself as a human, go up to the food hall—'

'Is he here?'

Lucy raised her finger to her lips again and then pointed it towards the ceiling. 'He's up there, on the roof with all the other reindeer,' she whispered. 'As soon as the store closes on Christmas Eve, we're going to load up the sleigh and off they'll go.'

'Really?' she whispered back, eyes like saucers.

'Elf's honour,' she said, crossing her heart.

'Can I see him?'

Oh, good grief... 'He's resting, Dido. Building up his strength. It's a big job delivering presents to all the children in the world.'

'I 'spose...' For a moment her little face sagged with disappointment, then she said, 'Was it a carrot? His favourite snack? We always leave a carrot for Rudolph.'

'Well, carrots are good, obviously,' she said, wondering what the rest of the poor reindeer had to sustain them. 'Great for his eyesight as he flies through the night. Good for children, too.' *Good for you* was so boring, though. Christmas was about excitement, magic. 'But what Rudolph really loves when it's cold is a handful of chilli-flavoured cashew nuts to warm him up.' She paused. 'They're what make his nose glow.'

'Wow! Really? That is so cool...'

'That's a very special secret,' Lucy warned. 'Between you, me, Rudolph and Santa.'

'So I can't tell Cleo? She's my big sister.'

'The sister who tried to tell you that Santa doesn't exist? I dooooon't think so.'

The child giggled.

'Only a very small handful, though. If Rudolph has too many his nose will overheat...'

Stop! Stop it right there, Lucy Bright!

'Dido... It's time to go,' her mother said, rescuing her.

Mouthing a silent *thank you* over her daughter's head. 'Say bye-bye.'

'Bye-bye.' Then she whispered, 'Say hi to Rudolph.'

'I will.' Lucy put her finger to her lip, then said, 'Merry Christmas.'

'Merry Christmas.'

Whew. The magic restored to one little innocent. Clap if you believe in fairies…

Not her.

Not fairies. Not fairy tales.

Lesson learned.

She looked up, saw the Chief Elf watching her from his little window and, as ordered, began picking up toys that had been picked up and dropped, restoring them to the shelves. Holding the hands of children who'd momentarily lost sight of their mothers.

When all was calm and ordered, she hitched herself onto the vacant stool and began buttoning teddies into jackets and trousers. While her fingers moved on automatic, she found herself wondering not about her future, or where she was going to spend the night, but about the man on the stairs. The way he'd caught her, held her for what seemed like minutes rather than seconds.

The broad support on his hand at her back. Dangerously mesmerising grey eyes that had locked into hers, turning her on, lighting her up like the national grid. She could still feel the fizz of it. She'd never understood why men talked about taking a 'cold shower' until now.

'Any trouble evicting the bodyguards?' Nat asked, dropping in at the security office in the basement. It was hopeless hunting through the store, but he might catch a glimpse of her on the bank of screens being fed images from CCTV cameras around the store.

'No, although they were on the phone calling up rein-
forcements before they were through the door. Whoever
replaces them won't be as easy to spot.'

Women. He'd use women, he thought, scanning the
screens but she'd gone to earth. Found a hiding place.
Or perhaps she really had slipped back out into the dark
streets. That should have been his hope; instead, the idea
of her out there, alone in the cold and dark, filled him with
dread.

'Have you seen them before?' he pressed. 'Any idea who
they work for?'

Bryan Matthews, his security chief, frowned, clearly
puzzled by his interest, but shook his head, keeping whatever he was thinking to himself.

'They didn't say anything? Offer any explanation?'

'No, they were clam-mouthed professionals. They must
have been in a flat panic to have drawn attention to themselves like that. Any idea who they've lost?'

'Maybe. It's possible that she's about this high,' he said,
his hand level with his chin. 'Short pale blonde hair, green
eyes, wearing a black knitted dress with a big collar.' He
looked at the shoe he was still carrying. 'And no shoes.'

'You saw her?'

He'd done more than that. He'd not just seen her, but
caught her, held her and she'd filled up his senses like a
well after a drought. There had been a connection between
them so physical that when she'd run it had felt as if she'd
torn away a chunk of his flesh and taken it with her.

'I saw someone who seemed to be in a bit of a state,' he
said. 'Pass the word to keep alert for anything out of the
ordinary, especially at the store exits. When she does leave
I want to be sure it's her decision. Any problem, call me.'

'I'll pass the word.'

He nodded. 'I'll be in my office.'

He glanced once more at the screens, not knowing whether to be relieved or disappointed when he came up empty.

The common sense response would be relief, he reminded himself as he strode through the electrical department, heading for the lift. But this was about more than the smooth running of the store. It was rare for a woman to catch his attention with such immediacy.

Her fear had only sharpened his reaction, taking it beyond simple interest in an attractive woman. A snatched moment that had raised his heart rate, leaving him not just breathless, but exposed, naked, defenceless. The kind of feelings he hated, did everything possible to avoid. But still he wanted to know who she was. What, who, she was running from. Wanted to taste lips that had been close enough to tantalise his memory, send heat spiralling down through his body...

He came to an abrupt halt as he realised that she was there. Right there in front of him. Not just once, but over and over, her face looking out from dozens of silent television screens banked up against the wall. Her hair was longer, her face fuller and she was smiling so that those green eyes sparkled. The heat intensified as he focused on her lips. How close had he come to kissing her?

Close enough to imagine how it would feel, the softness of her lips, how she tasted as her body softened beneath him...

Whoever she was, it seemed that her disappearance was important enough to make the national news.

Or maybe just dramatic enough.

He reached the nearest set and as he brought up the sound the picture switched to a ruckus at a press conference.

'...*scenes of total confusion as she very publicly ended*

her engagement to financier, Rupert Henshawe, accusing him of being a liar and a cheat...'

The camera caught Henshawe's startled face, moving in for a close-up of a trickle of blood that appeared on his cheek, before swinging wildly to catch the green-eyed girl clutching a file against her breast with one hand, while swinging her bag, connecting with the jaw of a man who was trying to hang on to her with the other.

The picture faded to the familiar figure of business tycoon, Rupert Henshawe, making a statement to camera.

'I blame myself. I should have realised that such a change in lifestyle would lead to stress in someone unused to the difficulty of being always in the public eye—'

His phone rang. He ignored it.

'Meeting Lucy was a life-changing moment for me. She's encouraged me to see the world in a new light...'

Lucy. Her name was Lucy.

'...her passionate belief in the fair trade movement has given a new ethical dimension to our fashion chain, which today I'm relaunching under the new name, Lucy B, in her honour...'

That was why she'd looked familiar, he realised as Henshawe paused, apparently struggling to keep back the tears.

He'd seen something in the papers about a romance with some girl who worked in his office—about as likely as Henshawe becoming a planet-hugger, he'd have thought...

'Yes?' he snapped, finally responding to the phone's insistent ring, never taking his eyes from the screen.

'It's Pam Wootton, Nat—'

'...I realise that I have been too wrapped up in all these new initiatives, visiting overseas suppliers, to give her the

support she so desperately needed. To notice how tired
she has become, her lack of appetite, her growing depen-
dence on the tranquillisers that were prescribed after the
press drove her to move out of the flat she shared with
friends—'

Tranquillisers?

Nat felt a cold chill run through him. History repeating
itself...

'She needs rest, time to recover, all my best care and,
as soon as I have found her, I will ensure—'

'Nat?'

The voice in his ear was so insistent that he realised it
wasn't the first time his PA had said his name.

'Sorry, Meg, I was distracted,' he said, still staring at the
screen. Then, as the news moved on to another story and
he forced himself to concentrate, 'Pam Wootton? What's
the matter with her?'

'She's collapsed. She was down in the grotto when it
happened and Frank Alyson has called an ambulance, but
I thought you'd want to know.'

'I'll be right there.'

'What are you doing?'

Lucy, teddy-dressing on automatic while her brain frantically free-wheeled—desperately trying to forget the man
with the grey eyes and concentrate on thinking about where
she could go when the store closed—looked up to find a
small boy watching her.

'I'm wrapping this teddy up in a warm coat. It's snowing,' she said, glad of a distraction. Short of a park bench,
she was out of ideas. 'It will be very cold on Santa's
sleigh.'

'Can I help?'

'James, don't be a nuisance,' his mother warned. She

had two smaller girls clutching at her skirts, half scared, half bewitched. Lucy smiled reassuringly.

'He's fine,' she said. 'Do you all want to give me a hand?'

Within minutes she was surrounded by small children dressing teddies, grinning happily as she helped with sleeves and buttons.

How long had it been since she'd done that? Not a posed for the camera smile, the kind that made your face ache, but an honest-to-goodness grin?

She'd been so busy shopping, being interviewed by the gossip magazines, having her photograph taken, that there hadn't been any time to catch her breath, let alone enjoy the crazy roller coaster ride she was on. Or maybe that was the point.

She hadn't wanted time to stop and think because if she had, she would have had to listen to the still small voice whispering away in the back of her mind telling her that it couldn't possibly be real.

Mental note for diary: always listen to still small voice. It knows what it's talking about.

Being here reminded her of how much she'd missed working in the day-care nursery. Missed the children.

'Your turn for a break,' one of the elves said, as it was time for the children to get back on the sleigh, and she began to gather up the bears. 'Through the office, turn left. Coffee, tea, biscuits are on the house. There's a machine with snacks if you need anything else.'

The tea was welcome and although Lucy wasn't hungry she took a biscuit. Who knew when she'd get the chance to eat again? With that thought in mind, she stocked up on chocolate and crisps from the machine.

Rather than get involved in conversation with the other staff, she took a moment to check her phone, although what she was expecting to find, she didn't know. Or rather she did. Dozens of missed calls, all of which she ignored. Texts, too. And hundreds of tweets, all demanding to know the whereabouts of Cinderella.

They couldn't all have been from Rupert's stooges. But how could she tell the real from the phoney? If someone was hoping to entice her into trusting them, they wouldn't be leaping to his defence, would they?

She was considering whether to send a tweet to reassure the good guys that she was safe—at least for now—when something made her look up. The same prickle of awareness that had made her look around on the stairs.

And for the same reason.

There, not ten feet away, talking to Frank Alyson, was the man with grey eyes. The man who'd caught her, held her in one hand as easily as if she were a child and who had, for one brief moment, made her forget everything. Where she was, why she was running...

She could still feel the imprint of his hand on her back, the warmth of his breath against her cheek and, as she sucked her lower lip into her mouth to cool it, she almost believed that she could taste him on her tongue.

CHAPTER FOUR

GREY EYES was head to head with the Chief Elf and Lucy scarcely dared breathe as she watched the pair of them.

One look and the game would be up.

It was one thing keeping her identity a secret from people who weren't looking for her, didn't expect to see her, but anyone who knew her, or was looking for her, wouldn't be fooled for a moment by her disguise. And he had to be looking for her. Didn't he?

The thought filled her with a mixture of dread and elation. While her head was afraid, she had to restrain her body from leaning towards him, from shouting *Look! Here I am!*

But, standing back like this so that she could see all of him—the broad shoulders, the long legs—she could also see that he was wearing an identity tag just like the one Pam had been wearing, which meant that he wasn't a customer, someone just passing through.

He worked in the store and if Rupert's bodyguards had elicited help from the management in finding her she was in deep trouble because one thing was obvious. He wasn't junior staff.

His pinstriped suit was the business, his tie, navy with a tiny pattern, was eye-wateringly expensive; she'd bought one like it in the store just yesterday. And, even without the designer gear, he had that unmistakable air of authority.

But if she'd thought he'd seemed intense as he'd held her balanced above the stairs, now he looked positively grim.

'Keep your eyes open, Frank.' His voice was low; he didn't need to raise it to make a point.

As she watched, pinned to the spot, he took a step back, glanced around, his eyes momentarily coming to rest on her. She'd left it too late to move and she lowered her lashes, opting for the if-I-can't-see-you-then-you-can't-see-me scenario. Holding her breath as she waited for the *got you* hand on the shoulder.

Her heart ceased to beat for the second or two that he continued to stare at her, but after a moment she realised that, while he was looking at her, he wasn't actually seeing her. He wasn't even in this room, not in his head, anyway.

Then someone put his head around the corner. 'Whenever you're ready, sir.'

Without a word, he turned and walked away. Which was when she realised that he was gripping something in his hand. A shoe.

Her shoe.

Had it fallen out of her bag when she'd stumbled?

Well, duh… How many red suede peep-toe designer shoes were there lying around Hastings & Hart? How many dumb females whose coach had just turned into a pumpkin were there fleeing up the H&H stairs scattering footwear in their wake?

How many men who could stop your heart with a look?

Stop it!

Enough with the fairy tales.

She was done with fairy tales.

'Wh…who was that?' she asked, as casually as she could, once she'd finally managed to retrieve her heart from her mouth and coax it back into life.

Frank gave her a weary look and she remembered, too late, that he didn't like inquisitive elves.

'That, Miss Mop and Bucket,' he replied, 'was Nathaniel Hart.'

'Hart?' She blinked. 'As in…' She pointed up at the building soaring above them.

'As in Hastings & Hart,' he confirmed.

'No…' Or, to put it another way, *Nooooooo!*

'Are you arguing with me?'

'No!' And she shook her head, to make sure. 'I just hadn't realised there was a real Mr Hart.' It certainly explained the air of authority. If he looked as if he owned the place it was because, well, he did. 'I thought that most of these big stores were owned by big chains.'

'Hastings & Hart is not most stores.'

About to ask if there was a Mr Hastings, or even a Mrs Hart, she thought better of it. She was having a bad enough day without feeling guilty about lusting after some woman's husband.

'Is that all?' Frank asked with a sardonic lift of the brow. 'Or are you prepared to honour us with another teddy-dressing class for the under fives?'

'I'm sorry. It got a bit out of hand,' she said, fairly sure that was sarcasm rather than praise. 'I won't do it again.'

'Oh, please don't let me stop you. You are a hit with the children, if not with their mothers.'

Definitely sarcasm and she had been feeling rather guilty since several of the children had refused point-blank to surrender their bears to the rigours of a freezing sleigh ride and insisted they come home with them in a nice warm taxi. Not that it should worry Frank Alyson. It was all the more profit for Nathaniel Hart, wasn't it? Which was all men like him cared about.

But all the practice she'd had smiling in the last few months stood her in good stead and she gave him one of her best.

He looked somewhat startled, as well he might—she didn't imagine he got too many of those—and, satisfied with the effect, she returned to her stool, where she would be safely out of sight of Mr Nathaniel Hart, unless he borrowed Frank Alyson's Chief Elf robes.

But, while the children kept her busy, her brain was fizzing with questions. Had Grey Eyes been contacted directly by one of Rupert's minions? Asked to organise a discreet search for her? Or even perhaps by Rupert himself? They probably knew one another—billionaires united was a very small club—because he seemed to be taking a personal interest in the search.

He hadn't sounded at all happy when, having belatedly come to her senses, she'd taken off up the stairs, leaving only her shoe behind.

And it would explain why he was carrying it around with him. He assumed that she had the other one tucked away in her bag and, obviously, she would need two of them if she was going to walk out of here.

Tough. He should have kept his mind on the job.

Or maybe not. Even now, her heart flipped at the memory as she absently sucked on an overheated lip.

Having been assured by the paramedics that Pam was suffering from nothing worse than the latest bug that was going around, Nat drove her home and insisted that she stay there until she was fully recovered.

'But how will you cope? There's so much to do and—'

'Pam, we'll manage,' he insisted. 'And the last thing we need at this time of year is an epidemic.'

'Sorry. I know. And no one's indispensable. Petra will manage. Probably.' She rubbed at her temple. 'There was something I was meant to be doing...' He waited, but she sighed and said, 'No, it's gone.'

'Can I get you anything? Tea? Juice?'

'You're a sweet man, Nathaniel Hart,' she croaked. 'You'd make some woman a lovely husband.'

An image of the woman on the stairs, her scent, the softness of her dress, disturbingly real, filled his head...

'I'm just a details man,' he said, blanking it off. 'Go and get into bed. I'll make you a hot drink.'

'You should get back to London before the roads get any worse,' she said. Then, as headlights swept across the window, 'That's Peter home.'

'Closing time, Lou.' The elf sitting on the next stool stood up, eased her back. 'Reality beckons.'

'I'll just finish dressing this bear.'

'You're keen. See you tomorrow.'

It was a casual throwaway line, needing no answer, and Lucy didn't reply. Tomorrow would have to take care of itself; it was tonight that was the problem.

She tucked the teddy into a pair of striped pyjamas and a dressing gown, putting off the moment when she'd have to face a cold world. Because no amount of thinking had provided her with an answer to where she could go. Certainly not the flat she'd shared before she'd met Rupert. That would be the first place anyone would look.

She had a little money in her purse that would cover a night at some cheap B&B. The problem with that was that her face would be all over the evening news and someone was bound to spot her and call it in to one of the tabloids for the tip-off money.

The sensible answer, she knew, would be to contact one of them herself, let them take care of her. They'd stick her in a safe house so that no one else could get to her and they'd pay well for the story she had to tell. That was the reason they'd been grabbing at her, chasing after her. Why Rupert would be equally anxious to keep her away from them.

The problem with going down that route was that there would be no way back to her real life.

Once she'd taken their money she'd be their property. Would never be able to go back to being the person she had been six months ago.

Instead she'd become one of those pathetic Z-list celebrities who were forever doomed to live off their moment of infamy, relying on ever more sleazy stories to keep themselves in the public eye. Because no one would employ her in a nursery or day-care centre ever again.

But this reprieve was temporary. Out of time, she placed the teddy on the shelf and went to the office.

Frank looked up from his desk, where he was inputting figures into a computer. 'Are you still here?'

'Apparently. I was looking for Pam.'

He pulled a face. 'She collapsed not long after you arrived,' he said in an I-told-you-so tone of voice.

'Oh, good grief. I'm so sorry. Is she going to be all right?'

'It's just a bug and an inability to accept that we can manage without her for a day or two. Mr Hart took her home a couple of hours ago. Why did you want her?'

'Well…'

About to explain about the swipe card, it occurred to her that if Pam had collapsed not long after she'd mistaken her

for an elf, she might not have had time to do the paperwork.
Make her official. Log her in.

'It's nothing that won't wait. Although…'

She couldn't. Could she?

'She didn't mention what time I'm supposed to start
tomorrow,' she added, as casually as she could.

'The store opens at ten. If you're honouring us with your
presence, you'll need to be in your place, teddy at the ready
at one minute to. Is that it?'

'Er…yes. Ten. No problem.'

He nodded. 'Goodnight.' Then, as she reached the
door, 'You did a good job, Louise. I hope we'll see you
tomorrow.'

'Thanks,' she said. 'Me, too.'

Nat switched on the radio as he drove back through thick
swirling snowflakes that were beginning to pile up on the
edges of the road. The footpaths were already white.

He'd hoped to catch an update about Henshawe's missing
fiancée—ex-fiancée—on the news, but it was all weather
warnings and travel news and the bulletins focused on the
mounting chaos as commuters tried to get home in weather
that hadn't been forecast.

She'd got lucky. But not as lucky as Henshawe. An embarrassing story was going to be buried under tomorrow's
headlines about drivers spending the night in their cars,
complaints about incompetent weather forecasters and the
lack of grit on the roads.

They'd probably be reunited and back on the front cover
of some gossip magazine by next week, with whatever
indiscretions she was accusing him of long forgotten, he
told himself. Forget her.

By the time he returned to the store it was closing. The
last few shoppers were being ushered through the doors,

the cloakrooms and changing rooms thoroughly checked in a well rehearsed routine to flush out anyone who might harbour ideas of spending the night there.

He parked in the underground garage, removed the shoe from the glove compartment and walked through to the security office.

Bryan looked up as he entered.

'Anything?' he asked.

'Not a sign. She probably slipped out under cover of the crowds. She's certainly not in the store now.'

'No.' He looked at the shoe and, instead of dropping it in the lost property box, held onto it.

'Are you going straight up to the tenth floor?'

He nodded. 'I'll be in the office for a while. You're working late?'

'We're a couple of men down with some bug that's going around.'

'Let me know if it becomes a problem.'

But it wasn't the likelihood of staff shortages at their busiest time of year that was nagging at him as he headed for the lifts. It was something he'd seen, something telling him that, despite all evidence to the contrary, his fugitive hadn't gone anywhere. That she was still here.

It was stupid, he knew.

She'd undoubtedly used the phone she'd been clutching in the hand she'd flung around his neck to call a friend, someone to bring her a change of clothes and whatever else she needed.

He needed to put the incident out of his mind. Forget the impact of her eyes, the flawless skin, long lashes that had been burned into his brain like a photograph in that long moment when he'd held her.

What was it? What was he missing?

He walked through the electrical department, but the

television screens that had been filled with her larger-than-life-size image were all blank now.

Her hair had been darker in that photograph. She'd been wearing less make-up. It was almost like seeing a before and after photograph. The original and the made-over version. Thinner, the image expensively finished, refined, everything except a tiny beauty spot above her lip that could not be airbrushed out of reality...

He stopped.

The beauty spot. That was what he'd seen. He scanned his memory, fast-forwarding through everything he'd seen and done in the hours since that moment on the stairs.

And came skidding to a halt on the elf.

The one who'd been standing so still by the drinks machine while he was talking to Frank. She was the right height, the right shape—filling out the elf costume in a way it hadn't been designed for. And she'd had a beauty spot in exactly the same place as the girl on the stairs.

Coincidence? Maybe, but he spun around and headed into the grotto.

While everyone else raced to change, get away as quickly as possible, Lucy dawdled and it had taken remarkably little time for the locker room to empty.

It was a little eerie being there on her own, the motion-sensitive lights shutting down all around her, leaving her in just a small area of light. And, while she was grateful to be off the streets, in the warm, she wasn't entirely sure what to do next.

Where she would be safe.

While the locker rooms would be free of cameras—she was almost certain they would be free of cameras—there would undoubtedly be a security presence of some sort.

Would it be high-tech gadgetry? Motion sensors, that

sort of thing. Patrols? Or just someone tucked up in an office with a flask of coffee, a pile of sandwiches and a good book while he monitored the store cameras?

At least she would be safe in here for a little while and she could use the time to take the shower she'd longed for. Wash off the whole hideous day. Wash off the last few months and reclaim herself.

And if someone did happen to come in, check that everyone had left, she could surely come up with some believable reason for staying behind to take a shower after work.

A hot date?

Actually, she did have one of those. Well, a date, anyway. Rupert didn't do hot, but neither would he cancel the Lucy B launch dinner at The Ritz just because she'd caused him a little embarrassment. She had no doubt that his PR team had already put some kind of spin on that. Stress. Pre-wedding nerves.

Of course if she turned up in the elf costume—the paparazzi would certainly be on the job tonight—it would wipe the smug smile off all their faces.

For a moment she was sorely tempted but, recalling the scrum at the press conference, she decided to give it a miss.

No. If she needed an excuse for being in the shower so late, she'd stick to the second job story. Everyone needed extra money at Christmas and a waitress—her own particular preference when she'd needed the cash to finance her studies—had to be clean and fresh.

She reclaimed her dress from the locker and then, having folded her costume neatly and left it on the bench, she took a towel from the rack and stepped into one of the stalls.

The water was hot and there were shampoo and soap dispensers. Hastings & Hart staff were very well taken care of, she decided, as she pushed the pump for a dollop of soap. Maybe she should reconsider her career options.

Could being an elf in a department store be considered a career? What did Santa do for the rest of the year? And would she get to meet the boss again?

Cold shower, cold shower!

She squeezed some shampoo. Her hair didn't need washing—she'd spent two hours in the salon having it cut and pampered earlier in the day—but she felt the need to cleanse herself from top to toe, rid herself of the past few months, and she dug in deep with her fingers, washing away the scent of betrayal, rinsing it down the drain.

Then, in no hurry to stop, she reached out to adjust the temperature a touch.

The grotto, Santa's workshop, was deserted. Nat walked through to Frank's office, hoping he might find a staff list, but the man was too well organised to leave such things lying about. Besides, he knew he had to be wrong. It had to be a coincidence. There was no way Lucy could have transformed herself into an elf.

It was ridiculous. He was becoming obsessed, seeing things.

Hearing things…

A deluge of ice water hit Lucy and she let out a shriek that would have woken the dead. She groped blindly for the control which, having spun at the merest touch, was now stuck stubbornly on cold.

She gave one last tug. The control knob came off in her hand and, freezing, she burst out of the shower stall, dripping, naked, eyes closed as she grabbed for the towel.

She wiped her face, took a breath, opened her eyes and discovered that she was not alone.

Nathaniel Hart—the man with his name above the front door—had obviously heard her yell. More of her 'openness and lack of guile', obviously. Not her best move if she wanted to keep below the radar.

She didn't scream, despite the shock. Her mouth opened; her brain was sending all the right signals but nothing was getting past the big thick lump that was blocking her throat.

He took the control from her hand, reached into the shower stall, screwed it deftly back into place and turned off the water, giving her a chance to gather her wits and wrap the towel around her before he closed the door.

Then he helped himself to one, dried his hands and only when he'd tossed it onto the bench behind her did he give her his full attention.

'Making yourself at home, Cinderella?' he enquired after what felt like the longest moment in her life while a slow blush spread from her cheeks and down her neck, heating all points south until it reached her toes.

Cinderella.

He knew...

It took forever to unglue her tongue from the roof of her mouth, making her lips work.

She took a step back, slipped on a floor awash with cold water. Torn between grabbing for safety and hanging onto the towel, she made a grab for the shower door.

No doubt afraid that she'd bring that down on them, Nathaniel Hart reached for her arm, steadying her before the towel had slipped more than an inch.

An inch was way too much. The towel, which when she'd first picked it up had seemed perfectly adequate for decency, now felt like a pocket handkerchief.

'This is the women's locker room,' she finally managed.

As if that was going to make any difference. This was

his store and she was trapped. Not just shoeless this time, but 'less' just about everything except for a teeny, tiny towel that just about covered her from breast to thigh. Not nearly enough when this close to a man who'd sizzled her with a look when she'd been fully dressed.

He was looking now—which dealt with freezing...

'You shouldn't be here,' she said, finally managing to get her voice to work and going for indignant. She failed miserably. She just sounded breathless. She felt breathless...

With good reason.

She was naked, alone and at the mercy of a man who almost certainly meant her no good. But, far from fleeing, his touch was like an electric charge and all her instincts were telling her to forget modesty, let the towel fall and cooperate with whatever he had in mind. One hundred per cent.

Nooooo!

She forced herself to take a step away, put some distance between them, get a grip. Regretting it the minute she did. There was something about his touch that made her feel safe. Made her feel...

'And that's not my name,' she added, cutting off the thought before she lost it entirely.

'No?' He flipped something from his pocket and offered it to her. 'If the shoe fits...'

He was still carrying her shoe?

'What do you think this is?' she demanded, ignoring the shoe. 'A pantomime? I'm all through with the Cinderella thing, Mr Hart.'

'You know who I am?'

'Mr Alyson told me. You're Nathaniel Hart and you own this store.'

'I run it. Not the same thing.'

'Oh.' She wasn't sure why that was better, but somehow

it was. She was totally off billionaire tycoons. 'I just assumed...'

'Most people do.'

'Well, if the name fits,' she said and thought she got the tiniest response. Just a hint of a smile. But maybe she was imagining it. 'What do you want, Mr Hart?'

'Nothing. On the contrary, I'm your fairy godmother.'

She stared at him but said nothing. She was in enough trouble without stating the obvious.

'I know what you're thinking,' he said.

'I promise you, you haven't got a clue.'

'You're thinking where is the frilly skirt? Where are the wings?'

No... Not even close. 'Trust me, it would not be a good look for you. Take my advice, stick with the pin-stripes.'

'Well, I'm glad you take that view.'

The barest suspicion of a smile became a twitch of the lips, curling around her, warm, enticing. Tempting. Heating up bits that it would take a very long cold shower to beat into line and she was very glad indeed that he hadn't got a clue.

'Hastings & Hart takes its role as an equal opportunities employer very seriously,' he assured her.

'We have to take our fairy godmothers wherever we can find them in these enlightened days,' she agreed, firmly resisting the temptation to fling herself into his arms and invite him to make free with his magic wand. Instead, she tightened her lips, keeping them pressed down in a straight line. A smile meant nothing, she told herself. Anyone could smile. It was easy. You just stretched your lips wide...

But he was really good at it. It wasn't just the corner of his mouth doing something that hit all the right buttons. It had reached all the way up to his eyes and the warmth of it reached deep within her, turning her insides liquid.

She clutched the towel a little tighter. 'I guess the real test comes with Santa Claus? Would you employ a woman for that role?' she asked a touch desperately.

The lines carved into his cheeks became deeper, bracketing his mouth. And the silver sparks in his eyes had not been reflections of the Christmas decorations, she realised, but were all his own. It was all there now. Every part of his face was engaged and while it wasn't a pretty smile, it was all the more dangerous for that.

'Not my decision, thank goodness. Human Resources have the responsibility of employing the best person for the job and keeping me on the right side of the law.'

She tutted. 'Passing the buck.'

'There has to be some advantage to go with the name,' he replied, 'but, as far as fairy godmothers go, right now I'm not just your best option, I appear to be the only one.'

'Oh?' she said, putting on a brave front. If she was going down, she refused to be a pushover. 'Why do you think that?'

'Because if there had been anyone you could ask for help you wouldn't be hiding out in Santa's grotto dressed as an elf. You'd have used the phone you were carrying to call them.'

'Who says I'm hiding?' she demanded. 'That I need help.'

'The fact that you're here, prepared to risk getting caught on the premises after closing, speaks for itself.'

She couldn't argue with his logic. He had it, spot on, but she still had the backup excuse. 'I'm just late leaving,' she said. 'I needed a shower before I start my other job.'

He shook his head.

'You're not buying it?'

'Sorry.'

'Oh, well. It was worth a shot.' She managed a shrug

even though her heart was hammering in her mouth. 'So. What happens now?'

'I congratulate you on your ingenuity?' he suggested. 'Ask how you managed to get yourself kitted out with an elf costume so that you could hide out in Santa's grotto?'

'I'm smart?'

'Obviously. But, if you managed it, there are security issues involved.'

'Oh, look, it wasn't anyone's fault,' she said quickly. Clearly the game was up for her, but she couldn't allow anyone else to suffer. 'I was mistaken for a temp who was expected but never turned up and it was too good an opportunity to miss. Pam won't get into trouble, will she? She was desperate. Not just desperate but sick,' she stressed. 'Well, you know that since you took her home.'

'Don't worry about Pam, worry about yourself,' he said, the smile fading.

She shivered. Not from fear. This man was not a bully. He wasn't crowding her, there was no suggestion of the physical threat that had seemed so real in the press conference. Why she'd run.

He was much more dangerous than that.

He could bring her down with a look. As if to prove it, he reached for a dry towel and draped it around her shoulders, assuming that she was cold. His touch tingled through her and she knew that all he had to do was put his hand to her back and she'd put up her hands, surrender without a struggle.

Fortunately, he didn't know that.

'What were you planning to do next?' he asked, not lingering, but taking a step back, putting clear air between them.

'Get dressed?' she suggested.

'And then?' he persisted.

'I thought I might bed down in one of your tents.' There seemed little point in lying about it. 'I noticed them yesterday when I was Christmas shopping. I've never been camping,' she added.

'It's overrated. Especially in the middle of winter.'

'I don't know. I could brew myself some tea on one of those little camp stoves. Fry a few sausages for my supper. I'd leave the money for the food on the till in the food hall.' She clutched the towel a little more tightly against her bosom. 'Maybe have a bit of a sing-song to keep my spirits up,' she added a touch recklessly. 'I did work for three hours for nothing. And I was planning to work tomorrow on the same terms. Bed and breakfast seems a reasonable exchange.'

'More than reasonable,' he agreed. 'Which one did you have your eye on?'

'I'm sorry?'

'Which tent? I can recommend the one-man Himalayan. I'm told that it's absolutely draught-proof.'

'Oh. Right. Well, thanks.'

'I'd strongly advise against the cooking, though. The security staff are based on the same floor and the smoke alarms are extremely sensitive.'

CHAPTER FIVE

LUCY swallowed hard. Was he joking? It was impossible to tell. When he wasn't smiling, Nathaniel Hart could give lessons in how to do a poker face.

'Well, thanks for the tip,' she managed. 'I've got a bag of crisps and a chocolate biscuit that I bought from the machine. They'll keep me going.'

He shook his head and a lick of thick dark hair slid across his forehead.

'That won't do,' he said, combing it back with long fingers. 'Chocolate biscuits and crisps aren't going to provide you with your five-a-day.'

Her five-a-day? She stared him. Unreal. The man was not only conspiring with her to trespass in his department store, but was concerned that she was eating healthily. Consuming the government's daily recommended five portions of fruit and vegetables...

Or had he already summoned Rupert and was simply amusing himself at her expense while he waited for him to arrive and remove her?

Of course he was. Why was she even wasting time thinking about it?

'Who are you? The food police?' she demanded crossly. At least that was the intent but his hand was still on her

arm, his fingers warm against her goosepimply skin and
she didn't sound cross. She sounded breathless.

'Hastings & Hart take a close interest in staff welfare.
We have a cycle to work scheme—which is why you have
the luxury of shower facilities—'

'Luxury!' Finally she got her voice back. But then there
wasn't much luxury in an unexpected ice-cold dunk.

'—and subsidised gym membership as well as a healthy
options menu in the staff canteen.'

And he'd driven Pam Wootton home when she was taken
ill, she reminded herself. That was taking staff welfare
very seriously indeed. Not many men in his position would
have done that. It suggested that he was unusually kind,
thoughtful and, about to tell herself that Rupert would never
have done that, it occurred to her that he had. Done exactly
that. And, as she'd just discovered, he was neither kind nor
thoughtful.

'Impressive, Mr Hart, but I'm only a temp. Temps don't
get fringe benefits.'

Not just a temp, but an illicit one at that. He might be
a great employer but she had no more reason to trust him
than he had to trust her.

'Besides, the crisps are made from potatoes,' she said,
playing for time as she tried, desperately, to think what to
do next. Pull away from his hand, for a start, obviously.
Put some space between them…'And they're cheese and
onion flavour.'

There were no windows down here, but even in the basement there had to be a fire escape. Or would Rupert have
learned from her last dash for freedom and have those
covered before he moved in?

Was that what all the time-wasting was about?

'So potato and onion, that's two of my five,' she added,
wishing she'd spent more time thinking about her escape

instead of day-dreaming about a dishy stranger while she dressed teddy bears. 'There's the protein from the cheese, too, don't forget.'

Think... *Think!*

'And it's an orange chocolate biscuit.'

'Is that it?' he asked. 'All done?'

'All done,' she admitted. She was out of ideas. Out of excuses. Out of flavourings.

'Nice try—'

There was the smile again. The whole works. Crinkles fanning out from the corners of his eyes, something magical happening to his mouth as the lower lip softened to reveal the merest glimpse of white teeth. And then there were his eyes...

His eyes seemed to suggest that he was as surprised as she was to find he was smiling and, as quickly as it had appeared, it vanished.

And she could breathe again.

'—but no cigar,' he said. 'I'm sorry to be the bearer of bad news but potatoes don't count as a vegetable.'

'They don't?' She made a good fist at surprised.

'Not as one of your five-a-day.'

He didn't look sorry.

'You're telling me I'm going to have to stop counting fries?' she demanded, hoping to make him forget himself again and actually laugh. Get him on her side. 'Well, that's a swizz.'

'And you can forget the flavourings, too.'

'I was afraid that might be stretching it. I did have orange juice with my breakfast,' she assured him, as if determined to prove that she wasn't a complete dietary failure. Playing the fool in an attempt to lull him into believing that she'd bought his act.

'Good start. And since breakfast?'

'I had green beans with my lunch and I'm fairly sure that the fruit in the dessert was the real thing.'

'Apple tart, right?'

'How on earth do you know that?'

'The cinnamon was the giveaway.'

'Cinnamon?' Had he been that close? Mortified, she smothered a groan. Time to put a stop to this. 'What about you, Mr Hart?'

'Nat.'

'Nat?'

'Short for Nathaniel. A bit of a mouthful.'

'But nicer than Nat, which is a small spiteful insect which takes lumps out of you when you're innocently enjoying a sunset.'

'Very nearly,' he agreed, rewarding her with a flicker of a smile that went straight to her blush. And too late she realised her mistake. 'What about me?'

She'd thought she was being clever, keeping him talking, while she scoped out the shower room, hoping to pick up the faint illumination of an emergency exit, but it was hopeless. This was the basement and there was no escape, but she could still let everyone know where she was. What was happening. If only she could convince him that she wasn't going to make a run for it so he'd leave her to get dressed...

She shook her head. 'It doesn't matter. My name is Lucy, by the way. Lucy Bright. But you already know that.'

'I caught the Lucy on the news. Not the Bright. It explains the B in Lucy B.'

News?

That hideous scene had been on the news? Well, of course it had. The unveiling of the new look for his fashion chain, taking it upmarket, providing aspirational clothes for the career-minded woman. Clothes for work and play.

Clothes with a touch of class and a fair trade label was a big story. Providing new jobs both here and in the Third World.

'How d'you do, Lucy Bright?' he said, finally removing his hand from her arm and offering it to her.

She clutched the towel with one hand, placed her other in his, watching as his long fingers and broad palm swallowed up her own small hand. A rush of warmth warned her she was doing the head to toe blush again.

'To be honest, I've had better days, Nathaniel Hart.'

'Maybe I can help. Why don't you get dressed and then we'll go and see what's good in the Food Hall? I'm sure I can find something more enticing than crisps and chocolate for your supper.'

What?

'There is nothing more enticing than crisps and chocolate.'

Healthier, maybe, but right now she was in the market for high carb, high calorie comfort food.

'And we do need to discuss your camping arrangements,' he continued, ignoring the interruption, 'because, even if you manage to evade the security cameras, I'm afraid the cleaners will spot you.'

'They clean inside the tents?'

'That's probably a push of the vacuum too far,' he admitted, 'but they will certainly notice one zipped up from the inside. You don't imagine you're the first person to have that idea, do you?' He didn't wait for her answer. 'Take your time. No rush,' he said, surrendering her arm, leaving a cold spot where his hand had been, using it to take a phone from his pocket as he turned and walked away, finally leaving her to get dressed.

* * *

Appointments...
20:00 Camping out for the night in H&H outdoors
department.
20:30 Or maybe not.

Nat finished his call, then leaned back against the wall
opposite the locker room door and waited, closing his eyes
in an attempt to block out the image that was indelibly
imprinted upon his mind.

Lucy Bright backing naked out of the shower stall, water
pouring off her shoulders, back, the deliciously soft curve
of her backside. Her determined chin as she'd faced him
down despite the hot pink flush that had spread just about
everywhere.

Her struggle not to smile, when a smile would, undoubtedly, have been in her best interests.

A drop of water sliding slowly around a curl released
from its airy hold, hanging for a moment before it finally
fell. Lying for a moment in the hollow above her collarbone
before it was joined by another and had gathered sufficient
weight to overcome inertia and trickle down between her
breasts.

Smooth shoulders lifted in the merest shrug as she ad-
opted a carelessly casual response to the awkwardness of
the situation.

Like a swan, all appeared serene on the surface, while
her brain had clearly been whirring like the freewheeling
cogs of a machine as she tried to engage gear and figure
out how to escape him for a second time. Work out her next
move.

Or maybe his.

Good question. What exactly *was* he going to do?

Until five minutes ago, he'd thought it was simple. He

would deliver her to friends and walk away. No more, no less complicated than driving Pam home this afternoon.

But it wasn't simple. Simple had become a fantasy from the moment he'd touched her, looked into her green-gold eyes. From the moment he'd glimpsed her luscious curves.

While his head was demanding that he call a cab, dump her in it and send her on her way, do what he could to help without getting involved, his heart—mostly his heart—wasn't having any of it.

That foolish organ demanded that he scoop her up, carry her to his apartment and keep her safe from harm.

Neither was an option.

It was clear that she didn't trust him further than she could throw him, and why would she? In her shoes, he'd be expecting the police to arrive at any minute to remove her from the premises.

What he had to do was keep his head, keep his distance—despite arms aching to wrap her up, keep her safe—but, most important of all, keep her from running.

He had no idea what had caused the row with Rupert Henshawe, or why he'd sent his heavies after her, but he did know that while she was here, under his roof, no harm would come to her. And that, he told himself, was all that mattered.

He looked at the shoe he was still holding, hoping that without it she'd think twice about making a dash for it the first chance she got.

Not so easy with the store closed but she was right, she was smart and, like the involvement issue, he wasn't banking on it.

We?

Lucy caught sight of herself in one of the mirrors and snapped her jaw shut. For a moment there she'd almost succumbed to the fantasy that he might be a good guy.

Perhaps the atmosphere in the grotto was rubbing off on her and, like the little girl in the lift, she wanted to believe.

Had they seen that in her? Rupert's PR people. The longing for something that had always been out of reach. Not the glamour, the clothes, but something deeper. A need for love so desperate that she would be emotionally seduced by the fairy tale of the beast tamed by the innocent.

In other words, a sucker.

Because only an idiot would have fallen for it. She knew she wasn't special. Not tall and elegant or the slightest bit gorgeous. She wasn't an 'It' girl, or a model, or an actress. Nothing like the kind of woman billionaires were usually seen with. Not the kind of woman Rupert had dated in droves—even while remaining determinedly uncommitted—before he'd apparently been bowled over by her innocent charms.

So innocent that he'd insisted on waiting until they were married before they moved their relationship beyond a few kisses.

How many women would have been dumb enough to fall for *that* fairy tale?

Forget the still small voice in the back of her head. The fact that he found it so easy to resist temptation, the fact that she was perfectly happy to go along with it, wasn't panting with frustration, should have sent not just warning bells clanging but klaxons wailing an ear-splitting warning.

It was so obvious, faced with reality, that she was in love with the idea of being in love, the fairy tale, rather than the man. While Rupert...

Well, his motives were clear enough.

He could have paid a celebrity to be the face, the figure

to relaunch his fashion chain, but he wanted a real woman who he would transform with his new 'look'. An ordinary woman.

Apparently she was a breath of fresh air. Real. That was how the PR people had described her in their report. Not a model or a star, but someone who every women in their sales demographic would instantly relate to, aspire to be. Would believe.

So far, so simple. And the rest of it had started as a throwaway line scribbled in the margins of a report.

And she'd fallen for it, believed him, because it had never once occurred to her that it was all a big fat lie. What, for heaven's sake, would be the point of that?

Innocent was right.

The point, of course, was money. A lot of money. Now she knew the truth, she could bring the whole edifice crashing down. It would cost him millions and he wasn't about to let that happen.

She dug out her phone and with shaky fingers she keyed in a tweet while she had a chance.

Lies, lies, lies…

She stopped. There was no signal. Had she been cut off? Or was it just because she was in the deepest part of the basement, surrounded by concrete? She'd had one a couple of hours ago by the coffee machine…

It didn't matter. Whatever the cause, she was, for the moment at least, totally on her own.

Nothing new there. She'd been on her own for most of her life. And if she was trembling by the time she tugged a comb through her damp hair it was with anger rather than fear.

She was absolutely furious with Rupert for lying to

her, with Nathaniel Hart for making her want to believe him, but most of all with herself for being so gullible, so stupid.

Diary update: Everything was going so well. I was safe for the night. All I had to do was keep my head down, stay out of the way of security patrols and I was home dry. Well, wet, actually, because I couldn't resist taking a shower...

Oh, for goodness' sake, she thought, closing the phone. What was the point?

She was up the creek without a paddle and going nowhere. At least not for the moment. Once she was out of the basement all bets were off, but for now the best she could do was get dressed and be ready to take advantage of the slightest opportunity.

She lifted the towel from her shoulders and began vigorously rubbing at her hair. The last thing she needed was pneumonia. In fact... She gave up on the hair and sorted through the pile of discarded elf clothes, picking out the tights, bootees and even the hat, pushing them into the depths of her bag.

The bootees weren't going to be snow-proof, but they would be a lot better than bare feet.

Guilt warred with a sense of triumph as she finished towelling herself off. Triumph won as she stepped into fragile lacy underwear which would do nothing to keep the cold out. She fastened her bra and then reached for her dress.

Her hand met the bare slats of the bench and she turned to look.

Her dress, along with the towel tossed aside by Nathaniel Hart, had slipped to the floor.

She made a wild grab for it but both dress and towel had been lying there quite long enough to soak up water like a sponge and, as she lifted it from the floor, it dripped icy-cold water down her legs.

In desperation she squeezed it. Rolled it up in a dry towel. The towel got wet. The dress did not get noticeably drier.

It was the elf costume or nothing.

She groaned. She might be in a mess but the dress did things to her figure that the elf costume could never hope to achieve. She *knew* what effect the dress had on Nathaniel Hart. Wearing that, she had a chance of distracting him but, while her underwear would have undoubtedly done the job with bells on, she could hardly make her escape in a couple of scraps of lace.

Too late to do any good, she moved to the far end of the bench where it was dry and climbed back into the only warm clothes she possessed. The elf suit. The gorgeous stripy green tights. The tunic that was a little too tight. The neat little belt with the pouch to keep her acorns in. Or whatever it was that elves ate. The flat, floppy around the ankles bootees.

Terrific.

At least she could put on some make-up. And she wasn't talking about freckles.

Five minutes later, lips pink, eyes smudgy, blusher discreetly applied and her damp hair released from the iron grip of hair straighteners and curling ridiculously around her head, she tugged on the tunic and sighed.

This was so not a good look. Her only hope was that some persistent paparazzo would snatch a snap of her leaving the store, being bundled into Rupert's car.

Or did that come under the realms of fantasy, too? There was an underground car park and that was where he'd pick her up, out of sight. Drive her away in a car with blacked-out windows. Or just shoved to the floor out of sight. No need for pretence.

She gathered her coat and bag, scared but determined not to let it show. Then, with her hand on the door, she paused. She still had the file and that gave her an edge. Bargaining power. Removing it from her bag, she stowed it in an empty locker, then looked around for a place to hide the key.

Once that was done, there was nothing more she could do but face the music—or, more accurately, the deliciously elegant Nathaniel Hart.

She gave one more tug on the hem of the tunic, reminding herself that it could be worse—at least she was wearing more than a damp towel. Actually, come to think of it, that might not be…

No. Telling herself to behave, be brave—she had more to worry about than how she looked—she took a deep breath and opened the door.

No poker face this time.

Between the elf costume and her wet hair sticking out at all angles, it was not her finest fashion hour, at least if the eyebrow gymnastics were anything to go by.

Making the most of a bad job, she pasted on a bright smile and gave him a twirl. 'What do you think?' she asked. 'Does my bum look big in this?'

There was a long moment—too long–while he considered the matter and her smile began to wobble. What kind of idiot drew attention to her worst bits?

'What happened to your dress?' he finally asked, avoiding her question.

'Are you referring to the world's most expensive floor cloth?' she responded, giving herself a mental slap for asking a question to which she already knew the answer.

'I don't know. Am I?'

'The dress that some idiot man managed to knock into a freezing puddle with a badly tossed towel?' She didn't wait for him to answer that one. 'You don't think I'd be wearing this if there was any choice, do you?'

'You were happy enough to grab it this afternoon,' he reminded her, 'although I have admit that it is rather—'

She glared at him, daring him to say the word *tight*.

'—green.' He opened the door that led into the electrical department. 'It goes with your eyes,' he added, taking her elbow as he fell in beside her. Not in a frog-marching way. Just a touch, a guiding hand, rather like a gentleman escorting a lady in to dinner in some Jane Austen movie, but she wasn't fooled by that. Or his attempt at gallantry. She knew he was simply keeping contact so that if she decided to make a run for it all he had to do was tighten his grip.

She'd do it, too, at the first chance of escape.

For the moment, however, she forced herself to relax so that she wouldn't telegraph her intentions. She'd already witnessed the lightning speed of his reactions when he'd stopped her from falling on the stairs. Lightning in every sense of the word. That moment while something seemed to fuse between them had been like a lightning strike. For a moment they had both been a little dazed. She wasn't dazed now, though—well, not much—and carrying her kicking and screaming through the store was an entirely different kettle of fish. And if she decided to play hide and seek she might be able to hold out until morning.

Not so easy when the store was empty. There were cameras everywhere. But that worked both ways. His security people, the ones he'd warned her about, would be watching...

She realised that he was looking at her.

'What?' she demanded.

'Nothing. I was just speculating on Frank Alyson's response to the liberties you've taken with your elf costume.' He sounded grave, but a smile was tugging at the corner of his mouth. 'Your belt is a little too tight and your make-up is definitely non-regulation. Where are the rosy cheeks and freckles?' he asked. 'And you must know that you're improperly dressed without your hat.'

Okay, he was teasing and, despite everything, she was sorely tempted to smile. Instead, she reminded herself that they were *his* security people. They would believe whatever he told them and she couldn't deny that she was on the premises illegally.

Cool. She had to play it cool. Wait her chance.

'So…what? He'll feed me to the troll?'

'Troll?' he asked, startled into a grin and set off a whole new wave of sparks flaring through her body.

Maybe she could set off a fire alarm, she thought desperately, doing her best to ignore them. Or there were the cleaners. They would be arriving soon; he'd said so. They had to get in. And get out again.

'It's what he does to underachieving elves,' she replied, deadpan. 'But I'm off duty so I'm afraid you're going to have to live with "improper", at least until my dress dries,' she said, as if her clothing disaster was the only thing on her mind. 'Always supposing it survives the dunking.'

'I'm sorry about the dress. For some reason I didn't notice it.'

Well, no. He'd been too busy not noticing her towel slipping all over the place…

'I'll replace it, of course.'

'It was a one-off. A designer original.'

'Oh. Well, let's hope it dries out.'

'It had better. Everything else I own is packed up in a couple of boxes. Along with my life.'

The life she'd had before she met Rupert Henshawe. It hadn't been very exciting, but it had been real. Honest. Truthful.

Her clothes, including the most expensive suit she'd ever bought, the one she'd bought for her interview at the Henshawe Corporation—she'd been so determined to make a good impression. It had done its job, but of course it hadn't been good enough for Lucy B.

There was an ancient laptop she'd bought second-hand. All the letters were worn off the keys but it had seen her through her business course. A box of books for her college work. A few precious memories from her childhood.

She'd left pretty much everything else behind when the constant presence of the media on the doorstep of the tiny flat she'd shared with two other girls had made it impossible to do even the simplest thing. When even a trip to the corner shop for a bottle of milk had become a media scrum.

Her kettle, radio, her crocks and pots. The bits and pieces she'd accumulated since she'd left the care system.

She was now worse off than she'd ever been. No job, nowhere to live. She was going to have to start again from scratch.

How much did she have left in her old account? Enough for the deposit on a room in a flat share?

There had been a time when she'd have known to the last penny.

'I didn't plan this very well, did I?' she said, trying to keep the panic out of her voice.

'I've no idea what you've done, Lucy.'

Nothing. She hadn't done a thing...

'I missed the start of the news bulletin but you wield a mean handbag.'

'That man grabbed me,' she protested. 'He wouldn't let me go.'

'I wasn't criticising. It must have been terrifying to be caught up in that kind of media mayhem. I didn't catch the wrap up,' he prompted. 'As you're aware, Pam collapsed and I was called away.'

'Is she going to be okay?' Lucy asked.

'Just a seasonal bug. She should have stayed at home, but it tends to get hectic at this time of year.'

She glanced at him. 'You saw me, didn't you? When you were talking to Mr Alyson.'

'I saw the costume,' he said. 'Not you. I was looking for a girl in a very sexy black dress.'

At least he didn't deny that he'd been looking for her.

'It was only later,' he added, glancing down at her, 'when I remembered your beauty spot, that I realised it was you.'

'My what?'

'Your beauty spot,' he repeated, pausing, turning to face her. 'Here.'

'That's not...'

Her voice dried as he touched his fingertip to the corner of her lip. He was close, his eyes were dark, slumberous as he looked down at her, and for a moment she thought he was going to kiss her, finish what he'd started on the stairs.

Her heart rate picked up, hammering in her throat; all she could see was his mouth, bracketed by a pair of deep lines and, as his lower lip softened, she finally understood the depth of Rupert's betrayal. Just how shockingly she had been fooled. Because this was how it should be. The entire body engaged, every cell focused on the desire for the touch, the taste of that mouth against hers. Nothing else. And, as a finger of heat spiralled through her, a tiny, urgent gasp escaped her lips.

The sound, barely audible, was enough to shatter the spell. He raised heavy lids, lifting his gaze from her mouth to her eyes and dropped his hand.

'It's j-just a mole,' she said quickly, taking a step back, putting an arm's length between them before straightening her shoulders, lifting her chin. 'Rupert wanted me to have it removed. Just a little bit too warts-and-all ordinary for him, apparently.'

'If Henshawe thinks you're ordinary he needs to get his eyes tested.'

'Does he?' she asked, for a moment distracted by the unexpected compliment. But only for a moment. 'Well, green striped tights do tend to make you stand out from the crowd,' she said in an attempt at carelessness that she was a long way from feeling. And then wished she hadn't as he gave her legs the kind of attention that they could do without at the moment.

'True,' he said, finally dragging his gaze away from them, 'but I noticed you before you morphed into an elf,' he reminded her as he retrieved her elbow and headed briskly for the stairs.

'It's hard to miss someone falling over their own feet right in front of you,' she said, stumbling a little in the soft boots as she struggled to keep up with him.

He slowed, a consideration that she was sure neither Rupert nor his men would show her.

'Of course I have spent the last few months being buffed and polished and waxed,' she rushed on, trying not to think about how much 'notice' he'd taken of her. How close he'd just come to 'noticing' her again—this time in an empty store with none of the constraints of shoppers pounding past them. He was the enemy, for heaven's sake, and while she wanted to throw him off the scent, she wasn't entirely sure who would be distracting who... 'My hair has been streaked, my eyelashes dyed, my eyebrows threaded and I've lost weight, too.'

'Don't tell me. You had a personal trainer.'

'Good grief, no. I've just been too busy to snack between meals.' She gave him an arch look, ran a finger over one of her well-tended brows. 'You have no idea how much time it takes to look this groomed.'

He glanced at her, taking a long look at her messy hair and clothes that not even a catwalk model could make look good.

'Forget I said that,' she said hurriedly. 'I've been deprived of chocolate for too long and it's affecting my brain.'

Suddenly desperate for the instant gratification of chocolate melting on the tongue, she stopped, forcing him to do the same, dug the chocolate finger biscuit out of her elf pouch—so much more satisfying than acorns—and unwrapped it. As she raised it to her mouth she realised that she had an audience and she snapped it in half, offering one of the fingers to Nathaniel Hart.

He shook his head, not bothering to hide a smile. And she was right. The distraction was mutual. 'Your need is greater.'

She wasn't arguing and she bit into it, struggling to contain a groan of sheer pleasure.

'Better?'

'Marginally. Don't get me wrong,' she said, licking her fingers—she'd been carrying the chocolate next to her body and it was soft. 'I enjoyed it all. The gorgeous clothes. Being made over, every single bit of me being made as perfect as humanly possible without the intervention of surgery. Who wouldn't?'

That, after all, was the dream she was selling. Buy your clothes from this store and you too can have all this.

'Surgery?'

'I drew the line at the boob job. And the spray tan. I like my orange in a glass. Or chocolate-flavoured.'

She tossed a glance in his direction, but he shook his head. 'No comment.'

'Oh, please. Everyone has an opinion.' From the editor of a magazine who was desperate to do a step-by-step photo feature of a silicone implant—and had really struggled to hide her annoyance when she'd refused to play along—to the woman who did her nails. Everyone, apparently, wanted a bigger cup size. Everyone except her. She put her hands to her waist and pushed out her chest, straining the buttons to the limit. 'Apparently my naturalness and lack of guile wasn't, when push came to shove, quite enough. But that's the Cinderella story, isn't it? She had to be transformed before she was fit for the prince. All imperfections disappearing with a wave of a magic wand. Or the modern equivalent.'

He lifted an eyebrow.

'Photoshop.'

'But he still wanted her when he saw her as she really was. In her rags and covered with ashes from the hearth.'

'Oh, please! He didn't even recognise her.' She looked at the elegant red suede shoe he was still carrying, then up at Nathaniel Hart. 'Do you want to risk it?' she asked. 'If the shoe doesn't fit, will you let me go?'

'The shoe fell out of your bag, Lucy.'

'Did you see it fall?'

'Well, no...'

'Then I believe that is what's known in legal circles as circumstantial evidence.'

'Not if I find the matching one in there.'

'The matching one is jammed in a grating two streets away.' Then, unable to bear the suspense, the teasing pretence a moment longer, 'Shall we cut the pretence? How long have I got?'

His dark brows drew together in a puzzled frown. 'I'm sorry? How long have you got for what?'

'There's no need to pretend. I know you've called him. Rupert,' she added when his frown only deepened. 'I saw you. As you left the locker room.'

'The only person I've spoken to in the last twenty minutes—apart from you—is my chief security officer. To inform him that, rather than going straight to my office, I was still in the store.'

They'd reached the Food Hall and he released her elbow, snagged a trolley and headed down the nearest aisle.

Not Rupert?

Lucy firmly smothered the little flicker of hope that he was for real, ate the second finger of biscuit for comfort and went after him.

'Nice try,' she said when she caught up, 'but you were following me. On the stairs.'

'We were going in the same direction,' he conceded, picking up a box of eggs, glancing back at her. 'What made you look back?'

'Sheer paranoia? When I ran out of that hotel I had a dozen or so people on my tail. I knew I wasn't far enough ahead to have evaded all of them. I was trying not to draw attention to myself,' she said. 'Waiting for the hand on my shoulder.'

'And you thought I was the hand?'

'Aren't you? I heard you tell Frank Alyson to keep a

look out…' She faltered as he stopped by a shelf containing breakfast cereals. She was beginning to sound paranoid. Could she have got it wrong? That he didn't have a clue what she was talking about…'You will tell me if I'm making a total idiot of myself, won't you?'

CHAPTER SIX

'YOU'RE making a total idiot of yourself,' Nathaniel said obligingly, 'but it's okay. You're scared. I don't know why and you don't have to tell me. And I had the people following you escorted from the store.'

'You did? But how did you know?'

'They weren't discreet.' The muscles in his jaw tightened momentarily. 'Of course it's likely they were replaced but you should be safe enough now that the store is closed. They'll have to accept that you aren't inside and go away.' He continued to examine the shelf. 'Be glad to in this weather, I should think.'

'I suppose.'

'As for me, I was just doing my afternoon round of the store. It was pure chance that I happened to be following you up the stairs. What's your favourite cereal?' he asked, looking back at her.

'Mr Hart…'

'Nat. This one looks interesting,' he said, taking a box from the shelf. 'It has fruit pieces and something called clusters.'

'Nathaniel…'

'What are "clusters"?'

'Not one of your five-a-day,' she snapped, beginning to lose it. No. She'd lost it the minute he'd looked at her. He was looking at her now and her mouth dried. 'I haven't the faintest idea. I've never bought fancy breakfast cereals in my life. I always have porridge.'

'Always?'

'It's cheap, filling and good for you.' And, even when you had a platinum credit card with your name on it, old habits died hard.

'It also requires a saucepan and heat,' he pointed out.

'I was quite content with the crisps and the chocolate.'

'You've eaten the chocolate,' he reminded her, replacing the fancy cereal with its fruit and clusters on the shelf. 'Porridge it is.'

'No! I don't want anything.'

But he'd tossed a smart tartan box into the trolley.

It bore about as much similarity to the jumbo pack of own-brand oats she bought from the supermarket as the Lucy B version of the cashmere dress she'd abandoned, and she was sure the packaging reflected the price.

'And, just so there's no misunderstanding,' he continued, scanning the shelves as they moved on, 'the only thing I was asking Frank to keep an eye open for was anyone else showing signs of the bug that laid Pam low.'

'But—'

'The last thing I need at this time of year is an epidemic. Staff passing it on to the children visiting the grotto.'

She looked up at him, searched his face. He submitted patiently to her scrutiny, as if he understood what she was doing. He looked genuine but so had everyone else she'd met in the last few months. All those nice people who had been lying to her.

She could no longer trust her own judgement.

'Can I believe you?'

'It doesn't really matter what I say, does it? If I've called Henshawe to tell him where you are there is no escape. If

I haven't, then you're safe. Only time can set your mind at rest.'

'So,' she asked, a wry smile pulling at her lip, 'is that a yes or a no?'

His only response was to reach for a bottle of maple syrup and add it to the trolley.

'Suppose I insisted on leaving?' she persisted. 'Right this minute.'

'I'd find you some warm clothes and then drive you wherever you wanted to go.'

'Why?'

'Because, interesting though that outfit is, I imagine you'd rather leave wearing something that doesn't look as if you've escaped from a pantomime.'

Lucy discovered that she couldn't speak.

'Because you're under my roof, Lucy. Staff, temp, customer, you're my responsibility.'

She shook her head in disbelief.

'You're afraid I'd trick you? That I'd take you to him?'

He didn't appear to take offence which, considering the way she'd been casting doubt on his character, was suspicious in itself and Lucy shook her head again. Her entire world had been turned upside down for the second time in months, but this time not for the good.

'I can't trust anyone. I thought I knew Rupert. I thought he cared for me. I don't and he doesn't. The only thing he appears to care about is his profit and loss statement.'

'Are you sure? I don't know Henshawe, other than by reputation,' he continued when she didn't say anything. 'What I've read in the financial pages. Frankly, he's not a man I'd want to do business with, but love can change a man.'

'Well, that's just rubbish and you know it,' she declared.

'The only time you can change a man is when he's in nappies.'

She saw him pull his lips back tight against his teeth, doing his best not to smile. His eyes let him down.

'It's not funny!' But she found herself struggling with a giggle. 'Rupert Henshawe is not, and never was, in love with me. What we had was not a romance, I discovered today, but a marketing campaign. That's why I gave him back his ring.'

'A masterpiece in understatement, if I might say so. You have a good throwing arm, by the way. Have you ever played cricket?'

'They showed that on the news?' She groaned, mortified at the spectacle she'd made of herself. Then she sighed. 'What does it matter? It'll be on the front page of every newspaper tomorrow morning. The only story about our relationship that wasn't carefully stage-managed by his PR team.'

'You and the PR team got lucky. Tomorrow's headlines will all be about the weather.'

'It's still snowing?'

'Deep and crisp and even,' he said. 'Traffic chaos from one end of the country to the other. It's no night for an elf to be out.' He paused. 'Especially not in something that doesn't cover her—'

'I've got the picture.' She tugged on the back of the tunic. 'Thank you.'

When she still didn't move he took her hand and pressed his phone, warm from his pocket, into it.

'If you can't trust me, take this, call Enquiries and ask for a cab firm, although I warn you you'll have a long wait in this weather.'

Calling her bluff. He knew she had nowhere to go. She

opened it, anyway. Keyed in the number for Enquiries but, before it was answered, she broke the connection.

'We both know that if I had anywhere to go, anyone to call, I wouldn't be standing here in this ridiculous outfit,' she said. 'I'd be long gone.'

Nat watched her accept the bitter truth and felt his heart breaking for her. No one should be so alone. So friendless.

'I'm sorry. It's tough when you love someone and they let you down.'

'Love is a word, not an emotion, Nathaniel. We're sold on it from the time we're old enough to listen to fairy tales. Songs, movies, books… It's a marketing man's dream. I was in love with the idea of being in love, that's all. Swept up in the Cinderella story as much as anyone buying the latest issue of *Celebrity*. It's not my heart that's in a mess. It's my life.' About to hand the phone back to him, she said, 'Actually, would you mind if I sent a message?'

'You've thought of someone?'

Why didn't that make him feel happier?

'Half a million someones,' she replied. 'My Twitter and Facebook followers. Some of them must be genuine.'

'It seems a fair bet,' he admitted. 'What will you say?'

'Don't worry, I'm not about to ask them to descend en masse on Hastings & Hart and rescue me.'

'Pity. It would make this the best Christmas H&H have ever had,' he said, then wished he hadn't.

'Sorry. While I'd like to oblige you by delivering a store full of customers at opening time, right now I'm doing my best to stay beneath the radar while I figure out what to do.'

'It's your call. What will you say?'

'*Trust no one*…springs to mind. Or does that sound a touch paranoid?'

'Just a touch.' He turned away, giving her a moment to think while he pretended to scan the shelf. 'And since Henshawe, in his statement to camera regarding your outburst, managed to imply that you not only had an eating disorder but were mainlining tranquillisers to deal with the stress of your new lifestyle, that might not be in your best interests.'

'He did *what?*'

'He was touchingly sincere.'

Her eyes narrowed.

'I'm just saying. Having met you, I can see how unlikely that is. At least about the eating disorder,' he added, tossing a packet of chocolate biscuits into the trolley. The ones with really thick chocolate and orange cream in the middle. Maybe they'd tempt her to stay.

'Thanks for that!'

Lucy noted the chocolate biscuits. The man was not just eye candy. He paid attention…

'Any time. And, let's face it, you're a bit too sparky to be on tranquillisers.'

'Sparky?' She grinned. Couldn't help herself. '*Sparky?*'

'I was being polite.'

'Barely,' she suggested. 'You're right, of course. It was my mouth that got me into all this trouble in the first place. But I can see how his mind is working and that does scare me.' And, just like that, she lost all desire to smile.

'He blamed the press for causing the problems by hounding you out of the flat you shared with your friends.'

'If you're attempting to reassure me, I have to tell you that it's not working.'

'You didn't feel hounded?'

Nat added some crackers to the trolley, then crossed

to the cold cabinet and began to load up with milk, juice, salads, cheese.

'A bit,' she admitted, trailing after him. 'I couldn't move without a lens in my face, but since it was his PR people who were orchestrating the hysteria it seems a bit rich to blame the poor saps wielding the cameras. But I have fair warning what to expect when Rupert catches up with me.'

Nat glanced at her.

'I'll be whisked into one of his fancy clinics for my own good,' she said, responding to his unasked question.

'He has clinics?'

'He has a finger in all kinds of businesses, including a chain of clinics that provides every comfort to the distressed celebrity. A nip and tuck while you're drying out?' she said, pulling on her cheeks to stretch her mouth. 'No problem. A little Botox to smooth away the excesses of a coke habit? Step right in. Once he's got me there, he'll probably throw away the key.'

Lucy attempted a careless laugh, but he suspected that she was trying to convince herself rather more than him that she was joking.

He was more concerned why Henshawe would want her out of the way that badly—or why she'd think he would—and when he didn't join in she stopped pretending and frowned at the phone.

'How about, *I'll be back!*…?' she offered.

'Will you?' he asked. 'Go back?'

'To Rupert?' She appeared puzzled. 'Why would I do that?'

'Because that's what women do.'

'You think this is just some tiff?' she demanded when he didn't answer. 'That it'll blow over once I've straightened myself out? Got my head together?'

'It happens,' he said, pushing her, hoping that she might volunteer some answers.

'Not in this case.'

She snapped the phone shut without sending any kind of message and offered it back to him.

'Why don't you hang on to it for now?' he suggested. 'In case you change your mind.'

She looked at him, still unsure of his motives. Then she shrugged, tucked the phone into the pouch at her belt.

'Thanks.'

Her voice was muffled, thick, and he turned away, picked up a couple of apples and dropped them in the trolley. Giving her a moment. Sparky she might be, but no one could fail to be affected by a bad breakup. Especially one that had been played out in the full gaze of the media. Tears were inevitable.

After a moment she picked up a peach, weighed it in her hand, sniffed it. Replaced it.

'No good?' he asked, taking one himself to check it for ripeness.

'They are a ridiculous price.'

'I can probably manage if you really want one. I get staff discount.'

That teased a smile out of her, but she shook her head. 'Peaches are summer fruit. They need to be warm.'

And, just like that, he could see her sitting in the shade of an Italian terrace, grapes ripening overhead, her teeth sinking into the flesh of a perfectly ripe sun-warmed peach straight from the tree. Bare shoulders golden, meltingly relaxed.

Her lips glistening, sweet with the juice...

'I get why you ran out of the press conference, Lucy,' he said, crushing the image with cold December reality. 'But, having dumped the man so publicly, I don't understand why he's so desperate to find you.'

She swallowed, managed a careless shrug. 'I thought you didn't want to know.'

He didn't. If he knew, he would be part of it, part of her story. But, conversely, he did, desperately, want her to trust him and the two were intertwined.

'I have something of his. Something he wants back,' she admitted.

The file, he thought, remembering the glossy black ring binder she'd been holding up in the news clip. That she'd been carrying in her bag.

It wasn't there now, he realised.

'Maybe you should just give it back,' he suggested. 'Walk away.'

'I can't do that.'

Before he could ask her why, what she'd done with it, she was distracted by the sound of voices coming through the arch that led to the butchery.

'It's just one of the cleaning crews,' he said quickly, seizing her wrist as panic flared in her face and she turned, hunting for the nearest escape route. 'Good grief, you're shaking like a leaf. What the hell has he done to you? Do you need the police?'

'No!' Her throat moved as she swallowed.

'Are you sure? What about this?' he demanded, releasing her wrist, lifting his hand to skim his fingertips lightly over the bruise darkening at her temple.

She stared at him. 'What? No! A photographer caught me with his camera. It was an accident. Nothing to do with Rupert.' She looked anxiously towards the archway, the voices were getting nearer. 'Please…'

'Okay.' He wasn't convinced—he'd heard every variation of the bruise excuse going—but this wasn't the moment to press it. 'We're done here,' he said, heading for the nearest lift.

'You can't take the trolley out of the food hall,' she protested as the doors opened.

'You want to stay and pack the groceries into carriers?' he asked, stopping them from closing with his foot.

A burst of song propelled her into the lift. 'No, you're all right.'

'Doors closing. Going up...'

'What?' She turned on him. 'Where are you taking me?'

'Believe me, you'll be a lot safer on the top floor than the bottom one,' he said quickly. 'There'll be no security staff. No curious cleaners wondering why you look familiar. Where they've seen you before.'

She opened her mouth, closed it again, her jaw tightening as she swallowed down whatever she was going to say.

'You'd never have got away with it, Lucy.'

'You don't know that,' she declared, staring straight ahead. 'And it would test your security staff. If they found me you'd know they're as good as you think they are.'

'Believe me, they are. And you'd spend the night in a police cell.'

'Oh, but—'

'They don't call me when they find intruders, Lucy. They call the local police station and then the game would be up. If you're so sure that the cleaners would recognise you, I think it's a fair bet to assume that whoever turned up to arrest you would, too.'

She slumped back against the side of the lift. 'You're right, of course. And the elf costume would confirm everything that Rupert was saying about me. That I'm one sandwich short of a picnic.'

'It wouldn't look good,' he agreed. 'But if you really do have your heart set on spending the night in a tent, I'll go and fetch one of those pop-up ones. You can set it up on the bedroom floor.'

The lift came to a halt. *'Tenth floor... Customer services. Accounts. Doors opening...'*

'Bedroom floor?' She frowned. 'I thought the bedroom department was on the fifth...'

She stopped, blushing, remembering too late how she knew that.

'Forget the bedroom department,' he said, leading the way past the customer services department, down a corridor past empty offices. 'Have you never heard of living over the shop?'

'Over the corner shop, maybe,' she said as he used a swipe card to open a door that led to an internal lobby containing a private lift from the car park and a pair of wide double doors. 'But not...'

He keyed a number into a security pad, opened the door and, as he stood back to allow her to precede him, her protest died away.

Ahead of her was the most striking room Lucy had ever seen. Acres of limed floor. A pair of huge square black leather sofas. Starkly modern black and steel furniture. Dove-grey walls. No paintings, no colour, not a single thing to distract from the view through the soaring wall of glass in front of her. Constant movement, the ever-changing vibrant colour of the cityscape against the monochrome room.

'Wow!' she exclaimed, gazing out over a London lit up and laid out at her feet like fairyland. 'You actually live here?' she asked, moving closer.

There were lights everywhere.

Not just the Christmas lights, but every famous landmark

floodlit to show it at its best. There was traffic crossing bridges, strings of lights along the Thames. Even the aircraft coming into land, navigation lights winking, added to the drama.

And Christmas trees, everywhere there were Christmas trees.

Big ones in squares, rows of small ones atop buildings, every shape and size in gardens and shining out of windows. The colours reflected in the big soft flakes of snow falling like feathers over the city, settling on parks, covering trees, rooftops. Wiping the world clean.

He hadn't answered and she turned to him, expecting to see him smiling, amused by her totally uncool reaction.

But his face was expressionless.

'When I'm in London,' he said. 'There are stores all over the country, as well as abroad. I seem to spend a lot of time in hotels.'

'They don't all have apartments like this on the top floor?'

'No. I can say with confidence that this is unique. It was commissioned by my cousin, Christopher Hart, as part of the refurbishment of the Hastings & Hart flagship store.'

'It's amazing. I bet you can't wait to get home.'

'This isn't home...' He bit off the words as if they'd escaped before he could stop them. And when she waited for him to tell her why, 'It's a long story.'

'Is it? Well, here's the deal. You tell me yours and I'll tell you mine.'

'Long and very boring. Make yourself at...'

'Home?' she offered, filling the gap.

He managed a smile. He had an entire repertoire of them, she discovered. Sardonic. Amused. The one that lit up her insides, fizz, whoosh, bang, like a New Year firework display.

And then there was this one. The blank-eyed kind you cranked up when you didn't want anyone to know how you were really feeling. The shutters had come down so fast she almost heard them clang, excluding her. And now they were down she knew how much she wanted to go back two minutes.

'Or not,' she said when the silence had gone on for far too long.

'My problem, not yours, Lucy. Look around. Find yourself a room—there are plenty to choose from. I'll be in the kitchen.'

He didn't wait to see if she accepted his invitation, but returned to the trolley, disappeared through a door. Something had touched a raw nerve and while every instinct was urging her to go after him, put her arms around him, kiss it better, he might as well have painted a sign saying *keep out* on his back.

Instead, she took him at his word and looked around. The small flat she'd occupied at the top of Rupert's townhouse had been elegant, comfortably furnished, but this was real estate on an entirely different level.

It was the kind of apartment that she'd seen featured in the 'at home' features in *Celebrity*. So tidy that it looked as if no one lived there.

This was a somewhat extreme example, she decided. There was no Christmas tree here, no decorations. Not so much as a trace of tinsel.

Maybe, she decided, when you worked with it all day, you needed to escape. Maybe.

This might be a stunning apartment but he'd said himself that it wasn't home. So where was? She wanted to know.

Her fingers trailed over the butter-soft leather of the sofa as she turned, taking it all in and, looking up, she saw an open gallery with the same stunning view of the city. It was reached by a circular staircase and, taking Nathaniel at his word, she went up, finding herself in a space wide enough for casual seating. Armchairs in more of that soft black leather.

There was a single pair of black panelled doors. Assuming that they led to an internal lobby where she'd find the bedrooms, she opened one and stepped through.

For a moment all she could see was the blinking of the navigation lights of a plane passing overhead, then soft concealed lighting, responding to movement, gradually revealed the room she'd stumbled into.

The dark, asymmetrical pyramid of glass above her that would, by day, light the room. The tip of a landmark that rose like a spear into the sky. Silver in the rain. Bronze, gold, fiery red when struck by the sun. Never the same.

Below it was the largest bedroom she had ever seen, perfect in every striking detail. The walls were a soft dove-grey and, apart from the bed, a vast space of pure white, the only furniture was a cantilevered slab of black marble that ran the entire width of the room behind the bed.

Unable to stop herself, she opened a door that led to a pair of dressing and bath rooms. His and hers.

Nathaniel's?

No. Despite an array of the most luxurious toiletries, the designer suits, couturier dresses, in the walk-in wardrobes, it was obvious that neither of them was in use. It wasn't just the fact that all the clothes were cocooned in plastic covers.

There was no presence here. Like the rest of the apartment, it was visually stunning, austere, silent.

But here the silence was a hollow, suffocating emptiness.

Even the art was monochrome. Just one piece, a black-framed architectural impression of the Hastings & Hart building that filled the space above the bed.

The only point of colour in the room was a single crimson rose in a silver bud vase gleaming against the black marble.

She touched a velvety petal, expecting it to be silk, but it was real. The one thing in the room, in the entire apartment, as far as she could tell, that was alive and she shivered as she stared up at the drawing.

The building was a thing of light, energy, leaping from the earth. While this…

'This isn't home…'

And then her eyes focused on the signature on the drawing.

Nathaniel Hart.

Nat emptied the groceries onto the central island of the vast kitchen that he rarely used for anything other than making coffee.

He'd offered to pitch Lucy a tent but wasn't that what he was doing? Camping out. Living here but doing his best not to touch anything.

As if by not making an impression, not disturbing anything, maybe one morning he would wake up and he'd be back in his own life. The nightmare over.

Lucy closed the doors, quietly retraced her steps down to the lower floor, found the kitchen.

Nathaniel was standing with his back to the door, arms spread wide, hands gripping the counter so hard that his knuckles were white. Certain she was intruding, she took an instinctive step backwards, but he heard and half turned, his face as empty as the room upstairs.

'I'm lost,' she said quickly.

'Lost?'

'Not so much lost as confused. I went upstairs. It seemed the obvious thing to do.' She lifted a shoulder in an embarrassed little shrug.

'My fault.' He straightened, dragged both hands through his hair. 'I should have given you the guided tour instead of leaving you to find your own way around.'

'I could have found my own way. I just didn't want to blunder in anywhere else that's private.'

'It's not private. It's just…' He shook his head. 'Come on, I'll show you around.' He grasped her hand and led the way to a wide corridor with a series of doors, all on one side.

'Linen cupboard,' he said, keeping her hand tucked in his. 'Bedroom, bedroom, bedroom…' opening doors to reveal three empty bedrooms, all decorated with the same pale walls, black marble night tables, white linen as the room upstairs. 'Bedroom,' he repeated, opening the last door to reveal yet more of the same, finally releasing her hand, leaving it for her to decide whether or not to follow him inside because this was not just another bedroom.

'This is your room,' she said.

'The master suite upstairs spooked you and you don't know me.' He turned to face her. 'I wanted you to see for yourself that I have nothing to hide.'

'You don't feel like a stranger,' she said, following him, placing her hand in his. Foolish, maybe, especially considering the way her heart leapt whenever he was within ten feet of her. Yes, the room upstairs had spooked her, but it didn't seem to be doing much for him either, and his fingers closed about hers. Almost as if they were uniting against the world.

The word dropped into her chest with a thunk, but for once she kept her mouth closed, her thoughts to herself.

United...

That was what it had felt like when he'd held her on the stairs. Instinctive. Natural. There had been no barriers between them, only an instant and mutual recognition, and in another place somewhere private, they'd have been out of their clothes, not caring about anything but the need to touch, to hold and be held, feel the heat of another human body.

Not just lust at first sight. Something far deeper than that.

Slightly shocked at the direction her mind was taking, she forced herself to retrieve her hand, ignore the cold emptiness where his palm had been pressed against hers and concentrate on the room.

Square, with long, narrow floor to ceiling windows on two sides, it occupied the corner of the building.

Nathaniel had barely made an impression on it. There were a few books piled up on the marble ledge beside the bed and, taking advantage of his invitation, she ran her fingers down the spines. Art. Design. Management. Psychology. No fiction. Nothing just for fun.

The only thing that set this room apart from the others was a drawing board and stool, tucked up into the corner. As far out of the way as possible.

There was nothing else that gave any clue to the man.

A bathroom. A wardrobe-cum-dressing room, smaller than the ones upstairs. At least his clothes were lived in, used and, unable to help herself, she lifted the sleeve of one of maybe a dozen identical white shirts.

She turned, saw that he was watching her. 'Fresh air,' she said. 'It smells of fresh air. Like washing hung out on a windy day.'

'You're wasted as an elf. You should be writing copy for the manufacturers of laundry products.'

'Not me!' She shook her head. 'Sorry, I didn't mean to snap, but I'm right off the whole idea of marketing right now.'

She dropped the sleeve, stepped past him, back into the bedroom.

'Tell me, Nathaniel,' she asked as she looked around, 'did you get a discount for buying in bulk?'

'Bulk?'

'The paint. The marble. I know you designed the building. I saw your drawing. In the room upstairs.'

'I designed the building. The store,' he confirmed. 'But the apartment was private space, decorated to client specification. The idea was that nothing should distract from the windows. The colour, the movement. The concept of the city as living art.'

'Right.'

'You don't like it?'

'The initial impact is stunning. The views are incredible, but...' She hesitated as she struggled to find the words to explain how she felt.

'But?'

'But everything with colour, life, movement is happening somewhere else. To someone else. Up here, you're just...' she gave an awkward little shrug '...a spectator.'

CHAPTER SEVEN

'How long have you been here, Lucy?'

'I don't know. Twenty minutes?' She looked across at him. 'Do you want me to leave now?'

'You're not going anywhere. And I'm not offended. I was merely calculating how long it had taken you to see the fatal flaw in a design that wowed the interior design world. Was featured in a dozen magazines.'

'And was cousin Christopher pleased about that?' she asked, sensing that he wasn't entirely happy with what had been done with the amazing space he'd provided. 'He is the man whose clothes are shrouded in the dressing room upstairs, I take it?'

'He was torn, I'd say. He'd thrown open the doors to the likes of *Celebrity* magazine, wanting the world to see his eyrie. He'd forgotten that I was the one who would be credited with its creation.'

And the impression she'd gained that he didn't like the man much, even if he was kin, solidified.

'I'll bet you a cheese omelette that they all focused on the windows. That's if you'd allow anything that yellow to brighten the monochrome perfection of your kitchen.'

'I let you in,' he reminded her, 'and I promise you no one has ever looked greener, or more out of place.'

'Dressed like this,' she replied, reprising the twirl, 'I'd look out of place anywhere except your basement.'

'True.'

'Maybe you should have left me down there.'

'Maybe you should get out of it.'

Something about the way he was looking at her sent a tremor of longing through her. It was as if something had become unhinged in her brain. Shock—it had to be shock. She didn't do this. But, before she could do something really stupid, she said, 'I think we'll stick with the plan.'

Plan! What plan?

When he didn't answer she crossed to the drawing board to take a look at what he was working on. It wasn't a big project, just the front and side elevations of a single-storey house.

There was a photograph clipped to the corner of the board. Taken from a rocky ledge, the land fell away to a small sandy cove. The site for the house?

The edges of both photograph and drawing were curling slightly, as if they hadn't been touched in a long time. Yet it was here, he kept it close, and she ran a hand over the edge of the photograph in an attempt to smooth it.

'This is nice,' she said, looking back at him. 'Where is it?'

He didn't look at the picture.

'Cornwall.'

'I've never been to Cornwall.'

'You should,' he said, his face devoid of expression and for a moment she thought she'd put her foot in her mouth. Right up to her ankle. 'It's... nice.' Then she saw the tiny betraying flicker at the corner of his eye. 'And full of Cornish piskies. Dressed like that, you'd be right at home.'

He was teasing her?

'I'm not a pixie,' she said, mock indignantly, to disguise the rush of pleasure, warmth, that threatened to overwhelm her. 'I'm an elf.'

'Piskies, not pixies.' Then, abruptly, 'That's the lot. You've seen it all now. Choose a room, Lucy. Make yourself at home. I'll go and make a start on that cheese omelette I owe you.'

'You're admitting I was right?' she demanded, not wanting him to go.

'Smart as paint,' he agreed, leaving her in his room. A gesture of trust? Because she was a stranger, too. Or because he felt the same tug of desire, heat?

Except they weren't. Strangers. They might never have met before but, from the moment their eyes had met, they had known one another, deep down. Responding to something that went far beyond the surface conventions.

She looked again at the photograph.

Nice.

What a pathetic, pitiful word to describe such a landscape. To describe a house designed with such skill that it would become a part of it.

It wasn't *nice*; it was dramatic, powerful, at one with its setting.

It was extraordinary. Twenty minutes. That was all it had taken her to see through surface veneer to the darkness at the heart of the apartment.

He'd designed it as a gift for Claudia, his cousin's wife. Envisaged it filled with light, colour, life—reflecting the light, colour, life of the city. He'd been forced to watch, helpless, as Christopher had taken his vision and sucked the life right out of it. Just as he'd sucked the life right out of the woman he loved.

* * *

Lucy didn't bother to look at each room before deciding which to choose. They were all as soulless as the room upstairs.

She dumped her bag on the bed and checked out the en suite bathroom. Like those upstairs, it was supplied with all the essentials, including a new toothbrush which she fell upon with gratitude.

She'd replace it first thing...

She caught her reflection in the mirror. *First thing* suggested that she was staying. That she had taken him at his word. Trusted that bone-deep connection...

'Not bright, Lucy B,' she said. 'You are such a pushover. One smile and he's got you wrapped around his little finger.'

One look and she'd seen her engagement to Rupert for the sham it was.

But, even if he was as genuine as her instincts—and just how reliable were those dumb whoosh, flash, bang hormones anyway?—were telling her, this was, could only ever be, a very temporary stopgap.

Breathing space.

She took out her own phone and it leapt into life. Of course. Why would Rupert cut her off when it was the one way he could contact her?

There were dozens of voicemails. She ignored them. There was no one she could think of who'd have anything to say that she wanted to hear. But she opened Rupert's last message:

Henshawe 20:12. We need to talk.

Blunt and to the point, it didn't escape her that he'd waited until the store was closed, all the doors were locked and there was no chance that she was still inside before calling her.

Proof, if she needed it, that he'd had someone watching all that time, just in case.

No doubt he'd had everyone out checking anywhere else she might have taken cover, too. She guessed some of the messages were from her former flatmates, the owner of the nursery where she'd worked. Everyone who had touched her life since the day her mother had abandoned her.

No apology, but at least there was no pretence. Forced to accept that she'd somehow slipped through his fingers, he was ready to talk.

The problem there was that there was nothing he had to say that she wanted to hear.

Or maybe one thing, and that was unintentional.

Not that, in her heart of hearts, she'd needed confirmation that Nathaniel really was on the level. That he'd seen she was in trouble and hadn't hesitated to step forward.

That he was one of the good guys.

But it was good to know that her judgement wasn't terminally damaged. Not as crap as she'd thought.

She logged into Twitter. There were hundreds of messages now. And a new hashtag: *#findLucyB*

No prizes for guessing who'd come up with that one, she thought, as she logged into her diary.

Nathaniel Hart is on the side of the angels. Not only can he make the world go away with a look, but he doesn't ask unnecessary questions. Which doesn't mean I'm not going to have to tell him everything. I am. I will. But not yet.

Right now, I'm a lot more interested in his story. The man is clearly a genius architect, so what the heck is he doing running a department store—stores?

And if those clothes upstairs in the creepy

bedroom belong to his cousin, the one who com-
missioned this apartment, where is he?

'Can I help?'

Nat, emptying the trolley, turned at the rare sound of
another human voice in his kitchen. Lucy was standing in
the doorway, a discordant slash of garish green against the
cool grey of the slate and marble surfaces of the kitchen.

A discordant note in his life, knocking him off balance,
sending a fizz of expectancy racing through his veins.

'Shall I put these away?' She didn't wait for an answer,
but picked up a bag of salad leaves and, as she turned, he
saw that she'd taken off the felt boots and striped tights,
that the tunic barely covered her satin-skinned thighs and
that her toenails were painted a bright candy-red that would
have all the boy elves' heads in a spin. Not to mention the
CEO of this department store.

She opened one of the doors to the stainless steel fridge
and he saw her pause for a heartbeat as she realised that,
apart from bottled water, it was empty.

'You don't do a lot of entertaining, do you?'

'I usually eat in one of the store restaurants,' he said.
'It keeps the staff on their toes, knowing I might drop in
at any time.'

'Right.'

'There are eight of them to choose from,' he said, needing to prove that he wasn't totally sad. 'Everything from
Italian to Japanese.'

'Sushi for breakfast?' She didn't wait for an answer.
'The store doesn't open until ten, does it? I don't know
about you, but I'd be gnawing my fingers off by then.'

'It's just as well I ignored your demands to put the porridge back on the shelf, then.' He took one of her hands,

rubbed a thumb over the back of her slender fingers, perfect nails. 'It would be a pity to spoil these.'

'Nathaniel...' The word came out as a gasp.

'Fortunately, the staff canteen opens at seven,' he said, cutting off the little thank you speech he could see she was working up to, letting go of her hand. He didn't want her thanks. He didn't know what he wanted. Or maybe he did. He just wasn't prepared to let go of the past. Admit it. 'It takes time to get everything pitch perfect for the public.'

'Well, that makes sense, I suppose.' She sounded doubtful. 'If you don't like to cook.' She turned back to the island, continued putting away the cold food. 'What are you planning to do for Christmas? I don't imagine the store is open on Christmas Day.'

'No. Obviously, I've tried to persuade the staff that it's a good idea, purely for my own convenience, you understand, but for some reason they won't wear it.'

Bad choice of words.

She wasn't wearing nearly enough. If she was going to stay it was essential that she cover those shapely legs. Those sweet little toes with their shiny red nails. Or he wouldn't be answerable.

Nathaniel frowned and Lucy swallowed. Hard. She was totally losing it.

'I'm sorry. That was unbelievably rude of me. You've probably noticed, but I tend to say the first thing that comes into my head. Obviously, you've got family, friends.'

A cousin, at least.

'I'm never short of invitations,' he agreed, 'but, by the time the big day arrives, all I want to do is open a tin of soup.'

'You can have too much of a good thing, huh?'

'Remind me again,' he invited, 'what exactly is good about it?'

'You don't like Christmas?'

'I repeat, what's good about it?'

'Lots of things. The fun of choosing gifts for the people you love.' No response. He didn't love anyone? No... 'Planning the food?' she offered quickly, not wanting to think about the red rose in the room upstairs. 'Oh, no. You don't cook. How about a brass band playing Christmas carols in the open air? The sense of anticipation. The faces of little children.' She didn't appear to be making much impression with the things that she loved about Christmas so she tried a different tack. 'How about the profits, Nathaniel? Remind me, how much does it cost to take a sleigh ride to Santa's grotto?'

If she'd hoped to provoke him into a show of emotion, she would have been disappointed.

'Would you care to see a breakdown of the costs involved in designing and creating a visual effects spectacular that will satisfy children who've been brought up on CGI?' he enquired, clearly not in the least bit excited by the cost or the finished product. 'You're right, Lucy. Christmas is a rip-off. A tacky piece of commercialism and if I could cancel it I would.'

'I didn't say that!'

'No? Forgive me, but I thought you just did.'

'What I was doing was offering you a personal reason to enjoy it.'

'The profit motive? Sorry, you're going to have to try harder than that.'

'Okay. Come down to the grotto and listen to the little ones for whom it's all still magic, the wonder still shiny-bright.'

'At a price.'

'I know. And I wish every child had the chance to see it.' She reached up for an egg basket, hanging over the island. 'Actually, I wouldn't mind seeing it myself.' Then, because he was a cynic and she was a fool, 'Should any of them ask you, by the way, the reindeer are parked on the roof.'

'They are?'

'Well, obviously. Santa's here so where else would they be?'

'Good point.'

'And you might warn Groceries that there's likely to be a rush on chilli-flavoured cashew nuts. You wouldn't want to miss a sale.'

'That would be tragic.' Nat felt the tension ease from his jaw as his mouth hitched up in the makings of a smile. 'I know I'm going to hate myself for asking this, but why would there be a rush on chilli-flavoured cashew nuts?'

Lucy responded with a careless shrug and he found himself holding his breath, wondering what was coming next.

'I happened to let it slip that Rudolph eats them to keep his nose bright. Dido promised to keep it secret but I can't guarantee that she won't try a little one-upmanship on her sister.'

'What an interesting day you've had, Lucy Bright.'

'It's had its ups and its downs,' she admitted. 'That was definitely an up.'

'Why cashew nuts?'

'Oh, well, peanuts can be a problem. You know. Allergies…' She regarded him steadily, waiting. Then, 'Come on, Nathaniel Hart. Get with the plot.'

Realising he'd missed something, he lifted his brows, inviting her to provide the punchline.

'Elf and safety?'

It took a moment but then he shook his head. 'I do not believe you just said that, Lucy Bright.'

'Actually, neither do I,' she said solemnly. And then she snorted with laughter.

The sound rippled around the kitchen, bouncing off doors, windows, an array of steel tools hanging from the four-sided rail above the island.

Waking everything up, Nat thought, setting up a hum that seemed to vibrate through him until he was laughing, too.

'Do you have a kettle, do you know?' she asked once she'd recovered. Then, as he reached for it, 'I don't need to be waited on.'

'I do know how to boil a kettle. Tea?' he offered. 'Or would you prefer coffee?'

'Oh, tea, I think. Camomile, if you've got it. It's a bit late for coffee.'

Only if you were able to sleep.

She transferred the eggs from the carton to the basket while he filled the kettle, switched it on. Stretched up on her toes to replace it.

Her hair had dried into a froth of little tendrils that curled around her face, against her neck. All she needed were wings and a white dress and she'd look more at home on the top of a Christmas tree than dressed as an elf.

Eggs safe, she picked up a punnet of baby plum tomatoes and looked at them for a moment, then at the plain white china mugs he'd taken from the cupboard, a tiny frown buckling her forehead.

She wasn't beautiful, there was nothing classic about her features, yet there was a sparkle in her green eyes that made everything right. Made something inside him begin to bubble, catch like a motor that hadn't been used in a while, that had to be teased into life with a touch, a smile, laughing lips that begged to be kissed.

Like a limb that had gone to sleep, the return to life hurt.

He turned away, almost with relief, as the kettle boiled and reached for one of a row of polished black canisters.

'It's not camomile,' he apologised, extracting a couple of tea bags. He rarely drank tea and discovered that they were disconcertingly beige in this monochrome world. 'I'm afraid Earl Grey is the best I can do.'

'That will be lovely,' she said, joining him. A warm presence at his side.

He dropped the bags into the mugs, poured on boiling water, looked up.

'You've settled in?' he asked, trying to forget about the kiss.

She nodded.

'You've got everything you need? Toothbrush? Toiletries?'

'Yes, thanks. Everything for the guest who forgot to pack her toilet bag,' she assured him. 'Even a bathrobe. I'll replace the toothbrush.'

'No need.'

'I'd have to buy one, anyway.'

'You'll need more than a toothbrush. You'll need some clothes.' And, before she could object, 'A change of underwear, at least.'

'You have a washing machine, I imagine?'

'There was one included in the specification,' he admitted. 'Along with every other modern convenience known to man.'

'Specified by your cousin. The man with the Gothic taste.'

'Gothic?'

'How else would you describe that room upstairs? It's pure Addams family. All it needs is a belfry for the bats.'

'It would spoil the lines. And let in the rain.'

'Heaven forbid.'

He saw the question in her eyes, then the uncharacteristic hesitation as she decided against it.

'Actually, it's all black and white, glass and brushed stainless steel in the store, too, isn't it?' she said, changing tack. 'I hadn't realised before, but of course down there it's a frame for all that colour. It works.'

'Thanks for that. I think,' he said, but it gave him an opportunity to revisit the subject of clothes. 'Actually, I was wondering, in the interests of aesthetics, if I could encourage you to change into something a little less…green.'

'In the interests of aesthetics?' Her exquisitely threaded eyebrows rose in a pair of questioning little arches. 'Is that an architectural get-out-of-your-kit line, Nathaniel Hart?'

'I wasn't suggesting you stripped off here and now.' Although the idea had considerable appeal.

'Are you sure? It sounded rather like it.'

He managed a shrug. 'I was merely pointing out that they're working clothes. If you're planning to keep up the act, continue to hide out in the grotto, you're going to need them fresh and clean in the morning. House rule,' he said.

'Is that right?' For a moment he thought she was truly offended. Then she grinned. 'Well, snap, Mr Pinstriped Suit. Off with your jacket. Off with your tie and cufflinks!'

Grinning back, he said, 'I'll change if you will. Let's go shopping.'

She was still smiling, but she was shaking her head. 'Until I get a proper job, I won't have any money. And I can't take anything from you, Nathaniel.'

Why not? Presumably, she'd allowed Henshawe to dress her. Which answered that question. But didn't help with the problem.

'Be reasonable, Lucy. You can't live in that.'

'It will be a challenge,' she admitted, but there was a steely glint in those green eyes now, and he battled down the frustration of having an entire store full of clothes he would happily give her, aware that this wasn't about him. This was about her. Her need to re-establish her self-esteem. Recover what had been stolen from her.

'You've got a proper job,' he reminded her, 'at least until Christmas. I'll sub you until the end of the week.'

'You're really going to let me work here?'

'Why not? You seem to have nothing better to do and an elf with a close personal relationship with Rudolph is a real find. Besides,' he pointed out, 'you owe Pam.' It wasn't playing fair, but he was prepared to use every trick in the book to keep her safe. Keep her close.

'Pam might have other ideas if she knew the truth,' she reminded him as she opened a carton of milk, poured a little into each mug. 'What is the going rate for an elf?'

He told her.

'Sorry...' she was going to turn him down? '...that's actually not bad, but even so I wouldn't be able to afford your prices.'

'There's a generous staff discount,' he said.

'For temps?'

'I'm a temp, too.' Long-term, until death us do part...

'Are you?' For a moment it was all there in her eyes. The questions that were piling up, but when he didn't answer all she said was, 'I bet you're on a better hourly rate than me.'

She handed him one of the mugs and turned to lean back against the counter to sip at her tea. He could feel the warmth of her body and he wished he'd taken her advice, taken off his jacket so that there was only his shirt sleeve between them.

'I wonder what happened to the real elf?' she said after a moment. 'The one from Garlands.'

'Maybe, given time to think about it, she didn't want to spend December in a windowless basement,' he said, sipping at his own tea and deciding there were more interesting ways of heating up his, her lips. How close had they been to a kiss on the stairs? An inch, two?

'Maybe. Or maybe, when it started to snow, she decided she'd rather go home and make a snowman.'

'Is that what you'd have done, Lucy?'

'Me? Fat chance. Every minute of every day is fully booked. Or it was. This afternoon I had a meeting with a wedding designer to explore ideas for my fantasy wedding.'

'It may still happen,' he said, glancing down at her, the words like ashes in his mouth.

'Nope. The word "fantasy" is the clue. It means illusory. A supposition resting on no solid ground.'

He wanted to tell her that he was sorry. But it would be a lie and actually she didn't look that upset. The brightness in her green eyes was not a tear but a flash of anger.

'So what should you be doing this evening? If you weren't here, tearing my life's work to shreds.'

'Now?' She pulled a face. 'I should be gussied up in full princess mode for a gala dinner at the Ritz, to celebrate the unveiling today of Lucy B.'

'With you as the star? Well, obviously, that would have been no fun,' he teased.

'Not nearly as much as you'd think. Speeches, smug PR men and endless photographs,' she said. 'Being an elf beats it into a cocked hat.'

'So you're saying that your day hasn't been a total write-off?'

'No,' she said, looking right at him. 'Hand on my heart, I'd have to say that my day hasn't been a total write-off.'

Any other woman and he'd have said she was putting a brave face on it, but something in her expression suggested that she was in earnest.

'Shame about the snowman, though,' she said, turning away as if afraid she'd revealed more of herself than she'd intended. She abandoned her mug. 'It doesn't often snow in London, not like this. I hope the missing elf did seize the day and go out to play.'

'It's not too late.'

'Too late for what?'

'To go out to play.' And where the hell had that come from? 'Build a snowman of your own.'

'Nathaniel!' she protested, but she was laughing and her eyes, which he'd seen filled with fear, mistrust, uncertainty, were now looking out at the falling snow with a childlike yearning and, crazy as it was, he knew he'd said the right thing. And, as if to prove it, she put a hand behind her head, a hand on her hip, arched a brow and, with a wiggle that did his blood pressure no good, said, 'Great idea, honey, but I haven't got a thing to wear.'

'Honey,' he replied, arching right back at her. 'You seem to be forgetting that I'm your fairy godmother.'

Before he could think about what he was going to do, he caught her hand and raced up the stairs with her.

The emptiness hit him as he opened the door, bringing him to an abrupt halt. Lucy was right. This wasn't a bedroom, it was a mausoleum. And that hideous rose...

'Nathaniel...' Her voice was soft behind him, filling the room with life, banishing the shadows. Her warm fingers tightened on his as if she understood. 'It doesn't matter. Leave it.'

'No. Seize the day,' he said, flinging open the door to

the dressing room with its huge walk-in wardrobe filled with plastic-covered ghosts. The colours muted. No scent. Nothing.

He pulled off covers, seeking out warm clothes. Trousers. He pulled half a dozen pairs from hangers. A thick padded jacket. Opened drawers, hunting out shirts, socks. Sweaters. Something thick, warm...

As his hand came down on thistledown wool, it seemed to release a scent that had once been as familiar as the air he breathed and, for a moment, he froze.

Carpe diem.

The words mocked him.

When had he ever seized the day? Just gone for it without a thought for the consequences; been irresponsible? Selfish? Maybe when he'd been eighteen and told his father that he wasn't interested in running a department store, that he was going to be an architect?

Had it taken all the courage, all the strength he possessed to defy, disappoint the man he loved, that he had never been able to summon up the courage to do it again?

'Nathaniel, this is madness,' Lucy called from the bedroom. 'I can't go outside. I don't have any shoes.'

He picked up the sweater, gathered everything else she was likely to need, including a pair of snow boots that he dropped at her feet, doing his best to ignore her wiggling toes with their candy nails.

'They'll be too big,' she protested.

'Wear a couple of pairs of socks.' Then, 'What are you waiting for? It'll all have disappeared by morning.'

'Madness,' she said, but she leapt to her feet and gave him an impulsive hug that took his breath away. She didn't notice, was already grinning as she began to tug the tunic over her head, offering him another glimpse of those full, creamy breasts, this time encased in gossamer-fine black lace.

Breathless? He'd thought he was breathless?

'Downstairs in two minutes,' he said, beating a hasty retreat.

CHAPTER EIGHT

LUCY scrambled into a shirt that didn't quite do up across the bust. Trousers that didn't quite meet around the waist, were too long in the leg. It was crazy stupid. But in a totally wonderful way.

She picked up the thistledown sweater, held it to her cheek for a moment, trying to catch a hint of the woman— thinner, taller than her—who'd owned it. What was she to Nathaniel? Where was she?

Nothing. Not even a trace of scent.

Relieved, she pulled it over her head. It was baggy and long enough to cover the gaps. She tucked the trousers into a pair of snow boots that swallowed the excess and the feather-light down-filled coat, the kind you might wear on a skiing holiday, had room enough to spare.

Hat, scarf.

She didn't bother to check her reflection in the mirror. She didn't need confirmation that she looked a mess. Some things it was better not to know. Instead, she picked up the gloves and, leaving behind her a room that no longer looked cold but resembled the aftermath of a jumble sale, she stomped down the stairs in her too-big boots.

By the time she'd re-applied lipstick to protect her lips from the cold, picked up her phone and purse, Nathaniel was impatiently pacing the living room.

'Two minutes, I said!'

About to reiterate that this was madness, the words died on her lips. He'd abandoned the pinstripes for jeans, a jacket similar to the one she was wearing. The focused, controlled businessman had been replaced by a caged tiger scenting escape.

'Yes, boss,' she said cheekily, pulling on her gloves as they used the private lift which took them straight to the underground car park.

He boosted her up into the seat of a black Range Rover, climbed up beside her.

'Better duck down,' he said as they approached the barrier.

'You don't think...?'

'Unlikely, but better safe than sorry.'

The traffic was light; no one with any sense would be out in this weather unless is was absolutely necessary.

'I think you might be optimistic about it thawing by morning,' she said.

'Want to risk leaving it for another day?'

'No way!'

'Thought not.'

Neither of them spoke again until he'd driven through Hyde Park and parked near the Serpentine Bridge.

'Oh, wow,' she said, staring across the utterly still, freezing waters of the lake. The acres of white, disappearing into the thick, whirling snow. 'Just...wow,' again as she unclipped the seat belt, opened the door, letting in a flurry of snow.

She didn't stop to think, but slid down, spun around in it, grinning as Nathaniel caught her hand and they ran across the blank canvas, leaving their footprints in the snow.

She picked up a handful and flung a snowball at him,

yelling as he retaliated, scoring a hit as snow found its way inside her jacket.

Lucy was right, Nat thought as they gathered snow, piling it up, laughing like a couple of kids. This was crazy. But in the best possible way. A little bit of magic that, like the kids visiting the grotto, was making a memory that would stay with him.

They rolled a giant snowball into a body, piling up more snow around its base before adding a head.

Drivers, making their way through the park, hooted encouragement but, as Lucy waved back, he caught her hand, afraid that someone might decide to stop and crash their snowman party.

He wasn't afraid that she'd be recognized. They were far enough from the street lights and the snow blurred everything. It was just that, selfishly, he didn't want to share it, share her, with anyone.

She looked up, eyes shining, snowflakes sticking to her lashes, the curls sticking out from beneath her hat, clinging for a moment to her lips before melting against their warmth.

'Are we done?' he said before he completely lost it and did in reality what he'd imagined in his head a dozen times: kiss her senseless. Or maybe that was him. The one without any sense. 'Is it big enough?'

'Not it. She. Lily.'

'A girl snowman?'

She added two handfuls of snow, patting it into shape, giving her curves.

'She is now.' She grinned up at him. 'Equal opportunities for all. Fairy godmothers. Santas. Snowmen. I wish we'd brought some dressing up clothes for her.'

He removed the pull-on fleece hat he was wearing and tucked it onto Lily's head.

'Oh, cute,' she said and draped the scarf she was wearing around her like a stole. Then she took her phone from her pocket and took a picture.

'Give it to me. I'll take a picture of both of you.'

She crouched down, her arm around the snow lady, and gave him a hundred watt smile. Then she said, 'No, wait, you should be in it, too. A reminder of how much trouble you can get into when you catch a stranger on the stairs.'

'You think?' he said, folding himself up beside her, holding the phone at arm's length. 'Closer,' he said, putting his arm around her, pulling her close so that her cheek was pressed against his and he could feel her giggling.

'We must look like a couple of Michelin men.'

'Speak for yourself,' he said, turning to look at her. Her eyes were shining, lit up, her mouth just inches from his own in a rerun of that moment on the stairs when the world went away.

Had it ever come back?

He fired off the flash before he forgot all his good intentions.

'How's that?' he said, showing her.

'Perfect,' she said, looking over his arm. 'Can I send them to my diary?'

'As a reminder of a crazy moment in the snow?'

'As a reminder that not all men are mendacious rats,' she said. 'That once in a while Prince Charming is the real deal.'

'No…' Not him. Wrong fairy tale. He was the Beast, woken by Beauty from a long darkness of the soul.

But she had fallen back in the snow, laughing as she swept her arms up and down to make a snow angel.

'Come on. You too,' she urged, laughing, and he joined in, sweeping his arms up and down until their gloved hands met. He looked across at her, lying in the snow, golden curls peeping out from beneath her hat, laughing as the huge flakes settled over her face, licking them from her lips.

'What do they taste of?' he asked.

She didn't hesitate. 'Happiness.' And then she looked at him. 'Want to share?'

She didn't wait for his answer, but rolled over so that her body bumped into his, her face above him.

There were moments—rare moments, perfect moments—when the world seemed to pause on its axis, giving you an extra heartbeat of time.

It had happened when he'd caught her on the stairs and, as her laughing lips touched his, a simple gift, and cold, wet, minty-sweet happiness seeped through him, warming him with her passionate grasp on life, it happened again, more, much more than any imagined kiss.

The world stood still and he seized the moment, lifting his hands to cradle her head, slanting his mouth against hers as the warmth became an inferno hot enough to touch the permafrost that had invaded his soul.

Her kitten eyes were more gold than green as she raised her lids. Then touched her lips to his cheek, tasted them with her tongue.

'One of us is crying,' she said.

He rubbed a gloved thumb over her cheek. 'Maybe we both are.'

'With happiness,' she declared.

'Or maybe it's just our eyes watering with the cold. I need to stand up before my butt freezes to the ground.' And, before he could change his mind, he lifted her aside, stood up.

'I've messed up your snow angel,' she said as he reached out a hand to help her to her feet.

'That's okay. I'm no angel,' he said.

'Who is?'

'If I had a Christmas tree, I'd put you on top of it,' he said and, beyond helping himself, he touched his knuckles to her cheek, kissed her again. Just a touch, but somehow more intense for its sweetness. A promise... 'Do you want a picture of your angel?' he asked, forcing himself to take a step back.

'Please.' Then, as if she, too, needed to distract herself from the intensity of the moment, 'I don't suppose you have such a thing as a piece of paper?'

He searched through his pockets, found an envelope. 'Will this do?'

'Perfect.' And, using a lipstick, she wrote in big block capitals: LUCYB WOZ HERE!

She propped it on the front of the snow lady, put out her hand for the phone and took a snap.

'Great. Tweet time, I think,' she said, pulling off her glove with her teeth and, struggling with cold fingers, keyed in a message.

Thanks for the good vibes, tweeps. Here's a tweetpic, just to let you know that I'm safe. #findLucyB
LucyB, Wed 1 Dec 22:43

Lucy lifted the phone, looking over her shoulder at him. 'What do you think? Will that have them all running around in the snow?'

'Is that the plan?' he asked as she pressed 'send'.

'I don't have a plan,' she said, lifting her hand to his cheek, pressing her lips against it. Then, as she looked up at him the smile died, 'Thank you, Nathaniel.'

'I should be thanking you. If it wasn't for you, I'd be inside going through the daily sales figures instead of finding my inner child.'

'Inside in the warm,' she said, turning away to give the

snow lady a hug. 'Stay cool, Lily.' Then she looked up. 'It's stopped snowing.'

'I told you. It'll all be gone by tomorrow. Everything will be back to normal.'

'Will it?'

She sounded less than happy at the prospect. Which made two of them.

'We've still got tonight. Are you hungry?'

Her eyes lit up. 'Absolutely starving.'

Diary update: *Fun and frolics in the park with Nathaniel. I didn't see that coming and neither, I suspect, did he. I have to admit that making a snow-man—snow lady—in the park at ten o'clock at night in a blizzard is probably not the most sensible thing I've ever done. And it's getting hard to top the stupid ones I've done today.*

And then he kissed me. No, wait, I kissed him. We kissed each other. Lying in the snow.

'I know what this is all about, you know.' Lucy gave him a sideways grin as they stood on the Embankment overlooking the river, tucking into hot dogs. 'Why we're having hot dogs. You just don't want all that nasty bright yellow eggy, cheesy stuff in your kitchen.'

'It's not that.'

Nat took out his phone and snapped her as she sucked a piece of onion into her mouth.

'Hey, not fair!'

'One more for your fans,' he said, lifting it out of reach as she made a grab for it. 'The truth of the matter, Lucy B, is that I couldn't make an omelette to save my life.'

For some reason she seemed to think that was funny. They'd laughed a lot.

She'd laughed at a couple of outrageous Santa incidents he'd shared from way back in the history of the store. He'd laughed at her stories about a day-care nursery where she'd worked. It was obvious how much she loved the children she'd worked with. From a momentary wistfulness in her look, how much she missed them.

As she'd talked, laughed, all the strain had seeped out of her limbs and her face and she'd told him enough about her character—far more than she realised—to reassure him that she was on the level.

'Actually, this is great. Crazy perfect.' She bumped shoulders with him. 'Thank you.'

'My pleasure,' he said, wrapping his arm around her waist, wanting to keep her close. And it was. Golden curls peeped out from beneath her hat, framing a face lit up, almost translucent in the lamplight.

And, as the strain had eased from her face, the knots deep in his own belly had begun to unravel, at least until that second kiss. At which point they had been replaced by a different kind of tension.

'I hope the missing elf had as much fun as we have,' she said. 'I owe her a lot.'

'Me too,' he said. 'I'll check with HR first thing to see if there were any messages. Deflect any problems.'

'Why?' she asked, her tongue curling out to catch an errant onion. 'Why would you do that? Any of this?'

Good question.

She looked up. 'What happened, Nathaniel? On the stairs.'

Another good question.

'I don't know,' he admitted. That something had happened—something momentous—was beyond doubt. 'I can tell you why I noticed you.'

'That's a start.'

'It was your hair… The way it seemed to float around your head like a halo. It reminded me of someone.'

Quite suddenly, Lucy lost her appetite. What had she expected him to say? That he'd been captivated at a glance. Lie to her? She'd had enough lies to last her a lifetime.

'The woman these clothes belong to?' she asked, pushing it.

'Claudia. Her name was Claudia. She was my cousin's wife.'

'You were in love with her?' Stupid question. Of course he was.

'We both were. I met her at university, dated her, but when I brought her home she met Christopher and after that it was always him. It didn't stop Chris obsessing that we were having an affair when we worked together on the store design.'

She lifted her hand to the bruise at her temple, gently rubbing her fingers over the sore spot, remembering his concern.

'He was abusive,' she said.

'I believe so. She used to brush aside any concern, say she bruised at a touch. Was always walking into things. Maybe she was. She wasn't eating properly, fighting an addiction to tranquillisers. Then one day I caught her running, terrified. I held her,' he said. 'Just held her, begged her to leave him. Not for me. For herself. And then Chris caught up with her, held out his hand to her and, without a word, she took it. Walked away with him. It was as if she had no will.' He glanced at her. 'It was just the hair, Lucy. You're not a bit like her.'

'No,' she said. 'I'm shorter, fatter…' He frowned and she rushed on, 'You're talking about her in the past tense.'

'There was an accident. Chris always drove too fast, even though he knew it terrified her. Probably *because* it terrified her. It's all about control, isn't it?' He looked away for a moment, but then looked back. 'She died instantly. He's in a wheelchair, paralysed from the neck down.'

She shivered, but not with the cold, and he turned to her, put his arms around her. Held her. Just as he'd held Claudia, she thought and, much as she wanted to stay there, in his arms, she pulled away.

'I have no reason to protect Rupert Henshawe, Nathaniel. He does not control me.'

'Doesn't he?' He shook his head, as if he knew the answer. 'Reason has nothing to do with it,' he said. Then, before she could deny it, 'It was my fault. I should never have come back. Never accepted the commission.'

'Why did you?'

'Family. Guilt. I turned my back on family tradition and it broke my father's heart. It was a way to make up for that.'

'And, after the accident, you stepped in to look after things?'

'There was no one else.'

'No one else called Hart, maybe. Is Christopher punishing you for what happened to him?' she asked. 'Or are you punishing yourself for not saving Claudia?' He didn't answer. Maybe he didn't know the answer. 'Who is it who leaves the rose, Nathaniel?'

'That's enough, Lucy,' he said sharply.

'It's him, isn't it? A daily reminder that she loved him. He can't abuse his wife any more, frighten her, hurt her, because she's beyond his reach,' she continued, recklessly ignoring the warning. 'So he's abusing you instead.'

There was a long moment of silence.

So not bright, Lucy Bright.

Blown it, Lucy Bright.

And then he touched her cheek with his cold hand. A gesture that said a hundred times more than words.

'Bright by name, bright by nature. Good guess, but you're not entirely right. I'm punishing myself for failing to protect her. But I'm punishing him, too. Even while it gives him pleasure to know that I've been jerked back into the family business, robbed of something I loved, at the same time it's eating him alive to know that I'm in control. In his place.'

'He had Claudia.'

'Yes, he had Claudia. His tragedy, and ultimately hers, is that he never believed that she could love him more than me. That he always thought of himself as second choice in all things.'

'Let it go, Nathaniel. If you don't, it will destroy you and then he'll have killed you both.'

'I know,' he said, looking at her. 'I know.' And somehow she was the one holding him. Hugging him to her, holding him safe. She could have stayed there for ever, making their own warm, safe space in an icy world. Then he dropped a kiss on the top of her head. 'Your turn, Lucy.'

'Mine?' She looked up at him.

'That was the deal. I tell you mine and you tell me yours. Tell me what happened on the stairs.'

'I...' About to deny it, she thought better of it. 'I don't know. I was in a bit of a state, confused. An emotional basket case.'

'That would explain it,' he replied dryly, 'but I have to tell you that, between your criticism of the penthouse and the basket case explanation of a stop-the-world-moment, you are not doing a lot for my ego.'

'I didn't mean...'

Lucy faltered. She didn't know what she meant. She was more confused now than she had been then. When he'd caught her, their eyes had met and the instant connection had entirely bypassed her brain.

Her response to him had been entirely physical, without thought or reason. Completely honest. Without guile. Innocent.

'I wanted you to kiss me,' she said. Then, because being honest really mattered, 'I wanted you.'

Even in the light from the street lamps, Nat could see the blush heat Lucy's cheeks. Felt an answering and equally primitive rush, a desire to recapture that atavistic moment of connection. The caveman response, with no need for words or complicated ritual.

Her honesty shamed him. He'd wanted her, too, with a raw urgency that shocked the civilised man. It was the same primal instinct that urged him to protect her. They were two sides of the same basic need for survival. Take the woman, plant your seed and then protect her against the world because she was your future. And he would. From what, he wasn't entirely certain, only that this time he wouldn't stand back. Wouldn't fail. No matter what the cost.

The 'no involvement' mantra had gone right out of the window the moment he'd suggested this mad adventure.

That first life-changing encounter had given him back something of himself. The kisses they'd shared in the snow had broken through a barrier. More would have them naked, in bed. That was why he'd stopped by the hot dog stall instead of taking her straight home.

'"I wanted you",' he repeated thoughtfully. 'Maybe it could do with a little work. I was thinking that it was one of those perfect, never to be repeated, once-in-a-lifetime moments when everything seems to drop into place.'

She pulled a wry smile. 'You'd think so, wouldn't you. But they will keep happening to me.'

'You're telling me that you keep meeting strangers you want to kiss?' he asked, his voice even, but the caveman response was, he discovered, a lot more powerful than the civilised veneer would suggest.

'Oh, not *kiss*.' Her smile deepened. 'That was a bonus feature. And of course last time it wasn't a chance encounter, but stage-managed, so actually you're right. Once-in-a-lifetime it is.'

'Stage-managed?'

'You want the story.' She nodded as if she'd been expecting that. 'I warn you that it's long. You'll probably want another hot dog. Extra onions for me.'

He returned with two fresh hot dogs, dripping with mustard and onions, and leaned back against the wall, his shoulder just touching hers. Just so that she'd know he was there.

Giving her courage to tell her story. Face the betrayal head-on.

'The Henshawe Corporation's High Street fashion chain had lost market share,' she began. 'It was no longer hot so they made the decision to give the stores a new look, a new name. Re-brand it. Take it upmarket.'

Lucy bit into the bun, chewed it for a while, watching a police launch moving slowly up the river, the lights dancing on the water, while she gathered her thoughts.

Nathaniel slipped his arm around her shoulder as if it was the most natural thing in the world.

'They went to their PR company, as you do,' she said, 'and commissioned them to come up with a strategy to launch the new brand. One that would not only garner maximum media coverage, but engage their target consumer audience of young women who read gossip magazines and aspire to be the wife, or at least the girlfriend, of a top sports star.'

'Or, failing that, one of the minor royals,' he said, raising a smile.

'You've got it.'

'So far, so standard.'

'Their first step was to set up focus groups to find out what that group were looking for. Get feedback on likely "names" to launch the new brand.'

'Classy, stylish, sexy clothes. Good value. A label with cachet. You don't need a focus group to tell you that,' he said.

'No, but they were surprised to discover that concerns were raised about sweatshop labour. And then someone said wouldn't it be great if they used an ordinary girl, someone like them, rather than a celebrity to be the face of the store.'

'What they meant was one of them.'

'Undoubtedly,' she said. 'But it gave the PR firm their hook. Their media campaign. All they needed was an ordinary girl.'

'So how did they find you, Miss Ordinary?' he asked.

'They advertised for a junior clerical assistant.'

'Interesting approach,' he said dryly. 'You ticked all the boxes?'

'Good grief, no. I wasn't thin enough, tall enough, pretty enough or even smart enough.'

It was all there in the file. Painful reading.

'I thought they wanted ordinary.'

'Ordinary in quotes,' she said, using her fingers to make little quote marks.

'You must have had something.'

'Thanks for that,' she said, waving towards the road, where the cars were moving slowly past in the slushy conditions.

'Who are you waving to?'

'My ego and yours, hand in hand, hitching a ride out of here,' she said, her breath smoking away in the cold air. Her mouth tilting up in a grin. Because, honestly, standing here with Nathaniel, it did all seem very petty. Very small stuff. Except, of course, it wasn't that simple.

'Actually, I happen to think you're pretty special,' he said, capturing her hand, wrapping it in his. 'But we both know that you're not classic model material.'

'You're right. I know it, you know it, the world knows it. But I had three things going for me.' They'd handily itemised them on a memo. 'First, I had a story. Abandoned as a baby—'

'Abandoned?'

'The classic baby in a cardboard box story, me.'

He made no comment. Well, what could anyone say?

'I had a dozen foster homes,' she continued, 'a fractured education that left me unqualified to do anything other than take care of other people's children. Not that I was qualified for that, but it was something I'd been doing since I was a kid myself.'

'You truly were Cinderella,' he said, getting it.

'I truly was,' she confirmed.

The hot dog was gone and she reached for her coffee. Took a sip. It was hot.

'Second?' he prompted.

'I had ambition. I worked in a day-care nursery from eight-thirty until six, then evenings as a waitress to put myself through night school to get a diploma in business studies.'

'Cinderella, but not one sitting around waiting for her fairy godmother to come along with her magic wand.'

He was quick.

'Cinderella doing it for herself,' she confirmed. 'Not that

it did me much good. I didn't get a single interview until I applied for the Henshawe job.'

'It's tough out there.'

'Tell me about it. I really, really needed that job and when they asked me why I wanted to work for the company I didn't hold back. I let them have it with both barrels. The whole determination to make something of my life speech. Oscar-winning stuff, Nathaniel. They actually applauded.'

'They were from the PR company, I take it?'

'How did you guess?'

'HR managers tend to be a little less impressionable. You said you had three things.'

'My third lucky break was that some woman on the team was bright enough to realise that I was exactly the kind of woman who would be walking in off the street, desperate for something to make her look fabulous. Let's face it, if the gold-standard was a size-zero, six-foot supermodel, the reflection in the dressing room mirror was always going to be a disappointment.'

'But if they compared themselves with you... Who is this PR company? I could use that kind of out of the box thinking.'

'Oh, I don't deny they're good.'

'Sorry. Your story. So, having applauded your audition, they told you what the part would be?'

'No.'

'No?'

'You're missing the point. I was going to be a genuine "ordinary" girl who had been picked from among his staff. I had to believe in the story before I could sell it.'

'Did I say they were good?'

'Oh, there's more. Someone added a note on the bottom of their report to the effect that this was going to be a real fairy tale. And then they started thinking so far out of the box they were on another planet.'

His hand tightened on hers. 'It was all a set-up? Not just the job, the discovery...'

'I had a phone call the day after my interview, offering me the job. I started the following week and I have to tell you that it was the most boring week of my life. I was climbing the walls by Friday afternoon, wondering how long I could stand it. Then I was sent up to the top floor with a pile of files, got knocked off my feet by a speeding executive and there was Rupert Henshawe, perfectly placed to pick me up, sit me in his office, give me coffee from his personal coffee-maker while his chauffeur was summoned to take me home. And, while we waited, he asked me about my job, whether I liked working for the company. I'd heard he was as hard as nails. Terrifying if you made a mistake. But he was so kind. Utterly...' she shrugged '...charming.'

'I'd heard he was a smooth operator.'

'I had flowers and a note on Saturday. Lunch in the country on Sunday. Picture in the tabloids on Monday.'

CHAPTER NINE

'ARE you telling me that you didn't have a clue?'

'Not until today,' she admitted. 'Dumb or what?'

'Don't be so hard on yourself. You saw what he wanted you to see.'

'What I wanted to believe. Until today. I was late and, since I didn't have time to go home and pick up my copy of the wedding file, I decided to borrow the one in Rupert's office. That's when I stumbled across the one labelled "The Cinderella Project".'

She still remembered the little prickle at the base of her neck when she'd seen it.

'But the romance, the engagement?'

She understood what he was asking. 'There is no sex in fairy tales, Nathaniel. My Prince Charming okayed the plan, but only with the proviso...' written in his own hand '...that he didn't have to "sleep with the girl".' More of those quote marks.

'So he's gay?'

She blinked. 'Why would you say that?'

He shook his head. 'Just thinking out loud.'

She stared at him for a moment. Was he saying what she thought he was saying? That the only reason a man wouldn't want to sleep with her was because...?

'No...'

He responded with a lift of those expressive eyebrows. 'You'd have thought someone so good at the details would have made a little more effort. That's all I'm saying.'

'Yes... No...' She blushed. 'I wasn't exactly throwing myself at him.'

'No? How come I got so lucky?' She dug him in the ribs with her elbow. In response, he put his arm around her. 'You throw, I'll catch,' he said and, without stopping to think, she stood on tiptoe and put her arms around his neck. He didn't let her down, scooping her up so that she was off the ground, grinning as he spun her around, kissing her before he set her back on her feet.

'Thanks,' she said.

'Entirely my pleasure,' he assured her, still holding her close. 'But I don't understand. If there was no great romance, no passion, why did you accept his proposal, Lucy?'

'Because I bought the fairy story.'

She was still buying it, she thought, glancing up at Nathaniel. She really needed to get a grip on reality.

'The breakup scenario is already written, by the way,' she said, before he could say anything. Pulling away. 'Apparently, I'm going to call the wedding off because Rupert is a workaholic, too absorbed in business to spend time with me. True, as it happens. Sadness, but no recriminations. Nothing sordid. Just a quiet fade out of the relationship once the stores are open and the brand established.'

'You went seriously off message this afternoon.'

'I lost the plot big time, but that's what you get for employing amateurs.'

'I can see why he's desperate to get the file back. The tabloids would have a field day with this.' And, from looking deep into her eyes, he was suddenly looking at something in the distance above her head. 'I'm not just talking about his underactive libido.' She didn't miss the edge to his voice as he added, 'You could make a fortune.'

'Yes, I could. I could have phoned one of the tabloids this afternoon. But I don't want a drama, Nathaniel. I just want to disappear. Get my life back. Be ordinary.'

'But you're Lucy B,' he pointed out.

'I know. That's why I can't let him get away with what he's doing. Why I can't just disappear. Because that's not the end of it.'

'There's more?'

'He wants his file back because all that lovely stuff about fair trade fashion is a bunch of baloney.'

'Baloney?'

'Lies, falsehoods, untruths. There is a fair trade company, but it's just a front. The actual clothes, shoes, accessories will still be made by the same sweatshop workers he used for the old stuff. That's why he's desperate to retrieve the file.'

He said just one word. Then, 'I'm sorry...'

'No need to apologise. You've got it. The man has all the morals of a cowpat.' She stuffed her hands deep in her pockets. 'That's why I was so angry. Why I couldn't think straight. When the media circus took off like a rocket, bigger than anything they had imagined, and a headline writer shortened my name to Lucy B, Marketing ditched the names they'd been playing with and grabbed it. He's going to use my name—on the shop fronts, on the labels, everywhere—use me to sell his lie. That's what today's press conference was about. To unveil the look of the stores. Tell the world about the jobs he's creating, both here and in the Third World. Impress the public with his new caring image, impress the shareholders with profit forecasts.'

'That's...' For a moment he didn't seem to be able to find a word. And then he did. 'Dangerous.'

Not reassuring—she'd been a lot less bothered by the expletive—and, despite the down jacket, she shivered.

'You're cold,' he said. 'Let's go home. Get you back in the warm.'

Diary update: I have to admit that when Nathaniel asked me if I was hungry I didn't anticipate a hot dog from a stall on the Strand, but it was junk food at its finest. And the onions were piled up high enough to bring tears of joy to the eyes of the government's diet Tsar. But then it's been that sort of day. Surprises all round. Horrible ones, delicious ones and a man a girl could love. Not fairy tale falling in love, but the genuine article.

Will everything be back to normal tomorrow?

Can anything ever be normal again?

What is normal?

Nathaniel didn't say anything until they were near the store, then he reached out and, hand on her arm, said, 'Out of sight, I think.'

She didn't argue, but ducked down until the barrier clanged behind them and he'd pulled into a parking bay and switched off the engine. Released his seat belt.

'You saw something?' she asked as she slid down from the seat without waiting for him to help her.

Nat shook his head, put his arm around her shoulders and swept her towards the lift, wanting her inside, out of sight. Regretting the crazy impulse to go out in the snow. Anyone might have seen her.

The guy at the hot dog stall wouldn't forget two idiots who'd gone out to play in the snow, stood for ever, eating hot dogs and talking.

'What's bothering you?' she asked.

'I hadn't realised... This is a lot more serious than I thought, Lucy.'

He keyed in the code and breathed more easily when the door clicked shut behind them, shedding his coat and gloves, kicking off his boots. It was probably the first time he'd actually been glad to be home since he'd moved into the apartment. The first time it had felt like home. A sanctuary.

'You're scaring me,' Lucy said, cold hands fumbling with her zip.

He stopped her. Not cold, just shaking, he discovered and, instead of unzipping it for her, he put his arms around her, held her, because he was scared for her.

This wasn't simply some romance gone wrong. It wasn't even just an amoral PR campaign that meant heads would roll right up to boardroom level.

'Nathaniel? Now you're really worrying me!'

He let her go, unzipped her jacket, helped her out of it.

'Okay. While the fake romance would be an embarrassment to Henshawe, I've no doubt he could contain the damage, but the fair trade thing is fraud.'

'Fraud?'

'It's going to seriously damage him and the Henshawe Corporation when it gets out. The Lucy B chain will be history, his shareholders will want blood and he'll be facing a police investigation.'

'You're talking jail time?' she asked, shocked.

'He's probably shredding papers as fast as he can right now. Talking to his suppliers to cover his tracks. But, while you've got his file, written proof of what he did, he's not safe and I believe that a man who has the morals of a cowpat would go to any lengths to stop that from happening.'

'You're saying that I'm in danger?'

Before he could answer, the phone rang and he unhooked it from the wall. 'Hart.'

'Nat, it's Bryan. Sorry to disturb you, but I've just had a call from the police.'

His heart rate picked up. 'And?'

'It seems they've had a missing person report. A woman called Lucy Bright. The WAG of some billionaire. She was last seen heading this way just after four this afternoon and appears to have vanished off the face of the earth. I wouldn't have bothered you, but the timing is right and the description matches the woman you saw this afternoon.'

'Did you mention that to the police?' he asked, reaching out a hand as he saw the colour drain from Lucy's face.

'No. It might not have been her and I assumed that you wouldn't want policemen crawling all over the store talking to the staff. Or the ensuing press invasion. Not until we're sure, anyway.'

'Good call.'

'I searched the name on the internet and I'm about to send you a photograph as an email attachment. In the meantime, I've initiated a sweep of the premises, just to cover ourselves.'

'Right…' Then, 'You were in the force, Bryan. Isn't it unusual for them to get involved in something like this so quickly?'

'It depends who's missing. And why.'

Nat listened as he detailed all the likely reasons why the police had got involved so quickly. Suspected violence, theft… He never took his eyes off Lucy who, her free hand to her mouth, was watching him with growing apprehension.

'I'll get back to you. In the meantime, keep me posted.'

Lucy was numb. The minute Nathaniel had picked up the phone she'd known something was wrong. And when she'd heard him say the word police she'd known the game was up.

'The police? They've been here? Looking for me?'

'Just a phone call.'

Just!

'You've been reported missing and they're following up on a suggestion that you were last seen entering the store.'

'They're not going to give up, are they? I'm so sorry to have involved you in this, Nathaniel, but I can't believe that Rupert had the nerve to involve the police.'

'You stole a file,' he pointed out. 'One filled with sensitive commercial information.'

'I know, but...' Then, 'Are you saying that he's had the nerve to accuse me of stealing?'

'Not officially.'

'So what?'

'He could be using the fact that there has been a campaign by your fans on the social media sites to put pressure on them. Apparently, the most used hashtag in the last few hours has been #findLucyB.'

'Well, colour me surprised.'

'You're not impressed that you inspire such devotion?'

'Not desperately. I have no doubt that it was instigated by the Henshawe PR team. Why waste time looking for someone when you can persuade half a million people to do it for you? Get a little hysteria going. But I still don't understand. The police don't normally bother about missing persons unless there's blood on the carpet. Do they?' she pressed when he didn't immediately answer.

'Not normally. Not this soon. It must have been the call from your mother that did the trick.'

Lucy froze.

'My mother?'

'She gave an emotional doorstep interview, pleading with anyone who knows where you are to call her. It's probably online if you want to see it.'

'No! I don't. She's not my mother,' she said. 'I told you. I don't have a mother.'

'Lucy—'

'She's a fake,' she said quickly, all the peace, the pleasure of their evening together dissipating in that bitter reality. 'Just another lie dreamed up to keep the press engaged.' The worst one. The cruellest one. The rest she might abhor, but they, at least, had a purpose. 'What's a fairy tale without a wicked witch...?'

Except that she hadn't been wicked. She'd been fifteen. Abandoned by an abusive boyfriend. Alone and afraid.

Lies...

Before she could move, Nathaniel had his arms around her, holding her rigid body, murmuring soft calming sounds that purred through her until she finally stopped shaking. He held her while her silent, angry tears soaked his T-shirt. Held her until the tension seeped from her limbs and she melted against him.

Just held her.

It was a technique she used to calm distraught children, holding them tight so that they'd feel safe even when they fought her—her promise that, whatever they did, she would not let go. And, even as she broke down, buried her face in his shoulder and sobbed like a baby while his hands gently stroked her back, in the dark recesses of her mind, she recognized that this was something he'd done before.

That she shouldn't read more into it than a simple

gesture of comfort and gradually she began to withdraw. Ease away.

She was a survivor. She'd taken everything that life could throw at her and she'd take this, come through it. She lifted her head, straightened her shoulders, putting herself back together, piece by piece, something she'd done times without number.

But never before had the loss of contact felt so personal, the empty space between two bodies quite so cold.

Then, as she brushed her fingers, palms over her cheeks to dry them, Nathaniel took away her hands, tugged up the edge of his T-shirt and used it to very tenderly dab them dry.

'I'm sorry,' she said quickly, pulling away from him before the tears began to fall again. 'I didn't plan to weep all over you.'

His response was a crooked smile and, making a pretence of wringing out his T-shirt between his hands, making a joke of it, he said, 'Is that the worst you've got?'

She felt an answering tug at the corner of her own lips. She was still embarrassed at bawling her eyes out, but somehow it didn't seem to matter so much. Nothing seemed to matter when Nathaniel smiled at her.

And that was dangerous.

Not because he was trying to fool her, but because she was capable of fooling herself. Seeing only what she wanted to see. Hearing only what she wanted to hear.

'You have to call the police, Nathaniel. Tell them I'm here.'

'Do I?' he asked. 'I'm perfectly capable of looking a policeman in the eyes and telling him that you're not in the store.'

'No lies,' she insisted. 'Nobody lies…'

'So long as I do it before the store opens tomorrow, it will be the truth.'

'But it wouldn't be the whole truth and nothing but the truth, would it?'

'You care about that?'

'I've been living a lie for the last six months. This afternoon I lied to Pam...'

'You didn't actually lie to her.'

'I didn't tell her the truth, which is the same thing.' She'd actually congratulated herself on her cleverness, which, considering the way she'd berated Rupert for doing the same thing, was double standards any way you looked at it. 'You've been kind, Nathaniel. Not some fairy tale Prince Charming; you're the real thing. A "parfit gentil knyght". But you have the store to think about, your reputation. This is going to be messy and I don't want you involved.'

'It's odd, Lucy, but that's exactly what I told myself this afternoon when I delegated one of my staff to find you, return your shoe, offer you a pair of tights, whatever else you needed. Leave it to someone else to deal with, I thought. Don't get involved.'

'You did that?' For a moment she felt as if she was bathed in a warm blast, like opening an oven door. 'Well, I guess I will need a pair of tights—'

'I was still saying it when I had Henshawe's bullies evicted from the store,' he continued, taking her face in his hands.

'—and shoes. The boots are great, but—'

'And all the time I was driving Pam home and couldn't think of anything but the fear in your beautiful kitten eyes.' Instinctively, she closed them and felt the butterfly touch of his thumbs brush across her lids. His fingers sliding through her hair as he cradled her head. 'I was telling myself to forget it. Whatever it was. That it wasn't my problem. Don't get involved—'

'But, as to the rest,' she cut in, forcing her eyes open, refusing to succumb to his touch, his voice so soft that it seemed to be lost somewhere deep in his throat.

Forcing herself to take responsibility for what had happened. Step away.

'As to the rest,' she said as her retreat was halted by the bulk of the island unit, 'I'll swallow my pride, borrow some clothes and call that taxi. Go to the nearest police station and tell them the truth.'

It was fraud. A crime...

He'd moved with her, his hands still cradled her head, his train of thought unbroken.

'—don't get involved. Telling myself that by the time I got back you'd be long gone.'

'And in the morning,' she persisted, shutting her ears to temptation, 'you can tell the police that I'm not in the store.'

'And that's not being economical with the truth?'

'Only slightly.'

'The truth, since you're so keen on it, Lucy Bright, is that I was involved from the moment I saw you ahead of me on the stairs. Your hair floating like a halo around your head.'

'Well, that's history...'

She was trapped against the island. His hands were a gentle cradle for her face, his body was warming her from breast to knee, the silver glints in his eyes were molten.

'Now I just look like Harpo Marx...'

Not that she could have moved. Every cell in her body had given up, surrendered and, as his gaze slid down to her lips, it was only the counter at her back that was holding her up.

'Your neck...' His thumb brushed her jaw as his hand stroked her neck in a slow, lazy move that sent a wave of heat rippling down to her toes. 'Did you know that the nape of the neck is considered so erotic that geishas leave it unpainted?'

She managed a small noise, nothing that made any sense because, forget necks, napes or any other part of the anatomy, his voice, so low that only her hormones could hear, was doing it for her.

'The way your dress was slipping from your shoulder—'

'It was just a look,' she said in a last-ditch attempt to hang onto whatever sense she possessed. 'A once-in-a-lifetime, never-to-be-repeated look—'

'What are you prepared to risk on that, Lucy Bright? Truth, dare, kiss, promise...'

Her desperate protestations died as, not waiting for her answer, his eyes never leaving her lips, Nathaniel looked at her with that same intensity, the same liquid silver eyes that had turned her core molten, before slowly lowering his mouth to hers.

She watched in slow motion, knowing that it was going to happen, knowing that all she had to do to stop it was answer him.

Say just one word.

If only she could remember what it was. But her brain was lollygagging around somewhere. Out to lunch. Make that dinner...

She slammed her eyes shut a second before he made contact and her world was reduced to touch. The soft warmth of a barely-there kiss. A tingle as her lips demanded more. A breath—his, not hers. She'd sucked air in and it was stuck there as she waited for the promise.

The warmth became heat.

Her lower lip began to tremble.

Someone moaned and her tongue, too thick for her own mouth, reached for his. Touched his lip. Another moment of this torture and she was going to slither between his arms and melt into a messy puddle on the floor at his feet.

Was this the kiss? The promise? Or was it about the truth?

Right now, it didn't seem to matter much. It might be 'just a kiss' but she wanted it. Wanted it and everything that followed.

'You win,' she murmured against his mouth, her eyes still closed.

'Not entirely,' he replied, his voice more a growl than a purr as his hand abandoned her neck to capture her hip, pull her close, as the kiss became the briefest reality before he took a step back, leaving her hot and hungry for more. 'But you most certainly lost and I'm not going to be a gentleman about it. I'm claiming my forfeit.'

At which point her knees gave up the struggle and buckled beneath her.

Nat caught her as she slithered into his arms. 'Hey,' he said, 'it isn't going to be that bad.'

Her throat was thick and she had to clear it. 'It isn't?'

'What did you think? That I was going to demand your body?'

'Noooo…' Dry and thick with disappointment which if she could hear, so could he…'The police,' she muttered, grabbing for reality. 'We have to call them now.'

'You surrendered, Lucy. I won. Remember? Or shall we try that again?' He mistook her hesitation for reluctance. 'I'm going to call my lawyer,' he said, one arm propping her up, the other retrieving his phone from his jacket pocket.

'He'll call the police, reassure them that you're safe. That you'll be available for an interview, at a time convenient to you, if they want to talk to you.'

'Can you do that?'

'I can do that.'

And he did. Right after he'd caught her behind the knees and carried her through to her bedroom, set her down on the bed and pulled off the boots, taking the three pairs of socks she was wearing with them.

He'd stared at her toes for a moment, then flipped open the phone, got some lawyer out of his bed and told him exactly what he wanted. Not just straightening things out with the police—without revealing her whereabouts—but the retrieval of her belongings from the apartment in the Henshawe house.

'I'm running up a big bill, here,' she said when he'd finished.

'True. You're going to have to work right through until Christmas Eve.'

'That's not work. That's fun.'

He grinned. 'Christmas Eve two thousand and twenty.'

'That big, huh? And if I volunteer to cook Christmas lunch for you?'

'Christmas Eve two thousand and fifty.' And his smile faded. 'Here,' he said, handing her the phone. 'Keep this with you. Post the rest of your photographs. Give Henshawe a sleepless night.'

She would rather give Nathaniel one, she thought, but for once held her tongue, just watching him as he adjusted a dial on the wall and the glass darkened, blotting out the lights, the planes passing overhead.

'I'll find you something to sleep in.'

'I'll manage.'

'No doubt, but I'm not sure my blood pressure can take the strain.'

CHAPTER TEN

Diary update: *Okay, this is the last entry for today.
I just peeled off the jeans, which were pretty wet
around the knees. The snow had got down my neck,
too. I hadn't noticed until Nathaniel left me and suddenly I felt horribly cold, so now I'm dictating this as
I lie back in a gorgeously scented bubble bath...*

LUCY paused as she heard a tap on her bedroom door.

'Hello?'

'Room service.'

'I didn't—' she began, but the bathroom door opened a
crack—it hadn't occurred to her to lock it—and a glossy
Hastings & Hart carrier appeared, dangling from long
masculine fingers.

'Pyjamas, slippers and a selection of other female necessities, madam.'

She swallowed. 'Nathaniel...'

'Two thousand and fifty-one,' he said, before any of
the things bubbling up from her heart could spill over and
embarrass them both.

'Two thousand and fifty-one? They had better be designer necessities,' she replied. Keeping it light, light, light...

'Down to the last button,' he assured her, slipping the
handles over the door knob, where it would be safe from

accidental spills—the man learned fast—and closing the
door. She slid down a little lower in the bath, grinning to
herself.

She waited a minute, then clicked 'record' and continued
her diary update.

> *Right, where was I? Oh, thawing out in the bath.*
> *It's impossible to describe today, except that I'd be*
> *happy to cook Nathaniel Hart's Christmas dinner*
> *until the end of time. He is unbelievably special.*
> *And, I'm certain, deeply unhappy but tomorrow, as*
> *Scarlett O'Hara so famously said, is another day.*
> *Maybe it will bring a few answers. To my problems.*
> *And to his.*

That done, she checked her tweets.

> *@LucyB Loved the snow lady! One of the London*
> *Parks, right? Hyde, Regency, Green? More clues!*
> *#findLucyB*
> *jenpb, [+] Wed 1 Dec 23:16*

> *@LucyB Hyde Park. I can just make out the*
> *Serpentine Bridge in the background. U okay, sweet-*
> *ie? #findLucyB*
> *WelshWitch, [+] Wed 1 Dec 23:17*

She blinked, then quickly keyed in a response, posting
the pictures Nathaniel had taken.

> *@jenpb Hyde Park it is. Here's a pic of a snow angel*
> *I made. Tucked up safe, thanx, WW. #findLucyB*
> *LucyB, Wed 1 Dec 23:51*

* * *

@WelshWitch Safe & well fed as u can see in this pic.
Who needs dinner at the Ritz? Night tweeps. More
in the morning. #findLucyB
LucyB, Wed 1 Dec 23:54

Lucy climbed out of the bath, wrapped herself in the
bathrobe, brushed her teeth, did the whole cleanse, tone,
moisturise thing with the stuff provided.

Only when she was done with all that did she allow
herself the pleasure of opening the carrier.

The pyjamas were white—obviously—but they were
spattered with candy-red hearts and she couldn't wait to
scramble into them. Fasten the heart-shaped buttons.

The slippers, fuzzy soft ones that you pushed your feet
into, matched them. There was even a wrap that tied with
a big red bow.

Further down the bag she found underwear. Yummy,
silky, lacy underwear. And, right at the bottom, wrapped
in tissue, a pair of shoes. Red suede with peep toes, a saucy
bow and very high heels.

Not exactly like the ones she'd been wearing, but she
couldn't have chosen anything better for herself and she
was wearing a great big grin as, her arms full of wrap
and undies and shoes, she opened the door. And, for the
second time that day, had a heart-stop moment as she saw
Nathaniel, this time stretched out on her bed in a pair of
worn-thin joggers, a T-shirt so old that whatever had been
written on it had long since faded out, hair damp from the
shower, bare feet crossed at the ankle.

Exactly the kind of eye candy that any woman would
be delighted to find waiting for her after a delicious soak
in a scented bath.

Her pleasure was somewhat dimmed by the fact that he
was reading the file she'd carefully hidden in the locker

room, although she had to admit that the glossy black cover nicely matched the decor.

'I could have been naked,' she exclaimed. Again.

'A man doesn't get that lucky twice in one day,' he said, looking up, holding her gaze for so long that she forgot all about the file. 'But cute will do to be going on with.'

'The jammies *are* sweet,' she said when her heart had settled back into something like its normal rhythm and she could breathe again. 'I particularly love the red. It exactly matches my toenails.' She wiggled them. 'I had these done this morning. Pam made me remove the colour from my fingernails, but she missed these.'

'I can't think how,' he said, 'but I'm glad she did.' Then, 'Tell me, do you talk to yourself in the bath?'

'I was updating my diary. There was a lot to say.'

'It's been a busy day for Lucy B.'

'Buzz, buzz, buzz… Do you want to hear what I said about you?'

'Probably not.'

She told him anyway. 'I said that you were a great kisser, unbelievably special and deeply unhappy. I seem to have missed your talent with a lock pick.'

'I'm working on the happiness thing,' Nat said, grateful for the distraction of the file. 'And I didn't have to pick the lock. We keep a duplicate set of keys to the lockers. People are always losing them.'

'So? What? You wanted to check my story? See if I was telling the truth?' Her grin was long since history.

'If I'd even suspected that you were lying, Lucy, I'd have read the file in my office. I simply wanted to be sure that you had cast iron proof of Henshawe's guilt.'

'And have I?'

'Yes, fortunately. It's in the focus group section. The part where someone raised the fair trade question. There are detailed notes from the individual tasked to look into it and come up with a plan that would make them look good without compromising profits.'

'But—'

'There were a number of options. Higher prices. Lower margins. Cheaper materials. Or the handy solution that he went for. There's a handwritten note at the bottom over Henshawe's initials. "Option Four. Get on with it."'

Nat held it up for her to see and she sat down heavily on the side of the bed. 'So that's it, then. Lucy B down the pan.'

'Wishing you hadn't opened Pandora's box?' he asked.

'Good grief, no.' She looked down at him. 'You can't think that.'

'But you're not happy,' he said, leaving the question unanswered.

'How can I be? People are going to get hurt. Not Rupert. I don't care if he rots in jail,' she declared fervently and the last shreds of tension, doubt left him. She wasn't going to be seduced by the glamour, the millions. Her only thought was for the people who would be hurt when she brought the company down.

'Tell me about it,' he urged, dropping the folder and stretching out an arm, inviting her to lean back against his shoulder.

'It's always the innocents who pay,' she said, snuggling against him. 'I may have hated working there but hundreds of people—ordinary people—rely on the Henshawe Corporation to feed their families.'

'Right.'

'And it isn't just them. There are the shops. If they're not rebranded, they'll close. Hundreds of women will lose their jobs. I've met some of them and they're all so enthusiastic. So excited…'

She slipped down a little, getting more comfortable, her body heavier against him.

'Even the poor devils in the sweatshops will lose out,' he said, resting his chin on her head.

The scent of the soap she'd used was familiar, but on Lucy it was different, somehow.

'I know. But what choice do I have?' She fought a yawn. 'The man's a liar, a cheat and a crook.'

'List your options,' he suggested. 'One, you go to the police. Bring him and his company down.'

'It's too horrible to think about. Can I go to sleep now?' She closed her eyes.

'Okay. Two, you could sell him out to the tabloids, write a book, make a fortune.'

'Same result, except I get rich.'

'You could share the money amongst the people who lose their jobs.'

'Not rich enough to make a difference to them,' she said, her cheek pressed into his chest.

'No, not rich enough for that. There's option three, the one where you walk away and let him get on with it.'

'Nnngg.'

'No? How about threatening him with exposure? You could force him to clean up his act in return for playing out the role as written? Number four, sticking with the plan, but with you in the driving seat.'

'Wdntrstim,' she mumbled.

'No. Neither would I.' Then, 'What about me, Lucy? Could you trust me?'

No answer.

He didn't need one. She was curled up against him, defenceless as a baby. She'd seen through his guard, peered into his darkest places, knew him as few people did.

And he knew her, too. She lived who she was. Caring for others. even when her own world was crumbling around her.

He was, without question…involved.

And deeply happy to be so.

The engine had caught, the motor was running and the road ahead might have bumps in it but it was leading exactly where he wanted to be.

'Hey, into bed with you,' he said, tearing himself away. He didn't want to leave her, lose the soft warmth of her breast, her thighs curled against him. He wanted, for the first time in as long as he could remember, to lie beside a woman, sleep with her.

Just sleep.

Close his eyes and know she was there. Know she would be the first thing he saw when he woke. Know that he would be the first thing she saw when she opened her green-gold eyes and smile because that one thing made her happy.

But this wasn't about him. He pulled the cover from beneath her and she rolled into the warm space where he'd been lying, her face in the pillow.

'Big day tomorrow.'

'T'day…'

She was right. It was gone midnight. Or did she mean that it had been a big day today? Not just for her.

'Furs day rest life,' she mumbled.

He stood for a moment watching every scrap of tension leave her body as she melted into sleep almost before the jumble of words had left her mouth.

Today was the first day of the rest of her life. Or did she mean his?

He looked around at the room that, just hours before, had been sterile and empty. Clothes dropped where she'd left them. The bright red splash of her coat across the chair. A muddle. Untidy. Just like life.

There were no easy solutions, no perfect answers. You did what you had to do and got on with it. He'd been a successful architect, but he'd been raised to this. With no heart in it, he'd expanded the company out of all recognition. What could he do if he stopped looking back, regretting the life he'd lost and instead looked forward? Seized the day? Seized the life he'd been given?

Time to do a little homework. Arrange a meeting with the H&H trustees.

'Hey, sleepy-head.'

'Nnng…' She pushed her face deeper into the pillow. Today was not going to be fun and she was in no hurry for it to start.

There was a touch to her shoulder and, giving up, she opened her eyes, saw the tempting curl of steam rising from a bright red mug standing on the black marble, Nathaniel crouched down beside the bed.

'Nice mug,' she said.

'It matches your toenails.'

'So it does,' she said, rolling over onto her side. She was going to have to leave today and she didn't want to miss a minute of looking at Nathaniel. 'What time is it?'

'Nearly eight. I would have left you sleeping but I've got a meeting with the company trustees in a few minutes and I'm not sure how long it will take.'

'Shame,' she said. 'I was going to make you porridge for breakfast.'

'I'll cancel.' He made as if to move, but she caught his arm.

'No, you're all right. I've got until two thousand and fifty-one to convert you to oatmeal.'

'I warn you, it might take that long.'

For a moment neither of them spoke. She was thinking of forty years spent sharing breakfast with Nathaniel.

He was probably thinking *help!*

'Trustees?' she prompted.

'Hastings & Hart is controlled by a family trust. Much of the profit goes to charity.'

'That explains a lot.'

'Does it?'

It explained the sense of obligation. Why he couldn't walk away.

'I found the picture Pam took of you yesterday, by the way,' he said after a moment, 'and I've made an ID card for you, Louise Braithwaite.'

'Mmm... Yes. Sorry about that, but the name Lucy Bright was given to me by the nurses in the hospital, so that's made up, too.'

'I was going to talk to you about that. I did a little research on Henshawe last night and I saw the photographs. Are you sure that your mother is a fake?'

'It's in the file.'

'All it says is that it would make a great story if they found her.'

'And it did. Not a dry eye in the house.'

'Did you like her?' he asked. 'I mean, she did abandon you.'

'Fifteen years old with a boyfriend who'd done a runner at the word pregnancy. She could have done a lot worse, Nathaniel. I'm here. But not because of her. She's a fake. Another lie generated by Rupert's PR company.'

She threw the covers back, swung her legs out of the bed, but he didn't back off.

'Okay, I liked her. More than liked.' It wouldn't have hurt so much if she'd hated her on sight. Thought her the worst mother on earth and didn't give a damn. 'We fit.' Still he didn't move. 'I loved her, okay?'

'You look like her,' he said.

'They weren't going to pick someone who didn't, were they?'

'You've got the same hair.'

'The halo or the Harpo Marx? Hair can be fixed.'

'And eyes, Lucy. Look at her eyes. You can change their colour with contacts but not their shape. And, honestly, I know that His Frogginess is capable of it, but how could he get away with it? Truly. People know her. Her history. If she was a fake, her story was a lie, don't you think someone would have sold her out to the media?'

'Aren't you going to be late for your meeting?' she said.

'Just look, okay?' Then, letting it go, 'Your employee ID is in the kitchen with a swipe card to get you through the door between the store and the apartment. There's also a store account card in the same name so that you can get anything you need. And the keypad number for the door is two five one two.'

'Two five one two,' she repeated. 'Christmas Day? I think I can remember that.'

And she wiggled her toes at him, just to show him that she'd forgiven him for bringing up her mother.

Damn. She was doing it now.

Forgetting the quotes.

'The lawyer called first thing,' Nathaniel said. 'He's spoken to the police and also issued a short statement to the press to the effect that while you're sorting out your differences with Henshawe you're staying with a friend.'

She reached up, touched his cheek. 'A very good friend.' Then, 'Nice tie, by the way.'

He was dressed for work in a crisp white shirt and the uniform pinstripes, but the tie today was candy-red.

'I've decided that it's my favourite colour.'

'Good choice.' But, despite the tie, he looked tired and she said so. 'Did you get any sleep?'

'Not much,' he admitted. 'I had a lot of thinking to do.'

'Don't tell me—I've turned your life upside down. It's a bad habit I have.'

'No, Lucy. You've turned it the right way up. And the time wasn't wasted. I've come up with a fifth option.'

'What?' She was wide awake now.

'I'm going to be late for my meeting.' He leaned forward, kissed her cheek, headed for the door.

'Nathaniel!' She leapt out of bed and went after him. Then paused, suddenly shy. 'Your tie…' She reached up to straighten it, pat it into place, keeping her eyes on the knot, but he hooked his thumb under her chin, made her look at him.

'It'll be all right. I just need to straighten a few loose ends before I put it to you.' Then, apparently forgetting all about his meeting, he caught her close, kissed her, sweet and simple, before releasing her. 'Go back to bed, Lucy.'

'I will if you'll come too.'

'You make it hard for a man to leave.'

She grinned. 'I noticed.'

'You don't really have to be an elf, you know. You can stay here. Housekeeping will come in at about ten but, apart from that, no one will disturb you.'

Too late, she was already disturbed and the condition, she feared, was terminal.

'Frank is expecting me. I can't let him down.'

'Of course you can't. He'll feed you to a troll.' He kissed her again. 'I'll see you later.' And this time he did make it to the door, where he paused to look back at her. 'Don't do anything rash, will you?'

'The rashest thing I'm going to do this morning is put maple syrup on my porridge,' she promised.

Maybe.

Diary entry: *Woken by Nathaniel, all crisp and gorgeous and ready for a hard day making dreams come true in his palace of delights. Christmas shoppers. Children. And mine? And I'm not talking about Option Five. But I will have to decide what to do today.*

Nathaniel can't be right about my mother? Can he?

The meeting began just after eight.

Nathaniel began by offering his father, his uncles, what they wanted. A Hart fully committed to the company.

Only two men in the room did not leap to accept the gesture with gratitude, relief.

Christopher's father. And his own.

He wasn't surprised.

His uncle clung vainly to the hope that one day his own son would be able to resume his place.

His father had been hurt beyond measure that he hadn't wanted to follow in his footsteps and was sure there would be a proviso.

'What do you want in return, Nathaniel?' his father asked.

'Your agreement to a proposal.' He passed around a folder as he began to talk.

* * *

Lucy retrieved her costume from the upstairs bedroom. It seemed less daunting in the daylight, with clothes heaped untidily on the bed.

She left them where they were, but picked up the rose and took it downstairs, where she tossed it, bud vase and all, into the rubbish bin tucked beneath the sink.

Start the day with a positive action. And a proper breakfast.

She sat on a stool, spooning porridge sweetened with maple syrup into her mouth, sipping her orange juice. Flipping through her messages, reading tweets, messages on Facebook. Catching up.

There was nothing more from Rupert. Not a man to waste words on a lost cause.

There were a dozen or more from the woman who claimed to be her mother. She ignored them, instead flicking through the photographs stored on her camera. The informal snaps taken when she was off guard. Zoomed in on the eyes. Compared them.

Could Nathaniel be right?

She flicked back to her messages.

Do you want to send a message?

Did she? She thumbed in a text:

Tell me the truth. Who are you? Really?

Her thumb hovered over 'send'.

Two hours later, only Nat and his father were left in the room.

'You're in love with this girl?' His father had listened to his plan, added his opinion but, now they were alone, he'd gone right to the heart of the matter.

'I only met her yesterday.'

'You're in love with her?'

'It's a good plan.'

'Can I meet her?'

'Of course. She's down in the grotto, working as an elf.' He shrugged. 'It's a long story.'

'I've got all day.'

Lucy was sitting cross-legged on the floor, a semi-circle of children sitting around her, totally absorbed, as she sang them a song. They joined in the actions, roared with the lion, hooted with the owl, quacked with the duck.

Frank, watching with a smile stretching his face, turned as Nat joined him at the window. 'Will you just look at that?' he said.

He needed no encouragement. 'What's going on?'

'Santa's come down with the bug and I had to send him home. The replacement is suiting up, but there's a bit of a backlog. Lou sent some of the elves to organise coffee for the mothers and then rounded up the kids. I don't know where Pam found her but I'd like half a dozen more.'

'Sorry, Frank,' Nat said. 'She's a one-off and she's mine.' He turned to his father. 'And the answer to your question is yes.' Love at first sight was a concept he would have denied with his last breath. Until it happened. 'I know you'll think I'm a fool, that it's crazy, but I'm in love with her.'

'No. I don't think you're a fool. It happens like that sometimes. Magic happens. It was like that with your mother and me. Just one look was all it took.'

Just one look...

Yes.

'Any chance of you bringing her home for Christmas?'

Before Nat could answer, there was a movement from the inner sanctum and the children, almost reluctantly, began to trickle away.

'Can we borrow your office, Frank? We need to talk to her.'

'You're not going to take her away?'

'It's not up to me what she does; she's her own woman.' A romantic maybe, but strong, too. A woman who knew what she wanted, who never allowed anyone to control her, use her.

'Damn women's lib,' Frank muttered, stomping off to send her in.

'Nathaniel?' Lucy appeared in the doorway, hat slightly askew, curls wild, tunic rucked up behind. She tugged on it. 'Is anything wrong?'

'Nothing. My father wanted to meet you.'

'Oh.' She extended her hand. 'Hello, Mr Hart.'

'Hello, Lucy. I'm delighted to meet you. I'll leave Nathaniel to explain the situation.' He put his hand on his son's arm. 'Whatever you decide about the holiday. Your decision.'

'The holiday?' she asked when the older Hart had gone.

'We've been invited for Christmas.'

'We?'

'Us,' he said. 'It's okay. They ask me every year. They don't expect me to go.'

'Oh.'

'You sound disappointed. Sorry, but there's no way you're getting out of cooking Christmas dinner.'

'Shouldn't you check that I can cook before you commit yourself?'

'I don't actually care,' he said. Then told her about Option Five.

City Diary, London Evening Post
It was announced today that Hastings & Hart, continuing their expansion under the steady hand of Nathaniel Hart, have today acquired the Lucy

B chain from the Henshawe Corporation, who are withdrawing from the fashion business in order to concentrate on their core business.

Lucy Bright, the face of Lucy B, will be taking a more hands-on role in the business and is joining Hastings & Hart in January as a director of the Lucy B division with responsibility for fair trade development.

Rupert Henshawe is relinquishing the chairmanship of the Henshawe Corporation with immediate effect. Shares in the company were down in trading.

Slight wobble, tweeps, but the frog has been vanquished and LucyB is back and on target. Thanks for all the support.
LucyB, Fri 3 Dec 10:14

Lucy flicked through her followers, picking out the ones that were missing. Jenpb was gone. A couple of others. But *WelshWitch* was cheering her on and, on an impulse, she sent her a direct message. Something only she could read.

WelshWitch Want to meet for lunch? DM me.
Fri 3 Dec 10:16

There was just one more thing to do. She scrolled through the numbers in her phonebook and hit 'dial'.

'Lucy?'

'Mum...'

And then they were both crying.

* * *

Friday, 24th December
Appointments
09:30 Hair and stuff
11:00 Meeting with Marji from Celebrity
12:30 Lunch (with my mum!)
17:00 Reception for trustees in boardroom
20:00 Dinner in Garden Restaurant to celebrate
Hastings & Hart takeover of Lucy B launch

'Happy?' Nat said as they returned to the apartment after a Christmas Eve dinner for family and friends in the Garden Restaurant on the seventh floor—a celebration that her mother had been part of, too. Because, while Rupert Henshawe's ability to deceive had gone as far as pretending that he'd looked for her, she was the one who'd come forward when she'd read the story in the newspaper.

'Blissful,' she assured him. 'But what about you?' she asked, hooking her arm in his. 'Are you really prepared to let go of your career in architecture?'

'Says my biggest critic.'

'No. This building is amazing. The apartment is amazing. It just needs a little internal glow.'

He paused at the entrance, turned to her.

'You give it that, Lucy. It means light, doesn't it. Lucy?'

She nodded.

'Well, that's what you are. A light shining into all the dark places. You've lit up my life. Warmed my heart—'

'Nathaniel…'

'It's too soon to say this, you're going to think me a fool and, no, it's nothing to do with making you a director of Lucy B. You've earned that with your heart.'

'I'm terrified I'll get it wrong.'

'Terror is the default setting when you're at the top. But

you're not on your own.' He reached out to her hand. 'Never on your own.'

Her fingers wrapped around his and he felt the tension slide away as it always did when she was close. 'You are going to be wonderful. My father said so and he's no push-over for a pretty face.'

'I like your dad. And your mother. It was so kind of them to invite my mum for Christmas, too.'

'They knew that, wherever she was, you'd want to be, Lucy. That, wherever you were, I'd want to be, too.'

'I owe you a Christmas dinner,' she said, looking up. 'I guess that takes us to two thousand and fifty-two—'

'You think I'm letting you go that easily?' he growled. 'What I'm trying to say is that this is not a get-your-kit-off line. I love you. I loved you from the moment I first saw you.' With his other hand he reached out and touched her cheek, very gently, almost afraid that she would disappear under his touch. 'Just saying. You don't have to do a thing about it.'

'But, if I wanted to get my kit off, that would be all right?' she asked seriously. Looking up at him with those green-gold eyes, soft, filled with warmth, joy, happiness.

He swallowed. 'Your call.' Then, before she could move, 'But maybe you want to think about that. Give yourself some time.'

'And if I don't?'

'Then you can forget about flat-hunting. You won't be going anywhere.'

'If I stay here, I'll make changes,' she warned.

'You already have.' Pop music on the radio first thing in the morning. Pots of early jonquils brightening every surface. Laughter everywhere.

'Phooey. That's nothing. If I stay, I warn you, I'll want to paint the walls primrose-yellow.'

'I'll help you.'

'Hang pictures everywhere.'

'I've got a hammer.'

'Get a kitten.'

'Only one?' he asked.

'Well, they do get lonely without their brothers and sisters,' she said, a glint of mischief in her eyes. 'Two would be better.'

'Bring the whole damn litter.'

Her smile deepened momentarily and then, suddenly, she was serious. 'There's one more thing.'

'You want your mother to live with us?'

'You'd do that for me?' she asked. Then, shaking her head, she let him off the hook. 'It's not that. I want you to build the house in Cornwall.'

'For you—'

'No, Nathaniel; not for me. For you.' And, as if she knew that was the most difficult thing she'd asked, she lifted herself onto her toes and, coiling her arms around his neck, she kissed him. Giving him her courage, her strength, all her love.

There was no need. She'd been giving him that since the day she'd stumbled in front of him on the stairs. In that moment the fairy tale had changed from Cinderella to something entirely new. She'd brought the sleeping Beast back to life with a kiss, made him whole again. But he had one condition of his own.

'It's a house for a family, Lucy. I'll build it if you'll help me fill it.'

'Fill it?'

'With kittens, puppies, your mother. Our children.' There was a still moment when the world seemed to hold its breath. 'I love you, Lucy Bright. Will you marry me?'

'I...'

'It's a big decision. You'll need time to think about it.'

'Yes…' For a moment the world seemed to hang on its axis. Then she said, 'I've thought about it.' And, reaching for the single button holding together the green-gold silk Lucy B jacket that she was wearing, 'How soon can you get that door open?'

Lucy hadn't got it free when he pushed the door open, but this time he was the one who came to a shocked halt.

'A little extra glow,' she said as he took in the eight-foot Christmas tree laden with toys and candy canes and painted glass balls. A replica of the one in the grotto. Or had she just had it shifted? Frank would do anything for her.

There were swathes of greenery, a forest of plants sparkling with tiny white lights. Thick red pillar candles.

'I used my Louise Braithwaite store card,' she said. 'This is your Christmas gift from the elf.'

Then she let her jacket slip to the floor, raised her arms.

'But this one is from me. With all my heart, Nathaniel. All my love. All you have to do is unwrap it and enjoy.'

Lucy gazed at the familiar view. The rugged landscape, the deep blue of the distant sea. Familiar but different. And she smiled.

These days, when they bumped down the track in the big black Range Rover, the rocky ledge was topped by a long, low house that appeared to grow out of it. That over the years had become so much part of the landscape that it deceived the eye. The glass wall facing the sea a perfect reflection of the land. The rock and stone indivisible. One. Like the two of them.

Nathaniel turned to the rear. 'Out you get, boys. Let's get the car unloaded.' Then, as their two sturdy lads scrambled out, whooping to be free, eager to get at the sand, the sea, he reached across, laid his hand across her expanding waist, his eyes more silver than grey. 'Okay?'

'Absolutely. Our little girl and I will sit here and enjoy the view while you unload.'

'You're facing the house,' he pointed out.

'I know. It's my favourite view in all the world.' The house that he had designed for himself, built for her. More beloved than any palace. Just as he was so much more than any Prince Charming. Her rock. Her partner. Her beloved husband. The father of her children. A man at peace with life, with himself.

'Can we pitch the tent, Daddy?'

'I want to build a den.'

'What do you want, Lucy B?' Nathaniel asked, taking her hand, lifting it to his lips.

'I've got everything I ever wanted,' she said. 'How about you?'

'I have you, Lucy. Everything else follows from that,' he said, leaning across to kiss her.

A ROYAL BABY
FOR CHRISTMAS

SCARLET WILSON

This book is dedicated to my fellow authors
Kate Hardy, Tina Beckett and Susanne Hampton.
It's been a pleasure working with you, ladies!

PROLOGUE

May

HIS EYES SCANNED the bar as he ran his fingers through his hair. Six weeks, three countries, ten flights and thousands of miles. He'd been wined and dined by heads of state and consulate staff, negotiated trade agreements, arranged to be part of a water aid initiative, held babies, shaken hands for hours and had a number of tense diplomatic conversations.

All of this while avoiding dozens of calls from his mother about the upcoming royal announcement. His apparent betrothal to his lifelong friend.

All he wanted to do was find a seat, have a drink and clear a little head space. Il Palazzo di Cristallo was one of the few places he could do that. Set in the stunning mountains of Montanari, the exclusive boutique hotel only ever had a select few guests—most of whom were seeking sanctuary from the outside world. The press were banned. The staff were screened and well looked after to ensure all guests' privacy was well respected—including the Crown Prince of Montanari. For the first time in six weeks Sebastian might actually be able to relax.

Except someone was sitting in his favourite seat at the bar.

There. A figure with shoulders slumped and her head

leaning on her hand. Her ash-blonde hair was escaping from its clasp and her blue dress was creased. Two empty glasses of wine sat on the bar in front of her.

The bartender sat down a third and gave Sebastian an almost indiscernible nod. The staff here knew he liked to keep his identity quiet.

Odd. He didn't recognise the figure. Sebastian knew all the movie stars and celebrities who usually stayed here. She wasn't a fellow royal or a visiting dignitary. His curiosity was piqued.

He strode across the room and slid onto the stool next to hers at the bar. She didn't even look up in acknowledgement.

Her fingers were running up and down the stem of the glass and her light brown eyes were unfocused. But it wasn't the drink. It was deep contemplation.

Sebastian sucked in a breath. Whoever she was, she was beautiful. Her skin was flawless. Her features finer than those of some of the movie starlets he'd been exposed to. Being Prince of Montanari meant that a whole host of women had managed to cross his path over the last few years. Not that he'd taken any of them seriously. He had a duty to his future kingdom. A duty to marry an acceptable neighbouring princess. There was no question about it— it had been instilled in him from a young age it was part of his preparations for finally becoming King. Marriage was a business transaction. It wasn't the huge love and undying happiness portrayed in fairy tales. There were no rainbows and flying unicorns. It came down to the most advantageous match for the country and his parents had found her. Theresa Mon Carte, his childhood friend and a princess from the neighbouring principality. They were to be married within the year.

Part of the reason he was here was to get some time to resign himself to his fate. Because that was what it felt like.

But right now, he couldn't think about that at all.

He was entirely distracted by the woman sitting next to him. She looked as if she had the weight of the world on her shoulders. There was no Botox here. Her brow was definitely furrowed and somehow he knew this woman would never be interested in cosmetic procedures.

'Want to tell me about them?'

'What?' She looked up, startled at the sound of his voice.

Light brown eyes that looked as if they'd once had a little dark eyeliner around them. It was smudged now. But that didn't stop the effect.

It was like being speared straight through the heart.

For a second neither of them spoke. It was the weirdest sensation—as if the air around them had just stilled.

He was drinking in everything about her. Her forgotten-about hair. Her crumpled clothes. Her dejected appearance.

But there was something else. Something that wouldn't let him break their gaze. A buzz. An air. He'd never felt something like this before. And she felt it too.

He could tell. Her pupils dilated just a little before his eyes. He didn't have any doubt that his were so big right now the Grand Canyon could fit in them.

There was something about her demeanour. This woman was a professional. She was educated. And she was, oh, so sexy.

He found his tongue. 'Your worries.' He couldn't help but let the corners of his mouth turn upwards.

She gave the briefest rise of her eyebrows and turned back towards the waiting wine glass. Her shoulders straightened a little. He'd definitely caught her attention.

Just as she'd caught his.

He leaned a little closer and nudged her shoulder. 'You're sitting on my favourite bar stool.'

'Didn't have your name on it,' she quipped back.

Her accent. It was unmistakeable. The Scottish twang made the hairs on his arms stand on end. He could listen to that all day. Or all night.

She swung her legs around towards him and leaned one arm on the bar. 'Come to think of it, you must be kind of brave.' She took a sip of her wine. Her eyebrows lifted again. 'Or kind of stupid.'

He liked it. She was flirting back. He leaned his arm on the bar too, so they were closer than ever. 'What makes you think that?'

She licked her lips. 'Because you're trying to get between a Scots girl and the bar.' She smiled as she ran her eyes up and down the length of his body. It was almost as if she'd reached her fingers out and touched him. 'Haven't you heard about Scots girls?'

He smiled and leaned closer. 'I think I might need a little education.' He couldn't think of anything he wanted more.

Instant attraction. He'd never really experienced it before. Not like this. He'd wanted to come in here to hide and get away from things. Now, his sanctuary had become a whole lot more exciting.

A whole lot more distracting.

His stomach flipped over. What if he never felt like this again? Or even worse, what if he felt like this when he was King of Montanari and married?

Right now he was none of those things. The engagement hadn't been announced. He was about to step into a life of duty and constant scrutiny.

Theresa was a friend. Nothing more. Nothing less. They'd never even shared a kiss.

He hadn't come here to meet anyone. He hadn't come here to be attracted to someone.

But right now he was caught in a gaze he didn't want to escape from. The pull was just too strong.

Something flitted across her eyes. It was as if her confidence wavered for a second.

'What's wrong?' He couldn't help himself.

She sucked in a breath. 'Bad day at the office.'

'Anything to do with a man?' It was out before he thought.

She blinked and gave a little smile again, pausing for a second. 'No. Definitely nothing to do with a man.'

It was as if he'd just laid himself bare. Finding out the lie of the land. He couldn't ignore the warm feeling that spread straight through him.

He had no royal duties this weekend. There were no hands he needed to shake. No business he needed to attend to. He'd told Security he was coming here and to keep their distance.

If he lived to be a hundred he'd remember this. He'd remember this meeting and the way it made him feel. The buzz was so strong the air practically sparkled around her.

He was still single. He could do this. Right now he would cross burning coals to see what would happen next.

He leaned even closer. 'I came here to get some peace and quiet. I came here to get some head space.' He gave her a little smile and lowered his voice. 'But, all of a sudden, there's no space in my head at all.'

He took a chance. 'How about I stop searching for some peace and quiet, and you forget all about your bad day?'

She ran her fingers up the stem of her wine glass. He could tell she was thinking. She looked up from beneath heavy eyelids. 'You mean, like a distraction. An interlude?'

The warm glow in his body started to rapidly rise. He nodded. 'A distraction.'

She licked her lips again and he almost groaned out loud. 'I think a distraction might be just what I need,' she said carefully.

He tried to quieten the cheerleader squad currently yelling in his head.

'I've always wanted to meet a Scots girl. Will you teach me how to wear a kilt?' He waved to the barman. 'There are some killer cocktails in here. You look like a Lavender Fizz kind of girl.'

'I'll do better than that.' There was a hint of mischief in her voice. 'I'll teach you how to take it off.'

This wasn't her life. It couldn't be. Things like this didn't happen to Sienna McDonald. But it seemed that in the blink of an eye her miserable, lousy day had just got a whole lot better.

It was the worst kind of day. The kind of day she should have got used to in this line of work.

But a doctor who got used to a baby dying was in the wrong profession.

It had been little Marco's third op. He'd been failing all the time, born into the world too early with undeveloped lungs and a malformed heart; she'd known the odds were stacked against him.

Some people thought it was wrong to operate on premature babies unless there was a guarantee of a good outcome. But Sienna had seen babies who had next to no chance come through an operation, fight like a seasoned soldier and go on to thrive. One of her greatest successes was coming up on his fourth birthday and she couldn't be prouder.

Today had been draining. Telling the parents had been soul-destroying. She didn't usually drown her sorrows in alcohol, but tonight, in a strange country with only herself for company, it was the only thing that would do. She'd already made short work of the accompanying chocolate she'd bought to go with the wine. The empty wrappers were littered around her.

She sensed him as soon as he sat down next to her.

There was a gentle waft of masculine cologne. Her eyes were lowered. It was easy to see the muscled thigh through the probably designer trousers. If he was staying in this hotel—he was probably a millionaire. She was just lucky the royal family were footing her bill.

When he spoke, his lilting Mediterranean accent washed over her. Thank goodness she was sitting down. There was something about the accent of the men of Montanari. It crossed between the Italian, French and Spanish of its surrounding neighbours. It was unmistakeable. Unique. And something she'd never forget.

She glanced sideways and once more sucked in her cheeks.

Nope. The guy who looked as if he'd just walked off some film set was still there. Any second now she'd have to pinch herself. This might actually be real.

Dark hair, killer green eyes with a little sparkle and perfect white teeth. She might not have X-ray vision but his lean and athletic build was clear beneath the perfectly tailored suit. If she were back in Scotland she'd tell him he might as well have *sex on legs* tattooed on his forehead. Too bad she was in a posh kingdom where she had to be a whole lot more polite than that.

He hadn't responded to her cheeky comment. For a millisecond he looked a little stunned, and then his shoulders relaxed a little and he nodded slowly. He was getting comfortable. Did he think the game was over?

She was just settling in for the ride. She didn't do this. She didn't *ever* do this. Pick up a man in a bar? Her friends would think she'd gone crazy. But the palms of her hands were tingling. She wanted to touch him. She wanted to feel his skin against hers. She wanted to know exactly what those lips tasted like.

He was like every erotic dream she'd ever had just handed to her on a plate.

She leaned her head on one hand and turned to face him. 'Who says I'm a cocktail kind of girl?'

He blinked. Her accent did that to people. It took their ears a few seconds to adjust to the Scottish twang. He was no different from every other man she'd ever met. The edges of his mouth turned upwards at the sound of her voice. People just seemed to love the Scottish accent—even if they couldn't understand a word she said.

'It's written all over you,' he shot back. He mirrored her stance, leaning his head on one hand and staring at her.

There was no mistaking the tingling of her skin. Part of her stomach turned over. There was a tiny wash of guilt.

Today wasn't meant to be a happy day. Today was a day to drown her sorrows and contemplate if she could have done anything different to save that little baby. But the truth was she'd already done that. Even if she went back in time she wouldn't do anything different. Clinically, her actions had been everything they should have been. Little Marco's body had just been too weak, too underdeveloped to fight any more.

The late evening sun was streaming in the windows behind him, bathing them both in a luminescence of peaches and purples. Distraction. That was what this was. And right now she could do with a distraction.

Something to help her forget. Something to help her think about something other than work. She was due to go home in a few days. She'd taught the surgeons at Montanari Royal General everything she could.

She let her shoulders relax a little. The first two glasses of wine were starting to kick in.

'I don't know that I'm a Lavender Fizz kind of girl.'

'Well, let's see what kind of girl you are.' The words hung in the air between them, with a hundred alternative meanings circulating in her mind. This guy was good. He was very good.

She half wished she'd changed after work. Or at least pulled a brush through her hair and applied some fresh make-up. This guy was impeccable, which made her wish she were too. He picked up the cocktail menu, pretending to peruse it, while giving her sideways glances. 'No,' he said decidedly. 'Not gin.' He paused a second. 'Hmm, raspberries, maybe. Wait, no, here it is. A peach melba cocktail.'

She couldn't help but smile as she raised her eyebrows. 'And what's in that one?'

He signalled the barman. 'Let's find out.'

Her smile remained fixed on her face. His confidence was tantalising. She sipped at her wine as she waited for the barman to mix the drinks.

'What's your name?' he asked as they waited. He held out his hand towards her. 'I'm Seb.'

Seb. A suitable billionaire-type name. Most of the men in this hotel had a whole host of aristocratic names. Louis. Alexander. Hugo. Augustus.

She reached out to take his hand. 'Sienna.'

His hand enveloped hers. What should have been a firm handshake was something else entirely. It was gentle. Almost like a caress. But there was a purpose to it. He didn't let go. He kept holding, letting the warmth of his hand permeate through her chilled skin. His voice was husky. 'You've been holding on to that wine glass too long.' Before she could reply he continued. 'Sienna. It doesn't seem a particularly Scottish name.'

A furrow appeared on his brow. As if he were trying to connect something. After a second, he shook his head and concentrated on her again.

She tried not to fixate on the fact her hand was still in his. She liked it. She liked the way this man was one of the most direct flirts she'd ever met. He could have scrawled his intentions towards her with her lipstick on the mirrored gantry behind the bar and she wouldn't have batted an eyelid because this was definitely a two-way street.

'It's not.' She let her thumb brush over the back of his hand. 'It's Italian.' She lifted her eyebrows. 'I was conceived there. By accident—of course,' she added.

A look of confusion swept his face as the barman set down the drinks, but he didn't call her on her comment.

Sienna had a wave of disappointment as she had to pull her hand free of his and she turned to the peach concoction on the bar with a glimpse of red near the bottom. She lifted the tiny straws and gave it a little stir. 'What is this, exactly?'

Those green eyes fixed on hers again. 'Peach nectar, raspberry puree, fresh raspberries and champagne.'

She took a sip. Nectar was right. It hit the spot perfectly. Just like something else.

'Are you here on business or pleasure, Sienna?'

She thought for a second. She was proud to be a surgeon. Most men she'd ever met had seemed impressed by her career. But tonight she didn't want to talk about being a surgeon. Tonight she wanted to concentrate on something else entirely.

'Business. But it's almost concluded. I go home in a few days.'

He nodded carefully. 'Have you enjoyed visiting Montanari?'

She couldn't lie. Even today's events hadn't taken the shine off the beautiful country that she'd spent the last few weeks in. The rolling green hills, the spectacular volcanic mountain peak that overlooked the capital city and coastline next to the Mediterranean Sea made the kingdom one of the prettiest places she'd ever visited. She took another sip of her cocktail. 'I have. It's a beautiful country. I'm only sorry I haven't seen enough of it.'

'You haven't?'

She shook her head. 'Business is business. I've been busy.' She stirred her drink. 'What about you?'

He had an air about him. Something she hadn't encountered before. An aura. She assumed he must be quite enigmatic as a businessman. He could probably charm the birds from the trees. At least, she was assuming he was a businessman. He looked the part and every other man she'd met in this exclusive hotel had been here to do one business deal or another.

But for a charmer, there was something else. An underlying sincerity in the back of his eyes. Somehow she felt if the volcanic peak overlooking the capital erupted right now she would be safe with this guy. Her instincts had always been good and it had been a long time since she'd felt like that.

'I've been abroad on business. I'm just back.'

'You stay here? In this hotel?'

He laughed and shook his head. 'Oh, no. I live…close by. But I conduct much of my business in this hotel.' He gave another gracious nod towards the barman. 'They have the best facilities. The most professional staff. I'm comfortable here.'

It was a slightly odd thing to say. But she forgot about it in seconds as the barman came back to top up their glasses.

She took a deep breath and stared at her glass. 'Maybe I should slow down a little.'

His gaze was steady. 'The drink? Or something else?'

There it was. The hidden question between them. She ran her finger around the rim of the glass. 'I came here to forget,' she said quietly, exposing more of herself than she meant.

Her other hand was on the bar. His slid over the top, intertwining his fingers with hers. 'And so did I. Maybe there are other ways to forget.'

She licked her lips, almost scared to look up and meet

his gaze again. It would be like answering the unspoken question. The one she was sure that she wanted to answer.

His thumb slid under her palm, tracing little circles. In most circumstances it would be calming. But here, and now, it was anything but calming; it was almost erotic.

'Sienna, you have a few days left. Have you seen the mountains yet? How about I show you some of the hidden pleasures that we keep secret from the tourists?'

It was the way he said it. His voice was low and husky, sending a host of tiny shivers of expectation up her spine.

She could almost hear the voices of her friends in her head. She was always the sensible one. Always cautious. If she told this tale a few months later and told them she'd made her excuses and walked away...

The cocktail glass was glistening in the warm sunset. The chandelier hanging above the bar sending a myriad of coloured prisms of light around the room.

The perfect setting. The perfect place. The perfect man.

A whole host of distraction.

Exactly what she'd been looking for.

She threw back her head and tried to remember if she was wearing matching underwear. Not that it mattered. But somehow she wanted all her memories about this to be perfect.

She met his green gaze. There should be rules about eyes like that. Eyes that pulled you in and held you there, while all the time giving a mischievous hint of exactly what he was thinking.

She stood up from her bar stool and moved closer. His hand dropped from the bar to her hip. She brushed her lips against his ear. 'How many of Montanari's pleasures are hidden?'

There it was. The intent.

It didn't matter that her perfect red dress was hanging in the cupboard upstairs. It didn't matter that her matching lipstick was at the bottom of her bag. It didn't matter that her most expensive perfume was in the bathroom in her room.

Mr Sex-on-Legs liked her just the way she was.

He closed his eyes for a second. This time his voice was almost a growl, as if he were bathing in what she'd just said. 'I could listen to your accent all day.'

She put her hand on his shoulder. 'How about you listen to it all night instead?'

And the deed was done.

CHAPTER ONE

SHE STARED AT the stick again.

Yep. The second line was still there.

It wasn't a figment of her imagination. Just as the missing period wasn't a dream and the tender breasts weren't a sign of an ill-fitting bra.

A baby. She was going to have a baby.

She stared out of her house window.

Her mortgage. She'd just moved in here. Her mortgage was huge. As soon as she'd seen the house she'd loved it. It was totally too big for one person—how ironic was that?—but she'd figured she'd have the rest of her life to pay for it. It was five minutes from Teddy's and had the most amazing garden with a pink cherry blossom tree at the bottom of it, and a little paved area at the back for sitting.

It was just like the house she'd dreamed of as a child. The house where she and her husband and children would stay and live happily ever after.

She sighed and put her head in her hands.

She was pregnant. Pregnant to Seb, the liar.

It made her insides twist and curl. She'd never quite worked out when he'd realised who she was, while she'd spent the weekend in blissful ignorance.

A weekend all the while holed up in the most beautiful mountain chalet-style house.

The days had been joyful. She'd never felt an attraction like it—immediate, powerful and totally irresistible. Seb had made her feel like the only woman in the world and for two days she'd relished it.

It was too good. Too perfect. She should have known. Because nobody could ever be *that* perfect. Not really.

She'd been surprised by his security outside the hotel. But then, lots of businessmen had bodyguards nowadays. It wasn't quite so unusual as it could have been.

And she hadn't seen any of the sights of Montanari. Once they'd reached his gorgeous house hidden in the mountains, the only thing she'd seen was his naked body.

For two whole days.

She squeezed her eyes closed for a second. It hurt to remember how much she'd loved it.

How many other woman had been given the same treatment?

She shook her head and shuddered. Finding out who he really was had ruined her memories of those two wonderful days.

Of those two wonderful nights...

She pressed her hand on her non-existent bump. *Oh, wow.* She was pregnant by a prince.

Prince Sebastian Falco of Montanari.

Some women might like that. Some women might think that was amazing. Right now she was wondering exactly why her contraceptive pill had failed. She'd taken it faithfully every day. She hadn't been sick. She hadn't forgotten. This wasn't deliberate. This absolutely wasn't a ploy to get pregnant by a prince. But what if he thought it was?

Her mind jumped back to her house. How much maternity leave would she get? How much maternity pay would she get—would it cover her mortgage? She'd used her savings as the deposit for the house—that, and the little extra she'd had left to update the bathroom and kitchen, meant her rainy-day fund was virtually empty.

She stood up and started pacing. Who would look after her baby when she returned to work? Would she be able to return to work? She had to. She was an independent woman. She loved her career. Having a baby didn't mean giving up the job she loved.

She rested her hand against the wall of her sitting room. Maybe someone at the hospital could give her a recommendation for a childminder? The crèche at the hospital wouldn't be able to cater for on-calls and late night emergency surgeries. She'd need someone ultra flexible. There was so much to think about. So much to organise.

She couldn't concentrate. Her mind kept jumping from one thing to the other. Oh, no—was this the pregnancy brain that women complained about?

She couldn't have that. She didn't have time for that. She was a neonatal cardiothoracic surgeon. She was responsible for tiny lives. She needed to be focused. She needed to have her mind on the job.

She walked through to the kitchen. The calendar was lying on the kitchen table. It was turned to April—showing when she'd had her last period. It had been left there when the realisation had hit her and she'd rushed to the pharmacy for a pregnancy test. She'd bought four.

She wouldn't need them. She flicked forward. Last date of period, twenty-third of April. Forty weeks from then? She turned the calendar over, counting the weeks on the back. January. Her baby was due on the twenty-eighth of January.

She pushed open her back door and walked outside. The previous owners had left a bench seat, carved from an original ancient tree that had been damaged in a lightning strike years ago. She sat down and took some deep breaths.

It was a beautiful day. The flowers in her garden had

all started to emerge. Fragrant red, pink and orange free-sias, blue cornflowers, purple delphinium and multi-coloured peonies blossomed in pretty colours all around her, their scents permeating the air.

She smiled. The deep breathing was beginning to calm her. A baby. She was going to have a baby.

She closed her eyes and pressed her lips together as a wave of determination washed over her. Baby McDonald might not have been planned. But Baby McDonald would certainly be wanted.

He or she would be loved. Be adored.

A familiar remembrance of disappointment and anger made her catch her breath. For as long as she could remember her parents had made it clear to her that she'd been a 'mistake'. They hadn't put it quite in as few words but the implication was always there. Two people who had never really wanted to be together but had done 'what was right'.

Except it wasn't right. It wasn't right at all. Anger and resentment had simmered from them both. The expression on her father's face when he had left on her eighteenth birthday had told her everything she'd ever needed to know—as had the relief on her mother's.

She'd been a burden. An unplanned-for presence.

Whether this baby was planned for or not, it would always feel loved, always feel wanted. She might not know about childcare, she might not know about maternity leave, she might not know about her mortgage—but of that one thing, she was absolutely sure.

Her brain skydived somewhere else. Folic acid. She hadn't been taking it. She'd have to get some. Her feet moved automatically. She could grab her bag; the nearest pharmacy was only a five-minute drive. She could pick some up and start taking it immediately. As she crossed the garden her eyes squeezed shut for a second. Darn it. Folic acid was essential for normal development in a baby.

She racked her brains. What had she been eating these last few weeks? Had there been any spinach? Any broccoli? She'd had some, but she just wasn't sure how much. She'd had oranges and grapefruit. Lentils, avocados and peas.

She winced. She'd just remembered her intake of raspberries and strawberries. They'd been doused in champagne in Montanari. Alcohol. Another no-no in pregnancy.

At least she hadn't touched a drop since her return.

Her footsteps slowed as she entered the house again. Seb. She'd need to tell him. She'd need to tell him she was expecting his baby.

A gust of cool air blew in behind her, sending every hair on her arms standing on end. How on earth would she tell him? They hadn't exactly left things on good terms.

She sagged down onto her purple sofa for a few minutes. How did you contact a prince?

Oliver. Oliver Darrington would know. He was Seb's friend, the obstetrician who had arranged for her to go to Montanari and train the other paediatric surgeons. But how on earth could she ask him without giving the game away? Would she sound like some desperate stalker?

Oh, Olly, by the way...can I just phone your friend the Prince, please? Can you give me his number?

She sighed and rested her head backwards on the sofa watching the yellow ticker tape of the news channel stream past.

Her eyes glazed over. Last time she'd seen Seb she'd screamed at him. Hardly the most ladylike response.

It didn't matter that his lie had been by omission. That might even seem a tiny bit excusable now. But then, six weeks ago, rationality had left the luxurious chalet she'd found herself in.

It had been a simple mistake. The car driver—or, let's face it, he was probably a lot more than that—had given a nod and said *Your Highness* to something Seb had asked him.

The poor guy had realised his mistake right away and made a prompt exit. But it was too late. She'd heard it.

At first she'd almost laughed out loud. She'd been so relaxed, so happy, that the truth hadn't even occurred to her. 'Your Highness?' She'd smiled as she'd picked up her bags to go back in the house.

But the look of horror on Seb's face had caused her foot to stop in mid-air.

And just like today, the hairs on her arms had stood on end. Seb. Sebastian. The name of the Prince of Montanari. The person who'd requested she train the surgeons in his hospital. The mystery man that she'd never met—because he was doing business overseas.

Just like Seb.

She might as well have been plunged into a cold pool of glacier ice.

'Tell me you're joking?'

For the first time since she'd met him, his coolness vanished. He started to babble. *Babble.* His eyes darting from side to side but never quite meeting her gaze.

She dropped her bags at her feet on the stony path. 'You're not, are you?' He kept talking but she stopped listening. Her brain trying to make sense of what was going on.

'You're Sebastian Falco? *You're* the Prince?' She walked right up under his nose.

It must have been the way she'd said it. As if it were almost impossible. As if he were the unlikeliest candidate in the world.

He let out a sigh and those forest-green eyes finally met hers. His head gave the barest shake. 'Is that so ridiculous?'

The prickling hairs on her arms spread. Like an infectious disease. Reaching parts of her body that definitely shouldn't feel like that.

Although the rage was building inside her, all that came out was a whisper. 'It's ridiculous to me.'

He blinked. She could see herself reflected in his eyes. Hurt was written all over her face. She hated feeling like that. She hated being emotionally vulnerable.

Her mother and father had lived a lie for eighteen years. She'd always promised herself that would never be her life. That would never be her relationship.

She'd thrown caution to the wind and lost. Big style.

He'd made a fool of her. And she'd let him.

'How could you?' she snapped. 'How could you lie to me? What kind of woman do you think I am?'

As she heard the words out loud she almost wanted to hide. She knew exactly what kind of woman she'd been these last two days. One that acted as though this was nothing. She'd experienced a true weekend of passion and abandon. She'd pushed aside all thoughts of consequences and lost herself totally in him.

Ultimate fail.

Now she was looking into the eyes of a man who'd misled her. Let her think that this was something it was not.

He pulled his gaze away from hers, having the good shame to look embarrassed, and ran his hand through his thick dark hair.

But even that annoyed her. She'd spent all weekend running her own fingers through the same hair and right now she knew she'd never do that again.

He reached up and touched her shoulder. 'Sienna, I'm sorry.'

She pulled back as if he'd stung her and his eyes widened.

'Don't touch me. Don't touch me again. Ever!' She spun around and walked back inside.

She ignored everything around her. Ignored the soft

sofas they'd spent many an hour on. Ignored the thick wooden table that they'd eaten more than their dinner from. Ignored the tangled sheets in the white and gold bedroom that told their own story.

She grabbed the few things she'd brought with her—and the few other things she'd bought—and started throwing them into her bag.

Seb rushed in behind her. 'Sienna, slow down. Things weren't meant to happen like this. I'm sorry. I am. I came to the hotel to get away. I came to think about some things.' He ran his fingers through his hair again. 'And then, when I got there, there was just…' he held his hands up towards her '…you,' he said simply.

She spun back around.

'I didn't realise right away who you were. I'd asked Oliver if he could send a surgeon to help with training. I'm the patron of the hospital and they only come to me when there are big issues. The hospital board were unhappy about all our neonates having to be transferred to France for cardiac surgeries. It was time to train our own surgeons—buy our own equipment. But once I'd made the arrangement with Oliver I hadn't really paid attention to all the details. Our hospital director took care of all those because I knew I wouldn't be here. I didn't even recognise your name straight away.'

She felt numb. 'You knew? You knew exactly who I was?'

He sighed heavily and his tanned face paled. 'Not until yesterday when you mentioned you were a surgeon.'

She gulped. She knew exactly what he wasn't saying. Not until after they'd slept together.

'Why didn't you tell me? Why didn't you tell me you knew Oliver yesterday?'

He shook his head. 'Because we'd already taken things further than either of us probably intended. We were in our own little bubble here. And I won't lie. I liked it, Si-

enna. I liked the fact it was just you and me and the outside world seemed as far away as possible.' He took a
deep breath. 'I didn't want to spoil it.' He started pacing around. 'Do you know what it's like to have the eyes
of the world constantly on you? Do you know what it's
like when every time you even say hello to a woman it's
splashed across the press the next day that she could be
the next Queen?' The frustration was clearly spilling over.

'You expect me to feel sorry for you?'

He threw up his hands. 'The only time I've had a bit
of a normal life was when I was at university. The press
were banned from coming near me then. But every moment before that, and every second after it, I've constantly
been on display. Life is never normal around me, Sienna.
But here—' he indicated the room '—and in Il Palazzo
di Cristallo I get a tiny bit of privacy. Do you know how
good it felt to walk in somewhere, see a beautiful woman
and be able to act on it? Be able to actually let myself feel
something?'

Her throat was dry. Emotion and frustration was written all over his face. He couldn't stop pacing.

It was as if the weight of the world were currently sitting on his shoulders. She had no idea what his life was
like. She'd no idea what was expected of him. Her insides
squirmed. The thought of constantly being watched by
the press? No, thanks.

But the anger still burned inside. The hurt at being
deceived. How many other women had he brought here?
Was she just another on his list?

She stepped up close to him again, ignoring his delicious aftershave that had wound its way around her over
the last few days. 'So, everything was actually a lie?'

He winced. 'It wasn't a lie, Sienna.'

'It was to me.'

He shook his head and straightened his shoulders.
'You're overreacting. Even if I had introduced myself,

what difference would it have made?' He moved closer, his chest just in front of her face. 'Are you telling me that this wouldn't have happened? That we wouldn't have been attracted to each other? We wouldn't have ended up together?'

She clouded out his words—focusing only on the first part. It had been enough to make the red mist descend. 'I'm overreacting?' She dropped the clothes she had clutched in her hands. 'I'm overreacting?' She let out an angry breath as her eyes swept the room.

She shook her head. 'Oh, no, Seb. I'm not overreacting.' She picked up the nearest lamp and flung it at the wall, shattering it into a million pieces. 'This. This is overreacting. This is letting you know how I really feel about your deception.'

His chin practically hung open.

She stalked back to the bed and stuffed the remaining few items into her bag, zipping it with an over-zealous tug.

She marched right up under his nose. 'If I never see you again it will be too soon. Next time find someone else to train your surgeons. Preferably someone who doesn't mind being deceived and lied to.'

He drew himself up to his full height. On any other occasion she might have been impressed. But that day? Not a chance.

His mouth tightened. 'Have it your own way.'

'I will,' she'd shouted as she'd swept out of the chalet and back into the waiting car. 'Take me back to my hotel,' she'd growled at the driver.

Heavens. She hoped she hadn't got that poor man fired. He hadn't even blinked when she'd spoken. Just put the car into gear and set off down the mountain road. Her last view of Seb had been as he'd walked to the door and watched the car take off.

Now, it seemed all a bit melodramatic.

She'd never admit she'd cried on the plane on the way

home. Not to a single person. And especially not to a person she'd now have to tell she was carrying his baby.

Her eyes came into focus sharply and she leaned forward.

The tickertape stream of news changed constantly. Something had made her focus again.

She waited a few seconds.

Prince Sebastian Falco of Montanari has announced his engagement to his childhood friend Princess Theresa Mon Carte of Peruglea. Although the date of their wedding has not yet been announced it is expected to be in the next calendar year. The royal wedding will unite the two neighbouring kingdoms of Montanari and Peruglea.

Every single tiny bit of breath left her body. Her stomach plummeted as a tidal wave of emotions consumed her.

It was as if the glacier ice pool she'd imagined on the mountain of Montanari had followed her home. Nausea made her bolt to the bathroom.

This wasn't morning sickness.

This was pure and utter shock.

He was engaged. Sebastian was engaged.

As she knelt on the bathroom floor she felt momentarily light-headed. Could this be any worse?

She squeezed her eyes closed. Trying to banish all the memories of that weekend from her mind. Her body responded automatically, curling into a ball on the ground. If she didn't think about him, she couldn't hurt. She couldn't let herself hurt like this. She had a baby. A baby to think about.

She pressed her head against the cool tiles on the wall.

Pregnant by a prince. An *engaged* prince.

Funnily enough, no fairy tale she'd ever heard of ended like this.

CHAPTER TWO

December

SHE WAS LATE. Again. And Sienna was never late. She hated people being late. And now she was turning into that person herself.

It was easy to shift the blame. Her obstetrician's clinic was running nearly an hour behind. How ironic. Even being friends with the Assistant Head of Obstetrics around here didn't give her perks—but she could hardly blame him. Oliver had been dealing with a particularly difficult case. It just meant that now she wouldn't complete her rounds and finish when planned.

She hurried across the main entrance of the hospital and tried not to be distracted by the surroundings. The Royal Cheltenham hospital—or Teddy's, as they all affectionately called it—did Christmas with style.

A huge tree adorned the glass atrium. Red and gold lights twinkled merrily against the already darkening sky. The tea room near the front entrance—staffed by volunteers—had its own display. A complete Santa sleigh and carved wooden reindeers with red Christmas baubles on their noses. Piped music surrounded her. Not loud enough to be intrusive, but just enough to set the scene for Christmas, as an array of traditional carols and favourite pop tunes permeated the air around her.

Sienna couldn't help but smile. Christmas was her absolute favourite time of year. The one time of year her parents actually stopped fighting. Her mother's sister, Aunt Margaret, had always visited at this time of year. Her warmth and love of Christmas had been infectious. As soon as she walked in the house, the frosty atmosphere just seemed to vanish. If Margaret sensed anything, she never acknowledged it. It seemed it wasn't the 'done thing' to fight and argue in front of Aunt Margaret and Sienna loved the fact that for four whole days she didn't have to worry at all.

Aunt Margaret's love of Christmas had continued—for Sienna, at least—long after she'd died. Sienna's own Christmas tree had gone up on the first of December. Multicoloured lights were decorating the now bare cherry blossom at the bottom of her garden. She wasn't even going to admit how they got there.

It seemed that Mother Nature was even trying to get in on the act. A light dusting of snow currently covered the glass atrium at Teddy's.

This time next year would be even more special. This time next year would be her baby's first Christmas. A smile spread across Sienna's face.

Thoughts like that made her forget about her aching back and sore feet. At thirty-four weeks pregnant she was due to start maternity leave some time soon. Oliver had arranged for some maternity cover, and he'd had the good sense to start her replacement early. Max Ainsley was proving more than capable.

He'd picked up the electronic systems and referral pathways of Teddy's easily. It meant that she'd be able to relax at home when the baby arrived instead of fretting over cancelled surgeries and babies and families having to travel for miles to get the same standard of care.

She hurried into the neonatal unit and stuffed her bag into the duty room. She looked up and took a deep breath.

Every cot was full. An influx of winter virus had hit the unit a few weeks ago. That, along with delivery of a set of premature quads—one of whom needed surgery—meant that the staff were run off their feet.

Ruth, one of the neonatal nurses, shot her a sympathetic look. 'You doing okay, Sienna?'

Sienna straightened up and rubbed her back, then her protruding stomach. She was used to the sideways glances from members of staff. As she'd never dated anyone from the hospital and most of the staff knew she lived alone, speculation about her pregnancy had been rife.

The best rumour that she'd heard was that she'd decided she didn't need a man and had just used a sperm donor to have a baby on her own. If only it were true.

She'd stopped watching the news channel. Apart from weather reports and occasional badly behaved sportsmen, it seemed that her favourite news channel had developed an obsession with the upcoming royal wedding in Montanari early next year.

News was obviously slow. But if she saw one more shot of Seb with his arm around the cut-out perfect blonde she would scream. She didn't care that they looked a little awkward together. She just didn't want to see them at all.

She smiled at Ruth. 'I'm doing fine, thanks. Just had my check-up. Six weeks to go.' She waved her hand at the array of cots. 'I've got three babies to review. I'm hoping we can get at least two of them home for their first Christmas in the next few days. What do you think?'

As she said the words her Head Neonatal Nurse appeared behind Ruth. She'd worked with Annabelle Ainsley for the last year and had been more than a little surprised when it had been revealed that Annabelle was actually Max's estranged wife. She hadn't been surprised that it had only taken them a week to reconcile once he'd started working at Teddy's. For the last couple of weeks

Annabelle hadn't stopped smiling, so she was surprised to see her looking so serious this afternoon.

'There's someone here to see you.' The normally un-fazed Annabelle looked a little uncomfortable.

Sienna picked up the nearest tablet to check over one of her patients. 'Who is it? A rep? Tell them I don't have time, I'm sorry.' She gave Annabelle a smile. 'I think I should maybe hand all the reps over to Max now—what do you think?'

Annabelle glanced at Ruth. 'It's not a rep. I don't rec-ognise him and didn't have time to ask his name. He's insisting that he'll only speak to you and...' she took a breath '...he won't be kept waiting.'

Sienna sat the tablet back down, satisfied with the recordings. Her post-surgery baby was doing well. She shook her head. 'Well, who does he think he is?' She looked around the unit and paused. 'Wait? Is it a parent of one of the babies? Or someone with a surgery sched-uled for their child? You know that I'll speak to them.'

Annabelle shook her head firmly. 'No. None of those. No parents—or impending parents. It's something else entirely.' She handed a set of notes to Ruth. 'Can you check on little Maisy Allerton? She didn't take much at her last feed.'

Ruth nodded and disappeared. Annabelle pressed her lips together. 'This guy, he says it's personal.'

Sienna felt an uncomfortable prickle across her skin. 'Personal? Who would have something personal to talk to me about?'

The words were out before she even thought about them. Nothing like making herself sound sad and lonely. Did people at Teddy's even think she had a personal life?

Annabelle's eyes darted automatically to Sienna's pro-truding stomach, then she flushed as she realised Sienna had noticed.

Sienna straightened her shoulders. She'd never been

a fan of anyone trying to push her around. She gave Annabelle a wide smile. 'Oh, he's insisting, is he?'

Annabelle nodded then her eyes narrowed and she folded her arms across her chest. She'd worked with Sienna long enough to sense trouble ahead.

Sienna kept smiling. 'Well, in that case, I'll review my three babies. Talk to all sets of parents. I might make a few phone calls to some parents with babies on my list between Christmas and New Year, and then...' she paused as she picked up the tablet again to start accessing a file '...then, as a heavily pregnant woman, I think I'll go and have something to eat. I missed lunch and—' she raised her eyebrows at Annabelle '—I have a feeling a colleague I work with might *insist* I don't faint at work.'

Annabelle smiled too and nodded knowingly. 'Not that I want to be any influence on you, but the kitchen staff made killer carrot cake today. I think it could count as one of your five a day.'

Sienna threw back her head and laughed. 'You're such a bad influence but I could definitely be persuaded.' Her eyes went straight back to the chart. 'Okay, so let's see Kendall first. Mr I-Insist is just going to have to find out how things work around here.'

Annabelle gave a smile and put an arm at Sienna's back. 'Don't worry. Somehow I think you'll be more than a match for him. Give me a signal when you come back. I can always page you after five minutes to give you an escape.'

Sienna nodded. She didn't really care who was waiting for her—her babies would always come first.

Seb was furious. He kept glancing at his watch. He'd been in this room for over an hour—his security detail waiting outside.

The sister of the neonatal ward had seemed surprised at first by his insistence at seeing Sienna. Then, she'd ex-

plained Sienna was at another appointment and would be
back soon. What exactly meant *soon* at the Royal Cheltenham?

He'd paced the corridors a few times looking for her
with no success. The doors to the neonatal unit had a
coded lock, and, from the look of the anxious parents hur-
rying in and out, it really wasn't a place he wanted to be.

He'd been stunned when Oliver Darrington had phoned
him to discuss his own difficult situation—after a one-
night stand a colleague was pregnant. A colleague who
he had feelings for. Oliver had been Sebastian's friend
since they'd attended university together, even though
they were destined for completely different lives.

He hadn't told Oliver a thing about his weekend with
Sienna, so when Oliver had mentioned that Sienna too
was pregnant, Sebastian had felt as if he couldn't breathe.

His tongue had stuck to the roof of his mouth and his
brain had scrambled to ask the question he'd wanted to,
without giving himself away. According to Oliver she
was heavily pregnant—due to have her baby at the end
of January.

For a few seconds Seb had felt panicked. The dates
fitted perfectly. He didn't have a single doubt that her
baby could be his.

He could hardly remember the rest of the conversation
with Oliver. That made him cringe now. It was a complete
disservice to his friend.

He'd had things to deal with.

Since Sienna had stormed out of his chalet retreat his
life had turned upside down. He'd followed his parents'
wishes and allowed the announcement of the engagement.
Theresa had seemed indifferent. Uniting the kingdoms
had been important to her too. But marrying someone
she wasn't in love with didn't seem any more appealing
to her than it was to him.

If Sienna hadn't happened, maybe, just maybe, he

could have mustered some enthusiasm and tried to persuade Theresa their relationship could work.

But his nights had been haunted with dreams of being tangled in the sheets with a passionate woman with ash-blonde hair, caramel-coloured eyes and a firm, toned body.

She'd ignited a flame inside him. Something that had burned underneath the surface since she'd left. He'd been a fool. A fool to let his country think he would take part in a union he didn't think he could make work.

His parents had been beside themselves with anger at the broken engagement.

Theresa had been remarkably stoic about him breaking the engagement. She'd handed back the yellow diamond ring with a nod of her head. He suspected her heart lay somewhere else. Her voice had been tight. 'I hadn't got around to finalising the design for my wedding dress yet. The designer was furious with me. It's just as well really, isn't it?'

He'd felt bad as he bent to kiss her cheek. Theresa wasn't really upset with him. Not yet, anyway. She might be angrier when she found out about the baby. It could be embarrassing for her. He only hoped she would have moved on to wherever her heart truly lay.

The Head of his PR had nearly had a heart attack. He'd actually put his hand to his chest and turned an alarming shade of grey. And that had given Sebastian instant inspiration. In amongst breaking the news to both Theresa and his parents, Sebastian had spent the last two weeks doing something else—making arrangements to twin the Cheltenham hospital with the Montanari Royal General. He was already a patron of his own hospital; a sizeable donation would make him a patron of Teddy's too.

It was the perfect cover story. He could come to the Royal Cheltenham without people asking too many questions. Oliver had been surprised for around five minutes.

Then, he'd made him an appointment with the board. In the meantime, Sebastian could come freely to the hospital with his security and press team in tow. The announcement was due to be made tomorrow. Seb was hoping he could also make an announcement of his own.

He glanced at his watch again as the anger built in his chest. Sienna hadn't even contacted him. Hadn't even let him know he was going to be a father. Was her intention to leave his child fatherless? For the heir of Montanari not to be acknowledged or have their rightful inheritance?

That could never happen. He wouldn't *allow* that to happen. Not in his lifetime.

He heard a familiar voice drifting down the corridor towards him. It sent every sense on fire. That familiar Scottish twang. The voice she'd invited him to listen to all night...

'No problem. I'll be along to review the chest X-ray in five minutes. Thanks, Max.'

The footsteps neared but he wasn't prepared for the sight. Last time he'd seen Sienna she'd been toned and athletic. This time the rounded belly appeared before she did.

Her footsteps stopped dead in the doorway, her eyes wide. It was clear he was the last person she'd been expecting to see.

She took his breath away. She didn't have on a traditional white coat. Instead she was dressed in what must be a maternity alternative to a suit. Black trousers with a matching black tunic over the top. It was still smart. Still professional. Her hair was gleaming, a bit longer than he remembered and tucked behind her ears. A red stethoscope hung around her neck, matching her bright red lipstick.

'Sebastian.' It was more a breath than a word.

Her hand went automatically to her stomach. His reply stuck in his throat. He hadn't been ready. He hadn't been ready for the sight of her ripe with his child. Even under her smart clothes he could see her lean body had changed totally. Her breasts were much bigger than before—and they suited her. Pregnancy suited her in a way he couldn't even have imagined.

But now he was here, he just didn't even know where to start.

This wasn't happening. Not here. Not now.

She'd planned things so carefully. All her surgeries were over. Any new patients had been seen jointly with Max. He would perform the neonatal surgeries and she would do later follow up once she was back from maternity leave.

But here he was. Right in front of her. The guy she'd spent the last six months half cursing, half pining for.

Those forest-green eyes practically swept up and down her body. Her palm itched. That thick dark hair. The hair she'd spent two days and two nights running her fingers through. Those broad shoulders, filling out the exquisitely cut suit. The pale lilac of the shirt and the shocking pink of his tie with his dark suit and good looks made him look like one of the models adorning the billboards above Times Square in New York. Imagine waking up with that staring in your hotel window every morning.

Her breath had left her lungs. It was unnatural. It was ridiculous. He was just a man. She sucked in a breath and narrowed her gaze. 'Congratulations on your engagement.'

He flinched. What had he expected? That she'd welcome him here with open arms?

Part of her felt a tiny twinge of regret. Her hand had picked up the phone more times than she could count. She'd tried to have that conversation with Oliver on a number of occasions. But it was clear that he'd never realised what was behind her tiny querying questions. The thought that his friend might have had a liaison with his colleague obviously hadn't even entered his mind.

Was it really such a stretch of the imagination?

Sebastian let out a sigh and stepped towards her. She held up her hand automatically to stop him getting too close—last thing she needed was to get a whiff of that familiar aftershave. She didn't need any more memories of the past than she already had. Baby was more than enough.

The royal persona she'd seen on the TV news seemed to be the man in the room with her now. This wasn't the cheeky, flirtatious, incredibly sexy guy that she'd spent two days and two nights with. Maybe her Seb didn't really exist at all?

There was something else. An air about him she hadn't noticed before. Or maybe she hadn't been paying attention. An assurance. A confidence. The kind of persona that actually fitted with being a prince.

He caught the hand she held in front of her.

The effect was instant, a rush of warmth and a pure overload of memories of the last time he'd touched her.

If she hadn't been standing so squarely she might have swayed. Her senses were alight. Now, his aftershave was reaching across the short space between them like a cowboy's rope pulling her in. Her hand tingled from where he held it. His grip initially had been firm but now it changed and his thumb moved under her palm, tracing circles—just as he'd done months ago.

Her breathing stalled. No. No, she wasn't going to go here again.

This was the man that had announced his engagement a few weeks after they'd met. An engagement to a childhood friend. Had he been seeing her the whole time? She'd checked. But the media wasn't sure. Had he been sleeping with them both at the same time?

She had no idea.

But no matter what her senses were doing, thoughts like that coloured her opinion of the man. He hadn't been honest with her. They hadn't promised each other anything, but that didn't matter.

She snatched her hand back.

'I'm not engaged, Sienna. I broke off my engagement when I heard the news you were pregnant.' His voice was as smooth as silk.

She felt herself bristle. 'And what am I supposed to feel—grateful?'

He didn't even blink. He just kept talking. 'I heard the news from Oliver. He called me about something else. A woman. Ella? Do you know her?'

Sienna frowned. 'Yes, yes, I know her. She's a midwife here.' She paused. Did Sebastian know the full story?

'They're engaged,' she said carefully, missing out the part that Ella was pregnant too. She wasn't sure just how much Oliver would have told Sebastian.

A wide smile broke across Sebastian's face. 'Perfect. I'll need to congratulate him.' His focus came back on Sienna. 'Maybe we could have a joint wedding?'

'A what?' Someone walking past the door turned their head at the rise of her voice. 'Are you crazy?'

Sebastian shook his head. 'Why would you think I'm crazy?'

He drew himself up in front of her. 'You're carrying the heir to the Montanari throne. We might still have things to sort out, but I'd prefer it if the heir to the throne was legitimate. Wouldn't you? If you come back with me now we can be married as soon as we get there. We can tell the world we met when you came to work in Montanari Royal General. Everything fits.'

He made it all sound so normal. So rational. So matter-of-fact.

She wasn't hearing this. She wasn't. It was some sick, delusional dream. She thought back to everything she'd eaten today. Maybe she'd been exposed to something weird.

He reached into his pocket and pulled out a ring. 'Here.'

She wasn't thinking straight and held out her hand. 'What is it?'

One of the ward clerks walked past and raised her eyebrows at the sight of the way-too-big diamond. Perfect. Just perfect. She was already the talk of the place and Polly was the world's biggest gossip. She just prayed that Polly hadn't recognised Sebastian.

She flinched and pulled her hand away. 'What am I supposed to do with that?'

'Put it on,' he said simply, glancing at her as if it were a stupid question. 'You need to wear an engagement ring.' He paused for a second and looked at her face. 'Don't you like it? It's a family heirloom.' His forehead wrinkled. 'I'm sure I can find you something else in the family vault.'

She shook her head and started pacing. 'It doesn't matter if I like it. I don't want it. I don't need it. I'm—' She stopped and placed her hand on her stomach. '*We're* going nowhere. I have a job here. A home. The very last place I'm going is Montanari. And the very last thing I'm doing...' she paused again and shook her head, trying to make sense of the craziness around her. She drew in a deep breath and stepped right up to him, poking her finger in her chest. 'The very last thing I'm doing is marrying you.'

Now Sebastian started shaking his head. He had the absolute gall to look surprised. 'Why on earth not? You're expecting our child. You're going to be the mother of the heir to Montanari. We should get married. And as soon as possible.' He said it as if it made perfect sense.

Sienna put her hands on her back and started pacing. 'No. No, we absolutely shouldn't.'

Sebastian held out his hands. 'Sienna, in a few years you get to be the Queen of Montanari. What woman wouldn't want that?'

She shuddered. She actually shuddered. 'Oh, no. Oh, no.'

Sebastian's brow creased. 'What on earth is wrong? We can have a state wedding in Montanari...' he glanced at her stomach and gave a little shrug '...but we'll need to be quick.'

Sienna took a step back. 'Okay, were you really this crazy when I met you in Montanari and I just didn't notice? Because this is nowhere near normal.' She put her hand on her stomach. 'Yes, I'm pregnant. Yes, I'm pregnant with your baby. But that's it, Sebastian. This isn't the Dark Ages. I don't want your help—or need it.' She ran her fingers through her hair, trying to contemplate all the things she hadn't even considered. 'Look at me, Sebastian. I live here. In the Cotswolds. I came here from Edinburgh. I purposely chose to come here. I've bought my dream house. I have a great job and colleagues that I like and admire. I've arranged a childcare for my baby and cover for my maternity leave.' She could feel herself getting agitated. Her voice was getting louder the longer that she spoke. 'I won't keep you from our baby. You can have as much—or as little—contact as you want. But don't expect to waltz in here and take over our lives.' She pressed her hand to her chest. 'This is my life, Sebastian. *My life.* I don't need your money and I don't need your help. I'm perfectly capable of raising this baby on my own.'

Polly walked past again. It was obviously deliberate. Not only was she spying, now she was eavesdropping too.

With a burst of pure frustration Sienna kicked the door closed.

Sebastian raised his eyebrows.

She took a deep breath. 'I need you to go. I need you to leave. I can't deal with this now.'

Her lips pressed tight together and resisted the temptation to say the words she was truly thinking.

Sebastian seemed to have frozen on the spot. The air of assurance had disappeared.

It was then she saw it. The look. The expression.

He'd actually expected her to say yes.

He hadn't expected her to reject him. He hadn't expected a no.

Sebastian Falco was hurt.

Now, it was her that was surprised. It struck her in a way she didn't expect. She could almost see a million things circulating around in his brain—as if he was trying to find a new way to persuade her to go with him.

She could see the little vein pulsing at the base of his throat.

Her mouth was dry.

If she were five years old—this would be her dream. Well, not the pregnancy, but the thought of a prince sweeping in and saying he would marry her, presenting her with a huge diamond ring and the chance to one day be Queen.

But it had been a long time since Sienna had been five.

And her ambitions and dreams had changed so much they could move mountains.

Sebastian folded his arms across his chest. 'Why didn't you call me, Sienna?' His voice was rigid. 'Why didn't you phone and tell me as soon as you knew you were pregnant?'

Oh. That.

She should have expected it to come up.

'I was going to. I meant to. But the day I did my pregnancy test was the day your engagement was announced on the national news.' She looked at him directly, trying to push away the tiny part of guilt curling in her stomach.

'Between that, and finding out I was pregnant, it kind of took the feet out from under me.'

He broke their gaze for a second, his words measured. 'Theresa was a friend. It wasn't going to be a marriage of love. It was going to be a union of kingdoms. Something my parents wanted very much.'

'How romantic.'

She couldn't help herself. She'd been a child of a loveless marriage. She knew the effects it had. She raised her eyes to the ceiling. 'Well, your parents must be delighted about me. I guess I'm going to be the national scandal.'

She'd been delusional. She'd thought she knew this man—even a little. But nothing about this fitted with the two days they'd spent together. The Sebastian she'd known then was a man who actually felt and thought. He'd laughed and joked and made her the coffee she craved. He'd cuddled up beside her in bed and taken her to places she'd never been before. He'd gently stroked the back of her neck as she'd fallen asleep. He was someone she'd loved being around.

Too bad all of it had been a lie.

The man in front of her now was the Sebastian that appeared on the news. The one with a fixed smile and his arm around someone else.

That was what it was. That was what she'd always noticed. Even though she'd tried not to watch him on the news—she'd tried to always switch channel—on the few occasions she had seen pictures of him, something had never seemed quite right.

She'd always tried not to look too closely. Her heart wouldn't let her go there. Not at all.

But little things were falling into place.

The smile had never reached his eyes.

Now, the look in his eyes seemed sincere. His tone much softer. 'You can be whatever you want to be, Sienna. I'd just like you to do it as my wife.'

This look was familiar. She'd seen it so many times on the weekend they'd spent together. In between the flirting, fun and cheekiness there had been flashes of sincerity.

That had been the thing that made his untruthfulness so hard to take.

The room was starting to feel oh-so-small.

'Why didn't you call me later?'

It didn't matter that she'd just sipped some water. Her mouth felt dry. He wasn't going to let this go. He was calling her on it.

She licked her lips. 'I wanted to. I thought about it. But we didn't exactly exchange numbers. How easy is it to call a royal palace and ask to speak to the Prince?'

He shifted a little uncomfortably, then shook his head. 'You could have asked Oliver. You knew we were friends. He was the one who recommended you. He would have given you the number whenever you asked.'

'And how would that work out? "Oh, Oliver? Can you give me Seb's mobile number, please? I want to tell him that I'm going to ruin his engagement by letting him know I'm pregnant. You know, the engagement to his child-hood sweetheart?" At least that's the way it sounded in the media.'

He smiled. He actually smiled.

'You think it's funny?'

'No. Not at all. But that's the first time you've called me Seb since I got here.' He stepped forward.

She sucked in a breath.

She hadn't even noticed.

Seb was too close again. She needed some space, some distance between them.

He touched her arm. Her bare skin almost caught fire. There was no opportunity to flinch or pull away. His palm surrounded her slim wrist. 'I've told you. It was never like that with Theresa. We just didn't think of each other that way. And we'd never been childhood sweethearts. We were friends. Just friends.'

'You've told her about the pregnancy?'

He gave a little grimace. 'Not exactly. Not yet anyway.' He ran his fingers through his hair. 'I wasn't quite sure how to put it.'

'You were sleeping with us both?'

She couldn't help it. It just came out.

'What? No.' Sebastian shook his head again. 'I've never slept with Theresa. I've told you. It wasn't that kind of relationship. I don't sleep with my friends.'

She hated the way that relief flooded through her. The sincerity was written all over his face. He might have lied by omission before but she was certain he wasn't lying now.

She met his gaze. 'How will she feel when she finds out? It will look to the world as if you've made a fool of her. As if *we've* made a fool of her. I hate that. I don't want anyone to think I'd have an affair with someone else's man.'

He sucked in a deep breath and reached up towards her face. 'But I wasn't in a relationship with Theresa. I was single. I was free when we were together. And if I'd known you were pregnant I would never have let my parents force me into announcing an engagement.' His hand brushed her cheek and his fingers tangled in her hair.

This was what he'd done when they'd been together. This was how he'd pulled her into *that* first kiss.

The touch should have been mesmerising. But his words left her cold.

Forced. He'd never really mentioned his parents in their short time together.

'They forced you? I didn't think you'd let anyone force you to do anything.' There was an air of challenge in her voice.

He recognised it and raised his eyebrows. He gave her a half-smile. 'You haven't met my parents—yet.'

It was her first truly uncomfortable feeling. The King and Queen of Montanari. They wouldn't like her. They wouldn't like her at all. She'd ruined the plan to unite the neighbouring kingdoms and was going to give Montanari an illegitimate heir. Her face was probably currently fixed to a dartboard or archery target in their throne room.

'And are they forcing you to do this too?' The words came out in a whisper. Every muscle in her body was tensed.

Duty. That was what she was sensing here.

He might be sincere. But there was no love—no compassion here. Tears threatened to fill her eyes. She licked her dry lips and stepped back, out of his hold. He hadn't answered her question and she couldn't quite believe how hurt she felt.

'I think you should go back to Montanari, Sebastian. I'll let you know when the baby arrives and we can sort things out from there.'

He looked surprised, his hand still in the air from where he'd touched her hair. He stared at it for a second, then shook his head. 'Who says I'm going back to Montanari?'

She concentrated on her shoes. It was easier than looking at him. 'Well, you will, won't you? You'll have—' she waved her hand '—princely duties or something to do. You can't stay here. There's been enough tittle-tattle about who the father of my baby is. The last thing I want is for someone to realise who you are and gossip about us. I'm the talk of the steamie already.'

He shook his head in bewilderment. 'The what?'

'The steamie. You know—the washhouse.'

He shook his head. 'I have no idea what you're talking about. But you know what? Just keep talking. I'd forgotten how much I loved the sound of your voice.'

Ditto.

'The steamie. It's a Scottish term for an old wash-house—the place where people used to go and wash their clothes before everyone had washing machines. It was notorious. The women used to always gossip in there.'

'So, that's what we could be? The talk of the steamie?'

She nodded again. 'And I'd rather not be. It would be easier if you left. We can talk. We can make plans about access arrangements when the baby arrives. We have another six weeks to wait. There's enough time.'

'Oh, no, you don't,' he replied promptly.

She had a bad feeling about this. 'What do you mean?'

'I'm not going anywhere. I've already missed out on things. I'm not missing out on anything else.'

'What do you mean by that?' she asked again.

He leaned against the door jamb and folded his arms across his chest. There was a determined grin on his face. 'I've got work to do here.' He mimicked her hand wave. 'Princely duties. I need to sort out the twinning of our hospitals and iron out all the details. Get used to me being around.' He gave her a little nod. 'I'm your new best friend.'

CHAPTER THREE

IF HE DIDN'T love his friend so much he'd be annoyed by
the permanent smile that seemed to have fixed itself to
Oliver's face. Even sitting at a desk swamped with paperwork, Oliver still had the smile plastered on his face.

'Sebastian!' Oliver jumped to his feet, strode around
the desk and engulfed Sebastian in a bear hug.

Sebastian returned the hug and leaned back. 'You're
engaged? Do I get to meet the lucky lady?'

Oliver slapped his arm. 'You get to be my best man!'
His smile wavered for a second. 'Are you here for the
announcement tomorrow? I thought I would have heard
from you.'

Sebastian gave a brief nod. He pushed his hands into
his pockets and looked at Oliver. 'Not just that. It seems
you and I are about to experience some changes together.'

Oliver's brow furrowed at the cryptic line. 'What do
you mean?'

Sebastian glanced around. There was no one hovering near the door. Oliver's office seemed private enough.
'We're both about to be fathers.'

For a few seconds Oliver's expression was pure surprise. 'Theresa's pregnant? Congratulations. I had no
idea—'

Sebastian held up his hand to stop him. Of course he

was surprised. He knew Sebastian's real feelings about that engagement.

He shook his head. 'It's not Theresa.'

Oliver paled. 'It's not?'

They were good friends. He'd experienced Sebastian's parents. He knew exactly how focused and overbearing they could be. They'd spent many hours and a number of cases of beer contemplating the pressures of being an heir, along with Sebastian's personal feelings and ambitions.

The grin that spread over Oliver's face took Sebastian by surprise. He let out a laugh and walked back around the desk, pushing his wheeled chair back, putting his feet on the desk and crossing his arms. 'Oh, this is going to be good. Tell me all about it.'

Sebastian shook his head and leaned on the chair opposite Oliver. 'You find this amusing?'

Oliver nodded. 'I find this very amusing. It's only taken you thirty-one years to cause a scandal. I hope it's a good one.'

Sebastian made a face. 'You might change your mind when you find out the rest of it.'

'What's that supposed to mean?'

Sebastian shook his head again. 'Is everything set for the board meeting tomorrow?'

Oliver nodded. 'It's just a formality. They've already agreed to twin the hospitals and develop the training programme. You realise as soon as it's announced there'll be around forty staff queued outside my door trying to get their name on the reciprocal swap programme?'

Sebastian took a deep breath. Was there even a chance in a million that Sienna might consider something like that?

He was still smarting about her reaction earlier. What was wrong with making the heir to the Montanari throne legitimate? It made perfect sense to him.

Why was she so against it? He'd still felt the chemistry in the air between them—even if she wanted to deny it. He could admit that the timing wasn't great. But he'd dealt with things as best he could.

At the end of the day it was his duty to marry the mother of his baby. Maybe he could work on her, get her to reconsider?

'I plan on being around for the next few days—maybe longer.'

Oliver glanced at him. Sebastian's visits were usually only when he flew in and out of the UK on business and usually only lasted a couple of hours.

'Really, why?'

He'd picked up a pen and was scribbling notes.

Sebastian lowered his voice. 'Because I have to convince the mother of my child to marry me.'

The pen froze and oh-so-slowly one of Oliver's eyebrows rose. 'Say that again?'

Sebastian sat back in the chair and relaxed his arms back. He felt better after saying it out loud. It didn't seem quite so ridiculous a thought.

'Sienna—the mother of my child. I have to convince her to marry me.'

The pen flew past his ear. Oliver was on his feet. 'What? What do you mean, Sienna?' His head turned quickly from side to side. 'I mean, you? Her? The baby? It's yours?' It was almost as if he were trying to sort it all out in his mind. Then his eyes widened and he crumpled back down into his seat.

'Oh, no.' He looked as if he were going to be sick on the desk. 'How did you find out?' He didn't even wait for an answer. His head was already in his hands.

Sebastian gave a nod, reached over and clapped the side of one of Oliver's hands. 'Yep. It was you. You phoned about Ella and mentioned Sienna and how pregnant she was.'

Oliver's head shot back up. 'I thought you'd gone quiet

when we spoke but I just assumed it was because you were surprised when I said Ella was pregnant.'

'It wasn't Ella's pregnancy that surprised me.'

Oliver ran his hand through his hair. 'Yeah, obviously.'

He wrinkled his nose and a smile broke out on his face. 'You and Sienna, really?'

Sebastian was curious. 'What's so strange about me and Sienna?'

Oliver threw up his hands. 'It's just…it's just…she's so… *Sienna*.' He shook his head and laughed. 'Your parents will hate her. She'd be their ultimate nightmare for a queen.'

Sebastian felt a little flare of protective anger. 'What's that supposed to mean?'

Oliver shrugged. 'Where will I start? She's a surgeon. She's *always* going to be a surgeon. Sienna would never give up her job—she's just too good and too emotionally connected. Surgery is in her blood.' He was shaking his head. 'As for tactfulness and decorum? Sienna's one of the most straight-talking doctors I've ever known. She doesn't take any prisoners. She wouldn't spend hours trying to butter up some foreign dignitary. She'd tell them exactly what she expected of them and then move on to dessert.' He tapped his fingers on the table and stared up to the left for a second. 'It's almost like you picked the person least like your mother in the whole world. Except for looks, of course. Your mother was probably born knowing she'd one day be Queen. I bet even as a child Sienna never played dress-up princesses or looked for a prince. She'd have been too busy setting up her dolls' hospital.'

Sebastian had been about to interrupt, instead he took a breath. Oliver had absolutely nailed it.

Sienna was a career woman. His mother had always taken a back seat to his father in every way.

Sienna hadn't been scared to shout at him. He'd never heard his mother raise her voice in her life.

Sienna hadn't been afraid to be bold and take him up on his proposition. Her comment *How about you listen to it all night instead?* had haunted his dreams in every erotic way possible. His mother would have a heart attack if she ever knew.

Just as well Sienna was a doctor really.

The reality of his future life was starting to crash all around him. Sebastian didn't panic. He'd never panicked. But he felt wary. If he didn't handle things well this could be a disaster.

Could Sienna McDonald really be the future Queen of Montanari?

He leaned back and folded his arms. 'She's the mother of my child. Montanari needs an heir. It's my duty to marry her.'

Oliver raised his eyebrows. 'Please tell me you didn't just say that?'

When Sebastian didn't answer right away, Oliver shook his head. 'More importantly, please tell me you didn't say that to Sienna?'

Sebastian ignored the comment. 'Montanari needs change. Sienna will be just the breath of fresh air it needs. Who couldn't love her? She's a neonatal surgeon. She eats, breathes and sleeps her job. People will admire her intelligence. They'll admire her dedication. I know I do.'

Oliver started tapping his fingers on the table again. 'And what does Sienna have to say about all this?'

He was good. He was too good. He clearly knew Sienna well.

'Let's just say that Sienna and I are a work in progress.'

Oliver let out something resembling a snort. He stood up again. 'You're my oldest friend, Sebastian, but I'm telling you right now, I'm not choosing sides. She's one of my best doctors. Upset her and you'll upset me.' He gave a little shudder. 'She'll kill me when she finds out it was me that told you.' He leaned against the wall for a second. 'Why didn't she tell you herself?'

Sebastian shrugged slightly. 'Timing, she says. I'd just got engaged.'

Oliver rolled his eyes then narrowed them again. 'And why didn't you tell me that you'd got in a compromising position with one of my doctors?' He wagged his finger at Sebastian. 'Can't trust you for two minutes. I'll need to rethink this whole hospital-twinning thing. Can't have us sending all our doctors over there to get seduced by Montanari men—royal or not.'

Sebastian stood up. 'I have a baby on the way. My priorities have changed.' He headed to the door. 'I'll see you at the board meeting tomorrow—and for the press announcement.'

Oliver gave a nod. He tipped his head to one side. 'So, what's your next plan?'

Sebastian shot him a wide smile. 'Charm. Why else be a prince?'

Sienna stuck her head outside the doors to the paediatric ICU, then ducked back inside, keeping her nose pressed against the glass. The tinsel taped to the window tickled her nose and partially blocked her view.

'What are you doing?' asked an amused Charlie Warren, one of her OBGYN colleagues.

'I'd have thought that was clear. I'm hiding.' Her ever-expanding belly was stopping her from getting a clear view.

Charlie laughed. 'And who are you hiding from?'

'You know. Him.'

'Him, who?'

Sienna sighed and turned around, leaning back against the door.

'Sebastian.'

Charlie nodded slowly. 'Ah...now I see.'

Sienna brushed a lock of loose hair out of her eyes. 'I see the Teddy's super-speed grapevine is working as well as ever. He's been here less than twenty-four hours.'

Charlie leaned against the door with her and gave her a knowing smile.

'What are you grinning at?' she half snapped.

She'd always liked Charlie. They got on well. All her colleagues had been so supportive of her pregnancy. She stared at him again.

'There's something different about you.'

'There is? What?' He had a dopey kind of grin on his face.

She pointed. 'That. You've got the same look that Oliver is wearing.'

'I don't know what you mean.'

She poked her finger in his chest. 'Oh, yes, you do. What's her name?'

She was definitely curious. She'd spent the last week so wrapped up with preparations for Christmas and trying to keep her energy up that she'd obviously missed something important. Charlie was a widower. For as long as she'd known him there had been veiled shadows behind his eyes.

They were gone now. And it made her heart sing a little to see that.

He gave her a sheepish smile. 'It's Juliet.'

Sienna's mouth dropped open. 'No.' Then she couldn't help but grin. 'Really?' She got on well with the Aussie surgeon who'd performed *in-utero* surgery to save the life of a quad born at Teddy's last week.

His smile said it all. 'Really.'

She leaned against the door again. 'Oh, wow.' She flicked her hair back. It was really beginning to annoy her. 'First Oliver and now you. Lovesick people are falling all over the place.' She gave him a wicked glare. 'Better phone Public Health, it looks like we've got an infectious disease here.'

He nodded. 'Don't forget Max and Annabelle. This thing is spreading faster than that winter virus.' He gave her a cheeky wink. 'And from what I saw this morning at breakfast, others might eventually succumb.'

Heat rushed into her cheeks. She'd come in early this morning and walked along to the canteen for breakfast. She'd barely sat down before Sebastian had ambushed her and sat down at the other side of the table with coffee, toast and eggs.

It had been excruciating. She could sense every eye in the canteen on them both and it had been as quick as she could bolt down her porridge and hurry out of there.

Normally she loved breakfast in the canteen at Christmas time. Christmas pop tunes were always playing and the menu food got new names like Rudolph's raisin pancakes or Santa's scrumptious scrambled egg.

'I don't know what you mean,' she said defensively to Charlie, who was obviously trying to wind her up.

He laughed as he pulled open the door and looked out for a second. 'He seems like a nice guy. Maybe you should give him a chance.'

She laid her hand on her large stomach. 'Oh, I think it's pretty obvious I've already given him a chance.'

He just kept laughing. 'Well, he's on the charm offensive. And he's winning. Everyone that's met him thinks he's one version of wonderful or another. Including Juliet's daughter.'

'He's met her daughter?'

Charlie nodded. 'She loves him already. He gave her some kind of doll that the little girls in Montanari love. A special Christmas one with a red and green dress. She was over the moon.'

Sienna wrinkled her nose. 'You shouldn't let her speak to strangers.'

Something flashed over Charlie's face. 'If I didn't know any better, Sienna, I'd think you were a woman reaching that crabby stage just before she delivers.'

She shook her head fiercely and patted her stomach. 'Oh, no. No way. I've got just under six weeks. This baby is not coming out before then.'

'If you say so.' Charlie stuck his head out of the door again. 'Okay, you can go. The coast is clear. Just remember to be on your best behaviour.' He held the door before her as she rushed outside. 'And just remember... I recognise the signs.'

The coast wasn't clear at all.

Sebastian was waiting outside the unit, leaning against the wall with his arms folded.

'I'm going to kill Charlie with my bare hands,' she muttered.

It didn't help that he was looking even sexier than before. When he'd joined her this morning at breakfast he'd been wearing a suit and tie. Something to do with a business meeting. She hadn't really been paying attention.

Now, he'd changed into jeans, a leather jacket and a slim-fitting black T-shirt. His hair was speckled with flecks of snow.

'What are you doing here?' she asked as she made her best attempt to sweep past.

Sebastian was having none of it. He fell into step beside her. 'Waiting for you.'

She stopped walking and turned to face him. She wanted to be angry with him. She wanted to be annoyed. But he had that look on his face, that hint of cheek. He was deliberately taunting her. They'd spent most of the weekend in Montanari batting smart comments back and forth. This felt more like sun-blessed Montanari than the snow-dusted Cotswolds.

She stifled her smile. 'This better not get to be a habit. I'm busy, Seb. I'm at work.'

His grin broadened and she realised her error. She'd called him Seb again.

'When do you finish work?'

'Why?'

'You know why. I'd like us to talk—have dinner maybe. Do something together.'

His phone buzzed in his pocket. He shifted a little on his feet but ignored it.

'Aren't you going to get that?'

He shook his head. 'I'm busy.'

'How long—exactly—have you been standing out here?'

He smiled. 'Around two hours.' He lifted one hand and shrugged. 'But it's fine. The people around here are very friendly. They all like to talk.'

'Talk is exactly what they'll do. You might be a public figure, Seb, but I'm not. I'm a pretty private person. I don't want anyone else knowing about our baby.'

The look on his face was so surprised that she realised he hadn't even considered that.

How far apart were they? Had he not even considered that might put her under stress? Not exactly ideal for a pregnant woman.

And it didn't help that wherever Seb was, men in black were permanently hovering in the background.

He'd already made the assumption that she would want to marry him. Maybe he also thought she would be fine about having their baby in the public eye?

Oh, no.

She gave a sway.

'Sienna? What's wrong? Are you okay?'

He moved right in front of her, catching both her arms with his firm hands. He was close enough for her to see the tiny lines around his eyes and the little flecks in his forest-green eyes.

'You're a prince,' she breathed slowly.

He blinked. There was a look of amusement on his face. 'I'm a prince,' he confirmed in a whisper.

'I slept with a prince.' It was almost as if she were talking to herself. She knew all this. None of it was a surprise. But all of a sudden things were sinking in fast.

Before, Sebastian Falco hadn't featured in her life. Apart from the telltale parting gift that he'd left her, there was really no sign of any connection between them. No one knew about their weekend together. No one knew that they'd even met.

When she'd come back, it was clear that even though Oliver was Sebastian's friend, he'd had no idea about their relationship.

That was the way things were supposed to be. Even though, in her head, she'd known she should tell Seb about the baby, once the engagement was announced she'd pushed those thoughts away.

She'd pushed all memories of Sebastian and their time together—the touch of his hands on her skin, the taste of his lips on hers—away into that castle of his that she'd never seen.

A castle. The man lived in a castle. Not in the mountain retreat he'd taken her to. Her stomach gave a little flip as she wondered once more how many other women had been there.

'Sienna, honey? Are you okay? Do you want to sit down?'

Honey. He'd just called her honey as if it were the most natural thing in the world to do.

He wanted them to get married. A prince wanted to marry her.

Most women would be happy. Most women would be delighted.

Marry a prince. Live in a castle. Wasn't that the basis of every little girl's favourite fairy tale?

Not hers.

She wasn't a Cinderella kind of girl. Well, maybe just a little bit.

She definitely wasn't Rapunzel. She didn't need any guy to save her.

And she so wasn't Sleeping Beauty. She'd never spend her life lying about.

She looked around. They were three floors up. The glass atrium dome above them and the Christmas decorations directly underneath them. People flowed all around them. The Royal Cheltenham Hospital was world renowned. People begged to work here. Posts were fiercely contested. Three other surgeons she respected and admired had interviewed for the job that she'd been appointed to.

That had been the best call of her life.

She sucked in a breath. Teddy's was her life.

She loved her job, loved the kids, loved the surgeries and loved the people.

A gust of icy wind blew up through the open doors downstairs. The chill felt appropriate.

The kids' book character in front of her right now was threatening all that.

Would she really get any peace once people found out her child was the heir of Montanari?

Her hands went protectively to her stomach. 'What happens once he or she arrives?'

He looked confused. 'What do you mean?'

So much was spinning around in her head that the words stuck in her throat. After her childhood experiences she'd always vowed to be in charge of her own life, her own relationships and her own destiny.

Finding out she was pregnant had only made her sway

for a second or two, then it had just put a new edge to her determination to get things right.

She'd made so many plans this Christmas—almost as if she were trying to keep herself busy. Carolling. Helping on the children's ward. Wrapping presents for army troops stationed away from home. Oh, her house was decorated as usual, and she opened the doors on her advent calendar every day. But she'd pictured spending this Christmas alone so was scheduled to be working over the holiday. She hadn't counted on Sebastian being around.

Seb was still standing straight in front of her, looking at her with concern in his eyes. He reached up and brushed her cheek with the gentlest of touches—the most tender of touches. It sent a whole host of memories flooding through her.

Seb. The man she'd shared a bed with. The man who kissed like no other. The man she'd thought was someone else entirely.

The man who'd thought he could walk in here and sweep her off her feet.

She shivered. She actually shivered.

'What are the rules in Montanari? Did you propose to me because an illegitimate child can't inherit the throne?'

He shook his head. 'No. No, of course I didn't. And no. There's no rules like that in Montanari. I'm the heir to the throne, and my firstborn son, or firstborn daughter, will be the heir to the throne once I'm King.' He gave an almost indiscernible shake of his head. 'But let's face it, it would be much better if we were married.'

'Better for who?'

He held up his hands, but she wasn't watching his hands, she was watching his face.

'Better for everyone. I have a duty—a duty to my people and my country. I want to introduce our son or daughter as the heir to the throne.' His gaze softened. 'And I'd like to introduce you as my wife.'

She had an instant dual flashback. One part caused by his word 'duty'. An instant memory of just exactly how both her parents had felt about their 'duty' and the look of absolute relief on her father's face as he'd packed his bags and left. The second part was caused by the first. A memory from months ago—those first few weeks when apparent morning sickness had struck at any second of the day or night. She wanted to be sick right here, right now. Right over his brown boots.

Duty. A word that seemed to have an absolute chilling effect that penetrated right down to her soul. Every time she heard people use the word in everyday life she had to try and hold back her instant response—an involuntary shudder.

Her insides were curled in knots. He'd just told her he wanted to marry her—again.

But not for the right reasons.

It didn't matter that her back had ached these last few days, she drew herself up to her full height and looked him straight in the eye.

It was almost like putting blinkers on. She wouldn't let those forest-green eyes affect her in the way they had before.

'I have a duty. To myself and to my child. We aren't your duty. We belong to ourselves. No one else. Not you. Not your parents. Not your people. I spent my childhood watching two people who should have never got together barely tolerate each other.' Fire was starting to burn inside her. 'What did you get for your eighteenth birthday present, Sebastian?'

The question caught him unawares. He stumbled around for the answer. 'A car, I think. Or a watch.'

'Well, good for you. Do you know what I got? I got my father packing his bags and leaving. But that didn't hurt nearly as much as the look of complete relief on his face. As for my mother? Two months later she moved to

Portugal and found herself a toy boy. I can honestly say I've never seen her happier.' She pressed her hand to her chest. 'I did that to them, Sebastian. I made two people who shouldn't have been together spend eighteen years in what must have been purgatory for them.' She shook her head fiercely. 'I will never, *ever* do that to a child of mine.'

Sebastian pulled back. He actually pulled back a little.

She'd done it again. Twice, in the space of two days, she'd raised her voice to Sebastian in a public place. Perfect. The talk of the steamie again.

But she couldn't help it. She wasn't finished.

There was no way Mr Fancy-Watches-For-His-Birthday could sweep in here and be part of her and her baby's life.

While she might have had a few little day dreams about the guy who was engaged to someone else, her reality plans had been way, way different.

This was why she'd negotiated new hours for the job she loved. This was why she'd visited four different nurseries and interviewed six potential childminders. This was why she'd spoken to her friend Bonnie—a fellow Scot who'd transported to Cambridge—on a number of occasions about how best to handle being a single mum.

This man was messing with her mind. Messing with her plans.

She didn't need this now. She really didn't.

She held up her hand. She knew exactly how to get rid of him. And not a single word would be a lie.

'I don't want this, Sebastian. This isn't my life. This isn't my dream. I will never, ever marry a man out of duty.' She almost spat out the word.

She lifted her hands towards the snow-topped atrium. 'When, and if, I ever get married, I'll get married to the man I love with all my heart. The man I couldn't bear to spend a single day without in my life. The man who would walk in front of a speeding train for me or my child without a single thought for himself—just like I would for him.' She took a few steps away from him. She was aware that a few people had stopped conversations around them to listen but she was past the point of caring.

'You don't know me, Sebastian. I want the whole hog. I want everything. And this, what you're offering? It doesn't even come close. I want a man who loves and adores me, who will walk by my side no matter what direction I take. I want a man who can take my breath away with a single look, a single touch.'

She could see him flinch. It didn't matter she was being unfair. Sebastian had taken more than her breath away with his looks and touches, but he didn't need to know that, not right now.

'I want a husband who will be proud of me and my career. Who won't care that I'm on call and he might need to reorganise his life around me. Who'll help around the house and not expect a wife who'll cook him dinner. Public Health may well have to do investigations into my cooking skills.'

She was enjoying herself now, taking it too far. But he had to know. He had to know just how fast to run.

'I will never accept anything less. I've been the child of a duty marriage. I would never, ever do that to my child. It's a form of torture. Growing up feeling guilty? It's awful.' She pressed her hands on her stomach again. '*My* child—' she emphasised the word '—is going to grow up feeling loved, blessed and, above all, wanted. By me, at least. There will be rules. There will be discipline. But most of all, there will be love.'

She walked back up to stand right in front of him. 'Whoever loves me will know how much I love Christmas, will want to celebrate it with me every year. Will know the songs I love, the crazy carols I love to sing. They won't care that I spend hours wrapping presents that are opened in seconds, they won't care that I buy more Christmas decorations than there is space for on the tree, they won't care that I have to have a special kind of cake every Christmas Eve and spend a fortune trying to find it. They'll know that I would only ever get married at Christmas. They would never even suggest anything else.'

She took a deep breath and finally looked at him—really looked at him.

Yip, she'd done it. He looked as if she'd just run over him with an Edinburgh tram. This time she lowered her voice. 'You might be a prince. You might have a castle. But I want the fairy tale. And you can't give it to me.'

And with that, she turned and walked away.

CHAPTER FOUR

'Are you coming down with something?' Oliver was staring at him in a way only a doctor could.

'What? No. Don't be ridiculous.'

Oliver gave a slow, careful nod. 'The board paper was excellent. They love the idea. It looks like the Falco charm has done its magic.'

'Except where it counts.'

'What's that supposed to mean?' Oliver rolled his eyes. 'No. Please. I'm not sure I want to know.' He walked around the desk and leaned against the wall.

Sebastian sighed loudly. He couldn't help it. 'I thought once I came here, Sienna might be happy to see me again. I didn't expect her to be quite…quite…'

'Quite so Sienna?' Oliver was looking far too amused for his liking.

Sebastian let out a wry laugh. 'Yeah, exactly. Quite so Sienna. I still can't believe she didn't let me know.'

Oliver shook his head. 'Doesn't sound like her. She's fierce. She's independent. She's stubborn—'

'You're not helping.'

Oliver laughed. 'But she's also one of the kindest-hearted women I know. She's always been professional but I can't tell you how many times I've caught her sobbing in a dark corner somewhere when things aren't going well with one of her patients. Working with neonates is the toughest area for any doctor. They're just getting started at life. They deserve a chance. And Sienna needs to be tough to get through it. She needs to be determined.' He paused for a second and his steady gaze met Sebastian's. 'Sienna puts up walls. She's honest. She's loyal. If she didn't let you know about the baby—she must have had a darn good reason.'

Sebastian bit the inside of his cheek. All of Oliver's words were striking chords with him. 'She said it was the engagement announcement. It put her off. She didn't want to destroy my engagement and cause a scandal.'

Oliver's brow creased. 'That's very considerate of her.' He stood up straight and took a few steps towards Sebastian. 'Quick question, Seb. Did you believe that?'

Sebastian was surprised. It hadn't occurred to him to doubt what Sienna told him. 'What do you mean?'

Oliver started shaking his head. 'I guess I just think it could be something else.'

'What do you mean?'

Oliver began walking around. 'It all sounds very noble. But would Sienna really deny you the chance to know your child? She could have spoken to me—she knows we are friends—I could have found a way to get a discreet message to you.' He gave Sebastian a careful look. 'I wonder if there was something else—a different kind of reason.'

Sebastian shifted in his chair. He couldn't get his head around what Oliver was saying. 'What do you mean? You think the baby might not be mine?'

Oliver held up his hand. 'Oh, no. Sienna wasn't seeing anyone. I couldn't even tell you when she had her last date. She's totally dedicated to her work. You don't need to worry about that.'

Thoughts started swirling around his head as relief flooded through him. Sienna had nailed exactly why he had come here. Duty. That was how he always lived his life.

It had been instilled in him from the youngest age.

He might not have loved Theresa. But she would have fulfilled the role of Queen with grace and dignity.

Sienna? Her personality type was completely different. She was intelligent. She was a brilliant surgeon. But she hadn't been brought up in a royal family. She didn't know traditions and protocols. He wasn't entirely sure she would ever follow them or want to.

He was pushing aside the way his heart skipped a beat when he saw her. The way his body reacted instantly. Passion like that would never last a lifetime no matter how pleasurable.

But that passion had created the baby currently residing inside Sienna. His baby. The heir to the throne of Montanari.

He stared back at Oliver. Knowing there were no other men in Sienna's life was exactly what he needed to hear. His press team were already wondering how to handle the imminent announcement about the baby.

'Then what on earth are you talking about?' He was getting increasingly frustrated by Oliver talking around in circles.

Oliver ran his hand through his hair. 'Let's just say I recognise the signs.'

'The signs of what? By the time you actually tell me what you mean this baby will be an adult.'

Oliver laughed again and started counting off on his fingers. 'Do you know what I've noticed in the last day? Sienna's twitchy. She's on edge. She's different. Throughout this whole pregnancy she's been as cool as a cucumber.'

'You think I'm having a bad effect on her?'

Oliver put his hand on Sebastian's arm. 'I think you're having *some* kind of effect on her. I've never seen her like

this.' He gave a little smile. 'If I didn't know any better—
I'd say Sienna McDonald likes you a whole lot more than
she admits to.'

Sebastian was stunned. 'Really?'

Oliver raised his eyebrows. 'It's such an alien concept to you?'

A warm feeling spread all over Sebastian's skin, as
if the sun had penetrated through his shirt and annihi-
lated the winter chill. When he'd proposed marriage the
other day it had been an automatic reaction—something
he'd planned on the flight over. But it had been precipi-
tated by duty. Their baby would be the heir to the throne
in Montanari.

Part of him was worried. She did actually like him?
Was that why Sienna was acting the way she did?

He stood up and started pacing. 'She told me outright
she'd never marry me. She told me she wanted everything.
Love, romance, marriage, a husband who would love and
adore her. She told me being a prince wasn't enough—
not nearly enough.'

'And you thought it would be?' Oliver's face said it all.
'How come I've known you all these years and never realised how stupid you were?'

He stood up, stepped forward and poked his finger into
Sebastian's chest. 'How do you feel about Sienna? How
do you feel about her in here?'

His answer came out automatically. 'What does that
matter? A marriage in Montanari is usually about a union.
On this occasion, it's about a child. Feelings don't come
into it.'

It was an uncomfortable question. Memories of Sienna
McDonald had swirled around his head for months. The
most obscure thing—a smell, a word—could conjure Sienna front and foremost in his mind again. The briefest
thought could send blood rushing all around his body. His

first sight of her—pregnant with his child—had affected him in ways he hadn't even contemplated.

From the second he'd met her Sienna had got under his skin.

The sight of her, the taste of her, the smell of her was irresistible. The way she responded to his teasing. He did care about her. He did care about this baby. But could it be more?

How would someone like him know what love was anyway? It wasn't as if he'd spent a life exposed to it. He'd had teenage crushes. A few passionate flings. But marrying for love had never really been on his radar. Sienna's words and expectations the other day had taken him by surprise.

Oliver folded his arms and raised his eyebrows. He knew Sebastian far too well to take his glib answer at face value.

'I... I... I...' He threw up his hands in frustration. 'I don't know. She confuses me. I never contemplated having emotional ties to the woman I'd marry. Sienna has just mixed everything up.'

Oliver shook his head. 'Then hurry up and decide. Hurry up and decide how you feel about the mother of your child. A beautiful, headstrong and highly intelligent member of my staff *and* a friend of mine.' He took a step closer and held up his finger and thumb almost pressed together. 'Do you want to know how much Sienna McDonald will care about you being a prince? Do you want to know how much a palace will impress her? This much.'

Oliver walked away and sat down behind his desk. He looked at Sebastian carefully. 'The trouble with you is that you've had too much help in this life.'

'What's that supposed to mean?'

Oliver waved his hand. 'Someone to do this for you, someone to do that. You didn't even do your own grocery shopping when we were students together.'

Sebastian looked embarrassed.

'Sienna doesn't have that. Sienna has never had that. Everything for this baby, she's worked out for herself. She's juggled her schedule. Worked out her maternity leave to the second. Put plans in place for every patient.' He put his elbows on the desk. 'Everything to do with her house—what we'd call a fixer-upper—she's sorted out herself too. She's spent years saving to get the house she really wants. It's not a house to her—it's a home. Do you know how crazy she is about Christmas? Do you know that she's a fabulous baker?' Oliver sighed.

Sebastian shook his head. 'All I know about Sienna is what I learned on that weekend back in Montanari, and what I've learned in the last few days. Everything's a mess. She's still angry with me—angry that I was engaged to someone else. She told me exactly what she wanted in this life and it was the whole fairy tale.' He dropped his voice slightly. 'She also told me I wasn't part of it. I have no idea how to connect with this woman, Oliver. I have no idea how I can manage to persuade her to give the thought of us a chance. Sometimes I think she doesn't even like me.'

Oliver frowned. 'Oh, she likes you—I can tell.'

'She does?' It was the first thing that gave him some hope.

Oliver leaned back again and looked his friend up and down as if he were assessing him. 'In the past she's been very selective. Guys who don't live up to her expectations?' He snapped his fingers and gave Sebastian a wicked grin. 'Gone. Just like that.'

Sebastian had started to feel uncomfortable. But Oliver was his friend—he couldn't keep up his serious face for long. It was obvious he cared about the welfare of Sienna. And Sebastian was glad about that, glad to know that people had her back.

He folded his arms across his chest and leaned against

the wall. Some of the things that Oliver had said had struck a chord. There were so many things about Sienna that he didn't know. Things he wanted to know.

The bottom line was—could Sienna really be Queen material?

One weekend was not enough. It would never be enough. But he wasn't sure he wanted to say that out loud now. At least not to his friend.

'So, how do I get to know the real Sienna McDonald—the one behind the white coat?'

Oliver smiled. 'Eh, I think you've already achieved that.' He raised his eyebrow. 'There is evidence.'

Sebastian started pacing. Things were rushing around in his mind. 'Stop it. What about the other stuff? The Christmas stuff? What she takes in her tea?' His footsteps slowed. 'How she wants to raise our kid?' His voice got quieter. 'If she actually might more than like me...'

He stopped. Sienna. He needed to be around Sienna.

Oliver gave him a smile. 'I guess you should go and find out.'

It was an Aston Martin DB5. She'd seen one in a James Bond movie once. Even she could recognise it. A classic machine. She should have known he'd own something like this. He opened the door of the pale blue car revealing a red leather interior and she sucked in her breath.

She'd never been a show-me-your-money-and-I'll-be-impressed kind of girl. But this was a bit different. This was pure class. She'd watched enough car shows in her time to know that owning a car like this was a labour of pure love.

Just looking at it made her tingle.

The streets were dusted with snow. People were crossing the car park and staring, nudging each other and pointing at the car.

Christmas lights lit up the street opposite. Every shop

had decorations in its windows. She could hear Christmas pop songs drifting out of the pub across the road. At the end of the road was a courtyard where a giant tree was lit with gold and red lights. It was paid for by the local council and the kids on the paediatric ward could see it from their windows. The lights twinkled all night long.

'What are you doing, Sebastian?'

He smiled. He was dressed for the British weather in a pair of jeans, black boots and his black leather jacket. She gave a little gulp as her insides did some weird little flip-flop.

He smiled. Oh, no. The flip-flop turned into a somer-sault. 'I came to pick you up. Someone told me you had car trouble. I thought I could drive you home.'

She bit her lip. Tempting. Oh, so tempting.

'I can call for roadside assistance. I really need to get my car sorted. It shouldn't take too long.'

He waved his hand. 'Albie, the porter, said if you leave your keys with him he'll get your car started later. It's too cold to hang around and wait for roadside assistance.' He stepped a little closer.

There it was. That familiar aroma. The one that took her back to Montanari, and sun, and cocktails, and...

'We could pick up a little dinner on the way home.'

Her stomach let out a loud growl. It was almost as if her body were conspiring against her. She scrambled to find a suitable excuse but her stubborn brain remained blank. 'Well, I... I...'

'Great. That's sorted, then.' He took her car keys from her hand and walked swiftly back to the hospital, leaving her to stare at the pale blue machine in front of her, gleaming as the sun dipped lower in the sky.

She was still staring a few seconds later when he returned. He stood alongside her and smiled. 'Like it?'

She couldn't help the smile as she met his proud gaze. 'I guess I'm just a little surprised.'

'By what?'

She waved her hand towards the car. 'I guess I thought you might be in something sleek, low-slung and bright red.'

He laughed out loud. 'You think I'm one of *those* kind of guys?'

She nearly laughed herself. He really didn't need to elaborate. But as she kept staring at the car she felt a wave of something else. 'I guess I don't really know, do I?'

She turned to look at him, her warm breath frosting the air between them. Those dark green eyes seemed even more intense in the darkening light. He held her gaze. She could see his chest rise and fall as he watched her, searching her face.

All of a sudden she felt a little self-conscious. Was there any make-up even left on her skin? When was the last time she'd combed her hair?

This time Sebastian wasn't smiling. He was looking at her in a way she couldn't really fathom. As if there were a thousand thoughts spinning around in his head.

He would be King one day. He would be King of his country. She'd tried not to think about any of this. It had been easy before. He was engaged. He was getting married. He was with someone else.

But now he was here.

Here, in the Cotswolds, to see her. Her, and their baby.

He leaned forward and she held her breath, wondering what would happen next.

His arm brushed against hers as he pulled open the car door. 'Then let's do something about that,' he said huskily.

Snowflakes started to fall around her. She looked up at the now dark purple streaked sky. She could almost swear that there was something sparkling in the air between them.

As she took a step towards the car he turned towards her again, his arm settling at the side of her waist.

'In case you haven't noticed, I'm not a flashy kind of guy. I like classics. Things that will last a lifetime. Something that every time you look at it, it makes your heart flutter just a little. Because you know it's a keeper. You know it was made just for you.'

She couldn't breathe. She couldn't actually breathe. Large snowflakes were landing on his head and shoulders. His warm breath touched her cheek as he spoke— he was that close. Her hand rose automatically, resting on his arm. They were face to face. Almost cheek to cheek. If she tilted her chin up just a little...

But she couldn't. Not yet. Maybe not ever. She needed her head to be clear around Sebastian. And right now it was anything but clear.

It was full of intense green eyes framed by dark lashes, a sexy smile and sun-kissed skin. She could smell the leather of his jacket mingling with the familiar scent of his aftershave. She could see the faint shadow along his jaw line. The palm of her hand itched to reach up and touch it.

She hadn't moved. And he hadn't moved either. Being this close was almost hypnotic.

But she had to. She had to look away. She broke his gaze and glanced back at the car. 'It's blue,' she said. 'I thought all these cars were silver.'

Cars. A safe topic. A neutral topic. Something that would stop the swell of emotion currently rising in her chest.

He blinked. His hand hadn't moved from her currently non-existent waist. He gave a nod. 'A lot of them were silver. James Bond's was silver. But mine? Mine is Caribbean blue. As soon as I saw it, and the red leather interior, I knew it was perfect. I had to have it.'

He held her gaze again and she licked her lips anxiously. *I had to have it* echoed in her head. Why did it feel as if he wasn't talking about the car?

There was a screech behind them. A bang. A huge shattering of glass. And they both jumped apart.

Two seconds later the air was filled by a blood-curdling scream.

Sebastian didn't hesitate. He ran instantly towards the scream.

The doctor's instinct in her surged forward. She glanced towards the hospital doors. She could go and ask for help but Teddy's only took maternity and paediatric emergencies. It wasn't a district general and she didn't even know what was wrong yet.

She started running. Running wasn't easy at her current state of pregnancy. The ground was slippery beneath her feet as snow was just starting to settle on the ground.

As she reached the road that ran alongside the hospital she could see immediately what was wrong. One car had skidded and hit a lamp post. Another car had mounted the pavement and was now embedded in the dress shop's window. The Christmas decorations that had decorated the window were scattered across the street. She winced as her foot crunched on a red bauble. Sebastian was trying to talk to the woman who was screaming. He had his hands on both of her shoulders and was trying to calm her down.

Sienna's eyes swept over the scene, trying to make sense of the situation. An air bag had exploded in the car that had hit the lamp post. A young woman was currently slumped against it.

The other driver was slumped too. But there was no airbag. It was an older car and his head and shoulders were over the steering wheel of the car. The windscreen was shattered and shards of glass from the shop's window frame were directly above him.

The woman on the pavement was obviously in shock. She'd stopped screaming and was talking nonstop between sobs to Sebastian.

He turned towards her, his eyes wide. 'Her kid. Her kid is under the car.'

Another bystander stepped forward and put his arm around the woman, nodding towards Sebastian and Sienna. 'I've phoned an ambulance.'

Sienna gulped. She was familiar with obstetric emergencies. She was often called in for a consult if there could be an issue with the baby. Paediatric emergencies took up half of all her days. Neonates had a tendency to become very sick, very quickly and she needed to be available.

But regular emergencies?

She dropped to her knees and peered under the car. There was a mangled pushchair, and further away, out of her reach, a little figure.

Her heart leapt. Sebastian dropped down next to her, his head brushing against hers as he looked under the car.

He pressed his hand over hers. It was the quickest movement. The warmth of his hand barely had time to make an impact on her. 'I'll go.'

She hardly had time to speak before Sebastian was wriggling his way under the car. She opened her mouth to object just as baby gave her an almighty kick. Her hand went automatically to her belly. Of course. There was no way she could possibly fit under the body of the car—Sebastian was already struggling.

She edged around the front of the vehicle, watching the precarious shards of glass hanging above the car and staying on the ground as low as she could. The slush on the ground soaked her knees and legs, her cream winter coat attracting grime that would never be removed. She slid her arms out of the coat and pulled it over her head—at least she'd have some protection if glass fell.

'Can you try and feel for a pulse?' she said quietly to Sebastian, then added, 'Do you know what to do?'

There was a flicker of light. Sebastian had wriggled

his phone from his pocket and turned on the torch, lying it on the ground next to him.

In amongst the darkness and wetness, Sienna thought she could spot something else. The little boy was still tangled in part of the buggy and her view was still partially obscured.

She turned to the people behind her. 'Can someone find out the little boy's name for me, please?'

Sebastian's face was grim; he had a hand up next to the little boy's head. 'Yes, I've got a pulse. It's fast and it feels faint.'

Truth was, so did she.

She nodded. 'What position is he in?'

Right now she so wished she could be under there. Her frustration at not being able to get to the child was building by the second.

'He's on his back. Wait.'

She couldn't see what Sebastian was doing. He was moving his hand and holding up the torch to the little guy's face.

A voice in her ear nearly made her jump out of her skin. 'Gabriel. The little boy's name is Gabriel.'

She sucked in a breath. 'Sebastian, tell me what's wrong. What can you see? His name is Gabriel. Is he conscious?'

The wait must only have been a few seconds but it felt like so much longer.

Sebastian's face was serious. He held up one hand, palm facing towards her, and held his phone with the other so she could see. It was stained red.

'There's blood, Sienna. Lots of it. He's pale but there's something else—his lips are going a funny colour.'

Sienna turned to the crowd again, searching for the man's face she'd seen earlier. 'Any news about the ambulance?'

The man shook his head. 'Someone has run over to the hospital to try and get more help and some supplies.'

She nodded. 'I need swabs. Bandages. Oxygen. A finger monitor if they've got one.'

'I'll go,' said a young woman and ran off towards the hospital entrance.

Sienna felt in her pocket. All she had was an unopened packet of tissues. Not exactly the ideal product—but at least they were clean.

She threw them towards Sebastian. 'It's all I've got. Try and stem the flow of blood. Where is it coming from?'

Sebastian moved his body, blocking her view again, and she almost whimpered in frustration. She felt useless here. Absolutely useless. She couldn't check the child properly, assess any injuries or provide any care. It was the only time in her life she'd regretted being pregnant.

But Sebastian was calm. He wasn't panicking. He hadn't hesitated to slip under the car and help in any way that he could. As she watched he tore open the packet of tissues and tried to stem the flow of blood.

'It's coming from the side of his neck. I think he's been hit by some of the glass.' He paused for a second and she instantly knew something was wrong.

'What is it? Tell me?'

Sebastian kept his voice low. 'His lips are blue, Sienna.'

She hated this. She hated feeling helpless. 'Do you know what the recovery position is? Turn him on his side, Seb. Open his mouth and try and clear his airway. Check there's nothing inside his mouth. He's not getting enough oxygen into his lungs.'

The noise around them was increasing. There was a faint wail of sirens in the distance. The volume of the murmuring voices was increasing. People were always drawn to the scene of an accident. She could hear someone shouting instructions. A voice with some authority attached to it. She could only pray it was a member of the hospital staff dealing with one of the drivers.

The driver. She should really look at him too. But her first priority was this child. If Gabriel didn't breathe he would be dead. If his airway was obstructed he would be dead. She had no idea the extent of his other injuries but no oxygen would certainly kill him. If she had a team around her right now they would take time to stabilise the little guy's head and neck. But she didn't have a team— and there wasn't time.

All she had was Sebastian—the Prince from another country who was under there trying to be her right-hand man.

She could hear him talking to the little boy, coaxing him, trying to see if he could get any response. Shadows were shifting under the car; it was still difficult to see what was going on.

'Sebastian? Have you stopped the bleeding? What about his colour? Have you managed to put him in the recovery position yet?'

'Give me a minute.' The voice was firm and steady.

He doesn't have a minute. She had to bite her tongue to stop herself from saying it out loud. There was a clatter beside her. 'Sorry,' breathed a young woman. 'More help is coming.'

Sienna looked at the ground. There was a plastic tray loaded with supplies. She grabbed for the pulse oximeter. It was one of the simplest pieces of equipment they had—a simple little rubber pouch with a sensor that fitted over a finger and gave you an indication of someone's oxygen levels. She switched it on and reached as far under the car as she should, touching Sebastian's back.

'Here. Take this. Put it over his finger and tell me what the number is.'

Sebastian's position shifted. 'Come on, Gabriel,' he was saying encouragingly. He'd moved his torch. It was right at Gabriel's face, which was now facing away from her. For the briefest second she could see Sebastian's face reflected in the glass. He was focused. Concern and anxiety written all over his face.

She held her breath. His hand reached behind him to grab hold of the monitor. He'd heard her. He was just focusing on Gabriel.

She could almost swear her heart squeezed. If she were under the car right now, that was exactly how she'd be.

Focused on Gabriel. Not on any of the noise or circumstances around them.

'Watch out!' came the shout from her side.

There was a large crash and splinters of glass showered around her like an explosion of tiny hailstones. Her reaction was automatic: she ducked even lower, pulling the coat even further over her head. There were a few shrieks around her. Sebastian's head shot around. 'Sienna?'

His gaze met hers. He was worried. And he wasn't worried about himself. And for the tiniest second he wasn't thinking about Gabriel. He was thinking about her.

She didn't have time. She didn't have time to think about what that might mean. The cramped position was uncomfortable and baby wasn't hesitating to let her know it.

'His colour. How's his colour, Sebastian?'

Sebastian quickly looked back to Gabriel. 'It's better,' he said. 'He's still pale but the blueness is gone.'

Sienna breathed a sigh of relief. 'Put the monitor on his finger and tell me the reading.'

The sirens were getting much louder now; the ambulances must be almost there.

Sienna started grabbing some more of the supplies. Swabs, tape, some saline. She unwound the oxygen mask from the canister.

'Ninety-one. His reading is ninety-one. Is that good?'

She could see the anxiety on his face. His steady resolve was starting to fade a little.

If she were in a hospital she'd say no. But since they were cramped under a car with a little boy bleeding and on his side she remained optimistic. Sebastian had done a good job. She was surprised at how good he'd been. He had no background in medicine. No training. But he hadn't hesitated to assist. And the weird thing was he'd been so in tune with her. He'd done everything she'd instructed. He'd been calm and competent, and somehow she knew inside that she wouldn't have expected Sebastian to act in any other way.

She took a deep sniff. No smell of petrol. No reason to deny Gabriel oxygen. She switched on the canister and unwound the tubing, pushing the mask towards Sebastian. 'Try and hold this in front of his mouth and nose. Let's see if we can get that level up a little.'

Something green flashed to her side. The knees of a paramedic as he bumped down beside her. He lifted the edge of her coat. 'Hey, Doc, it's you.'

She jerked at the familiar voice and felt a wave of relief. Sam, an experienced paramedic she'd met on a number of occasions, gave her a worried smile. He glanced upwards. 'I'm getting you out of here. Tell me what I need to know.'

She spoke quickly. 'There's a little boy trapped under the car. He was in his buggy. He looks around three. His name is Gabriel. His mother is being cared for at the side by someone.' She almost stuck her head out from the coat to look around but Sam shook his head. She pointed under the car. 'He was blue. My friend had to move him into the recovery position and he's bleeding. His sats are ninety-one. There's oxygen under there too.'

Sam nodded solemnly. He didn't remark on the fact Gabriel had been moved. He just peered under the car. 'Who's your friend?'

She hesitated. 'Seb—Sebastian. He's just visiting.'

Sam had never been slow. 'Oh, the mystery Prince everyone's talking about. Is he a doctor?'

She pretended not to hear the first part of the conversation. 'No, he's not a doctor. He's just been doing what I told him to do.' She patted her stomach. 'I couldn't quite fit.'

Sam nodded and jerked his head. 'Right, move away and stay under that coat. Back away slowly. I'll get your friend to come out and I'll replace him.' Another siren came screaming up behind them. 'That'll be Fire and Rescue. They'll help with the car and the glass.' He gave her another look. 'Now move, pregnant lady, or I'll admit you with something or other.'

She gave a grateful smile. Sam wasn't joking. She backed away to let him do his job. She heard him give Sebastian a few instructions then, in the space of under a minute, Sebastian slid out from under the car and Sam replaced him. His colleague appeared with the Fire and Rescue crew and everything just seemed to move quickly.

Sebastian moved over to her and wrapped his arm around her shoulders. 'You okay?'

There was a tiny smudge of blood just above his eye. She felt in her pocket. No tissues. They'd used them.

She gave a nod. His jeans and jacket were muddy and dirty—as was her cream coat. Truth was, it would never recover. She shivered and pushed her arms into the damp coat. 'I'm fine. Give me a minute and I'll find something to clean your face.'

He shook his head, just as there was a shout and another shard of glass fell from the shattered shop window. Sebastian winced. But he didn't try and pull her away. He must have known she'd refuse. Instead they waited for another fifteen minutes as the Fire and Rescue crew worked alongside the paramedics and police to help all the victims of the accident.

Now she had time to take her breath she could survey

just how bad things looked. The two drivers were quickly extricated from the cars, neck collars in place, one conscious and one still unconscious.

A policewoman was standing with Gabriel's mum. The poor woman looked terrified. Once the hanging shards of glass had been safely cleared from the shop window, the fire crew surrounded the car and, on instruction, just bodily lifted it to allow Sam to slide out from underneath with Gabriel on a sliding board. The buggy was still tangled around his legs.

Sienna drew in a sharp breath as her baby kicked in sympathy. Half of her wanted to rush back over and offer to help, but she knew that Sam and his colleague were more than qualified to do emergency care. Gabriel didn't need cardiac surgery—trauma wasn't exactly her field, and part of being a good physician was knowing when to step back.

Sebastian didn't rush her. He didn't try to hurry her away from the site of the crash. As they watched all the accident victims being loaded into the ambulances he just kept his arm wrapped firmly around her shoulders.

She was glad of it. The temperature seemed to have dropped around them and the underlying shiver hadn't left her body.

A few of her colleagues who'd also helped at the scene came over and spoke to her. One of the midwives gave a wry smile. 'Can't remember the last time I treated a seventy-year-old man.' She shook her head as she headed back towards the hospital main entrance.

Sienna turned to Sebastian. 'I think it's probably time for us to go.'

He nodded and glanced down at their clothes and smiled. 'Somehow I think dinner should wait.'

She put her hand to her mouth. 'We can't go in that gorgeous car while we're so mucky.'

As they walked towards the car he let out a laugh.

'That's the beauty of a leather interior—any dirt will wipe clean. Don't worry about it.'

Her stomach gave a growl. 'Let's pick up some take-out,' she said quickly.

Sebastian gave a little frown. She almost laughed out loud. He was a prince. The last time he'd eaten take-out he'd probably been a university student. She made a note to ask Oliver about that. For all she knew, Sebastian had arrived at university with his own chef. It was time to show him how the other half lived.

He held open the door for her again. She shot him a wicked smile. 'What will we have—Chinese? Indian? Pizza? Or fish and chips?'

He made something resembling a strangled sound and gave a sort of smile. 'You choose,' he said as he closed the door and walked around to the other side of the car.

She waited until he'd climbed in. 'Pizza it is, then. There's a place just five minutes from where I live. It does the best pizzas around here.'

She settled into the comfortable seat. Even the smell in the car sent little shivers down her spine. It was gorgeous. It was luxurious. It just felt...different from anything she'd been in before.

Sebastian started the engine. It was a smooth ride; even the engine noise was soothing.

She gestured to the sleek black car following behind them. 'Do they follow you everywhere?'

He gave a little shrug. 'It's their job. They've learned to be unobtrusive. I promise, you won't even know that they're around.'

She smiled. 'Do you have to buy them dinner too?'

He laughed and shook his head. 'Don't worry. They'll make their own arrangements.'

She gave him directions, pointing him to the pizza shop.

When they pulled up outside she went to open the door

but he grabbed hold of her hand. 'No way. You stay where you are. I'll order. What would you like?'

Part of her wanted to refuse. But she'd spent so long outside in the freezing temperatures that her body was only just starting to heat up. She didn't answer straight away and he prompted again. 'What's your favourite pizza?'

'What's yours?'

Their voices almost came out in sync. 'Ham, onion and mushroom.'

Silence. Both of them stared at each other for a second and then both started laughing.

She shook her head. 'Seriously? Really?'

He nodded. 'Really.'

She held up her hand. 'Wait a minute. Deep pan or thin crust?'

He glanced outside at the thick snow that was falling around the car. 'Somehow, I think tonight has to be deep pan night.'

She gave a thoughtful nod. 'I think you could be right.'

She reached out and touched his hand, narrowing her eyes suspiciously. 'Seriously, when was the last time you ate pizza?'

He winked and climbed out of the car. 'That's for me to know and you to guess. Give me five minutes.' He slammed the door and ducked into the pizzeria.

She watched while he placed his order and talked away to the guys behind the counter. Within a few moments they were all laughing. She, in the meantime, was kind of fixated on the view from the back.

She was ignoring the grime and mud all down one side of his probably designer jeans and staring instead at the distinctive shape of his broad shoulders and muscled arms under his leather jacket. If she followed the gaze down to the jeans...

Her body gave an inadvertent shudder as baby decided

to remind her of his or her presence. It felt odd having the same urge of sensations she'd felt the last time she'd been around Sebastian. It seemed like a lifetime ago now. And yet…it felt as if it had just happened yesterday.

But it hadn't been yesterday, it had been months ago.

And months ago she hadn't been this shape. Months ago, she hadn't needed to adjust her position every few minutes in an attempt to try and get comfortable. Months ago her breasts hadn't virtually taken over her body. Months ago she hadn't spent her days considering where the nearest loo was.

Months ago she'd been happy to toss her clothes across the bedroom floor and let the sun streaming through the windows drench her skin.

She sighed and settled back into the seat.

Then sat straight back up again.

Her house. She would be taking Sebastian to her house.

Now they weren't having dinner at some random neutral venue. They were both covered in mud. She'd need to invite him in, and to clean up.

Sebastian. In her home.

The place where she'd made plans. The nursery that was almost finished. The wooden crib that had arrived and was still in its flat-pack box as she was so disappointed by it.

The drawer with tiny white socks and Babygros.

Her stomach gave another leap as she saw Sebastian give the guys a wave and pick up the large pizza box. How would it feel to have Prince Sebastian Falco in her home?

It was almost as if the atmosphere in the car had changed in his absence. Sienna seemed a little tense as he handed her the pizza box. She gave him stilted directions to her house and one-word answers on the five-minute drive.

He had to admit the smell from the pizza box wasn't too bad. The last pizza he'd eaten had been prepared by a

Michelin-starred chef. But somehow he knew that wasn't something he should share with Sienna right now.

Earlier, he'd felt the connection to her. It didn't matter he'd been completely out of his depth and—truth be told—a tiny bit terrified of doing something wrong under that car. But every ounce of his body had told him he had to help. There was no way he could leave an injured child under a car on his own, and, with Sienna's instructions, he'd felt confident to just do as she asked.

It didn't help that the whole time he'd been under there he'd been thinking about the perilous glass dangling directly above the car and Sienna's body.

They turned onto a tree-lined street. Each house was slightly different from the one next to it. Most were painted white, and most were bungalows. A few had sprawling extensions and others had clearly extended into the roof of their property.

Sienna pointed to the left and he pulled up outside a white bungalow with large bay windows and a bright red door. It was covered in a dusting of snow and there were little white lights strung around one of the trees in the front garden.

It wasn't a castle. It wasn't a mansion house. It wasn't even a chalet in the mountains. But he could sense her air of pride. He could instantly tell how much she loved this place.

He gave her a smile. 'It's lovely.'

She let out a deep breath as her eyes fixed on her home. 'Thank you. I love it.'

He walked around quickly, holding the door open for her and lifting the pizza box from her hands. She opened the garden gate and they walked up the path to the front door.

Warmth hit them as soon as she opened the front door. She gave him a smile. 'I have a wood-burning stove. Costs next to nothing. I stack it full in the morning and it burns all day. I'd hate to come home to a cold house.'

A cold house. There was just something about the way she said those words. Almost as if cold didn't only refer to the room temperature.

She walked through to the kitchen and took the pizza, sliding it into her bright red Aga stove. She bit her lip as she turned towards him. 'I don't really have anything you can change into. You can clean up in my bathroom if you want. There are fresh towels in there if you want to use the shower.'

He could tell she was a little uncomfortable. He had no problem taking a shower in Sienna's home—it might actually help warm up his bones a little—but he didn't want to make her feel any more uncomfortable than she already did. He tried not to stare at his surroundings. There was tinsel looped over the fridge. An advent calendar with doors open hanging on the wall, and an array of little Santa ornaments lining the window ledge. Sienna really did love Christmas.

'Do you want me to leave?'

He almost held his breath.

'No. No, I don't.' She slid her dirty coat from her shoulders. 'Look, I'm going to put this in the wash. Leave your dirty clothes at the bathroom door and I'll wash them too. There's a white bathrobe on a hook behind the door. You can wear that while we eat dinner.'

He gave a little nod and walked down the corridor depositing his jeans and T-shirt outside the bathroom door. By the time he'd showered—and scoped out the bathroom for any non-existent male accessories—the pizza was back out of the oven and she had some glasses on the table.

He almost laughed out loud. The dressing gown covered him. But not entirely. His bare legs were on display and, although he'd managed to tie the waist, it gaped a little across his broad chest. It was clear Sienna was trying to avoid looking too closely.

He sat down at the table opposite her and adjusted it as best he could. 'It's not like you haven't seen it all before,' he half teased.

Colour flushed her cheeks. She lifted up the diet soda and started pouring it into glasses. 'Yeah, but I haven't seen it sitting at my kitchen table. Things that happen in Montanari tend to stay in Montanari.'

He tried not to flinch. It was a throwaway comment. He pointed towards her stomach as she served the pizza onto plates. 'It seems that what we did didn't want to stay in Montanari. It wanted to get right out there.'

He was doing his best to lead up to something. He'd had four phone calls today from the royal family's publicist. The British media knew he was here. The whitewash about twinning the two hospitals had quickly came unstuck. Any investigative journalist worth their salt wouldn't take too long to find out why he was really here. He expected to be headline news tomorrow.

She set down his plate with a clatter and before she could snatch her hand away he covered it with his own. 'Sienna, are you okay?'

She shot him an angry glance and walked around to the other side of the table and sat down, staring at him, then the pizza, then him again.

He folded his arms. 'Okay, hit me with it. It's time we were honest with each other.'

She pressed her lips together for a few seconds, then blurted out, 'Why are you here, Sebastian? What is it—exactly—that you want from me?'

He sighed. 'I'm here because of you, Sienna. Even if I hadn't heard about the baby I would never have gone through with the marriage to Theresa. I'm not my parents. I can't live that life. No matter how much they want me to.' He stared at the woman across the table from him.

She had little lines around her eyes. Her hands were spotless but there was one tiny mud splash on her cheek. Her pale skin was beautiful. Her light brown eyes looked tired. Her blonde hair had half escaped from the pony-tail band at the nape of her neck. Her cheeks were a little fuller than when they'd been together last; her whole body had blossomed and it kind of suited her.

In short, he'd never seen anyone look so beautiful.

'Baby or not, I would always have come back for you, Sienna,' he said quietly. 'I thought marriage was about a union between countries. I thought I could tolerate a marriage to a friend. But as soon as it was announced I felt as if the walls were closing in around me. It wasn't enough. I'm not built that way. I just hadn't realised it. A marriage to Theresa would have made her miserable, and me miserable. It could never have lasted.'

There was silence in the room. The only sounds from the ticking clock on the wall and the rumble from the washing machine in the next-door utility room.

She licked her lips. Those luscious pink lips that he ached to taste again. 'I don't believe you,' she whispered. 'You want the heir to your kingdom. You don't want me. I was just the stranger to have sex with.'

There was hurt—hurt written all over her face. A face he wanted to cradle in his hands.

He took his time to choose his words. 'It was sex. It was great sex. With a woman who managed to crawl under my skin and stay there. A woman who has haunted my dreams—day and night—ever since. The baby is a bonus, Sienna. A wonderful, beautiful bonus that I'm still getting my head around and I get a little more ex-cited about every day.'

Part of what he'd said was true. She had got under his skin. He'd thought about her every single day. He'd just not ever considered making her his Queen.

But this baby? This baby was too important. In a way,

it would be easier if it weren't Sienna that was having his baby. Theresa had been easy to put in a little box in his head. She was a friend. She would only ever be a friend.

But Sienna? She was spreading out of any little box like a new and interesting virus. One that had started reproducing the first second that he'd met her. He couldn't squash her into some box in his head.

Because he *felt* something for her.

He just wasn't entirely sure what that was—or what it could be.

Fear flashed across her eyes and her hands went protectively to her stomach. 'This is my baby, Sebastian. Mine. I get to choose. I get to say what happens. You haven't been here. You can't just show up for the grand finale and expect to be the ringmaster at the circus. This is my life. Mine.'

He couldn't help it. Emotions were building inside him. He hated that she felt this way. 'But I want it be ours. I want it to be *our* lives. You're writing me off before we've even started. You have to give me a chance. Look at tonight. Look at how we fitted together. Do you think I could have done that with anyone else?' He shook his head. 'Not for a second, Sienna. Only with you.'

He stopped. He had to force himself. He picked up a slice of pizza even though his appetite had left him. 'Let's try and relax a little. It's been a big night. We need some down time.'

He could see a dozen things flitting behind those caramel eyes of hers.

'Stuff it,' she said as she stood up quickly. She marched to the fridge and brought out a white box that came from a bakery. She lifted out the biggest chocolate éclair he'd ever seen and put it on a plate and shrugged. 'Figure you might as well see how I deal with stress. It might give you a hint for the future.'

He sat quietly, trying not to smile as she devoured the

chocolate éclair with a fork and sipped her diet soda. The atmosphere slowly settled.

From the table he could see outside into her snow-covered back garden, framed by the now black sky. It was bigger than he'd expected with an unusual style of seat and a large tree. Next to the seat was a little bush with a string of glowing multicoloured lights that twinkled every now and then.

He smiled. 'You really do like Christmas, don't you?'

She raised her eyebrows. 'Wait until you see the front room.' She sighed as she stared at her back garden. 'I've been here less than a year. I have visions of what my back garden should look like. Our local garden centre has a whole host of light-up reindeers and a family of penguins.' She pointed at the large tree. 'And I wanted lights for that tree too, and a light-up Santa to go underneath. But if I'd bought everything I wanted to, I would have bankrupted myself. So, I've decided to just buy one new thing every year. That way, I can build myself up to what I really imagine it should look like in my head.'

He watched her as she spoke and couldn't help but smile. The more she spoke, the more of a drifting-off expression appeared in her eyes, it was almost as if she were actually picturing what she wanted her garden to look like.

'Why do you like Christmas so much?'

She gave a throwaway shrug. 'I just like what it means.' She paused and bit her lip. 'It was the one time of year my parents didn't fight—probably because my Aunt Margaret came to stay.' She smiled. 'It was almost as if she brought the Christmas spirit with her. She had so much energy. So much joy. When I was little she made every Christmas special. She was obsessed by it. And I guess I caught a little of her bug.'

It was nice seeing her like this. He stood up and lifted

his glass of diet soda. 'Okay, hit me with it. Show me the front room.'

She laughed and shook her head as she stood up. This time she didn't avert her eyes from the dressing gown that barely covered him. She waved her hand. 'Give me a second.' Then she walked along the corridor and bent down, flicking a few switches just inside the door. She smiled and stood back against the wall. 'I wanted to give you the full effect.'

He stopped walking. She was talking about her front room. He knew she was talking about her front room. But he was already getting the full effect. The full Sienna McDonald effect. Every time she spoke with that lilting Scottish accent it sent blood rushing around his body. Every time their gazes connected he felt a little buzz.

She looked excited. It was obvious she was proud of whatever he was about to see.

The main lights in her room weren't on. They weren't needed, because every part of the room seemed to twinkle with something or other.

He stepped inside. The tree took pride of place at the large bay window. The red berry lights twinkled alongside the red decorations. In the corner of the room were three lit-up white and red parcels of differing sizes. A backlit wooden nativity scene was set out on a wooden cabinet. The pale cream wall above her sofa was adorned with purple and white twinkling stars.

In the other corner of the room were a variety of Christmas village ornaments. All had little lights. He smiled as he noticed the school room, the bakery, the shop and Santa's Christmas workshop.

The one thing he noticed most about this place was the warmth. Nothing like his Christmases in the palace in Montanari. Oh, the decorations had been beautiful. But anonymous people had arrived and assembled them every year. There was no real connection to the family.

Everything was impersonal. Most of the time he was told not to touch. Sienna's home had a depth that he hadn't experienced before.

He turned to face her. 'It's like a Christmas grotto in here. How long did this take you?'

She shrugged. 'Not long. Well…maybe a few days.'

He stepped a little closer. Close enough to feel her swollen stomach against his. The rest of the room was dark. He reached up and touched the smudge on her cheek. 'You didn't get a chance to clean up, did you? I wonder how little Gabriel is doing.'

She froze as soon as he touched her cheek. Maybe it was too familiar a gesture? Too forward of him. The tip of his finger tingled from where he'd come into contact with her skin. He couldn't help but touch her again. This time brushing her cheek as he tucked a wayward strand of hair behind her ear.

Her eyes looked darker in here. Or maybe it was just the fact her pupils had dilated so much, they were currently only rimmed with a tiny edge of brown.

'I'll phone the hospital later.' Her voice was husky, almost a whisper. If she objected to his closeness she hadn't said.

He took in a deep breath. A deep breath of her.

There it was. The raspberry scent of her shampoo, mixed with the light aroma of her subtle perfume and just the smell of her. For Sebastian it was intoxicating. Mesmerising. And sent back a rush of memories.

His fingers hesitated around her ear. He didn't want to pull them away. He didn't want to be out of contact with her.

This felt like something he'd never experienced before.

Something worth waiting for.

She bit her bottom lip again and he couldn't stop himself. He pulled her closer and met her lips with his. Taste.

He could taste her. The sweetness of the éclair. Now, he truly was having a rush of memories.

The memory of her kiss would be imprinted on his brain for ever. Her lips slowly parted and his fingers tangled through her hair, capturing the back of her head to keep her there for ever.

Her hands wound around his neck as she tilted her head even further to his. Somehow the fact that her swollen belly was next to his was even better than he could have imagined. Their child was in there. Their child was growing inside her. In a few weeks' time he'd be a father. And no matter what his parents might think, he couldn't wish for a better mother for his child.

His hand brushed down the side of her breast and settled on her waist.

He felt her tense. Slow their kiss. He let their lips part and she pressed her forehead against his. Her breathing was rapid.

He stayed like that for a second, letting them both catch their breath.

'Sebastian,' she breathed heavily.

'Yes?'

She lifted her heavy eyelids to meet his gaze. 'You have to give me a minute. Give me a few seconds. I need to go and change.'

He stepped back. 'Of course. No problem.'

He'd no idea what that meant. Change into what?

She disappeared into the corridor and he sank down into her comfortable red sofa for a few minutes, his heart thudding against his chest.

Maybe she wanted him to leave. Maybe she wanted him to stay.

He'd always been confident around women. He'd always felt in charge of a relationship. But things were different with Sienna.

Everything was at stake here.

Sebastian didn't do panic. But right now, if he said the wrong thing, he could mess up everything. And what was the right thing to say to a pregnant woman who'd already told you she wanted the fairy tale?

He looked around the room. The Christmas grotto. Sienna's own personal fairy tale. No castle. No prince. Just this. He tried to shift on the sofa but it was almost impossible. It was one of those sink-in-and-lose-yourself-for-ever kind of sofas.

Sienna had a good life here. She had a house that she loved. Loyal friends and the job of her dreams. The truth was, she didn't really need him. If Sebastian wanted to have a place in her life he was going to have to fight for it.

And he had to be sure what he was fighting for.

He'd meant it when he told her he'd always have come back for her. At first, it had just been words. He just hadn't said the next part—he just wasn't entirely sure what he was coming back *for*.

Someone to have a relationship with? An affair?

Or something else entirely?

It hadn't even been clear in his head until that moment. But as he'd watched her face he'd had a second of pure clarity—sitting across the table was exactly what he wanted. Tonight had given him a new perspective. If he hadn't been there he didn't doubt that Sienna would have put herself in harm's way to try and help that child. It was part of what he admired so much about her.

This might not be the way he had planned it. But Sebastian was always up for a challenge.

Sienna walked back into the room. She glanced at the gaping dressing gown and looked away. 'Your jeans are washed. I've put them in the dryer. They won't be long.'

He nodded. 'Thanks. Now, come and sit down. It's been a big day. Sit for a while.'

He could see her hesitation. See her weighing up what

to do next. She'd washed her face, pulled her hair into some kind of knot and changed into what looked like pyjamas.

She walked over and sat down next to him, curling one leg up underneath her. He wrapped his arm back around her shoulder.

Sienna wanted things to be by her rules. He wanted to keep her happy.

'Tell me what you've organised for the baby. What would you like me to do?'

She looked at him in surprise. 'Well, I've pretty much organised everything. I've turned one room into a nursery. I just need to give it a lick of paint and some of the furniture has arrived. But I haven't built it yet.'

'Let me do that.'

She blinked. 'Which one?'

'Both. All of them. Do you know what colour you want for the nursery? I could start tomorrow.'

Had he ever painted anything in his life? What did he actually know about room decoration? It didn't matter. If that was what she needed for the baby, then he would find someone to do it. Money wasn't exactly an object for Sebastian. If he paid enough, he could get it done tomorrow.

She drew back a little. It was all he could do not to focus on those lips again. He was trying his best to keep her at arm's length. Even though it was the last thing he wanted to do. If he wanted a chance with Sienna and with his baby, he would have to play by her rules.

'Well, okay,' she said after what seemed like for ever. She pushed herself up from the sofa. 'Come and I'll show you the nursery.'

He tried to follow her and fumbled around on the impossible sofa. 'How on earth did you do that? This thing just swallows you up like one of those sand traps.'

She started laughing. 'It does, doesn't it? It was one of

the first things I bought when I got my own flat. I love the colour and, even though it needs replacing, I've never found another sofa quite the colour that I love. So I keep it. The removal men just about killed themselves carrying it down three flights of stairs when I moved from my flat to here.'

He gave himself an almighty push and almost landed on top of her. 'Oh, sorry.' His hand fell automatically to her waist again. It hadn't been deliberate. Not at all. But not a single part of his body wanted to move.

This was his problem. His brain was screaming a thousand things at him. He was getting too attached. He was beginning to feel something for Sienna. Something other than the blood rushing through his body. The rational part of his brain told him she didn't really want him, she didn't want to be part of the monarchy in Montanari. She was probably the most unsuitable woman to be his wife.

But little question marks kept jumping into his thoughts. Was she really so unsuitable? She was brilliant. She had a career. She was a good person. Yes, she was probably a little unconventional. She certainly didn't hesitate to speak her mind. But, after spending his life around people who didn't say what they meant, it was actually kind of refreshing. Add that to the fact that even a glimpse of her sent his senses into overload...

She pulled back a little from him so he dropped a kiss on her forehead and stepped away. 'Blame the sofa.' He smiled.

She showed him across the hall to the nursery. So far he'd seen the bathroom, the main room, the kitchen and the utility. Two other doors in the corridor seemed to glow at him. One of them must be her bedroom.

He waved his hand casually. 'This is a nice house. What's down there?'

She looked over her shoulder. 'Just my bedroom and the third room, which is a dining room/bedroom. I hadn't quite decided what I wanted to do with it yet. There's another sitting room at the back, but the house layout is a little awkward. I think the people that built the house added it on at the last minute. It ended up being off the utility room.'

Sebastian gave a nod as she flicked the switch on the room she'd designated the nursery.

It was a good-sized room. There was a pin board on the wall covered in messages and cut-out pictures. Some were of prams, some of other nurseries, some of furniture and a few of treehouses and garden play sets.

He smiled as he looked at them all. She pointed to one of the pictures. 'That one. That's what I decided on.'

It was lovely. A pale yellow nursery, with a border with ducks and teddy bears and with pale wooden furniture.

She nodded towards the flat boxes leaning against one wall. 'It only arrived yesterday.' There was a kind of sad twang in her voice.

He walked towards it. 'What's wrong?'

She sighed. 'Nothing. It's just not quite what I'd hoped for. I'm sure it will look fine once it's all built. But there was no point in building it until I'd painted the room and put the border up.'

One of the ends of the flat-pack furniture box was open and he peered inside, reaching in with his hand to touch the contents. He got it. He got it straight away. The furniture on the picture on her pin board looked like solid oak with delicate carving and professional workmanship. Furniture bought from a store would never compare. He knew exactly what he could say right now, but he had to be careful of her feelings. She'd worked hard to make preparations for their child.

'Do you know what shade of yellow you want?'

She pointed to the corner of the room. There were around ten different little squares of varying shades of yellow. 'Yeah, I picked the one three from the end. I've bought the paint, I was planning on starting tomorrow.'

She walked over to a plastic bag. 'I have the border here, along with the matching light shade and bedding.'

He took a deep breath as he walked a little closer. 'I really want to help. I really want to be involved. Will you let me paint the room for you tomorrow? And hang the border? Once that's done I can build the furniture, and if you don't like it we can see if there's something more suitable.'

This was the point where she could step away. This was the point where he could end up flung out of the house. But she stayed silent. He could see her thinking things through. The reserve that she'd built around herself seemed to be slipping a little, revealing the Sienna that he'd connected with in Montanari.

His finger wanted to speed dial someone right now. There had to be someone around here that could help make good on his promises.

She nodded slowly then met his gaze with a gentle smile. 'Do you know what? That might actually be good… thanks.' She narrowed her gaze and wagged her finger at him. 'But you're not allowed to bring in someone else to do it. You have to do it yourself. I don't want anyone I don't know in my house.'

There was a tiny wave of unease. She could read him like a book. 'Of course. Of course, I'll do it myself. It will be my pleasure.' He looked around the room. It would be nice with the pale yellow colour on the walls.

He'd tell her things on a need-to-know basis.

He walked back to the pin board and pointed at the prams. 'Have you ordered one yet?'

The two on the board were both brightly coloured with modern designs. Nothing like the coach-built pram he'd been pictured in as a child. He gave a little smile, thinking about his room as a small child with its dark furniture and navy blue drapes.

She stepped up next to him. 'What are you smiling at?'

He gave a sigh. 'I know nothing about prams. But they both look kind of funky. I'm sure I won't have a clue how to put them together.'

Her gaze changed. It was thoughtful. Almost as if she'd finally realised that he planned on being around. Planned on being involved.

'You can buy a plain black one if you want,' she said softly. There was something sad in her voice.

His hand reached down and he intertwined his fingers with hers. 'I'll be proud to push whatever red or purple pram you choose. Why don't you let me buy you both? That's if you haven't ordered one yet.'

She paused. She hadn't pulled her hand away. He started tracing little circles in the palm of her hand with his thumb. 'Sienna, I'm here because I want to be here. I want to be here for you, and for our baby. But…' he turned to face her straight on '…this might all get a little pressured. I have to tell my parents that they're going to be grandparents.'

Her eyes widened. 'They don't know?'

'Not yet. I wanted to speak to you first. To give you a little time.' He reached and tangled his fingers through her hair. 'Once I tell them, the world will know. You won't just be Sienna McDonald, cardiothoracic neonatal surgeon any more. You'll be Sienna McDonald, mother of Prince Sebastian Falco's child. I want to protect you from that. You'll be bombarded with phone calls and emails. Everyone will want a little piece of you.' He shook his head. 'I don't want that.' He gave her a sorry smile. 'There's not enough of you to go round.'

For a moment she looked terrified. Surely, she must have expected this at some point. Surely she must have realised that the press would be interested in their baby?

Maybe his concerns about her had been right.

Her response was a little shaky. 'I don't want people interfering in my life. I'm a surgeon. I do a good job. I've made plans on how to raise this baby.'

Something twisted inside him. He wanted to say everything he shouldn't. He might only have known about this baby for a couple of weeks but every sleepless night had been full of plans for this child too.

Somehow he had to find a way to cement their plans together. There would need to be compromise on each side. How on earth would Sienna cope with his mother?

His mother's idea of compromise would be to sweep this baby from under Sienna's nose, transport the baby to the palace in Montanari and bring up the child with the same ideals she'd had for Sebastian.

For about ten seconds that had been his plan too. Had he really thought Sienna would be happy to marry him and leave her job and friends behind?

He could see himself having to spend the rest of his life having to prevent Sienna and his mother from being in the same room together.

It didn't even bear thinking about. There would be time enough for all that later. He had to start slowly.

He looked around the room. Then he glanced at Sienna's stomach. He let the wave of emotions that he'd tried to temper flood through him. That was his baby in there. *His.*

He didn't want to be a part-time parent. He wanted to see this child every day. He wanted to be involved in every decision.

And the truth was, he wanted to be around Sienna too.

He touched her cheek. 'I want to be part of those plans, Sienna. That's all I'm asking.'

She stared at him for the longest time. Her gaze unwavering.

'Let me do something to try and help. Once I've spoken to my parents, can I get one of the publicists from the palace to contact you? To try and take the pressure off any queries you might get from reporters?'

She gave the briefest of nods. At least it was something. It was a start. He hadn't even mentioned the fact that he would actually have to hire security to protect her.

'You can come tomorrow. You'll need to be up early before I go to work.'

He smiled. 'No problem. I like to be up early.' He pointed to the pin board again. 'What about the prams?'

The edges of her lips turned upwards and she gave a little shake of her head. 'You've no idea how hard this is for me.'

'What?' He couldn't keep the mock horror from his voice as he put one hand to his chest. 'You mean letting someone else help? Letting someone else be involved?'

She nodded. She waved at the photos on the board. 'I'm running out of time. I need to order the pram that I want this weekend if it's going to be here on time.' She pulled a face. 'Trouble is, I still can't choose. And the lie-down pram, buggy and car seat all go together. At this rate, if I don't choose soon, I won't even have a way to get my baby home from hospital, let alone out of the house.'

He nodded. She hadn't taken him up on the idea of getting both. 'How about we go this weekend and look again?'

She gave him the strangest look. 'Have you any idea what these places are like? The guys in the giant nursery stores always look like they've been dragged in there kicking and screaming and can't wait to get back out.'

He raised his eyebrows. 'Well, I will be different. I can't wait to spend hours of my life helping you choose between a red and a purple pram set.' He gave a hopeful smile. 'Is there coffee in these places?'

She nodded. 'Oh, yes. But you need to drink decaf in

support of me. But there's also cake. So it might not be too bad.'

Finally, he was getting somewhere. Finally he felt as if he was starting to make inroads with Sienna. They'd made a connection today that felt like it had back in Montanari.

And this wasn't just about the baby—even though that was all they'd really talked about. This was about them too.

This would always be about them.

She walked back to the door of the nursery. 'Okay, thanks. Tomorrow it is. Now let me get your clothes. The dryer will be finished by now.'

His heart sank a little. It was time for him to go. It didn't matter how much he actually wanted to stay.

He followed Sienna down the hall as she pulled his clothes from the dryer. The jeans were still warm as he stepped into them and fastened them. He put the dressing gown on top of the dryer and turned to face her.

Her tongue was running along her top lip. She was watching him. Her eyes fixated on his bare chest. He took a step towards her.

'Sienna?'

He could act. He could pull her towards him and kiss her exactly the way he wanted to. But he'd already done that tonight. This time it was important for her to take the lead.

She put one hand flat on his chest and took a deep breath as she looked down at the floor. There was a tremble in her voice. 'You need to give me some time, Seb. It would be so easy just to fall into things again. To take up where we left off. But there's so much more at stake now.'

His heart gave a little jump. Seb. She'd just called him Seb again.

She lifted her head and met his gaze. 'I didn't expect to see you again. I didn't expect you to come.'

He placed his hand over hers. 'And now?'

'You asked me to give you a chance. I want to. I do. But I need to be sure about why we're both here. I've had more time to get used to the thought of our baby than you have. And the thought of being under the gaze of the whole world is something I hadn't even contemplated.' He gave her hand a squeeze. Now he couldn't help himself. He stepped forward and put his arms around her.

'Let me help. Let me get you some advice. We could release a press statement together if you wanted.'

She pushed back and shook her head. 'Release a press statement? Those are words I never thought I'd hear. Just give me a bit of time, a bit of space. One step at a time, Seb. If you want me to give you a chance, that's the way it's got to be.'

He was disappointed. He couldn't help it. He was rushing things. But being around Sienna and not *being* with her was more difficult than he could ever have imagined.

Now he felt a sense of panic. What about the press intrusion into Sienna's life? How would she cope? He was used to it. He'd been photographed since the day he was born. But, for Sienna, life was entirely different.

She loved her job. She'd trained long and hard to be a specialist surgeon. Would she be able to continue with the job she loved if she were his wife?

At first his only thought had been about duty. His duty to the mother of his child, and to his country. His proposal of marriage had only been about those things.

Now? Things were changing. Changing in a way he hadn't even contemplated. He gave a half-smile. Was this how Oliver felt around Ella?

He pulled his T-shirt over his head and reached for his leather jacket. She handed him a damp towel. 'Try and take some of the mud off it with this.'

She was so matter-of-fact. So practical. Ten seconds ago she'd been wearing her heart on her sleeve. He wiped the jacket as best he could and slid it on.

'My shoes are next to the door.' He paused; he really didn't want to leave.

She nodded. 'Okay, then. Be here early, around seven-thirty. I'll leave you a key to lock up when you're done.'

She followed him to the door and shivered as the icy blast hit as soon as he opened it. 'Stay inside,' he said quickly. 'Keep warm. I'll see you tomorrow.'

'Seb?'

He'd already gone down the first two steps and turned at the sound of her voice. 'Yeah?'

She closed her eyes for a second. 'Thank you,' she said softly, with one hand on her stomach.

He leaned forward and kissed her cheek. 'Any time. Any time at all.' Then he headed down the path back to his car.

CHAPTER FIVE

SHE DIDN'T SLEEP a single wink—just tossed and turned all night.

Eventually, she got up and phoned to check on Gabriel. It was a relief to find out he was stable and had regained consciousness.

Seb arrived early with hot pancakes for breakfast and a hire car for her to use. He was in a good mood and only teased her a little when she gave him a list of instructions, including where he was allowed to wear his shoes.

In a lot of ways he was easy to be around. It was easy to forget he was a prince. It was easy to forget he had a whole host of other responsibilities. Ones that would ultimately keep him away from her and their baby.

The first time she knew something was off was when she arrived at work. There was a TV van in the car park and a reporter was shooting a story opposite the main entrance to the hospital.

As soon as she turned into the staff car park one of the porters gave her a nod of his head. He walked quickly to her car. 'You might want to keep your head down and go in the side door.'

She picked up her bag. 'Why? What's happening?'

'You haven't seen it?'

Her phone started ringing. She glanced at the number. Seb. She'd only just left him. Why was he ringing her already? She silenced it as Frank held out his mobile towards her.

There was a photo. A photo of her house. A photo of her and Sebastian in her doorway looking intimate.

The headline wasn't much better.

Montanari's Baby Secret

She put her hand up to her mouth. 'No. No way. Who took that photo? That was last night. Someone was outside my house?' She didn't care about her ratty hair, or the fact she was wearing pyjamas in the photo. It looked as if she'd just fallen out of bed to show Sebastian to the door—that implied a whole lot of other things. All she cared about was the fact someone had been hanging about outside her house, waiting to take a picture. Why hadn't Seb's security people seen them?

Frank glanced over at the crowd in the car park. 'What's with the different car—did you know they'd be here? Trying to throw them off the scent?' He was smiling. It was almost as if he were enjoying the fracas.

'No. My car wouldn't start last night. Sebastian gave me a lift home. This is a hire car. My car's still in the other car park.'

Frank was still watching. 'Pull your hood up and duck in the side door. I'll walk next to you.'

She glanced around the car park. It seemed to be getting busier by the second. She pulled up her hood on her cream coat and walked alongside Frank with her head down. It only took five minutes to reach her office, close the door and turn on the computer. Her phone buzzed again. Seb.

As the computer started to kick into life she sank into her chair and put the phone to her ear. 'I've seen it. Reporters are all over the hospital. I've got a job to do. I don't need this.'

'I'll deal with it. I'll speak to Oliver and see what we can do. I'll phone you later once we have a press release ready.'

She put down the phone and watched as one headline after another appeared on screen. They had her name, her age, her qualifications. There was a report about the work she'd done in Montanari. There was speculation about how exactly she and Sebastian had met.

There was even more speculation about the timing. His sudden engagement and his wedding announcement, then his even quicker plans to cancel.

There was a camera shot of the King and Queen of Montanari from earlier on this morning. Sebastian's mother looked tight-lipped and quietly furious. He hadn't mentioned them at all. She could only imagine the kind of phone call that had been.

Oliver knocked on the door. 'Sienna? Can we talk?'

She sighed and rolled her eyes. 'Are the board complaining about the *femme fatale* on their staff?'

He snorted. 'Who cares? I'm worried about you. I've called Security. They'll keep an eye out for any reporters.'

'Thank you, Oliver.'

He paused for a second, hovering around the door as only a man who was struggling to find the words could.

She rolled her eyes again. 'What is it, Oliver?'

He pulled a face. 'I've no idea what happened between you before.' Then he shook his head and smiled. 'Well, actually the evidence is there. I've known him since we were at university. He was a few years younger than me but decided to join the same rowing club. We've been friends ever since. I just wanted you to know—I've never seen him like this.'

She frowned. 'Never seen him like what?'

Oliver hesitated again. 'Never seen him act like he's in love before,' he said as he retreated out of the door.

Her head started to swim. After a few seconds she actually put it down between her knees.

Last night had been overwhelming. Having Sebastian in her home, in a state of undress and then in the middle of their baby's nursery, had felt surreal.

She just hadn't pictured it happening in her head. It had seemed so far out of reach that she hadn't allowed her head room for it.

Now, it was a reality.

Now, the man that had haunted her dreams for months was finally only a fingertip away.

But how much was he actually offering?

When he'd told her he would always have come back for her, she'd really, really wanted to believe him. But words were easy. Everyone knew that.

And the fact was he'd left her warm bed and put an engagement ring on another woman's finger.

It didn't matter what the facts or circumstances were. It had still happened.

It had still hurt.

She would love to believe that one snowy day, out of the blue, Sebastian would have turned up on a white stallion to sweep her away from all this and declare his undying love.

But the word love had never been mentioned.

Maybe she was unrealistic. Maybe she was a fool to chase the fairy tale. But after being brought up by parents who clearly didn't love each other she could never do that to her child. Would it be even worse if she loved Sebastian and he never quite loved her? How would their son or daughter feel about being brought up in an uneven relationship blighted by unrequited love?

It was too hard to even imagine.

So, what exactly had Oliver meant? He'd never seen Sebastian in love before?

Her stomach gave a little swirl. When she'd looked into those forest-green eyes last night all she'd been able to think about was how much this guy could hurt her. How much of her heart he'd already stolen despite the walls she'd tried to put up around it.

Self-protect mode seemed easiest.

He was being kind. He was being considerate. But could it really be love and not duty?

Her head wouldn't even let her go there.

There was a knock at her door and Juliet Turner, the neonatal specialist surgeon, walked in with contraband in her hands.

'Sienna? Are you okay?'

Sienna pulled her head up from between her knees and smiled. 'Yeah. Sorry, I'm fine.'

Juliet frowned. 'It seems like I'm just in time. I thought the road to your favourite coffee shop might be lined with reporters this morning, so decided to take the hit for you. Don't worry—it's caffeine-and-sugar-free.'

She set down the coffee and a mystery package in a paper bag. 'Anything I can do for you?'

Sienna shook her head and waved at the contraband. 'You've already done it. Have I told you lately that I love you?' Juliet laughed as Sienna continued, 'How are the quads?'

Juliet smiled. 'Things are looking good. They seem to get a little stronger every day.'

Juliet's pager beeped. She glanced at it and her smile broadened. 'Charlie. Better go. Wedding plans are in the air.'

She practically danced out of the door as Sienna took a deep breath. It seemed that everyone else in this hospital had managed to find love just in time for Christmas. Max and Annabelle, Oliver and Ella and now Juliet and Charlie.

There was no way she could be that lucky too.

No way at all. The Christmas fairy dust had all been used up around here.

Her phone beeped. She opened the message. There was a photo attached that made her blink twice.

'Yuck,' she said out loud. It was from Sebastian. And it was apparently the colour she'd chosen for the baby's nursery. What she'd thought was pale yellow had actually morphed into something more neon-like. She smiled at the message.

Is this what you had in mind?

She glanced at her watch. Just over an hour and he'd already painted one wall. Too bad he'd need to paint it again.

She replied quickly.

Not quite.

Then she dabbed again.

Not at all!

Sienna jerked as her pager sounded. The caffeine-free skinny latte with sugar-free caramel toppled and some of the hot liquid spilled down her pale pink trousers.

She jumped up. 'Great.' She looked around her office. Of course. There was nothing to mop it from her trousers with—and by the time she found something the brand-new trousers would be stained for life.

She glared at the coffee Juliet had bought for her. 'That'll teach me,' she murmured.

The pager sounded again and she shook her head as

she stared at the number. Labour ward. Something must be wrong.

She left the coffee and the tiny cake decorated with holly Juliet had bought to go with it lying on the table. Her appetite had abated already.

She walked quickly down the corridor to the labour ward. She could have phoned, but they usually only paged if they actually needed her.

Kirsty, one of the younger labour-ward midwives, was looking a bit frantic. 'You looking for me?' Sienna asked. This striding quickly was getting a bit more difficult.

'I need you to look at a baby. Labour went perfectly—no concerns. But since delivery the baby has been kind of flat. I called the Paeds and they told me to page you.'

Kirsty hadn't paused for breath, her words getting quicker and quicker. Sienna reached over and put her hand on her arm.

'Kirsty, tell me what I need to know.'

Her eyes widened with momentary panic, then her brain kicked into gear and she nodded. 'Caleb Reed, thirty-six plus three weeks, five pounds eleven ounces. Born two hours. He's pale, irritable and his breathing is quite raspy.'

Sienna walked to the nearest sink and washed her hands. She glanced down at her trousers. If she had a little more time she could put on some scrubs. But best not to keep the paediatrician waiting. 'Which room?'

'Number seven.'

Kirsty walked to the room and stood anxiously at the doorway while Sienna dried her hands.

Sienna gave a nod and walked inside. Lewis Connell, one of her paediatric colleagues, told her everything she needed to know with one glance.

She gave a wide smile to the two anxious parents and held out her hand towards the father, who was perched at the side of the bed. 'Hi, there. I'm Sienna McDonald.'

She left her title out of the introduction. There was time enough for that later. The man warily shook her hand. 'John,' he said, and she held it out in turn to the mother. 'Dr Connell has asked me to come and take a look at your son. Congratulations. What have you called him?'

It didn't matter that she already knew. She was trying to get a feeling about the parents and how prepared they might be for what could come next.

The mother seemed a little calmer. 'Caleb. We've called him Caleb. And I'm Lucy.' She glanced at Sienna's stomach. 'When is your baby due?'

Sienna gave a little nod. 'Pleased to meet you, Lucy and John.' She patted her stomach. 'Not until the end of January. But if I follow your example I could have him or her any day.'

The mum gave an anxious laugh. 'My waters broke when I went to collect the Christmas turkey. Can you believe that?' She looked over to her baby with affection. 'I guess he couldn't wait for his first Christmas.'

Sienna nodded. 'I guess not. Do you mind if I examine Caleb?'

'No.' It came out as a little squeak.

Sienna smiled and walked to the sink and washed her hands again. Lewis had little Caleb lying in a baby warmer. He nodded to the chart next to him and she took a quick glance. Apgar scores at birth and five minutes later weren't too unreasonable. She was more concerned with the presentation of the baby in front of her now.

She unwound her stethoscope from her neck and warmed the end.

'Definitely cardiac,' murmured Lewis. 'But I'll let you decide.'

She trusted him. She'd worked with him for a long time. Lewis was one of the best paediatricians she'd ever worked with. His knowledge base was huge over a wide range of specialities.

Caleb was struggling. It was obvious. His skin was pale. His breathing laboured. She could see his accessory muscles fighting to keep oxygen pumping around his little body. His little face was creased into a frown and his whole body moving in little irritated twitches. The thing that she noticed most was the unusual amount of sweat glistening on his little body. Instinct told her it was nothing to do with the baby warmer. She lifted the chart and looked at the temperature. It was slightly lower than expected. The pulse oximetry readings were a little lower than expected too.

'Has he fed at all?'

She looked up to Lewis and both parents as she rested her stethoscope on the little chest. Lucy shook her head. 'The midwife tried to get him to latch on, but he didn't want to. He just didn't seem ready. She said we'd try again once the doctor had reviewed him.'

She gave a nod. 'No problem. Give me a moment while I listen to his heart.'

She scribbled a note to Lewis who nodded and disappeared out of the room to get what she'd just asked for.

She held her breath while she listened. There. Exactly what she expected. The whoosh of the heart murmur confirming the disruption of the heart flow. She felt for the pulses around the little body—in the groin and in the legs, checking the temperature of the skin in Caleb's lower body.

Lewis backed into the room again, pulling the machine.

'What's that?' John stood up.

She walked towards them. 'It's called an echocardiogram. It will let me check the blood flow around and through Caleb's heart.'

'You think there's something wrong with Caleb's heart?' Lucy gasped and held her hands to her chest.

The words she chose right now were so important.

She didn't want to distress the brand-new parents, but she wasn't going to tell any lies.

'I'm not sure. I think it's something we need to check out. He seems a little unsettled.'

John and Lucy shot anxious glances at each other. John moved over and put his arm around his wife.

Lewis had positioned the echocardiogram next to the baby warmer and was talking in a low voice to baby Caleb. Sienna gave the parents a little nod. 'Are you okay with me checking Caleb a little further?'

They both nodded. She could practically see the fear emanating from their pores. This was one of the worst parts of her job. In some cases, cardiac conditions were picked up during the antenatal scans, plans could be made in advance and parents prepared for what lay ahead. But in cases like these, there were no plans.

One minute parents were preparing for the exciting birth of their child—the next they were being told their brand-new tiny baby needed major surgery. She had a good idea that was what was about to happen for John and Lucy.

Lewis gave her the nod and she switched the machine on and spread some warmed gel on Caleb's chest. He was still grizzly. His colour hadn't improved and from the twitching of his arms and legs it was as if his little body knew something wasn't quite right.

While he'd been inside his mother and attached to the umbilical cord his cardiac system had had constant support. Now—outside? His little heart seemed to be struggling with the work.

'Hey, little guy.' She spoke quietly as she placed the transducer on his little chest wall and her gaze flickered between him and the screen. Her trained eyes didn't take long to see exactly as she suspected. She could see movement of the blood flow through the heart chambers and heart valves. She pressed a button to measure the direction and speed of the blood flow and then moved to the surrounding blood vessels.

There. Exactly as she expected. She took a deep breath and took her time. She had to be absolutely sure what she was seeing. The room was silent around her. But she'd dealt with this before. She had to make sure she had the whole picture before she spoke to the parents.

Finally, she gave a little nod to Lewis. 'Would you be able to contact Max and see if he is available?'

To his credit, Lewis barely blinked. He would know if she was looking for the other cardiac surgeon that she wanted to act promptly. He gave a brief nod and disappeared out of the room.

Sienna wiped Caleb's chest clean, talking to him the whole time, then lifted him from the baby warmer, wrapped him in a blanket and took him over to his parents. Once he was settled in his mother's arms she sat down on the bed next to them.

'Caleb has something called coarctation of the aorta. The aorta is the big blood vessel that goes to the heart.' She picked up Caleb's chart and drew a little picture on some paper for them. 'Caleb's aorta is narrower than it should be—like this. That means that his heart isn't getting all the blood that it needs. His heart has to work harder than it should to try and pump blood around his body. And this is something we need to fix.'

She paused, giving the parents a few minutes to take in her words.

'How...how do you fix it?' asked John.

She licked her lips. 'I need to do some surgery on him.'

Lucy let out a little whimper as she stared at her baby. Sienna put her hand on Lucy's arm.

'Right now, Caleb is getting a very good blood supply to the top half of his body. But his pulses are weaker in the bottom half of his body—to his legs and feet. If we don't do surgery to widen his aorta then his heart will be affected by working too hard and he could suffer from heart failure.'

Lucy was shaking her head. 'Why?' Her eyes were filled with tears. 'Why has this happened to our baby?'

Sienna nodded. These were natural questions for parents to ask. She chose her words carefully. 'There are lots of ideas around why some babies have problems with their hearts, but the truth is—no one really knows. It could be a family thing. It could be in your genes. The type of condition that Caleb has is called a congenital heart defect. Have you ever known anyone in either of your families to have something like this?'

They exchanged glances and both of them shook their heads. She gave a slow nod. 'Sometimes people think congenital heart defects can be caused by things in the environment, things around us. Other theories are it could be caused by things that we eat and drink or medicines a mum might take.' She gave Lucy's arm a squeeze. She had to be honest, but didn't want Lucy to blame herself for her baby's condition. It was important that they focused on Caleb right now.

'How often does this happen?' Lucy's voice had cracked already and tears had formed in her eyes.

This was always the hardest part—breaking the news to parents that something was wrong with the little person all their hopes and dreams were invested in.

She'd always found this bit hard. But not quite as hard as she was finding it today. She blinked quickly, stopped tears forming in her own eyes. It was hard not to empathise with them. In a few weeks' time she would be beside herself if something was wrong with her baby. It didn't matter how much she knew. It didn't matter what her skills were.

For the last few months she'd practically lived her life in a bubble. She'd been so focused on the plans. The plans about maternity leave, cover, nurseries, childminders, cribs, prams and car seats.

She hadn't really focused on the actual outcome.

The actual real live moment when she'd become a mother and her life would change for ever.

Sebastian had brought all that home to her.

Maybe it was having someone around who was so excited about their baby. She'd felt so alone before. So determined to make sure everything would be in place.

She hadn't let the excitement—or the terror—actually build.

But having Sebastian around had heightened every emotion she possessed in an immediate kind of way.

He talked about it so easily. Their baby being here. Their baby being loved. Their baby's future.

A horrible part of her thought that when he hadn't known it had actually been a little easier.

Because Sebastian wanted to be involved in *everything*.

And it was clear he had plans on going nowhere.

The door opened and Max came in. He didn't speak, just raised his eyebrows and walked over towards her.

She smiled gratefully. 'You asked how often this happens. It is rare. But not quite as rare as you might think. Around four out of every ten thousand babies born will have this condition. In some babies it's mild. For some people it's not picked up until they are an adult. Some children aren't picked up until their teenage years. John and Lucy, this is Max Ainsley. He's the cardiothoracic surgeon that is taking over from me while I go on maternity leave.'

Max didn't hesitate. He held out his hand, shaking both their hands but letting Sienna continue to take the lead.

'If you know about Caleb now, does that mean he's really bad?' John looked as though he might be sick.

Sienna moved her hand over to his arm. 'It means it's something that we need to fix, John. And we need to fix it now.' She scribbled something on Caleb's chart. 'I'm going to make arrangements to move Caleb up to the paediatric intensive care unit. You'll be able to go with him, but the staff will be able to monitor him better there. I'll arrange for him a have a few more tests—a chest X-ray and an ECG.'

Lucy's eyes widened. 'My dad had one of those when they thought he was having a heart attack.'

Sienna nodded. 'It gives us an accurate tracing of the heart without causing any problems for Caleb. Once we have all the test results Max and I will review them. The type of surgery we need to do is to widen the narrow part of Caleb's aorta. It's called a balloon angioplasty. We put a thin flexible tube called a catheter into the narrow area of the aorta, then we inflate a little balloon to expand the blood vessel. Sometimes we put a little piece of mesh-covered tube called a stent in place to keep the blood vessel open.' She paused for a second. 'If we think the angioplasty won't work, or it's not the right procedure for Caleb, then we sometimes have to do surgery where we remove the narrow part of the aorta and reconstruct the vessel to allow blood to flow normally through the aorta.'

She took a deep breath. 'I know all this is scary. I know all this can be terrifying. I understand, really, I do. But both Max and I have done this kind of surgery on lots of babies. It's a really specialised field and we have a lot of expertise.'

'Do some babies die?'

Lucy's question came out of the blue and Max glanced in her direction. It was clear he was happy to step in if she was finding this too difficult. And for the first time in her life, she was.

She gave a careful nod. 'There can always be complications from surgery. Caleb is a good weight. He isn't too tiny. The echocardiogram of his heart didn't show any other heart defects. Some babies with coarctation of the aorta have other heart conditions—but I don't see any further complications for Caleb.' She stood up from the bed; her back was beginning to ache.

'I have to warn you that surgery can take some time. We could be in Theatre for more than a few hours and I don't want you to panic. I'm going to bring you some information to read then we'll arrange to transfer Caleb upstairs for his tests. Both Max and I will come back and explain everything again, and answer any questions before you sign the consent form. Is there anything you want to ask me right now?'

Both John and Lucy shook their heads. They still looked stunned. Max put a gentle hand on her back. She'd done this kind of surgery on her own on more than thirty occasions but somehow, at this stage of her pregnancy, she was relieved she'd have a second pair of hands.

She gave a final smile at the doorway. 'Don't worry, we'll take good care of Caleb. I'll just go and make the arrangements.'

She ignored the stiffness in her back as she walked down the corridor. It was going to be a long day.

Sebastian was waiting at the end of the corridor. 'Hey,' she said. 'What are you doing here?'

He shrugged. 'I came to find you to see if we might actually make it to a restaurant tonight. I booked out a whole place so we might actually get some privacy. I thought we could try and make Christmas Eve special. But I just heard you're going into surgery.'

He made it all sound so normal and everything he'd said was true. But he was also worried about how she was, following the news story about them. Sienna seemed remarkably calm, however. She was focused. Her mind was on the job. And he admired her all the more for it.

She gave a little sigh. 'Christmas Eve is normally my favourite night of the year. I love the build-up. The expectation for Christmas the next day.' She squeezed her eyes shut for a second as Sebastian reached up and brushed his fingers against her cheek. She opened her eyes again and they met his. 'But this is the life of a surgeon,' she whispered. 'This is the life that I've chosen.'

She held her breath as he nodded slowly. Her heart thudding against her chest. He had to understand. He had to understand that this was her life. If he wanted to be part of it, he had to realise there were things she wouldn't give up—things she would never change.

He touched her cheek again and leaned forward, his lips brushing against her ear as he whispered back, 'I wouldn't have it any other way.'

Her heart gave a little swell as a few of the other staff walked past. She was jerked from their little private moment. She pointed to the elbow of his leather jacket. 'You touched the nursery wall, didn't you?' Then her mouth opened. 'You changed the colour, didn't you?'

He let out a laugh at the pale yellow stain on his jacket. A funny look passed over his face. 'Yip. I did. Those nursery walls have been painted with blood, sweat and even a few tears.' He grimaced. 'There might have been a bit of a problem with the border.'

'What do you mean?'

He made another face. 'Let's just say the painting I could just about handle. Border skills seem to have escaped me. I might need to buy you another.' He gave her a big smile. 'And I might have done something you won't be happy about.'

'What's that?' Her head was currently swimming with thoughts of the surgery she was about to perform. She didn't need distractions.

'I see what you mean about the furniture. I might have ordered a few alternatives.' He held up his hand quickly. 'But don't worry. If you don't like them, they can go back.'

His phone buzzed in his pocket. He pulled it out, silenced it and pushed it away again.

'Problem?'

He shook his head. 'Nothing I can't handle.'

'What is it?'

'Let's just say it's a mother-sized problem.'

Sienna's heart sank a little. 'How many calls have you had?'

He shifted from one foot to the other. 'I spoke to her this morning just as the press release went out. Since then, there's been another twenty calls.'

'And you haven't answered them?'

He shook his head firmly. 'I've already heard her opinion once. I don't need to hear it again.'

It was a horrible sensation. Like something pressing down heavily on her shoulders. 'Please don't fall out with your mother because of me.'

'Let me worry about my mother. You just worry about your surgery. Oliver said I can go into the viewing room and watch.'

'Oh.' She wasn't quite sure what to say. It was one thing inviting Sebastian into her home, but inviting him to watch her surgery was something else entirely. It seemed he was determined to be involved in both her personal and professional life. She wasn't sure quite how she felt about that.

He bent forward and kissed her on the cheek. 'Good luck. You'll be fantastic. They're lucky to have you.'

The doors swung open behind them and Max appeared in his scrubs. 'Let's go, Sienna. This could be a long one.'

She gave a quick nod and followed him to scrub. Right now she had a baby to focus on. Little Caleb deserved every second of her attention.

And he would get it.

The viewing gallery for the surgery was almost full. Sebastian had to squeeze his way between a couple of excited students.

Sienna appeared cool. She and Max had a long discussion with the staff around them to make sure everyone was on the same page. Then, she glanced up at the gallery as the anaesthetist put Caleb to sleep, and talked some of the students through the procedure they were about to perform. Even behind her mask he could see the brightness in her eyes—the love of her job shone out loud and clear. It made him wish he'd got to meet her while she'd been at the hospital in Montanari. 'Well, guys, I guess this isn't where any of us expected to be on Christmas Eve, but this is the life of a surgeon.' She pointed to the equipment next to her. 'We are lucky at Teddy's to have the best technology around. The whole time we perform this surgery cameras will record our every move. There are viewing screens in the gallery, which you'll be able to watch. You'll find that during surgery Max and I don't talk much. We like to concentrate on the intricacies of the operation—that's why we've explained things beforehand. We will, however, be available to answer any questions you have once surgery is over and we've spoken to Caleb's parents.'

There were a few approving nods around him.

Max walked to the opposite side of the operating table from Sienna. 'Ready?' he asked.

She nodded once and they began.

Sebastian had never seen anything like it in his life. He'd known exactly what her job was when he'd first met her, but he'd never actually seen her in action. He'd never realised just how tiny and intricate the procedures were that she and Max performed. The baby's vessels were tiny.

But Sienna was confident in her expertise. She and Max only exchanged a few words. They worked in perfect synchronisation. Little Caleb truly couldn't be in better hands.

Things started to swirl around in his head. Sienna had a gift. A gift she'd perfected over years of sacrifice and training. No matter how much his mother's words had echoed in his head this morning about duty and expectations for the mother of the heir apparent, he could never expect Sienna to fulfil the role that his mother had for the last thirty years.

Sienna had a skill and talent he could never ask her to walk away from. Not if he really loved her. Not if he really wanted her to be happy.

It came over him like a tidal wave. The plans he'd spent today making. The guilt that had washed over him as the decorator he'd hired had painted the first wall that hideous colour. He'd paid the man more than promised and sent him on his way. The hours of rolling yellow paint onto the walls. The aching muscles and spoiled, crumpled border. The emergency phone calls. The special orders. All because he'd realised this was about trust. This was about him, doing something for their child. This wasn't about duty at all. This was so much more than that. So much more than he'd ever experienced before.

All because he wanted to win a place in this woman's heart.

It finally hit him. She was worth it. She was really, really worth it.

He didn't want to live a single day without this woman in his life.

And he'd be lucky if he could capture a heart like hers.

Caleb's tiny vessel was even more fragile than expected. It took absolute precision to try and widen the vessel and insert the stent to make it remain patent. Having Max next to her was an added bonus. Normally, she would have performed this procedure unassisted, but they both knew that Max was likely to do Caleb's immediate follow-up care so it made sense that they worked together.

Baby wasn't taking kindly to her being on her feet so

long. Her back ached more than usual and her bladder was being well and truly kicked by some angry little feet.

'Sienna?'

Max's voice was much louder than usual. She glanced up sharply just as one of the instruments fell from her hand to the theatre floor.

She blinked. He was out of focus. A warm flush flooded her skin.

'Sienna? Catch her!' he shouted and it was the last thing she heard.

One second she was in the middle of an operation, the next second Sienna was in a crumpled heap on the floor. Sebastian was on his feet and racing down the stairs before he even had time to think. He banged on the theatre doors, which were protected by a code. A flurry of staff rushed past the inside of the doors towards the theatre she'd been operating in. A few seconds later two male scrub nurses were carrying her out of the theatre.

Sebastian banged the door again and one of the theatre nurses turned in surprise. She gave a little nod of her head, obviously realising who he was, and opened the door from the inside. 'I'm going to phone Oliver,' she said as she disappeared off to another room.

Sebastian rushed after the two male nurses. They were gently laying Sienna down on another theatre trolley. Their reactions automatic. One applied a BP cuff, the other stood next to her, talking quietly to her and trying to get a reaction.

It was all Sebastian could do not to elbow both of them out of the way. But they were better equipped to assist her than he was, and he had enough know-how to stand back and let them get on with it.

After a few seconds she started to come around. Groggy and—by the look of it—uncomfortable.

She took a few deep breaths, her hands going automatically to her stomach. One of the theatre nurses smiled at her. 'You decided to go on maternity leave, Sienna.'

She blinked and tried to sit up, but the other male nurse put his hand on her shoulder. 'Not yet. Give it another few minutes. Your BP was low. Let me get you some water to sip.'

Sienna groaned and put her hands to her head. 'Please tell me everything is okay with Caleb. Nothing else happened, did it? I can't believe I just stoated off the floor.'

'You what?'

Sebastian couldn't help it. Her accent seemed even thicker than normal.

The male nurse glanced at him with a smile. 'I think she means she fainted.' He moved out of the way to let Sebastian closer. 'And don't worry. Max is more worried about you than finishing off the surgery. I'll let him know you're okay. He just needs to close.'

Sienna turned to her side for a second, her face a peculiar shade of grey. 'I think I'm going to be sick.'

About ten arms made a grab for the sick bowls but they were all too late. Sienna tried to get up again. 'Don't anyone touch that. I'll clean it up myself.'

'No, you won't.' Oliver strode through the doors. 'Don't you dare move.'

Sebastian leaned across and touched her stomach to stop her getting up, just at the same second a little foot connected sharply with his hand.

'Oh,' he said suddenly, pulling his hand back.

'Try having it all day,' sighed Sienna. 'And all night.'

But Sebastian couldn't stop staring at his hand. That was his baby. *His* baby that had just kicked him.

Of course, he'd come over when he'd heard the news about Sienna—and her pregnancy bump was obvious. But he'd never actually touched it. Never actually felt his little baby moving beneath her skin.

Oliver walked around to the other side. 'I'll arrange

for you to go upstairs and have a scan. We need to make sure that everything is fine—that there aren't any complications.'

Sienna sat up this time and took the plastic cup of water offered by one of the theatre nurses. 'Oliver, honestly, I'm fine. There's no need to fuss. I hadn't managed to eat before I got called into surgery. That, and my back is aching a little because I'm getting further on. I'm fine. Once I go and get something to eat, I'll be good as new.'

'You'll be on maternity leave. That's it. No more patients. No more surgeries.' Sebastian almost smiled. It was clear from the tone of Oliver's voice that there would be no arguments.

Max came through the swing doors tugging his theatre cap from his head. 'How are you? Is everything okay?'

Her voice wavered a little. 'I'm so sorry, Max. Is Caleb okay? Have you finished?'

He waved his hand easily. 'Of course, he's fine. Don't worry about Caleb. I'll look after him.' He pointed to her stomach. 'You just worry about yourself and that precious cargo in there.'

She swung her legs off the side of the trolley. 'Let me go and get changed.' She glanced at Sebastian. 'Sebastian can take me home. I'll get take-out on the way.'

She had that determined lift to her chin but Oliver had obviously seen it before. 'No way. Not until I say. Scan first.'

She opened her mouth to argue but Sebastian cut her off. 'That would be great, Oliver. Thanks for organising that. It's really important to us to make sure that everything is fine with the baby. Those operating theatre floors are harsh.' He met her simmering gaze. 'We both want to be reassured that the baby has come to no harm.'

He'd chosen his words deliberately. There was no way she could refuse. It would make her look as if she didn't care—and that would never be Sienna, no matter how argumentative and feisty she was feeling.

She turned towards him and whispered under her breath. 'Don't tell me what to do. And I can do this myself. You don't need to be there. Why don't you wait outside?'

He felt himself bristle. He pasted a smile on his face and spoke so low, only she could hear. 'How many scans have I already missed, Sienna? Let me assure you, I have no intention of missing this one.'

She met his gaze for a second, as if she wanted to argue. Then seemed to take a deep breath and gave a tiny nod of her head.

One of the other nurses appeared with something else in her hand. 'From my secret chocolate supply. You're only getting special treatment because I love you and I expect you to call the baby after me—even if it's a boy.'

Sienna let out a little laugh and held her hand out for the chocolate. 'Thanks, Mary, I know you guard this stuff with your life. I appreciate it.'

Sebastian was trying his best to be calm. Now that Sienna had woken up, the panic in the room seemed to have vanished.

A porter appeared with a wheelchair and, after another check of her blood pressure, she was wheeled down the corridor towards the scan room.

Christmas Eve. The staff in the maternity unit were buzzing. Placing bets on who would deliver the first Christmas baby. The canteen would be closed later tonight and as they walked past one of the rooms, Sebastian could see plates of food already prepared for the night-shift workers.

The scan room was dark, the sonographer waiting for them. 'Hi there, Sienna. I heard you took a tumble in Theatre. Slide up on the trolley and we'll get a quick check of baby.'

Sienna had just finished eating her chocolate bar and she moved over onto the trolley and pulled up her scrub top.

Sebastian gulped. There it was. A distinct sign of exactly how they'd spent that weekend together in Montanari. He watched the ripples on Sienna's skin. Their baby currently looked as if it were trying to fight its way out from under a blanket.

The sonographer put some gel on Sienna's stomach and lifted her scanner. She paused. 'Do you know what you're having?'

Sienna shook her head. 'Let's avoid those bits if you can. I don't really want to know.'

For the first time in a long time Sebastian felt strangely nervous. He'd never been in a scan room before. Like everyone else in the world, he'd seen it on TV shows and news clips. But this was entirely different.

This was his baby.

No, this was their baby.

He watched as the black and white picture appeared on the screen. The first thing he noticed was the flickering. The sonographer held things steady for a second as she smiled at Sienna. 'Look at that, a nice steady heart-rate.'

Ah...that was the heart.

His eyes started to adjust to what he was seeing on the screen. The sonographer chatted easily as she swept the scanner around. 'Just going to check the position of the placenta and the umbilical cord,' she said simply.

'Why are you doing that?' He couldn't help but ask.

Sienna's eyes were fixated on the screen. 'She's checking to make sure the cord isn't twisted or the placenta detached.'

Neither of those sounded good. 'What would happen if they were?'

This time when she met his gaze she looked nervous. 'Let's just say I wouldn't be getting home for Christmas.'

He moved closer, putting his hand on hers. He looked back at the sonographer. 'And is everything okay?'

The sonographer waited a few seconds before turning to nod reassuringly. 'Everything looks fine.' She pointed to a few things on the screen, 'Here's baby's head, face, spine, thigh bone and...*oops*...let's go back up. Here are the fingers. The placenta looks completely intact and the cord doesn't appear to have any knots in it.' She placed the scanner at the side of the machine again and picked up some tissues to wipe Sienna's stomach. 'Everything seems fine.'

As the picture disappeared from the screen he felt a little pang. He'd missed out on so much already. He didn't want to miss out on another thing. The baby kicked again and even though the room was quite dark he could practically pick out the little feet and fists behind the kicks.

Sienna let out a nervous laugh. 'I guess they're beginning to get impatient. There can't be much room left in there now.'

The sonographer packed away some of her equipment. 'Five weeks to go? That's when it starts to get really uncomfortable. Watch out for some sleepless nights.' She gave Sienna a wink. 'I'll go and let Oliver know that everything is fine while you two get ready.'

Sienna shook her head. 'Yeah, thanks for that, Dawn. More sleepless nights. Just what I need.'

'You haven't been sleeping?'

She'd swung her legs off the trolley and was about to pull her scrub top back down. She looked up at him. 'You might not remember, Sebastian, but I like to sleep on my stomach—' she stared down '—and the munchkin is making it a bit difficult.'

She went to pull her top down and he put his hand over hers. The baby was still kicking. *His* baby was still kicking. 'Can you wait a minute?'

He bent down, kneeling until his head was just opposite her stomach. He watched her skin closely for each tiny punch or kick. He couldn't stop the smile. 'It's totally random. You never know where the next one will be.' He looked up at her. 'What does it feel like?'

She didn't answer for a few seconds. She was watching him with a strange look in her eyes. Eventually she stretched forward and took his hand, pressing his palm to her stomach. 'Feel for yourself.'

Sienna's skin felt different than he remembered. It was stretched tight, slightly shiny. There were no visible stretch marks, nothing that made it anything but a beautiful sight.

There. A little kick beneath his hand again.

He laughed and pulled it back. The kicks kept coming so he put both hands on her stomach. He felt something else, something bigger beneath his hand, and Sienna gave a little groan. 'What was that?'

She shook her head. 'I think that might have been a somersault. It certainly felt like it.' She placed her hands next to his and leaned back a little. 'Here, I think this is one of the shoulders. The baby's head should be down by now and it looked that way in the scan. But they can still turn if they want to. It's just not that comfortable when they do.'

Her belly felt warm. And the life contained within it was just a wonder to him.

He hadn't known it would feel like this. He didn't know it *could* feel like this. And this wasn't just about the baby. He couldn't imagine ever feeling this way about Theresa if she'd carried his child. This was about Sienna too.

'Do you have a picture?'

She frowned. 'Of what?'

'Of our baby when you got the first scan. Most people get a picture, don't they?'

She looked surprised but gave a nod. 'Yes, of course I have. It's in my bag.'

'Can I see it?'

She looked around and then shook her head. 'It's in my bag. It's in the locker room. I'll get it as soon as we get the go-ahead to leave.'

He gave what looked like a resigned nod as he stood back up and lifted his hands from her stomach. It surprised her how much she wished he'd left them there. So many things were surprising her about Sebastian.

This was all about the baby. Not about her. She had to try and put her feelings and emotions in a box and keep them there. The irony of that at Christmas time almost killed her.

She could imagine the box, with all her hopes and dreams of a fairy-tale true-love romance for her, Sebastian and the baby all wrapped in glittering red paper and silver foil sitting under her beautiful Christmas tree just waiting to be opened.

Something sank deep inside her. Reality check time.

Sebastian was interested in the baby. Yes, he'd made a few gestures towards her. But no more than she would expect from a well-brought-up prince, looking after the mother-to-be of his child.

She almost laughed out loud. Exactly how many princes did she know?

She didn't even want to admit the security she felt when he was next to her. She didn't want to acknowledge the fact that, the more he hung around, the more she lost a little piece of her heart to him each day.

She couldn't admit that. She just couldn't.

She wouldn't be her mother. The woman who'd spent her whole life with a man that had never really loved her. That wasn't a life. That wasn't a relationship.

If she'd learned anything from her parents it was that sometimes it actually was better if parents didn't stay together. The tortured strain of living in that household had become unbearable.

And although she hated her father for his actions, with her adult brain she might actually understand, just a little.

Maybe if they'd separated much earlier, she might actually have enjoyed a different kind of relationship with her parents. One where they both had the life they wanted, and she fitted around it. But would that have been any fairer to a child than the life she'd had?

Sebastian pulled his phone from his pocket. 'What do you want to eat?'

She pulled her scrub top down quickly. 'Chinese. Hong-Kong-style chicken with noodles.'

He nodded towards the door. 'Give me a minute. I'll make the call and we'll pick it up on the way home.'

The room had felt claustrophobic for a few minutes there. Once he'd felt the kick from his baby, once he'd seen his baby's heartbeat on the screen, it had all become so real.

What had started from the first second he'd seen Sienna McDonald pregnant with his child, continued with her independence and snarkiness, been embodied by her vulnerability and the kiss they'd shared and culminated in feeling his baby kick after she'd collapsed, had just all built to the tornado of seeing that flickering heartbeat and touching the stomach of the woman who currently held all his dreams.

His head just couldn't sort out where he was. Oliver had hinted at signs of love. Did his friend even know what he was talking about? The guy was running around in a pink-tinged cloud.

The conversation with his mother this morning would have poured *Titanic*-icy waters over even the most embraced by love, soul and spirit.

Duty. The word sent prickles down his spine.

He hated it. But he actually agreed. It was his duty to marry Sienna and make this child the rightful heir to the kingdom of Montanari.

He'd been brought up to believe that duty was more important than anything. It was hard to shake that off.

But the feelings he was having deep inside about this baby and Sienna? Duty didn't even come near them. These feelings were entirely different.

They penetrated his heart, his soul, his very essence.

They felt more essential than breathing.

He closed his eyes as the call connected and he placed the order in the calmest voice possible. A few people strolled past him in the corridor. As he opened his eyes again it was clear they recognised him. The TV reporters outside meant that any chance of privacy he and Sienna had was gone for now.

Something else flashed into his head—the other secret arrangements he'd made today. He just had no idea if they'd actually been pulled off. He made a quick call—sighing with relief when it ended.

Sienna appeared at the doorway with a smiling Oliver. Sebastian blinked. He hadn't even noticed him appearing. 'Take her home, feed her and don't let her come back until she's ready to deliver this baby,' he said. 'Let's go for the due date—twenty-eighth of January will be fine.'

Sienna looked a little more relaxed. 'Let me get changed. I'll just be a few minutes,' she said as she disappeared into the locker room a few doors down the corridor.

Sebastian looked at Oliver. He trusted his friend. He trusted his expertise. 'Everything okay?'

Oliver nodded. 'Everything is fine. She's had a good pregnancy. Her blood pressure is fine. But the truth is, she's thirty-five weeks. She could deliver now, she could deliver two weeks after her due date. We never know these things.' He paused. 'Are you going to be around?'

He didn't hesitate. 'Count on it.'

Oliver held out his hand towards him. 'Good. I'll see you soon.'

Sebastian shook his friend's hand. 'Can you tell Sienna I'll get the car and wait for her at the side door? It might be easier than having to face the paparazzi when we cross the car park.'

Five minutes later he was waiting right at the door in his DB5. He'd always loved this car but it wasn't exactly inconspicuous. They might be at the side of the hospital right now, but as soon as he tried to pull out of the car park, they would be spotted.

Sienna came out of the door a few minutes later, her hood over her head. She climbed into the car and closed the door. 'Oh, well,' she sighed. 'That's two cars I've abandoned in the car park now. The broken-down one and the hire car from this morning.'

Sebastian shrugged. 'Leave me to deal with it. Don't worry. Let's just get you home.'

He wanted some privacy. He wanted a chance to get her away from all this and talk about the things they should be talking about.

He stopped at the Chinese restaurant—would his stomach ever recover from this take-away food?—and collected their meal, before turning ten minutes later into Sienna's street.

She let out a gasp.

If he'd known she was going to be unwell, he probably wouldn't have put all the plans in place that he had this morning. But it was too late now.

It was all done.

Her eyes widened as the car drew closer to her house. Everything was just as he'd asked for. A large Norway spruce had been transported to her garden and covered with multicoloured twinkling lights.

Icicle lights had been hung from the eaves of her house and stars around her two large bay windows.

She put her hand to her mouth as they pulled up directly outside. She still hadn't said a word but the expres-

sion on her face said it all. 'Wait until you see the back.'
He smiled.

As they walked in the entrance hall he kept one hand
around her waist, leading her straight past the nursery and
down to the back door. He unlocked it and held it open.

It couldn't have been more perfect.

It didn't exactly look like a Santa's Grotto—more like
a little Christmas paradise. He'd added lights to the rest of
the trees and bushes. A heater next to her carved wooden
seat.

The light-up reindeers and penguins from the nearby
garden centre had been transported to her back garden.
And to make it even more perfect the whole garden was
dusted with snow, which was falling in large, thick flakes.

He kept his arm around her. 'Is it what you imagined?'

Her eyes were bright as she turned towards him. 'Oh,
it's even better than I imagined. I thought it would be
twenty years before it looked like this.' Her smile lit up
her whole face.

He let out the breath he'd been holding, waiting to see
what her reaction would be. He'd wanted to do something to make her happy. She'd already told him she loved
Christmas and this was the first time they would be together at Christmas.

He was praying it wouldn't be the last.

Showering her with expensive gifts would have been
easy. But he already knew that would make little impact
on Sienna.

He had to know what was important to her. And this
was part of the little bit of herself that she'd revealed to
him.

He only hoped the rest would go down so well.

He steered her back inside. 'Let's get this Chinese food
before it gets too cold. And I've something else to show
you.'

The words were casual but obviously sparked a memory in her brain. 'Oh, the nursery. You've painted it, haven't you? Let me see what it looks like.'

She walked quickly back inside the house, striding along the corridor enthusiastically. She flicked the switch at the doorway and stepped inside.

Now, he really did hold his breath again. Had he overstepped the mark?

She must have already had a vision in her head for how she wanted the nursery to look—he only hoped he'd captured that invisible picture.

She made a little noise—a sort of strangled sound. Was that good? Or bad?

Then she walked straight over to the new, specially carved oak cot. Ducks and bunnies were carved on both the outside ends of the cot and along the bottom bar. She ran her hand along the grain of the wood.

He heard her intake of breath. He'd taken the step of making up the cot with the bed linen she'd already bought. But along with the pale yellow walls, and the curtains that had almost been the death of him, he thought the new furniture fitted well.

She opened the new matching wardrobe and chest of drawers.

He'd replaced all the furniture she'd bought with hand-carved pale oak furniture. It was all exactly the same style, just a different quality with a price tag that most people couldn't afford. That, plus the on-the-day delivery, would have made the average man wince. But Sebastian didn't care. He wanted the best for Sienna. The best for their baby.

She let out a little laugh at the crumpled border in the corner of the room. Darn it. He'd forgotten to throw it away.

He couldn't help himself. 'What do you think? Do you like it?'

She stood for a few minutes, her eyes taking in the

contents of the room. He'd even added something extra, buying her a special cream nursing chair with a little table and lamp, and placed it in the corner of the room.

She walked back over to him, shaking her head slowly until she was just under his nose. Her eyes were glazed with tears when she looked up and his stomach constricted.

'I don't like it,' she said slowly, before opening her hands out and turning around. 'I love it! It's perfect. It just looks exactly as I'd imagined.'

'It is?'

'Yes!' She flung her arms around his neck. 'I can't believe you've done this all in one day. How did you manage?' Her hands were still around his neck but she pulled back a little. 'Did you have help?' She looked a little suspicious.

'The nursery was all me. The furniture came assembled. As for the outside decorations—I left very specific instructions.'

She raised her eyebrows. 'You can actually do some DIY?'

He laughed. 'Remember, I went to university with Oliver. The man that can barely wire a plug. So, yes, I can use a screwdriver and a paint roller.'

She was staring up at him with those light brown eyes. There was definite sparkle there.

'You did good,' she said simply.

'I did better than good,' he whispered. 'I found you.'

Her eyes widened and her lips parted a little. 'But you didn't mean to.' She glanced downwards. 'You didn't mean for this to happen.'

He shook his head. 'Neither did you. But this was always meant to happen, Sienna. I believe it. I was meant to meet you. You were meant to meet me. *We* were meant to be. This baby was meant to be. The more I see you every day, the more I can't imagine spending a single day without you.'

'But how can that be, Seb? How can that happen? I live here. You're part of a royal family in Montanari. You're the Prince, and one day you'll be the King. Somehow, I don't think I fit the job description.'

He shook his head. 'You don't get it, do you? It's up to me to think about the job description. And for me it's obvious. There's only one person I want by my side. Montanari needs to bring itself into the twenty-first century. A queen and royal mother that's a neonatal cardiothoracic surgeon? An independent, educated woman who is dedicated to her job? How can that be a bad thing? Why on earth would I ask you to give that up? I couldn't be more proud of the job that you do. I couldn't be more proud of the fact you came to Montanari to train our surgeons. I watched you in action today, Sienna. I don't think I've ever seen anything I admire more. You couldn't be more perfect if you tried.'

'I couldn't?' She looked stunned—as if it were the last thing she'd expected him to say. She looked as if she was about to say something else but he cut her off. He dropped a kiss on her perfect lips. Truth was, he'd thought about nothing else all day. She tasted sweet and as he kissed her and his fingers tangled through her blonde hair the fruity aroma from her shampoo swept around them. His hands went from her hair, to her shoulders and down her back.

He could feel their baby between them. It was stopping him getting as close as he'd like to. He intertwined his fingers with hers. 'Come here,' he whispered and pulled her through to the main lounge, sitting down on the swallow-you-up sofa and drawing her towards him.

She hesitated for the slightest second before moving forward and sitting astride him on the sofa. She looked at him for the longest time then finally lifted one hand and brushed her knuckles gently against the emerging shadow on his jawline. 'I don't know what to make of you, Seb,' she said in a throaty voice. 'I don't know what to make of any of this.'

He ran a finger down the bare skin on her arm. 'Tell me what you want.'

She shook her head. He saw the little shiver go up her spine as he ran his finger down her arm again. It was the gentlest of touches. The lightest of touches. They'd been intimate before. They'd been passionate before.

But not like this.

His hands settled on her stomach, feeling the baby lying under her skin. It seemed to be settled in one position. 'Do you think our baby is sleeping?' He smiled.

She arched her back, her stomach and breasts getting even closer. 'I hope so,' she murmured. 'But doubtless as soon as I go to bed they'll wake back up again. I think our baby is going to be a night owl and I have to warn you—' she leaned forward and whispered in his ear '—us Scots girls can get very crabbit when we have no sleep.'

He caught a strand of her hair and twisted it around one finger. 'Don't sell yourself short, Sienna. I seem to remember a couple of occasions when you managed quite well without sleep.' He released the strand of hair and let his hands brush against her full breasts then settle on her waist.

She closed her eyes and let out a little moan. Her hands pressed against his chest, her fingers coming into contact with the tiny hairs at the nape of his neck. He caught his breath. This was becoming more than he could have imagined. His body started to react.

Sienna smiled down at him. 'You like this? When I'm tired? Have an aching back? And, even though I haven't checked yet, probably puffy feet?'

'I think you're perfect just the way you are,' he said simply. He put his hands on her stomach again. 'Pregnant.

Not pregnant.' He lifted his hands higher. 'Big boobs. Small boobs. Swollen feet. Not swollen feet.'

'I'm not a queen-in-waiting, Seb.' She shook her head slowly. 'I've never wanted to be.'

'You want the fairy tale. I can give you that.'

She closed her eyes for a second. 'You can give me the palace, the lifestyle, the people.' She pressed her hand against her heart. 'But what's in here? You need some-one who wants to live that life. I don't think that can ever be me.'

He put his hands on her thighs. 'But our baby will be the heir. That's written in the stars, Sienna. You can't wipe that away. I want our child to grow up loving the country that they will eventually rule. I want them to respect and appreciate the people that live there. I want the people of Montanari to love my family.'

He sucked in a deep breath. 'We should get married, Sienna. Think about it. We could make this work between us, and we could make this work as a family. Don't dis-miss me out of hand like you did before. Take your time. Think about how we both want to bring our child up. Think about what's important to you.'

What was important to her? Right now her head was so muddled she couldn't think straight. Her breath had stalled somewhere in her throat. He had passion in his eyes when he spoke about Montanari. Just like the flicker she'd seen in his eyes a few moments earlier when they'd been locked in an embrace.

But when she'd pressed her hand against her heart, he just hadn't picked up what she'd meant. She wanted to know what was in *there*. In that heart that was beat-ing in his chest.

Because no matter how hard she'd tried to fight it, she'd developed feelings for Sebastian. Feelings that she just couldn't be sure were reciprocated.

He'd focused on part of her fairy tale—but not the most important part. The part that meant she and her Prince loved each other with their whole hearts. The part that she just couldn't live without.

Sebastian lit up her heart in a way she didn't want to admit. She couldn't put herself out there to find her love dismissed. The stakes were too high.

He was talking about Montanari. Making it sound as if that should be the place they have a future together. Lots of women might love that. A prince. A castle. A new baby.

But if he really knew her, he would know that a vital component was missing.

Something gripped her. Something tight, knocking her breath temporarily from her lungs. 'Oh.' She held out one hand towards Sebastian and gripped the other around her stomach.

'Sienna? Is everything okay?' He shifted position, moving her from his knees and onto the sofa.

She was stunned. 'I don't know. I've never felt anything like that before.'

His eyes widened. 'You don't think that...' His voice tailed off. His face paled.

She was still catching her breath, wondering where the sharp pain had come from and hoping against hope it was something else entirely.

She stood up and started pacing. Sebastian was right by her side. This couldn't be happening. It was too early. She was only thirty-five weeks.

'You had that fall today—do you think it could be anything to do with that?'

Sweat started to break out on her skin. She looked from side to side. 'I'm not ready. I'm not ready for this. I should have another five weeks to think about this—to make plans.'

Tears prickled in her eyes. 'It's Christmas Eve. I was

planning on watching some TV and wrapping some final presents.'

Sebastian glanced at the enormous pile under the tree. 'You have more?'

He slid his arm around her waist and she batted him on the chest. 'Stop it.'

He turned her around to face him.

One tear slid down her cheek. He brushed it away with his finger. 'Should I phone an ambulance? Oliver told me to phone if I was worried. Should I do that now?' He was babbling. The Prince was babbling.

It felt like an out-of-body experience. He'd always seemed so in control. Or at least he wanted the world to think that.

'Will our baby be okay? Will you be okay?'

Another tear slipped down her cheek. 'I'm thirty-five weeks today. They might give me some steroids to bring the baby's lungs on, and baby might be a little slow to feed. But there's nothing else we should worry about.' She slid her hands across her stomach. 'But, if I think I'm not ready, then I know for sure that you're *definitely* not ready.' Her heart started thudding in her chest. She'd operated on tiny babies. She'd been doing it for years and years. But she'd never actually *had* a baby before. And the truth was, she was scared.

Scared of what could lie ahead.

She broke out of his hold and started pacing again. 'I had everything planned. I knew what was happening. Then—' she turned to face him and held up her hand '—you come along with your kingdom and your press team, and your let's-twin-our-hospitals, and you've just confused me, stressed me—'

'You're saying all this is my fault?' She could see the pain and confusion written all over his face.

Then—*whoomph*. This time it was stronger. This time it made her bend double. *'Oohh.'*

'Sienna?'

Her hands went back to her stomach; she slid them under her loose top. This time there was no mistake. She could feel the tightening under the palms of her hands.

Sebastian strode towards her just as something else happened.

Something wet and warm. All over her living-room oak floor.

She closed her eyes.

'Is that what I think it is?'

She nodded and looked down at the darkening wet stain on her trousers. Thank goodness they were pale—otherwise she'd be panicking she couldn't tell the colour of the liquid. This liquid was clear.

'Start the car, Sebastian.'

'You don't want an ambulance?' There was an edge of desperation to his voice.

'On Christmas Eve? In the Cotswolds? We can get there much quicker on our own.'

In less than five minutes she'd changed and thrown some things into a bag; another contraction slowed her down. The front door was wide open, showing the snow-covered garden outside. Sebastian was standing with his jacket on, pacing at the front door. The car was running.

'Let's go. I'll lock up.'

She let him guide her out to the waiting car.

She groaned as he climbed in next to her. 'This wasn't what I imagined for Christmas Eve.'

He cleared his throat and shot her a nervous glance. 'Actually, I can't think of anything more perfect.'

'What?'

'We're having a baby.'

She took a deep breath and tried to clear her head. Focus. All she could focus on right now was the fact they were about to meet their child. She had to have some head space. She had to be in a good place.

'Truth is, I'm a tiny bit terrified,' she whispered, staring out at the snow-topped houses and glistening trees. Next time she came back here she'd have a baby with her.

His hand closed over hers. 'Then, let's be terrified together.'

CHAPTER SIX

'IT'S A GIRL!'

'It is?' Sienna and Sebastian spoke in unison.

Ella, the midwife in the labour suite and Oliver's new fiancée, smiled up at them as she lifted the baby up onto Sienna's chest. 'It certainly is. Congratulations, Mum and Dad, meet your beautiful new daughter.'

Sebastian couldn't speak. He was in awe. First with Sienna and her superwoman skills at pushing their baby out, and now with the first sight of his daughter.

She looked furious with her introduction to the world. Ella gave a little wipe of her face and body as she lay on her mother's chest and she let out an angry squeal. Ella laughed. 'Yip, she's here. Have you two thought of a name yet?'

A name.

His brain was a complete blank.

He still couldn't process a thought. He could have missed this. He could have missed this once-in-a-lifetime magical moment. That couldn't even compute in his brain right now.

His daughter had a few fine blonde hairs on her head the same shade as her mother. He had no idea about her eyes as her face was still screwed up.

'She just looks so...so...big,' he said in wonder.

Sienna let out an exhausted laugh. 'Imagine if I'd

reached forty weeks.' She looked in awe too as she ran her hand over her daughter's bare back. 'She's not big. She's not big at all. Ella will weigh her in a few minutes. But let's just wait.'

Sebastian shook his head as Ella busied herself around them. 'I have no idea about a name.'

He wanted to laugh out loud. For years in Montanari, the royal family were only allowed to pick from a specific list of approved names. His mother still thought that should be the case.

Sienna turned to him. 'I think we should cause a scandal. Let's call our daughter something wild—like Zebedee, or Thunder.'

Now he did laugh out loud. 'I think my mother would have a fit. It's almost worth it just to see the expression on her face.'

Sienna was still stroking their daughter's skin. 'Actually, I do have a name in mind.'

'You do?'

She nodded. 'I'd like to call my daughter after my aunt. She was fabulous with me when I was growing up and looked after me a lot when my mother and father were busy.'

She didn't say the other words that were circulating in her brain. *Or when my mother and father couldn't be bothered.*

It was an unfair thought and she knew that. But she was emotional and hormonal right now. She'd just done the single most important thing she would ever do in this life.

Her parents had never mistreated her. They just hadn't been that interested. Her aunt had been different. She'd always been good to her.

'What's your aunt called?'

Their daughter started to stir, squirming around her chest and making angry noises. 'Margaret,' she said quietly. 'My aunt was called Margaret.'

It was the last thing he'd really expected. A traditional name from an untraditional woman.

'Really?'

She looked up and met his gaze. Her hair was falling out of the clip she'd brought with her for the labour. Her pyjama top was open at the front to allow their baby on her skin.

He'd never seen anything more beautiful.

He'd never seen anything he could love more.

He blinked.

It was like a flash in the sky above him. He'd been trying to persuade Sienna to give him a chance for all the wrong reasons. He'd always liked her. The attraction had never waned.

But duty still ran through his veins. In his head he'd been trading one duty marriage for another. But Sienna had bucked against that.

She demanded more. She *deserved* more.

And it was crystal clear to him why.

He didn't want to have to persuade her to be with him. It was important to him that she wanted to be with him, as much as he wanted to be with her.

And she'd need to be prepared for the roller coaster that was his mother.

Sienna was more than a match for his mother—of that he had no doubt. But sparks could fly for a while in the palace.

His father—he was pretty sure he would love her as soon as she started talking in her Scottish accent and telling it exactly as it was.

Ella gave him a nudge. 'Do you want to hold your daughter? Sienna's work isn't quite finished yet.'

Sebastian gave an anxious nod as Ella first took their daughter from Sienna, weighed her, put a little nappy on her and supplied a pink blanket to wrap their daughter in. Two minutes later she gestured for him to sit in a comfortable seat she pulled out from the wall. 'Once she's delivered the placenta, we'll do another few checks. Oliver will arrive any minute. And I'll arrange for some food for you both. After all that hard work you'll both be exhausted. We have plenty to spare in the labour ward.'

He hardly heard a word. He was too focused on the squirming little bundle that had just been placed in his arms. The smile seemed to have permanently etched itself onto his face. It would be there for ever.

Her face was beautiful. He stroked her little cheek. The wrinkles on her forehead started to relax and her eyes blinked open a few times. He'd been told that all babies' eyes started as blue. His daughter's were dark blue; they could change to either green like his, or brown like her mother's. The blonde hair on her head was downy, it already had a fluff-like appearance and he could see the tiny little pulse throbbing at the soft centre in the top of her head.

He couldn't have imagined anything more wonderful. Less than twenty minutes ago this tiny little person had been inside Sienna, a product of their weekend of passion in Montanari. She might not have been planned but, without a doubt, it was the best thing that had ever happened to him.

They were the best thing that had ever happened to him.

Sebastian shook his head. 'Sienna did all the hard work. I was just lucky enough to be here.' He lifted one hand that had been thoroughly crushed for the last few hours. 'I might need a plaster cast, but I can take it.'

Ella smiled and went back to work.

By morning Sienna was back in a fresh bed with a few hours' sleep, showered and eating tea and toast. Margaret had finally opened her eyes and was watching him very suspiciously—as if she were still trying to work out what had happened.

Oliver came into the room to check Sienna over. 'Trust you not to hold on. You never did have any patience. I'm going to relish the fact that your daughter has obviously inherited your genes. Good luck with that, Sebastian,' he joked. He put his arm around Ella. 'Seriously, guys, congratulations. I'm delighted for you.'

He gave a nod towards the door. 'Word travels fast around here. There are a few more people who want to say hello.'

Ella looked to Sienna. 'How do you feel about that?'

Sienna glanced over at Sebastian, cradling their baby girl. 'Tell them to come in now. I want to try and give our daughter another feed. I think she'll get cranky quite soon.'

Ella gave a nod and Annabelle and Max, and Charlie and Juliet crowded into the room. Sebastian held his precious daughter while they all fawned over her, kissing Sienna and congratulating them both.

Charlie nodded at the clock on the wall. 'If you'd just held off for another few hours you could have had our first Christmas baby.'

Christmas. Of course. He'd almost forgotten this was Christmas Day now.

Sienna looked shocked for a second then threw back her head and laughed. 'Darn it! I completely forgot about that!' She looked suspicious for a second. 'Did any of you have a bet on me for the Christmas baby?'

Juliet shook her head. 'Not one of us. No one expected you to deliver this early.' She leaned over Sebastian's shoulder. 'But your girl looks a good weight for thirty-five weeks. What was she?'

'Five pounds, thirteen ounces,' answered Sebastian. Margaret's weight would be imprinted on his brain for ever.

Just as this moment would. Now he'd held his daughter, he didn't ever want to let her go.

* * *

Sienna's stomach grumbled loudly as she finished the toast. 'Sorry,' she laughed to her visitors.

She was trying to pay attention to them—she really was. But she couldn't help but be a little awed by the expression on Sebastian's face at the bottom of the bed. He was fascinated by their daughter. He could barely take his eyes off her.

She felt the same. She was sure she wouldn't sleep a wink tonight just watching the wonder of her little daughter's chest rising and falling.

'Here.' Annabelle thrust a little gift towards her. 'Something for your gorgeous girl.'

Sienna was amazed. 'Where on earth did you get a present on Christmas Day?'

Annabelle gave her a wink. 'I have friends in high places.'

Sienna felt her heart squeeze. Annabelle was the most gracious of friends. Sienna knew how hard she and Max had tried for a baby of their own; it had eventually broken down their marriage until their reconciliation a few weeks ago. And yet here they both were, celebrating with her and Sebastian over their unexpected arrival.

She opened the gift bag and pulled out the presents. A packet of pale pink vests, a tiny pink Babygro that had a pattern like a giant Christmas present wrapped with a bow, matching tiny pink socks and a pale pink knitted hat with a pom-pom bigger than Margaret's head. She laughed out loud.

She'd bought a few things for the baby's arrival but, with the rush, she'd forgotten to bring them from home. 'Oh, Annabelle, thank you, these are perfect. Now we have something to take our daughter home in.'

Sebastian looked up quickly, pulling the little bundle closer to his chest.

'We're going home?'

Oliver shook his head. 'No, sorry. Not tonight. The paediatrician wants to be sure that Margaret is feeding without any problems. I'm afraid you'll need to spend your daughter's first Christmas in hospital.' He glanced at Ella. 'Don't worry, the staff here are great. They'll make sure you're well looked after.'

Sienna sagged back against her pillows. 'I don't care. She's here, and she's healthy. That's all I care about. I might love Christmas. But it can wait.'

Max looked around the room. 'Let's say our good-byes, folks, and leave the new parents with their baby.' He rolled his eyes. 'Some of us have Christmas dinners to make.' Right on cue Margaret gave out a scream that made Sebastian jump.

Everyone laughed. They quickly gave Sienna and Sebastian hugs and left the room. Sienna pushed the table across the bed away and held out her hands. 'I think she must be hungry. Let's see if she's ready for a feed.'

Ella came back a few minutes later and helped Sienna position their daughter to feed. The first feed had been a little difficult. She gave Sienna a cautious smile. 'Sometimes babies that are born a little early take a bit longer to learn how to suck. They all get there eventually, but it can take a bit of perseverance.'

Sienna's eyes were on their daughter. 'It seems Margaret doesn't like to wait for anything. As a first-time mum I expected to have one of those twenty-hour labours.'

Ella shrugged. 'You might have done, if you'd reached forty weeks. You might be quite tall, but your pelvis is pretty neat.' She smiled up as Margaret latched on. 'Just remember that for baby number two.'

Almost in unison Sebastian and Sienna's heads turned to each other and their wide-eyed gazes met, followed by a burst of laughter.

Sienna waved her hand at Ella. 'Shame on you, Midwife O'Brien, mentioning another baby when the first one is barely out. You haven't even given me time yet to be exhausted!'

A warm feeling spread throughout Sebastian. His daughter's little jaw was moving furiously as she tried to feed. Sienna seemed calmer than he'd ever seen her, stroking her daughter's face and talking gently to her.

Ella looked up and met his contented gaze with a smile. 'I'll leave you folks alone for a while. Come and find me when you want some food, Sebastian. I take it you're staying all day?'

'Can I?' He hadn't even had a chance to discuss with Sienna what happened next.

Ella nodded. 'Of course. All new dads are welcome to stay with mum and baby. This is Teddy's. We're hardly going to throw you out on Christmas Day. This is a time for families.' She winked and left the room.

Sienna lifted her head and looked at the clock. 'I can't believe we had her on Christmas Eve. It all just seems so unreal. I thought I would spend today lying on my sofa, like a beached whale, watching TV and eating chocolates.'

A special smile spread across her face. 'I thought I wouldn't see you until next Christmas,' she whispered to their daughter. 'I'd planned to buy you one of those Christmas baubles for the tree with your name, date of birth and baby's first Christmas on it. I guess you've ruined that now, missy.'

Although she loved Christmas dearly, she'd been edgy about this year. Worried about what the future would hold for her and her baby. Sebastian showing up had brought everything to the forefront.

He was sitting in a chair at the end of the bed. Ever since her first labour pain he'd been great. After that first flicker of panic he'd been as solid as a rock. He'd rubbed her back, massaged her shoulders, and given her words of constant encouragement during the few short hours she'd been in labour. All without a single word of preparation. They hadn't even got around to the discussion about whether he would attend the labour or not.

He hadn't even blinked when she'd turned the air blue on a few occasions, and chances were he'd never regain the feeling in his right hand. She hadn't had time to think about whether he should be there or not. And the look on his face when he'd first set eyes on their daughter had seared right into her soul.

She'd never seen a look of love like it. Ever.

And that burned in ways she couldn't even have imagined.

'Seb?'

'Yes?' He stood up. 'Do you need something?'

She shook her head, trying to keep her wavering emotions out of her voice. 'I wouldn't ever have kept her from you. I would have told you about her as soon as she arrived,' she said quietly. She blinked back the tears.

She saw him swallow and press his lips together briefly. They were both realising he could have missed this moment. Missed the first sight of his daughter. Was it really fair that she'd even contemplated that?

She licked her lips. 'Your mother—what has she said about all this?'

For a few seconds he didn't meet her gaze. 'She's disappointed in me. That I didn't do things in a traditional way. She thinks I treated Theresa badly. She hasn't quite grasped the fact that Theresa was marrying me out of duty—not of love.' His eyes met hers and he gave a rueful smile. 'I think it's just as well I'm an only child. She would have tried to disown me at the beginning of the week because of the scandal I've caused.'

'But what does that mean? What does that mean for you, for me and for Margaret?'

Something washed over her, a wave of complete protectiveness towards her daughter. She wasn't going to let anyone treat Margaret as if she were a scandal—as if she weren't totally loved and wanted.

Sebastian sat down on the edge of the bed next to her and wrapped his arm around her shoulders. 'It means that I'll have to phone the Queen and tell her about her new granddaughter. She thought there would be a few weeks to try and manipulate the press. I guess our daughter had other ideas.'

The thought of the press almost chilled her. 'Can we keep her to ourselves for just a few more hours?' She hated the way that her voice sounded almost pleading. But this was their daughter, their special time. She wasn't ready to share it with the world just yet.

'Of course.' He smiled. His fingers threaded through the hair at the nape of her neck. It was a movement of comfort, of reassurance.

Her hormones were on fire. Her heart felt as if it had swollen in her chest, first with the love for her daughter, and next for the rush of emotions she'd felt towards Seb in the last few hours.

Everything that had happened between them had crystallised for her. His sexy grin, twinkling eyes and smart comments. The way his gaze sometimes just meshed with hers. The tingling of her skin when he touched her.

The way that at times she just felt so connected to him.

All she felt right now was love. Maybe she was a fool to expect more than he already offered. She could live in Montanari. He had no expectations of her giving up work—she could work with the staff she'd trained in their specialist hospital.

Margaret could be brought up in a country she would ultimately one day rule. And although that completely terrified Sienna, it was a destiny that couldn't be ignored.

Did it matter if Sebastian didn't love her with his whole

heart? He respected her—she knew that. And he would love their daughter.

This might be simpler if she didn't already know the truth.

She loved Sebastian. She'd probably loved him since that first weekend—she just hadn't allowed her brain to go there because of the betrayal that she'd felt. How hard would it be to live with a man, to stand by his side and know that he didn't reciprocate the love she felt for him?

Could she keep that hidden away? Would she be able to live with a neutral face in place in order to give their daughter the life she should have?

She pressed her lips together. Having just a little part of the man she loved might be enough. Having to look at those sexy smiles and twinkling eyes on a daily basis wouldn't exactly be a hardship.

And if he kept looking at her the way he did now, she could maybe hope for more. Another child might not be as far off the agenda as she'd initially thought.

She looked up at those forest-green eyes and her whole world tipped upside down. 'Your mother's name—it's Grace, isn't it?'

He nodded but looked confused.

She stared back down to her daughter's pale, smooth skin. 'I've had the name Margaret in my head for a while. But I had never even considered any middle names.' She looked up at him steadily. 'That seems a bit of a royal tradition, isn't it?'

He nodded again. She could see the calculations flying behind his eyes. 'What do you think about giving Margaret a middle name?'

The edges of his lips started to turn upwards. 'Seriously?'

She nodded, feeling surer than before. 'I chose our

daughter's first name. We never even had that discussion. How do you feel about choosing a middle name?'

She'd already planted the seed. Maybe the Queen wouldn't hate her quite as much as she imagined.

He looked serious for a second. 'Our family has a tradition of more than one middle name—how do you feel about that?'

She frowned. 'You mean you're not just Sebastian?'

He laughed. 'Oh, no. I'm Sebastian Albert Louis Falco.'

She leaned back against him. 'Okay, tell me what you're thinking. Let's try some names for size.'

He took a few seconds. 'If you agree, I'd like to call our daughter Margaret Grace Sophia Falco.' He turned to face her. 'Unless, of course, you want to call her after your mother.'

Something panged inside her. But the tiny feelings of regret about her relationship with her parents had long since depleted over time. 'No. I'm happy with Margaret. I think it's safe to say that my mother will play her grandmother role from a distance.' She glanced at the clock. 'I'll let both my parents know in a while about their granddaughter. I doubt very much that either of them will visit.' She gave a sad kind of smile. 'I might get some very nice flowers, though.'

She looked down at Margaret again, who'd stopped feeding for now and seemed to have settled back to sleep. 'Who is Sophia?'

Seb smiled. 'My great-grandmother. In public, probably the most terrifying woman in the world. In private? The woman I always had the most fun with. She taught me how to cheat at every board and card game imaginable.'

Sienna couldn't help but smile. 'You mean that the Falco family actually had some rogues?'

He whispered in her ear. 'I'll show you the family archives. We had pirates, conquerors and knights. We even had a magician.' He leaned over her shoulder and touched their daughter's nose. 'Happy Christmas, Margaret, welcome to the Falco family.'

Sienna turned to face him just as his lips met hers. 'Thank you, Sienna. Thank you for the best Christmas present in the world.'

She reached up and touched the side of his face. Her head was spinning. He was looking at her in a way she couldn't quite interpret. Her heart wanted to believe that it was a look of love, a look of hope and admiration. He hadn't stopped smiling at her—and even though she knew she must look a mess, he was making her feel as if she were the most special woman on the planet.

'Thank you,' she whispered as her fingers ran across his short hair. 'We made something beautiful. We made something special. I couldn't be happier.'

'Me either,' he agreed as he pulled her closer and kissed her again.

CHAPTER SEVEN

HE'D HARDLY SLEPT. He hadn't wanted to leave the hospital last night, but both he and Sienna had been exhausted. She only ever cat-napped when he was in the room and he'd realised—even though he hadn't wanted to be apart from them—that it would be better if he let her spend the night with their daughter alone.

Not that she would have had much time. He'd left the hospital at midnight and was up again at six, pacing the floors in her house, itching to go and see her and Margaret again.

His mother's voice had been almost strangled when he'd phoned with the news. But after a few seconds of horror, she'd regained her composure and asked if Sienna and baby were healthy after the premature delivery. He'd assured her that they were.

When he'd told her the name of her new granddaughter there had first been a sigh of relief and then a little quiver in her voice. 'I'm surprised that such a modern woman picked such a traditional name. It's a lovely gesture, Sebastian. Thank you. When will we see the baby?'

He sent his mother some pictures of Margaret and told her he'd invited both Sienna and Margaret to join him in Montanari. He hoped and prayed that they would, but placated his mother with the easy opt out about travelling so soon after delivery and making sure that Margaret's little lungs would be fit to fly.

He stood in the middle of the yellow nursery that Sienna had dreamed of for her daughter. If she agreed to join him in Montanari he would recreate this room exactly the way it was—anything to keep her happy.

Things had been good yesterday. They'd been better than good. Sienna and Margaret were his family, and that was exactly how they felt to him. He couldn't imagine spending a single day without them. He'd had a special item shipped yesterday from the royal vault at Montanari. It was still dark outside but the twinkling lights from the Christmas tree across the hall glinted off the elegant ruby and diamond engagement ring in his hand. He hadn't mentioned this to his mother yet. But with Margaret's new middle names, it was only fitting that Sienna wear the engagement ring of his great-grandmother Sophia.

The two of them would have loved each other.

He'd meant to go back to his hotel last night but Sienna had asked him to collect the baby car seat from the house so they could be discharged today. Once he'd arrived back at her house he'd decided just to stay. It had seemed easier. He should have brought some of his clothes from the hotel, because this was where they would come back to in the first instance.

He hurried outside to his car. It didn't really matter what time it was—the hospital would let him in any time. He just wanted Sienna to have had a chance to rest.

As soon as he pulled up outside the hospital alarm bells started going off in his head. Every TV station with a van was parked near the entrance. Every reporter he'd ever met was talking into a camera.

Someone spotted his car. All he could hear was shrieks followed by the trampling of feet. He got out of the car in a hurry. One of the reporters thrust a newspaper towards him. 'Prince Sebastian. Tell us about your new arrival.'

'Congratulations. What have you called your daughter?'

They surrounded him. Security. He hadn't considered security for his daughter. He stared at the news headline in front of him.

A NEW PRINCESS FOR MONTANARI!

The questions came thick and fast.

His hand reached out and grabbed the paper. He hadn't agreed to a press release. He had discussed it with his team and they'd planned an announcement for later today, once he, Sienna and baby Margaret had left Teddy's.

How on earth did the press know about Margaret already? He looked a little closer and felt his ire rise. There was a picture of his daughter. *His daughter.* Wrapped in a pink blanket, clearly lying in her hospital cot. Who on earth had taken that?

He started to push his way through the crowd of reporters. He didn't manhandle anyone but he didn't leave them in any doubt that he would reach his destination.

'Prince Sebastian, what about Sienna McDonald, the baby's mother? Are you engaged? Are you planning a royal wedding?'

Right now, he wished he could answer yes. But it seemed premature. Even though things were good between them, he hadn't asked her again yet. But the enthusiasm being shown for the birth of the new Princess was more than a little infectious. These people would hang around all day. It would be smarter just to give them a quick comment—he could find out about that photo later.

He turned around and held up his hands. 'As you know, my daughter was born a little earlier than expected on Christmas Eve. Both mother and baby are doing well and...' he paused for a second as he searched for the words '...I'm looking forward to us all being a family together very soon. Our daughter's name is Prin-

cess Margaret Grace Sophia Falco,' he finished with before turning around and walking through the main doors
of the hospital.

The noise behind him reached a crescendo.

The length of his strides increased in his hurry to reach
Sienna and his daughter. His hand slid into his pocket
and he touched the ring again. The box had been too
bulky to fit in the pocket of his jeans. But the ring was
still safely there.

A few of the midwives gave him a nod as he walked
towards Sienna's room. It was only Boxing Day so the
decorations were still all in place and Christmas carols
played in the background.

Hopefully, by the end of today, he could make things
perfect for everyone.

Sienna felt cold. She had been ignoring the TV in the corner of the room and just concentrating on her baby. The
midwives were great. Margaret had decided to have an
episode of colic at three a.m. After half an hour, one of
the midwives had told Sienna to get some sleep and she'd
walk the corridor with Margaret. Sienna hadn't wanted
to let her baby out of her sight, but she'd been exhausted.
Two hours later she'd woken with a peaceful Margaret
wrapped in her pink blanket and back in her crib.

By that time, she'd wanted to get back up. She'd had
a bath to ease her aching back and legs, and fed and
changed Margaret. Once Sebastian arrived she was hoping they would get the all-clear to take Margaret home.

Something caught her attention. A few words from
the TV. Sebastian.

She looked up as the TV reporters camped outside
the hospital all set off at a run to interview Sebastian on
live TV.

She still couldn't understand how they knew about the
baby. No one she worked with or trusted would speak to

the press. Sebastian had said he would talk to her about a press release.

She smiled as she caught sight of him on camera. His hair was a little mussed up. He obviously hadn't taken time to fix it. His tanned skin sort of hid the tiredness she could see in his eyes. His leather jacket—still complete with yellow smudge—showed off his broad chest and his snug jeans caused her smile to broaden. Sebastian Falco. Was she really going to agree to what he'd suggested last night?

Sebastian was a seasoned pro when it came to paparazzi. He wouldn't speak to them.

But actually, he stopped.

Just like Sienna's heart.

They were all firing questions to him about Margaret. Asking him to confirm the birth and her name. Someone thrust a newspaper towards him and she saw the tic in the side of his jawline. Whatever was in that newspaper had made him angry.

Another voice cut above the rest. 'Prince Sebastian, what about Sienna McDonald, the baby's mother? Are you engaged? Are you planning a royal wedding?'

A prickle ran down her spine. How could he answer that? They hadn't even finished that discussion.

Something flickered across his face, the edges of his lips turned upwards. 'As you know, my daughter was born a little earlier than expected on Christmas Eve. Both mother and baby are doing well and...' he paused for a second as a smile spread across his face '...I'm looking forward to us all being a family together very soon. Our daughter's name is Princess Margaret Grace Sophia Falco.'

Her heart plummeted.

Oh, no. Oh, no. Did he realise how that looked?

Sure enough the reporters had a field day. A woman in a bright red coat swung around and announced straight into the camera. 'We have a royal engagement *and* a royal wedding! It seems that Dr Sienna McDonald is about to become the wife of Prince Sebastian and the future of Queen of Montanari.'

The woman's bright red lips seemed to move in synchrony with the other reporters all around her, talking into their respective cameras.

A chill swept across her skin. The woman seemed to think she'd got the scoop of the century. She held her hand up to the sign of the Royal Cheltenham hospital. 'Looks like Teddy's is going to have to find another cardiac baby surgeon.' She said the words with glee. 'Once Sienna gets to Montanari she will have no time to worry about being a doctor.'

Fury swept around her. How dared they? How dared any of them assume that she would give up her job, her house, her life?

The door swung open and Sebastian strode in with a smile. 'You're up? You're awake?' He was still carrying the newspaper that had been thrust at him in his hand. 'Great. We need to talk. We need to make decisions.'

'Haven't you already just made all those for me?' She walked right up to him. 'Who on earth do you think you are?'

He pulled back and glanced towards their sleeping bundle in the corner. 'What on earth are you talking about?'

She flung her hands up in the air. 'Oh, come on, Sebastian. You're not naïve. You've been doing this all your life. You know better than to get pulled into things.' She couldn't stop the build of fury in her chest.

He'd tricked her. He'd sweet-talked her. He'd used all that princely charm. All to get exactly what he wanted.

All to get his daughter back to Montanari.

Sebastian shook his head. 'What do you mean?' He tried to step around her—to get to Margaret.

Sienna stepped sideways—stopping his path. 'You

practically just announced to the world that we were getting married.'

His tanned face blanched. 'I didn't.' It sounded sort of strangled.

She pointed to the yellow tickertape-style news headline that had now appeared along the bottom of the TV screen.

Prince Sebastian to marry Dr Sienna McDonald, mother of their daughter.

He flinched. Then something else happened. The expression on his face changed. He reached down into his pocket. 'Sienna, I didn't say we were getting married.'

'No. But with a smile on your face you just said that we were all going to be a family together soon. You practically told them we'd be moving to Montanari with you!'

He put his hands on her shoulders. 'What's wrong with you? Calm down. After last night, I thought things were good between us. I thought that maybe we were ready to take the next step.' He glanced over her shoulder. 'The right step for us—and our baby.'

She shivered. She felt as if she were in a bad movie with the villain in front of her. 'You did this,' she croaked as she looked frantically back to Margaret.

'What?' Confusion reigned over his face.

'The leak. It was you.' She pushed him away from her, forgetting for a second about Margaret as she strode forward and lifted the discarded newspaper. The picture of their baby brought tears to her eyes. 'You did this?' She couldn't actually believe it. 'To get what you wanted, you actually gave them a picture of my daughter without my permission?'

She couldn't think straight at all. She was just overwhelmed with emotions and a huge distinctive mothering urge. She'd been tricked. Manipulated. By a man she'd let steal her heart.

He'd left last night after telling her things could work. He'd introduce her to the family. Margaret could be brought up in Montanari and they could all live together as a family. He'd let her think they'd embrace a new-style queen—even though it wasn't a title she'd wanted. She could continue with the job she loved.

Sebastian looked utterly confused and shook his head again. 'What on earth are you talking about?' He took the paper from her hand. 'You think I did this? Really? Why on earth would I do that? We talked about this last night.'

'Yes. You said you'd wait. You said we'd agree to a statement. But that obviously wasn't good enough for you. You're used to getting your own way, Sebastian. You're used to being in charge. You lied to me last night. I was wrong to trust you. You made me think you would consider my feelings in all this.' She swung her hand to the side. 'Instead, you let the world know about our baby.' Tears sprang to her eyes. 'This is my time with my baby, mine. I don't want to share her with the world. I'm not ready.' She shook her head as everything started to overwhelm her. He was just standing there, standing there looking stunned.

She kept shaking her head. Now that they'd started, the tears just kept on coming. She was angry at herself for crying. Angry that she was standing here in her ratty pyjamas, hair in a ponytail and pale skin telling the Prince she wouldn't stand for this behaviour. She wouldn't be manipulated into more or less giving up her life and her daughter.

She'd thought there might just actually be some hope for them both. They could reconnect the way they had in Montanari. The memories that she had of the place would stay with her for ever.

There had been moments—fragments—when they'd

captured that spark again. But she'd been a fool. She'd been living the fairy tale in her head. Why? Why would a prince ever love her?

Things shouldn't be like this. If she were telling him to leave, she should be doing it in some magnificent building, wearing an elegant dress, perfect make-up and her hair all coiffured. She should be looking a million dollars as she told the fairy-tale Prince he couldn't manipulate her or deceive her. That she would bring their daughter up here, rather than be promised a lifetime without love.

Because that was what it really came down to.

That was what she wanted. What she'd always wanted.

For Sebastian to love her, the way her heart told her she loved him.

The clarity in her brain made her turn on him.

'You've deceived me. You've deceived me right from the start. You've spent the last few days trying to sweet-talk me. Trying to persuade me to bring our daughter to Montanari. And now? You think if you just leak the story to the press, then give them some kind of coy smile, and tell them we're about to be a family—then that's it. A fait accompli.' She flung her hands in the air again. 'Well, no, Sebastian. No. I won't have it. I won't get trapped into a life I don't want. I won't bring Margaret up in a marriage with no love in it.'

If Sebastian had looked stunned before, now his mouth fell open. He stepped forward then froze as she continued to rant.

She pressed her hand to her heart as the tears streamed freely. 'I won't do it. I just won't. I've been there. I've already spent eighteen years in a relationship like that. A relationship where I was tolerated and not really loved.' She shook her head. 'Do you know what that feels like? Really? Do you honestly think I'd bring my daughter up in a relationship like that? It's not enough. Not nearly enough. I love you. You love her. But you don't love me.

I don't want a loveless marriage. I want a husband that will love and adore me.' She looked off into the corner as she tried to catch her breath.

'A husband that will look at me as though I'm the most important person in the world. A husband that will trust me enough to always talk to me. To always be truthful with me. To support me in the job that I've trained to do since I was eighteen.' She took a step towards Sebastian. Looking into the face of the man that she'd thought would love her as much as she loved him. Being here in front of him made her stomach feel as if it were twisting inside out. It was hurting like a physical pain. That was how much she wanted this dream to come true. That was how much she wanted to be loved by him. It felt like the ultimate betrayal.

'You lied to me,' she said with a shaking voice. 'You said Montanari was ready for a new kind of queen. A queen who had a career. A queen who worked. You said that could happen. But according to the world outside, the expectation is that I give it all up. My years and years of training don't count. They don't matter. Well, they matter to me. And the environment I bring my daughter up in matters to me. I want Margaret to feel respected. To know she should work hard. To know that money doesn't grow on trees and you have to earn a living.'

She kept her voice as strong as she could. 'Your plan didn't work, Sebastian. I won't marry you. We won't be coming to Montanari.'

Sebastian felt as if he'd been pulled up in a tornado and dumped out of the funnel into a foreign land. He couldn't believe what she was saying. He couldn't believe what he was being accused of.

Worst of all were her words about being trapped inside a loveless marriage. Did she really hate him that much? She could never grow to love him even a little?

The ring felt as if it burned in his pocket. His plan had been to come in here this morning, tell her he loved her and would make this work, and propose. He'd felt almost sure she would grow to love him just as much as he loved her.

But her words of a loveless marriage were like a dagger to the heart. No matter what he promised her it seemed she couldn't ever imagine a life with him. A life with them, together as a family.

Had he really been so blind that he thought they were almost there?

Margaret gave a whimper from the crib. Twice, Sienna had stopped him walking towards her. Twice, she'd stopped him from seeing his daughter.

Sebastian felt numb.

'I'm done trying to force what isn't there. I'm done trying to be anything other than I am. You should have told me as soon as you found out you were pregnant. You should have let me know that I was going to be a father. The news blindsided me. You had months to get used to the idea. I had two weeks.'

He looked furious now.

He put his hand on his chest. 'And I wanted it, Sienna. I wanted it more than you could ever have imagined. I can't believe you're being so judgemental.' He shook his head. 'What did I say? I said I was looking forward to us all being a family together very soon. That's it. What's so wrong with that? They asked me if we were engaged and if we would get married and what did I do? I smiled. Because a tiny little part of me actually wanted that to happen.'

He started pacing.

'Do you know why? Because I was a fool. I was a fool to think we actually could have a life together. I was a fool to think you might grant me a scrap of that affection and passion you keep so tightly locked up inside you.'

He spun around towards her again.

'Well, I'm done. I'm done trying to force this. You clearly don't know how to love someone. Or if you do, it's clear that person will never be me. I won't spend my life tiptoeing around you. Margaret is my daughter, as much as yours. I'm not going to fight with you, Sienna. I will not have my daughter witnessing her parents rowing over her. If you're incapable of talking to me about her—if you're incapable of compromise—then we can talk via lawyers. You don't get the ownership on loving Margaret. She has the right to be loved by both her parents. I want to see her. I want to spend time with her. And, even though you clearly hate me, I won't let you stop me seeing her.'

He couldn't stop the words from coming out of his mouth. This woman, Sienna, who he'd hoped would make his heart sing, had just turned his world upside down. He loved her with his whole heart. He loved his daughter with his whole heart.

This morning, he'd thought he could turn this into something wonderful. He'd had the audacity to think that he and Sienna could love each other and it could last a lifetime.

Now…?

He just didn't know.

Sienna couldn't find any more words. Sebastian turned on his heel and walked outside.

She sagged on the bed out of pure exhaustion. What had happened? The tears continued to fall and her only comfort was lifting Margaret to her chest and holding the little warm body next to hers.

Her precious daughter. *Hers.* That was what she'd said to Sebastian. It didn't matter that it had been in the heat of the moment. She'd said it deliberately to exclude him. But Margaret wouldn't be here without Seb. The facts of life were simple.

The reporter in the red coat was still talking incessantly on the TV. Now, she was talking about how delighted Queen Grace was, how angry Princess Theresa was, how the people in Montanari were waiting for a formal announcement about their new heir, and how the Prince was clearly enthralled by his new daughter and fiancée since there had been no sign of him.

All she could think about was the expression on Sebastian's face. The hurt. The shock. The surprise. The words, 'I said I was looking forward to us all being a family together.'

She screwed her eyes closed for a second. When she'd challenged him on that he'd said he'd smiled because he'd hoped they could have a life together. They would get engaged. They would get married. Something tugged at her heart. The tone of his voice. The pain in his eyes. What did that mean? Did that mean he did care about her? He might actually love her?

There was a knock at the door and one of the midwives entered. She looked uncomfortable and pale-faced. She hesitated before talking. 'Seb... The Prince. He's down at the nursery. He asked if he could see Margaret before he leaves.'

'He leaves?' She felt sick. She stared down at her daughter's face. Margaret stared back and blinked. It was as if she was trying to focus. Already her eyes looked as if they would change colour. Change colour to the same as her father's forest green.

The midwife hesitated again. 'He asked if he could see her before he returns to Montanari.'

There.

She had what she wanted.

Sebastian was going to go.

It was like being rolled over by a giant tidal wave. The isolation. The devastation.

She started to shake as she gazed at Margaret. How would she feel if the shoe were on the other foot? How would she feel if someone stood between her and her daughter?

She'd chased him away. She'd said everything she probably shouldn't have said. But she couldn't think straight right now. Her heart was already wrung out by the birth of her baby.

When Sebastian had given that smile to the reporter she had instantly judged. She'd assumed he was being smug. She'd assumed he was calculating. But what if it had been none of those things? What if he'd been entirely truthful with her?

What if...what if he'd actually meant what he'd said? He'd believed they could have a life together. But did that life include love?

She started sobbing again. She didn't want him without love. She wanted everything. She couldn't let herself settle for anything less.

The midwife pulled tissues from a box that had miraculously appeared and handed her a few. She didn't say anything, just put a gentle hand on Sienna's shoulder.

She stared at her little daughter's face. He'd accused her of being incapable of love. She felt like just the opposite. As if she loved too much. She loved Margaret so much already. And right now? Her heart was breaking in two about Sebastian. She wasn't a woman incapable of love.

Far from it.

'What do you want me to tell him?' came the gentle voice of the midwife.

She nodded as a tear dripped from her face and onto Margaret's blanket. 'Yes. Tell him, yes. He can see Margaret.'

She handed her baby over with shaking hands.

She'd ruined everything and there was no way back.

* * *

The midwife took tentative steps down the corridor towards him, holding Margaret still wrapped in the pink blanket. His heart gave a little surge of relief. He turned back to the window of the nursery. The quads he'd heard everyone talking about looked tiny compared to Margaret. But he could see each of them kicking their legs and punching their tiny hands. Each fighting indignantly against their entry into the world. Their names were emblazoned over their plastic cribs. Graham, Lily, Rupert and Rose. He smiled. Traditional names, like Margaret. Maybe it was a new trend?

The midwife gestured with her head to the next room. 'Would you like to sit in here with your daughter?' He nodded and followed her inside, sitting in a large chair next to the window as she handed Margaret over. 'I'll wait outside,' she said quietly, then paused at the doorway. 'Sienna. She's very upset.' She sighed. 'I think you both need to take a deep breath.' She waved her hand. 'It's none of my business. I'd just hate you both to lose something that you love.' She turned and walked outside.

Sebastian stared at his daughter in his arms. His heart should be soaring. He should be celebrating. He should be rejoicing. But he'd never felt quite this sad.

This hadn't been the day he'd planned for.

This hadn't been the day he'd expected. In fact, it was so far away from what he'd thought would happen that he could barely even believe this was how things had turned out.

It was never meant to be like this between them. Never. Of that—he was sure.

But how on earth did they come back from this? He'd said some things he regretted. He'd said a lot of things he regretted.

He'd never been a man for emotional outbursts. He'd

spent a life of control, of restraint. But Sienna brought out a side of him he'd never thought he had.

Around her, his feelings ran stronger than he thought possible.

So, it was true.

Love could cause the greatest happiness.

And love could cause the greatest misery.

Margaret grumbled in his arms. Her little head turned from side to side, probably rooting for her mother.

Could he really go home? Could he really bear to leave them and not see them for how long—a few days, a week, a month?

He shuddered. He couldn't bear that. Not at all.

Life was precious. Life was fragile. Life wasn't supposed to be like this.

What would he do if he returned to Montanari? Probably fight with his parents. Probably take his frustrations out on those around him. All because he'd messed up the most important relationship of his life.

The relationship with the woman he loved with his whole heart.

He'd tried to forget about Sienna. He'd tried to follow his parents' wishes and get engaged to someone else.

In the end, it hadn't worked. It would *never* have worked.

His heart belonged to Sienna.

And he had to believe, he *had* to believe that part of her heart belonged to him too.

Margaret was important. Margaret would always be one of his priorities. But his other priority would be the woman he wanted as his wife.

Life ahead for him was formidable. Ruling Montanari would only be possible with a strong woman by his side. A woman whom he loved and respected. A woman who could help to lead Montanari into the modern world.

Everything about Sienna had captured his heart. Her wit. Her intelligence. Her stubbornness. Her determination. The look in her eyes when she'd first seen their daughter...

He had to win her. He had to win her back.

He'd never actually told her how he felt about her. He'd never actually put his heart on the line.

He'd been scared his feelings wouldn't be reciprocated. And that could still happen.

But he wasn't leaving her until he tried.

He stood up and walked to the door. The midwife stepped forward to take Margaret. 'No.' He shook his head. 'I'll take Margaret back to her mother.' He took a calm breath. 'I won't leave without talking to her.' He added quietly, 'I won't leave without putting up a fight for them both.'

The midwife gave a little nod of her head. 'Good luck,' she said quietly as he started down the corridor.

She'd finally managed to stop crying, wash her face and change out of the pyjamas into the clothes that Sebastian had set down in the corner for her earlier. She'd be going home soon.

Home with her daughter.

Right from when she'd started making her plans, she'd always expected to take Margaret home on her own.

But this last week, those steadfast plans had started to wobble.

Sebastian had slowly but surely started to creep his way around the edges and somehow into the middle of them all.

The night before last, when she'd seen the beautiful job he'd made of the nursery she'd been overwhelmed. It was almost as if Sebastian had climbed into her brain and seen the picture that she had stored in there.

He'd made the dream a reality.

His face when he'd looked at their daughter had taken her breath away. And when he'd then turned and met her gaze? She'd never felt so special. She'd never felt so connected or loved.

How could she go from that point to this?

She finished rubbing some make-up onto her face. Right now, she was paler than she'd ever been. She needed something—anything—to make her look a little alive again. She couldn't find her mascara, or any blusher, and there was only one colour of lipstick in her make-up bag, so she rubbed a little furiously into her cheeks and put some on her lips.

The door swung open behind her and she stepped out of the bathroom to get Margaret from the midwife. Her boobs were already starting to ache and Margaret was probably hungry again.

But it wasn't the midwife.

It was Seb.

For a second, neither of them spoke. They just stared. Finally Seb drew in a breath. 'You look…good.'

'That good, really?' It came out of nowhere. The kind of smart retort she'd got used to saying around him. Her eyes instantly started to fill with tears again—it was just as well she hadn't found mascara.

Margaret gave a little yelp and she held out her arms. 'Give me her. She needs to feed.'

He hesitated. And instead of handing Margaret over, he put her up on his shoulder. 'We need to talk.'

Sienna shook her head. 'We're done talking. We've said enough. We both need some space.'

He nodded. 'You're right. But just exactly how much space do you need?'

She frowned. 'What do you mean?'

He met her gaze. 'I mean, I don't want to leave. I don't want to go back to Montanari without the two people I love.'

She froze. Part of her wanted to believe. But part of her questioned everything.

'You just want Margaret. You don't want me. Don't panic, Seb. We'll work something out. You can see her.'

He stepped closer. Margaret seemed to be sucking at his neck. It wouldn't take her long to realise there was no milk there. He touched her arm. 'You're wrong. I do want you. I've always wanted you, Sienna—even when I didn't really know it myself. I would have come back. I would have always come back for you.'

She could hear what he was saying. He'd tried to say it before. But she just couldn't let herself believe it.

'But you didn't,' she whispered. 'You only came because of Margaret.'

He closed his eyes for a second. 'Sienna, you have to believe that even if Margaret wasn't here, *I* still would be.'

It was painful when she sucked in a breath. She shook her head. 'Words are easy. I'd like to believe you but, for all I know, you might just be saying this to persuade us both to come back to Montanari with you. This might all just be a trick to get Margaret back to your country.'

He reached over and touched her face. It was the gentlest of touches. 'Sienna, don't. Don't think like that of me. Is that really how you feel about me? I'm a liar? A manipulator?' He looked genuinely upset. His forest-green gaze held hers. 'Is that how the woman I love really feels about me?'

Her heart squeezed tightly in her chest. Her mouth was so dry she could barely speak. 'You love me?'

He stepped even closer. Margaret let out a few grumbles. His hand brushed back across Sienna's cheek and this time across her long eyelashes too.

'I love you so much I sometimes can't breathe when I think about you. I love you so much that the face I see when I close my eyes is yours. I can't let you slip through my fingers. I can't let the chance for this to become real get away because I'm emotional. You're emotional. And I'm a fool.'

She smiled. He knew how to charm a lady.

His fingers moved around her ear, tucking some stray strands of hair behind it. 'But I will, Sienna, if that's what you want. If you want me to leave—to give you space—I will. But know that I'll do it because I love you. Because you are the most important thing to me on this planet. Because I will always put what you want before what I want.'

Tears pooled in her eyes again and she took a step towards him. 'How can you do that, silly? You have a kingdom to look after. All those people. How on earth can I matter?'

He bent his head towards her. 'You matter because I say you matter. You and Margaret will always come first for me.'

This wasn't charm. This wasn't manipulation. This wasn't lies.

This was real.

'Oh, Seb,' she whispered. 'Can this really work?'

He took a deep breath. He was shaking. He was actually shaking. 'Only if you love me. Do you love me, Sienna?'

A tear dripped down her face. She reached up and touched the stubble on his jawline. Her lips trembled as she smiled. 'I do,' she whispered as she pulled his forehead towards hers.

His smile spread across his face. His eyelashes tickled her forehead. 'I think you've said that a little too early.'

She laughed as he fumbled in his pocket. 'Give me a second.'

She held her breath as he pulled out a glittering ruby and diamond ring—bigger than she could ever have imagined. He smiled at the ring. 'This is a family heirloom.

It belonged to my great-grandmother, Sophia, one of the most spirited women I've ever had the pleasure to know.' He gave her a special smile. 'She would have loved you, you know. She told me to give it to the woman that captured my heart and my soul. That's you. Will you marry me, Sienna?'

She lifted Margaret from his shoulder and tilted her lips up to his.

'A princess and a surgeon? Do you think you can cope?'

He slid his arms around her as his lips met hers. 'I can't wait to spend my life finding out.'

EPILOGUE

MONTANARI WAS COVERED in snow for the first time in twenty years. It was almost as if every weather system had aligned especially for the royal wedding.

Sienna looked at the snow-covered palace lawn, trying to hide the butterflies in her stomach. She kissed her ruby and diamond engagement ring and closed her eyes for a second.

This was it. This was when she married the man who had captured her heart, her soul and the very breath in her body. Sophia's engagement ring had been a lucky talisman for her. So much so that, when she couldn't decide on her wedding gown, late one night she'd trawled through the palace archives and found a picture of Sophia on her wedding day.

It had been perfect. A traditional gown covered in heavy lace was the last thing she would ever have contemplated. But somehow, the style reached out and grabbed her. The long-sleeve lace arms and shoulders were perfect for a winter wedding, as was the lace that covered the satin bodice and skirt. She'd taken the picture and asked the wedding designer to replicate the dress for her.

The door opened behind her and Juliet and her daughter Bea walked in. Both were wearing red gowns that matched their bouquets. Juliet gave her a smile. 'Ready, Princess?'

Sienna shook her head. 'Don't. I might just be sick all down this gown before anyone has had a chance to see it.'

Juliet walked over, her pregnancy bump clearly visible in her gown. Babies were in the air around here. She pulled at a strand of Sienna's curled hair. 'I spotted Sebastian earlier. He couldn't wipe the smile off his face. And you needn't worry about sickness. Margaret has just been sick on the Queen's outfit. I thought she was going to pass out with shock!'

Sienna threw back her head and laughed. 'Really? You mean, she'll actually have to change her outfit? Oh, I love that girl of mine. She knows exactly how to make her mother proud.'

There was a knock at the door and Oliver stuck his head inside. 'Sebastian asked me to give you a message.'

Her heart gave a little flutter. 'What is it?'

Oliver laughed. 'Hurry up and get down the aisle. He's done waiting. It's Christmas Eve tomorrow and Margaret's birthday. You have presents to wrap!'

Sienna gave a nervous nod. 'I'm ready. Tell him, I'm ready.'

Oliver walked across the room and gave her a kiss on the cheek. 'Ella and I couldn't be happier for you.'

She smiled as he left. Ella and Oliver had got married a few months before the birth of their baby, Harry. She'd never seen him happier.

Music drifted up the stairs towards them. Juliet gave her a nod and walked around, picking up the skirts of her dress.

The wedding was being held in the royal chapel, with the reception in the palace. She'd tried to memorise all the visiting dignitaries in the hope she wouldn't make some faux pas. Queen Grace had only thawed a little in the last year. She seemed a little interested in Margaret, and when she'd made a few barbed comments about the wedding plans Sienna had happily handed over the guest list and seating plan and told her to take charge, in case she seated some feuding families next to each other.

She was learning how to manage her mother-in-law and Sebastian was entirely grateful.

They reached the entrance to the chapel and Sienna sucked in her breath. The entire chapel was lit by candles, creating a beautiful ethereal glow. Juliet rearranged her skirts then set off down the aisle with Bea. Charlie watched them the whole way, his face beaming with pride. Their wedding plans had been put on temporary hold due to Juliet's pregnancy, but Sienna couldn't wait to attend the ceremony in the Cotswolds next summer.

Oliver held out his elbow. 'Two jobs for the price of one. Do I get double the salary for this?'

She bent over and kissed his cheek. 'You get my eternal thanks for being such a good friend. I couldn't have picked anyone more perfect to give me away, or to be Sebastian's best man.' She winked as the wedding march started. 'Just remember, the wedding speech will be watched the world over. I love you, but tell any Sienna-got-drunk stories and I will lace your dinner with arsenic.'

He laughed and patted her arm. 'I'll keep that in mind. Ready?'

She licked her dry lips and nodded.

As soon as they started down the aisle, Margaret started to call to her. 'Mama, Mama.' She was being held by Annabelle while Max held their daughter, Hope. Max and Annabelle had renewed their wedding vows and, after adopting Hope, were hoping to adopt two boys who were in foster care in North Africa.

Margaret was tugging at Annabelle's hair with one hand and waving at Sienna with the other. Her cream dress was rumpled—she crawled everywhere—and her headband was almost off her head. Margaret was destined to be the biggest tomboy in the world.

Sienna stopped to kiss her little hand, then carried on the last few steps to Sebastian.

He didn't hesitate. He took her hand immediately. 'You look stunning,' he said simply.

'You don't look too bad yourself.' She smiled. His athletic frame filled the royal dress uniform well, the dark green jacket making his eyes even more intense. Her heart skipped a few beats.

They fought regularly and made up even more passionately. He'd helped prepare her for the new role she'd have in Montanari and supported her in every decision she'd made. She'd started working between both hospitals but, to Oliver's disappointment, had made some plans recently to work permanently in Montanari. Sebastian didn't know that yet.

The music started to play around them for the first hymn and he leaned over and whispered in her ear. 'I didn't think it was possible, but I love you even more each day.' His thumb traced a circle in her palm. 'Ready for two to become one?'

She smiled at him with twinkling eyes. 'Actually, it's three becomes four.'

He blinked. Then his eyes widened and his smile spread from ear to ear as Sienna started to laugh.

And that was the picture that made the front page of every newspaper around the world.

* * * * *

UNWRAPPED
BY THE DUKE

AMY RUTTAN

This book is dedicated to my Aunt Margaret. She is the one who got me interested in everything to do with the British Royal Family. She sent me books, newspaper articles, magazines. Thank you, Aunt Margaret. So glad you shared your interest with me.

This book is also dedicated to my dad, who set me on the path to loving anything British or British comedy-related. So, Dad, and the rubber button is...?

CHAPTER ONE

"AND THIS IS WHERE you can change into your lab coat while you make rounds on our patients."

Geri nodded her head as she followed her father into the lounge all the surgeons and physicians at the hospital used. There were overstuffed sofas and a sparkling kitchen area. It was a comfortable enough room, more than comfortable, a lot different from the rooms in the inner-city Glasgow hospital where she'd done her residency. Those rooms usually had a couple of vending machines and a ratty old settee. Not that she'd spent much time in the doctors' lounge. She'd spent most of her time on the surgical floor.

Until a month ago when she'd given up her chance to be a surgeon.

She'd had every intention of finishing her surgical residency, but circumstances had changed after her last year on rotation and her father's offer to become a cardiologist had suited her just fine.

She'd been surprised at the opulence she found herself suddenly thrust into.

Of course, her father was a prestigious cardiologist, with a practice in Harley Street. Being a member of the peerage, he was used to working in more comfortable surroundings.

She was finding it all a bit overwhelming.

It had only been last year that her estranged father had

reached out to her and she'd gone from that young girl who'd grown up in a poorer district of Glasgow, studying hard to get scholarships and working two jobs to pay her way through medical school, to heiress.

Geri had spent her whole life doing everything in her power to make a better life for herself, to distance herself from her cold, detached mother who was now living in some commune in Israel. A mother who had no interest in a connection with her daughter anymore.

Which also suited Geri just fine.

So it had been a complete shock to her system to finally meet her father and find out that he was an aristocrat—a lord—and that she was a lady and the heiress to a family seat that stretched back to the time of King George III. And it wasn't just that. Her father was retiring and he was leaving his practice to her.

When he'd offered her the practice last year she'd turned him down. She'd been involved with Frederick and on her way to becoming a cardiothoracic surgeon.

Besides, she hadn't really wanted to get to know the man who hadn't given two figs about her existence until it had suited him.

Then Frederick had broken her heart and because of her relationship with him she'd became the laughing stock of the surgical program in Glasgow. She'd decided to take the easy way out and take her father up on his offer.

A secret shame she'd have to bear. Which was only fitting punishment for thinking herself in love with a surgeon she'd been learning from. For letting her emotions rule her heart.

Her mother had told her time and time again to hide away her feelings. Feelings served no purpose. They were a form of weakness.

So she'd left Glasgow for London to take over her father's share of the practice.

Surgery was the price she had to pay for her indiscretion. It wasn't a solo practice, as her father shared his practice with a cardiothoracic surgeon, but that didn't matter. It's what made her father's practice one of the top ones in Harley Street. In the same office you could meet with your cardiologist and one of the best cardiothoracic surgeons was just down the hall. Geri had yet to meet the infamous Mr. Ashwood, but she had read some of his research papers when she'd been doing her surgical residency. He was certainly an impressive and accomplished surgeon.

"Geraldine, you looked a little flustered. Are you sure you're well, my dear? We can save this walk-through for another time. You've only just arrived from Glasgow. Perhaps you should go back to my house and unpack. Rest."

"No, I assure you I'm fine." Geri smiled. "Please do continue."

She couldn't bring herself to call him "Father" just yet. He was still Lord Collins to her. She was staying at his home for now. Just until after Christmas when she could find her own place. It was awkward, to say the least. He walked around her like she was delicate china and was going to shatter.

They'd been together for a month and she felt like she didn't even know him. And she wasn't all that sure she wanted to.

Her father nodded, though he looked uncomfortable. Sometimes it was hard, being alone with him. It was awkward. They were too polite, but then there were other times when they enjoyed each other's company. Still, those times were few and far between.

He looked down at his pager. "Ah, a spot of trouble. One of my patients has just been admitted. Would you like to come meet her or would you rather stay here?"

"I'll stay here, I think. Just get my bearings. I'm sure I'll meet her soon enough."

Her father nodded. "I won't be a moment."

Geri breathed a sigh of relief when her father left her alone.

She was still trying to process it all. She couldn't quite believe she was here. It had always been a secret dream of hers to meet her father one day. Until each year had passed and those secret dreams of her father coming to rescue her from a lonely childhood had faded into nothing. At the age of eighteen she'd had his last name, known his first name was Charles, but had had no idea that he was a member of the aristocracy. And she couldn't be bothered to find out anything about him.

She'd had no idea he was a physician in Harley Street with a home at the posh end of Holland Park.

It was all a bit overwhelming. She sat on the edge of a couch and took a deep breath.

What am I doing here? I don't belong here.

"Excuse me, but are you lost?" It wasn't totally a question. It was a question mixed with annoyance.

Geri stood and turned around. She was taken aback by the tall, dark, handsome surgeon standing in the doorway, his face like thunder as he glared at her, letting her know in no uncertain terms she didn't belong there.

"Thank you for your concern, but I'm not lost."

He cocked his head to one side. "This room is for surgeons only. I think you're in the wrong place."

His voice was deep and husky, which sent a shiver of anticipation through her. She always fell for dark, brooding men. Frederick had been dark and brooding and look how that turned out.

Don't get carried away.

"I can assure you I'm not lost," she said again. "I was accompanying my father and he asked me to wait here until he returned. Besides, this is the physicians' lounge. Not the surgeons' lounge."

He snorted and moved past her into the room. "I'll have to have a talk with them, they'll let just about anyone in here."

"My, we're in a foul mood, aren't we?" She was tired of pompous, arrogant, rude people.

He poured himself a cup of coffee and then turned to look at her. "You're not from around here, are you?"

"Oh, and what was it that gave it away?"

He grinned. "That delightful accent you have. Somewhere in Scotland, I assume."

He was right, of course, but she wasn't going to let this holier-than-thou surgeon off the hook. He was presumptuous, conceited and haughty. And handsome, but never mind that. He needed to be taken down a peg or two.

"You know what they say about assumptions," she muttered under her breath.

He crossed his arms and leaned back against the counter, his eyes twinkling. "No, what do they say? Enlighten me, miss."

Darn.

He'd heard her. Well, two could play at this game.

"It's 'Doctor,' actually," she said, correcting him.

He cocked his eyebrows. "Is it really? Are you going to be working here, then?"

"In a manner of speaking." She tried to be evasive and end the conversation with him, but she wasn't that lucky. The way he'd asked if she was going to be working here made her feel nervous. Like suddenly she was a mouse and he was a cat, closing in for a kill.

He grinned, a lazy sort of grin that Geri knew all too well from the rogues she was used to dating. That smile was wolfish, almost predatory in nature, and as he set his coffee mug down and moved away from the counter towards her, Geri knew she was in deep, deep trouble.

"Well, my apologies, then. I had no idea that you were a new surgeon here."

"Just a doctor, actually. I'm not a surgeon." It stung to say that, but she didn't let it show. Her mother couldn't tolerate any show of emotion and she had learned well.

"I just naturally assumed you were a surgeon. You have an authoritative air about you."

"And only surgeons have the right to be authoritative?"

"Yes. I mean, lives are in our hands."

Geri rolled her eyes. Good lord, he was arrogant. "You're unbelievable."

"Why, thank you." He made a bow with a flourish.

"It's not a compliment. You're the most conceited, prideful man I have ever had the displeasure of knowing."

"Oh, come, now, darling. Surely not the worst?" He winked. "You've only known me for a few fleeting moments. Spend some more time with me and you'll no longer feel displeasure."

"Don't call me darling. I'm most definitely not your darling."

He leaned over and whispered in her ear, his hot breath fanning her neck, "Ah, but you could be."

It took all her strength not to slap him hard across the face or let him kiss her. It had been a long time since Frederick. A long time since she'd felt any kind of desire for a man.

"Geraldine, I'm sorry I took so long," her father said, coming into the room. She jumped back, silently thanking her father for his timing. "Ah, I see that I no longer have to seek you out, Thomas. Geraldine, I would like you to meet Mr. Thomas Ashwood. Thomas, this is my daughter, Geraldine Collins. She'll be taking over my position in the practice when I retire."

"Pardon?" Thomas said, sounding a bit dumbfounded. He was sure he'd heard the enchantress say the same thing the moment Charles Collins had dropped the bombshell on him. "What was that?"

"My daughter, Dr. Geraldine Collins. She's the cardiologist who is taking over my role in the practice. She'll be your partner."

Oh. God.

He'd been hitting on Charles's daughter? His competition, the bane of his existence since Charles had announced that he was retiring and leaving the practice. Thomas had thought that he was going to take over the practice in its entirety. He'd planned to hire an up-and-coming cardiologist and expand the surgical side of the practice. Take it to new heights, ones that he'd never been able to meet before.

But now he found himself with an unwanted new partner. The daughter of the great Charles Collins. He knew the type. Debutante. Spoiled, selfish and she would be all over him in a trice when she learned of his aristocratic background. Society women were out for money and blood.

It was all the same with women from the circles he moved in and he'd expected nothing different from Collins's daughter.

Until now.

She was nothing like he'd expected. She stood up for herself. She exchanged banter with him and didn't back down. He liked matching wits with someone. Not only was she a beauty, she was intelligent to boot. It was kind of exciting and also a bit bothersome. To her credit, Dr. Geraldine Collins didn't look exactly thrilled at the prospect of being his partner either.

"This is Mr. Ashwood?" Geraldine asked. Thomas couldn't help but notice the mild disgust in her voice. "This is *the* Mr. Ashwood who is your partner in your practice?"

Thomas bowed slightly at the waist. "One and the same, dear lady."

Geraldine's eyes shot daggers at him.

"Have I missed something?" Charles asked, apparently confused.

"No, nothing at all, Charles. I didn't exactly make my presence known to your enchanting daughter when I arrived. I'm afraid I took her a bit by surprise."

Charles Collins cocked his eyebrows. "Oh. Well, that explains everything."

"Aye?" Geraldine blushed and cleared her throat. "I mean, I suppose it does."

Thomas had been charmed the moment the "Aye" had slipped past her lips. She seemed refined, but she had obviously not been raised in the world he was used to, the world that both he and Charles came from.

And that intrigued him all the more, which was a dangerous thing indeed. He had to make an expeditious exit or he might do something he'd regret. And he thought too highly of Charles to besmirch the good name of Collins.

"Well, if you'll both excuse me..." As he was trying to make his excuse his pager and Charles's both went off. It was their patient, Lord Twinsbury. He was on his way to hospital and E.

"Blast," Charles said. "I have an office full of appointments."

"I can handle this, Charles," Thomas offered.

"I can assist," Geraldine said to her father. "You can head back to the practice and I can assist Mr. Ashwood."

No.

"That's an excellent idea," Charles said. "You met Lord Twinsbury last week when he visited. You're familiar with his file. What say you, Thomas? I mean, you'll eventually have to work together when I retire officially, so why not take the plunge now?"

"I don't think I'll need Dr. Collins's assistance in this matter." He was grasping at straws, but he really needed to get away from Geraldine. She piqued an interest in him that he hadn't felt in some time and he didn't like the way it made him feel.

"With all due respect, Mr. Ashwood, we don't even know if this is a surgical case," Geraldine said firmly. "And I *will* be present as we both examine Lord Twinsbury."

She had spirit. He liked that.

"You don't have hospital privileges."

It was a weak excuse.

"I do, as a matter of fact. I was granted them this morning." Geraldine crossed her arms, smiling very smugly.

"Now, instead of standing here and arguing, why don't we meet Lord Twinsbury in A and E and give him the attention he needs?"

Thomas was stunned as Geraldine moved past him and headed out into the hall. Even Charles looked a bit shocked but Thomas didn't have time to sit there and hash it out with him. Instead, he ran to catch up with Geraldine, who was marching away, her back ramrod straight and honey-brown strands of hair escaping that severe bun that was pinned at the back of her head. He couldn't help but admire her backside as she marched down the hall.

Don't think about her like that. She's off-limits.

"Do you even know where the A and E department is?" Thomas asked as he fell into step beside her.

She rolled her eyes at him. "Don't be silly. Of course I do."

"Good, because right now you're headed to the operating theater floor and A and E is this way." Thomas motioned over his shoulder in the opposite direction. He should've just let her go and get lost. Then he could deal with Lord Twinsbury himself, only something deep inside him, that nagging conscience he tried so often to ignore when it came to the opposite sex, was yelling at him to do the right thing.

She skittered to a stop and looked down the hall, her

hazel eyes sparkling with determination, annoyance and possibly embarrassment, her red lips pressed together in a firm line.

"Are you going to show me the right way, then, or am I to find the way myself?"

"If I was going to let you fend for yourself I wouldn't have stopped you and told you were going in the wrong direction."

Geraldine's shoulders relaxed and a small smile crept onto her face. "Thank you. I didn't think you would… That is to say…"

"There's no explanation needed." Thomas knew what she was trying to say, that she didn't think he would help her, and part of him was telling him not to. To let her flounder. She was, after all, the competition. Only he couldn't do that.

He might go by "the Dark Duke" in his social circle, the rake who seduced debutantes and left them the next day, but he was, after all, a gentleman above all else. Only, since the moment he'd first begun arguing with her, he'd been trying not to think about all the ungentlemanly things he wanted to do to her.

"It's this way," he said, motioning with his head.

She nodded and they walked side by side down the hall, not saying a word. He was truly impressed that she was able to keep up with his long easy strides in her tight pencil skirt and heels.

She was graceful, refined, but there was something hidden beneath that polished, emotionless surface. Something quite different from the women he was used to. She was tough, hardened but he had no doubt she was soft and feminine under that facade. He would like to find out, she intrigued him.

But he would not seduce Charles's daughter and since

settling down was out of the question for him, he would just have to keep a safe distance from Geraldine Collins.

They entered A and E and were waved over by the consultant in charge.

"He insisted on having his cardiology team come and look at him," Dr. Sears said, looking over at Geraldine, confused, before turning back to Thomas. "Where is Dr. Collins?"

"I am Dr. Collins." Geraldine pushed past him and Thomas shrugged, smirking. He had to admire her tenacity.

Lord Twinsbury was quite pale and lying back on the gurney. He smiled, though, when Geraldine came in.

"Ah, I thought I would be seeing your father but I assure you this is a better substitute."

Geraldine smiled. "Lord Twinsbury, you're a flirt."

"How many times do I have to insist you call me Lionel?"

Thomas cocked his eyebrows. Never in the thirty-odd years he'd known Lord Twinsbury personally and the five years he had been the man's surgeon had he been permitted to call him Lionel.

And Lord Twinsbury was one of his godfathers.

"Lionel, then." Geraldine smiled. "What seems to be the matter?"

Lord Twinsbury craned his neck and looked at Thomas. "Young fellow, they paged you as well. That's good."

"I would certainly hope that they would page me as well, my lord, or perhaps you'll allow me to call you Lionel, as well?"

Lord Twinsbury fixed him with a stare, much like his own dear departed father used to do. "I think not. You're not an attractive lady, like Geraldine is."

The stern smile softened as he looked over at Geraldine, who was taking Lord Twinsbury's blood pressure and frowning.

"Look at this, Mr. Ashwood," she said. Thomas leaned over to look at the reading and grimaced.

"Well? What's wrong? I can tell by your faces that my blood pressure isn't good."

"No, it's not, my lord." Thomas pulled out his stethoscope. "Do you mind if I have a listen?"

Geraldine helped Lord Twinsbury sit up as Thomas listened to the erratic sound of Lord Twinsbury's heart trying to pump blood through his clogged arteries. He had been warning Lord Twinsbury for years that his clogged arteries would only get worse. They had done several angioplasties at different times, but Thomas knew and had told him that one day it would come to open heart surgery.

It looked like that day had come.

"I can tell by your face, Thomas, that you're going to tell me something I really don't want to hear," Lord Twinsbury said.

"You can call me by my given name but I can't call you Lionel?"

"Your father would have a thousand fits knowing you're being so informal with me," Lord Twinsbury warned.

Thomas rolled his eyes. "My lord, you know what has to happen. I've told you this day would come. You need a coronary artery bypass graft and you need one today. Now. Or the next time you're speaking in the House of Lords you're liable to drop dead."

Geraldine gasped. "You have a terrible bedside manner, Mr. Ashwood."

Lord Twinsbury chuckled and patted Geraldine's hand. "Nonsense. I'm used to his behavior. I like his frank talk, my dear. It keeps me on my toes."

Geraldine frowned and Thomas winked at her.

"I'll have you admitted, Lord Twinsbury, and then we'll get you ready to go up to the operating theater today."

Lord Twinsbury nodded and then turned to Geraldine.

"I do hope you'll stay, my dear. Your father has been treating my heart for so many years and I want to make sure I have someone I can trust in there."

Thomas groaned and walked out of the room.

Lord Twinsbury was an eccentric character. He was also pompous and arrogant. Never took his advice. Probably because he still saw Thomas as that little boy who'd destroyed his Tudor hedge maze during Royal Ascot when he was ten.

"Mr. Ashwood, can I speak with you a moment?"

Good. Lord.

His day had been going so well. He'd done a great LVAD surgery to extend the life of a patient and was planning on returning to his office to get some charting done. He had not planned to deal with Charles Collins's daughter today.

He turned around. "How can I help you, Dr. Collins?"

"Do you treat all our patients in such a manner?"

"I do, as a matter of fact, because most of them I've known for quite some time. I haven't had any complaints yet."

"Do you think that he warrants a coronary artery bypass graft? Wouldn't another angioplasty or perhaps an endocardectomy work in this case? Is surgery really the answer for a seventy-three-year-old man in poor health?"

This was a little too much.

"Have I missed something, Dr. Collins? Are you or are you not a surgeon?"

Red tinged her cheeks and he'd hit a tender spot on her hardened walls. A chink in the armor, as it were. So perhaps there was a weakness, a crack in her icy facade. "I am a cardiologist so, no, I am not a surgeon."

"Then do not question my surgical opinion."

"Lord Twinsbury is as much my patient as yours."

"Your father would never question my surgical decisions," Thomas snapped.

"Perhaps he should."

Thomas took a step closer to her. "How long have you been treating Lord Twinsbury, Dr. Collins? A few hours, perhaps. I have been treating him for five years and over that five years I've done numerous angioplasties and made a failed attempt at a carotid endocardectomy, which almost killed him. I have informed my patient that he would need a coronary artery bypass graft. I have tried to keep the procedures as minimally invasive as possible for the sake of my patient, who has been in congestive heart failure for a long time, but there is no other option, so unless you're able to perform in the operating theater and have discovered a new, minimally invasive way of doing a coronary artery bypass graft, I would suggest you head back to our surgery in Harley Street and leave the surgical procedures to the qualified individuals."

He turned on his heel and left her, hating himself for taking her down like that in the hallway, in front of the A and E department and other physicians. Physicians she'd be working with.

He hated himself for making her feel that way.

If it had been anyone else, he wouldn't feel as bad as he did now. He'd given dressing-downs like that before and they had never eaten away at his conscience, but this was different.

He didn't know why, but it was and he didn't like it one bit.

CHAPTER TWO

I SHOULD LEAVE.

Geri bit her lip as she paced the viewing gallery of the operating theater where Thomas Ashwood was currently performing a coronary artery bypass graft on Lord Twinsbury. How she wished she could be in there, assisting. She'd read so many papers Mr. Ashwood had written. A few hours ago she would have given anything to learn from him.

Now she knew that would be a mistake. Just like Frederick had been a colossal mistake. She was here to start afresh. To prove herself. There was no way she was going to become entangled in a dalliance at work because the last time it had cost her her surgical career.

It didn't have to.

Geri shook that thought away and closed her eyes, thinking about the surgery and how she wished she was in that operating theater. Only Mr. Ashwood had made it perfectly clear that he did not want her around.

She'd been embarrassed and after her temper had cooled she'd realized he was right. She wasn't a surgeon; she may have seen and done surgeries during her residency, but she wasn't a full-fledged surgeon and she never would be. Besides, she'd only known Lord Twinsbury for a week and even though she read over his file she hadn't worked with him as long as Mr. Ashwood had.

She wanted to apologize to him.

"Apologizing is a sign of weakness."

Geri shook her mother's voice from her head. Apologizing in this case was not a sign of weakness but respect. She'd been wrong.

Geri had been less than thrilled to learn that the arrogant, pompous surgeon who had come sweeping into the doctors' lounge, making assumptions about her, was her new partner. And she'd been taken a little off guard by the fact that he was a devilishly handsome, well-spoken man of breeding. As well as a surgeon she admired.

Which meant he was completely off-limits.

Definitely.

She had been hoping that she wouldn't have to see him again, but to find out that he was the cardiothoracic surgeon and partner in the practice was too much to bear. She'd been expecting Mr. Ashwood to be someone like her father. Older and possibly on the verge of retirement.

If Mr. Ashwood was venerable she'd eat her hat and try to find out where he kept the youth elixir. She couldn't help but wonder what her father saw in him. Her father only seemed to associate with those of his own class, members of society, what would've once been affectionately referred to as "the *ton*" if all those historical romance novels she'd read as a girl were correct.

She had been surprised to see her father's partner was someone so young and his complete opposite. Her father was reserved, awkward and well-bred. Mr. Ashwood had a relaxed, devil-may-care attitude. A definite rogue. Then again, her father had partnered with her mother, a common daughter of a Glasgow teacher, and had produced her.

Yeah, but that didn't last too long, did it?

Geraldine paused in her pacing to look down at him,

operating on Lord Twinsbury. Even in the operating theater he had a commanding presence and she couldn't help but admire his technique. She may not be a surgeon, but she'd watched many surgeries and Mr. Ashwood knew exactly what he was doing and he was doing it with finesse.

"There you are, Geraldine."

Geri turned to see her father enter the observation room.

"I thought you went back to the office?" she said.

Her father shrugged his shoulders. "I was going to, but then I heard a rumor that Thomas gave you quite a dressing-down in the hall."

Heat bloomed in her cheeks. Great. She was already making the rumor mill here. She swallowed her pride. "And rightfully so. I stepped out of line."

"I should say so." A smile played on her father's lips and she couldn't help but smile secretly to herself. He was still handsome. Even at sixty-nine she could see why her mother had fallen for her father. Or had at least stuck around long enough to conceive her.

She just didn't see what her father had seen in her mother.

"I'm hoping he'll allow me to apologize to him," she said, rubbing the back of her neck.

"It's best not to bring it up. Don't let him see your soft underbelly. You gave an opinion, and though not the right one, it was still an opinion nonetheless. Thomas is ruthless. It's why I asked him to be a partner. He's talented but ruthless. If you want to survive in a successful practice with him you have to stand by everything you say. You have to bite back."

Geri cocked an eyebrow. "Bite back?"

Her father nodded. "It will blow over and you'll both find a rhythm of partnership. So why don't we head home? I had Jensen bring the car around."

Even though she was sorely tempted to leave and not

expose her soft underbelly to Mr. Ashwood, she couldn't leave things like they were. She had been wrong to question him.

And she wasn't going to run this time. She was here for the long haul.

"I think I'll stay if it's all the same to you."

"Are you sure, Geraldine?"

She nodded. "Positive."

Her father reached down and squeezed her shoulder. "Just call for the car when you need it, then. Jensen won't mind."

"Of course."

Only she wouldn't. She'd take the tube to Holland Park. She may not be from London, but she knew her way around public transportation just fine. She just wouldn't tell her father that. He would have a thousand fits if he knew that she was taking public transportation like a commoner. Only that was what she was.

She may talk in a refined way, because she worked hard to drop the rough accent she'd had since childhood, but she didn't belong in this world she'd just been thrust into.

The first time she'd had a formal dinner at her father's large Holland Park home she'd been so confused by the number of forks she'd made an excuse about not being hungry and had left the table.

Her father had been less than thrilled to find that she'd walked down the street to the local pub and had had something to eat there.

What am I doing here?

She tried to tell herself that she was getting to know her estranged father, taking the opportunity of a lifetime of inheriting a lucrative practice in Harley Street, but she wasn't sure that was it.

There was a buzz on the intercom, snapping Geri out of her reverie. She got up and pushed the button.

"Dr. Collins, I'm surprised to see you up there," Thomas said, not looking up at her.

"Well, Lord Twinsbury did mention that he wanted me close by."

Thomas glanced up and there was a twinkle in his eyes. "So he did. Why don't you scrub in and come down here? You can keep me company."

"I thought since I wasn't a surgeon my place wasn't in the operating theater."

He chuckled. "So I did, but I think this once I can make an exception for my new partner. Will you come down?"

"I'll be right there." Geri let go of the buzzer and made her way down to the change room, where she found some scrubs. A nurse led her to the scrub room, where she scrubbed down and then entered the operating theater. She kept a discreet distance so she didn't contaminate the sterile field. She'd missed being in the operating theater. It had been so long.

"I wanted to apologize, Mr. Ashwood," she said.

"Whatever for?" he asked absently, in that haughty way that drove her insane.

"I think you know."

He shook his head. "No apology needed. I might've been too harsh on you. You're allowed to have an opinion."

Geraldine was shocked. Frederick would've never admitted that to another surgeon or doctor.

"I really think—"

"No. It's done. More suction, please." Thomas didn't look at her as he continued the surgery. "Lord Twinsbury is a friend of my father's. I've known him for quite some time. I get a little overprotective of him."

"I see. Is your father friends with my father?"

Thomas smiled behind his mask, she could tell by the way his eyes crinkled. "No, in fact they were nemesis… or is that nemeses?"

Geri chuckled. "Rivals?"

"In some respects," Thomas said. "Although my father was not in the medical profession. I believe they were both rapscallions in their youth. Playing the field and going after the same women."

Geri's stomach twisted in a knot and she had a hard time picturing her father as a rapscallion. "Is that a fact?"

"Yes. I was surprised when your father brought me on when I completed my surgical residency. He had the most prestigious cardiology practice in Harley Street and I was willing to give my eyeteeth to work with him. I had to convince him that taking on a surgeon was a good business decision."

That was more believable. In the short time she'd known her father she'd gathered he wasn't one to take chances.

"Well, you seemed to have won him over."

"He never told me about you, though, not until a couple of months ago when he said you were joining us." This time he looked up from the surgery to fix her with those dark eyes that seemed to see past her facade into her very soul.

"My father and I don't have the best relationship. Or at least we didn't. I'm hoping to rectify that now." She hoped he didn't know she was lying through her teeth and under his hard stare she felt a bit uncomfortable.

"You're not even listed in *Debrett's*."

"Should I be?" Geri asked, hoping her voice didn't rise with her nervousness.

"Your parents were legally married."

"Briefly. I believe the divorce was finalized just after I was born. My mother left before she knew she was pregnant with me."

"So you should be in *Debrett's*, given that your father has a seat in the House of Lords."

"You seem to know a lot about me."

"I know nothing about you and that's the problem." He held out a hand while a scrub nurse passed him an instrument. "You're a complete mystery."

"Why are you even looking me up in *Debrett's*? What does it matter if I'm listed in there? It's a pretty useless publication, if you ask me." She crossed her arms, hugging herself, as if that would hide the fact that she was the estranged daughter of an aristocrat.

She'd read this story a million times in the romance novels she cherished. Only those novels were fiction and fantasy. This was real life.

And she was a doctor, a darned good doctor who was specializing in cardiology, and she had no interest, at the moment, in anything beyond medicine and helping her patients.

"It is that," Thomas agreed. "I mean, who needs to know who is thirty-seventh in line to the throne?"

"Exactly. I don't know and I really don't care."

"So what do you care about?" he asked.

"Medicine. It's all I care about."

He chuckled and shook his head. "You should've been a surgeon."

"And why is that?"

"You're cold. Detached. Vicious."

"I'll take that as a compliment," she said.

"I meant it as one," Thomas said. "But surely you have some interest beyond medicine. Reading, travelling...crochet?"

"Crochet?" she asked, trying not to laugh at the absurdity.

"It's good for the hands. Keeps the fingers strong and the mind sharp."

"Do you crochet, then?"

"Good lord, no."

"Then who told you that crocheting keeps the fingers strong and the mind sharp?"

"My grandmother, but then again she was a bit batty."

Geri couldn't help but smile. "So what do you do, then?"

"I paint."

Now she was intrigued. "What do you paint?"

"Nudes mostly." And he waggled his eyebrows at her over his surgical mask. She couldn't help but laugh along with the others in the room.

Frederick would never joke like this.

It was beneath him and Geri found herself liking this laid-back camaraderie. There was a light in the darkness of a serious surgery.

"I read a study once that said patients, although under general anesthesia, are aware of what is going on around them. Subconsciously. Better outcomes when the surgeon is happy."

Thomas stared at her and she regretted opening her mouth. Was he going to berate her again?

"I heard that too. And I believe it." He returned to his work and Geri watched him. Thomas was just as impressive as she'd always thought he would be.

Thomas laid down his instruments. "Dr. Fellowes, would you close up for me?"

"Yes, Mr. Ashwood." Dr. Fellowes stepped into the lead surgeon spot and began to close up the patient.

Thomas moved past her to the scrub room and Geraldine followed him as he peeled off his gloves, mask and surgical gown, placing them in the receptacle, before he began to scrub his hands.

Geraldine did the same.

"That was textbook surgery, if I do say so myself." There was a smug, satisfied smile plastered across Thomas's face.

"I'm glad it went so well."

"Well, the surgery went well. The next twenty-four hours will tell me the entire picture." Thomas dried his hands. "It's still touch and go. Recovery will be the key to success or failure."

"Will I see you tomorrow at the office?" Geri asked.

"No," he said. "I plan to stay close to Lord Twinsbury tonight. I will be monitoring him in the intensive care unit."

"Is it because he's a family friend or do you do that for all your patients?" She was teasing, she didn't really expect such a high-class surgeon to remain by his patient's bedside. Especially an elderly one like Lord Twinsbury, who, given his health, probably wouldn't have much of a shot of pulling through.

"All of them. Every last one."

She was stunned and was positive her mouth was hanging open by the way he grinned at her.

"Have a good evening, Dr. Collins."

Geri watched him walk down the hall. She shook her head. Every time she tried to fit Mr. Ashwood into a certain slot in her mind, he completely and utterly didn't fit.

And just as she'd surmised before, he was a danger.

A very sexy, tempting danger that she wanted no part of.

"You took the tube again didn't you?"

Geri hung up her coat on the coatrack in her father's office. "Well, you didn't wake me when Jensen took you to work."

"You got in late. I thought you'd appreciate the lie-in."

She had actually. "Yes, but today is clinic day. How am I supposed to get to know my new patients if I spend half the morning in bed?"

"Why didn't you call Jensen to bring you in?" her father asked. He sounded tense, as if he'd been worrying about her the whole time. Which was nice, but unwarranted. She was an adult.

"The Westway is jam-packed or didn't you hear about that?" she asked.

"Jensen could've taken the Bayswater Road. The Westway is always jam-packed at this time of day."

"I'm quite used to taking public transportation."

"I know, Geraldine, but your situation is different now." He returned to his work.

She took a seat in front of her father. "And how is it different? I still am the same person and no one knows me from Adam."

"You're a lady of means. An heiress," he said, not looking up.

Geri wrinkled her nose. "I'm a doctor."

Her father ran a hand through his hair and then sighed. "You're just as stubborn as your mother."

Geri shrugged. "I'll take that as a compliment." Though she really didn't think it was much of a compliment as she didn't want much association or comparison with her mother.

"Hmm." Her father then pulled out a cream-colored envelope and handed it to her. "You've been invited to your first social gathering."

She took the envelope and stared at the fancy calligraphy. "What's it for?"

"It's for a party after the London International Horse Show. We've both been invited. It's formal attire as the Duke of Weatherstone has been invited. You know he's in the line of royal succession."

Geri cocked her eyebrows and stared at the invitation. "How do I turn it down?"

"You can't turn it down."

"Why not?" she asked, flipping it over. "It's for this weekend."

"And what plans do you have for this weekend?"

She shrugged. "Christmas shopping."

"You're going. I've already told our hostess we'd be attending. Besides, it's a good way to get to know some of our patients. A lot of them will be there."

Before she could argue there was a knock at the door and Thomas stuck his head in. There were dark circles under his eyes, as if he'd been up all night, but that didn't deter from his general svelte and put-together appearance.

Good lord, he was handsome and a brilliant surgeon to boot.

Why did he have to look so good?

He's off-limits. Off. Limits.

"Am I interrupting?" Thomas asked.

Yes.

"No, Thomas, come in," Charles said.

Thomas opened the door and came in, jamming his hands in his finely tailored trouser pockets. "I wanted to report that Lord Twinsbury made it through the night."

Her father nodded and smiled. "That's excellent news."

"Wonderful," she said.

Thomas glanced at her briefly, his gaze landing on the cream-colored envelope. "Ah, I see the invitations for the Gileses' party have arrived."

"Yes, apparently the Duke of Weatherstone will be there," Geri teased.

A strange look passed across his face. "Well, I can tell you who won't be there—Lord Twinsbury. He'll still be in hospital for another week at least. At least he's out of the intensive care unit, but he's demanding to see his cardiologist."

Her father sighed. "I'll get Jensen to bring the car round."

"No, Charles. He wants the good-looking one." Thomas grinned at her. "He's asking for you, Dr. Collins."

Her father chuckled. "You'd better go, Geraldine. And please take Jensen."

"The Westway is completely jammed, though," Thomas said. "She could always take the tube."

Geraldine couldn't help but laugh at that, especially when her father glared at Thomas. "Only if you accompany her."

"Of course. I am a gentleman after all."

"That remains to be seen," her father mumbled.

Geraldine set down the invitation and grabbed her coat, heading out into the hallway with Thomas.

"So much for getting to know patients today." Geraldine followed him down to his office, where he grabbed his own coat and wrapped a scarf around his neck.

"You are getting to know a patient by going to the hospital and attending Lord Twinsbury. By doing so you're letting your other future patients know that you care."

"He just had surgery, you should be the one attending to him. Not me. I'm not the surgeon."

Which was a bitter pill to swallow.

"And I will be. I am accompanying you after all." Thomas cocked a head to one side. "You're not wearing a hat?"

"No, should I be?"

Thomas shrugged. "It's cold outside."

"I'm from Scotland. This is not cold for December. This is balmy," she teased.

"Balmy?"

"Yes. Exactly."

Thomas just shook his head. "Come on, then, my lady, I'm to be your escort to the tube."

Geri fell into step beside him and they walked down the street toward Regent's Park Underground Station.

"You know, it's been some time since I've taken public transport," he said offhandedly.

"Don't tell me you have a driver as well."

"Good lord, no. I find it a particular challenge to wrestle my way along the motorways on my daily commute."

"You're an interesting character, Mr. Ashwood," Geri remarked. "Wrestling motorways and painting people in the nude."

"Oh, yes, which is why you should get to know me better," he whispered huskily.

"Hmm, that remains to be seen."

"You still never told me what interests you beyond medicine, Dr. Collins."

"I do like reading."

"I do hope it's racy novels."

"Naturally," she teased, completely forgetting herself. *What're you doing?*

"Actually, I love Jane Austen."

"Most ladies do. I prefer Chaucer myself and Icelandic skalds."

"You're a man of many hidden depths."

"I could say the same about you, Dr. Collins. Except the man bit."

"I think since we're going to be partners you can call me Geri."

He cocked an eyebrow. "Geri? No, I think I'll call you Geraldine."

"Why? Only my father calls me Geraldine. No one else calls me Geraldine."

"Except me. Now. Geraldine. I like the sound of it. It's elegant."

"Hardly. I always hated the name."

"You shouldn't. It suits you."

"So what do I call you?" she asked.

"You can call me Thomas."

"Not Tom?" she teased.

"If you expect me to answer, no."

"You're so frustrating." Geri walked ahead of him. "I don't need an escort to the hospital."

She was hoping that he would take the hint and head back to the practice, only he didn't. He kept pace with her.

"Go back to the practice, Mr. Ashwood."

"I'm hurt. What happened to using our given names?"

"You became pedantic and annoyed me," Geri said, but a smile hovered on her lips. She was enjoying herself immensely. Which was a bad thing.

"I've been called many things, annoying especially, but never pedantic. That's a new one."

Geri couldn't help but laugh as they headed down to the underground at Regent's Park Station. When they were on the tube, crammed close together as they rode in silence, Thomas glanced down at her.

"Why don't you like Geraldine? It's a lovely name," he asked.

A hot flush crept up her cheeks. No one had ever called her name lovely before. She'd always hated it. Men would usually call her Geri. Geraldine was an old-fashioned name.

"I thought I'd name you Geraldine after your father's mother since that's the only thing you'll be getting from him."

Of course, Geri had never met her namesake.

"It's an old-fashioned name." It was an excuse. She did like her name, but preferred to be called Geri. When she'd learned Geraldine was a connection to her long-absent father who had never come to rescue her, she'd wanted to cut that tie.

She'd learned the hard way that she could rescue herself.

He shrugged. "So is Thomas, but I quite like it. Geri makes you sound like a singer in an all-girl pop band."

She laughed. "Well, I like Geri."

"And I like Geraldine. You'll see it my way soon enough

and you'll be begging me to say your name over and over." His voice was deep, like thick honey. Honey, which she pictured smearing over his body and licking off.

Blast.

"Are you propositioning me?"

He grinned, a smile that was dangerous and made her feel weak in the knees. "And if I was?"

"I would tell you to keep looking." She turned her back on him, but couldn't help but smile. It had been a long time since a man had flirted with her. When Frederick left her, no one had had anything to do with her. It had been as if she'd been a pariah.

And she'd known there had been a rumor going around that she was a cold fish in bed. Unfeeling. And that could be true. She'd never particularly liked sex. Yet when Thomas flirted with her, her pulse quickened and her body reacted to being so close to him.

He had some kind of spell over her. He was so tall, standing next to her on the tube, that longish dark hair styled so fashionably, the twinkle to his eyes and saucy smirk on his mouth. He was so confident.

She'd forgotten how much she liked the attention and she wished she had half the confidence and appeal he was oozing.

Don't think like that.

She wasn't going to get sucked in. She wasn't going to let another man affect her. This was her chance at something great. Geri was going to prove that she earned this partnership, just as much as she'd inherited it.

And nothing was going to get in her way.

CHAPTER THREE

THOMAS STOOD IN the hall, watching Geraldine with Lord Twinsbury. Before they had got to the hospital Lord Twinsbury's vitals had dropped and he'd had to remain in the ICU for the time being, but as he watched Geraldine talk with their patient, he could see color coming back into the old coot's cheeks.

And he couldn't help but grin. Geraldine may be a bit cold with him, but with patients she was gentle and kind. She had a good bedside manner. Even with Lord Twinsbury, who was a tyrant. Just like his own father had been. Tyrants didn't faze her. She held her own and he had to admire her spirit. She was strong. Stronger than any woman he'd ever known.

Most women in his circles wanted to be saved or acted helpless at times.

A dressing-down would've outraged them, but it hadn't bothered Geraldine one bit. In fact, she'd admitted her mistake and apologized.

It took a lot of gumption to do that. Now she was in there with Lord Twinsbury and handling him as if Lord Twinsbury was nothing more than a gentle kitten.

Which was far from the truth.

Lord Twinsbury had been as much of a reprobate as his father and Lord Collins had been. Thomas knew who the woman his father and Lord Collins had fought over was. He was staring at her daughter. He had been seven at the time, he just didn't know all the particulars.

His father had been widowed for three years and had been looking to find love again. His father had never talked much about the woman he'd been trying to woo, had said only that Lord Collins had come out from under him and swept the woman off her feet.

And it had always been a point of contention with his father that Geraldine's mother had chosen Lord Collins over him. His father had become bitter, even more so, and Thomas had resented that woman for making his father miserable. Of course, that hadn't worked out well for Geraldine or Lord Collins either.

He'd done research last night, checking on Lord Twinsbury, and that research had been Lord Twinsbury actually telling him a thing or two about what had happened.

Although Lord Collins had been head over heels in love with Geraldine's mother, the two had come from two different worlds and had not been suited. She had been a friend of a friend and had gate-crashed a party his father and Charles had both attended. And both of them had been enchanted by her. Apparently Geraldine's mother was cruel, emotionless, and had crushed Charles's heart.

Charles had never known until recently that his short-lived marriage had produced a daughter. According to Charles, his ex-wife had left not knowing she was pregnant and hadn't bothered to tell him she was carrying his child.

Thomas couldn't even begin to imagine the pain that must've caused Charles.

For Charles may have been a rascal and rogue in his younger halcyon days, but he knew Charles had suffered from an unimaginable heartache. He knew that Charles was trying to do his best to bridge the gap between him and Geraldine.

Only Geraldine was not meeting Charles halfway and he couldn't help but wonder why.

Thomas loved his father, but his father had always been a bit too distant, a bit bitter, and Thomas had spent most of his childhood at boarding school. He knew that his father had had a hard time looking at him because it had reminded him of his dearly departed wife. Thomas had had a lonely childhood, deprived of love.

"Ah, 'what tangled webs we weave,'" Thomas muttered under his breath.

You should keep moving. Stop staring at her.

Only he couldn't help but stare at her.

Unlike his father, he had never had his heart torn apart by grief, although he had experienced a disastrous infatuation in his youth. A woman who had been more interested in the title he was to inherit. The social status. She hadn't loved him for himself.

"Why do you need to work as a surgeon? Your family has enough money and land. Why not run your estates?"

"Cassandra, that's not what I want. I love medicine. I love surgery and saving lives is my passion."

She had never understood him. Not really, and he'd been blinded by lust. Then his father had died of undiagnosed hypertrophic cardiomyopathy and Thomas had found out he had the genetic predisposition for it too. He'd decided then and there that family was not for him. Especially when he'd seen how small a comfort Cassandra would be should the worst happen. Suddenly, to her, he had been defective. A lesser being. Being alone was far better.

Was it?

He shook his head in disgust with himself.

He'd only been around Geraldine Collins for a day and she was getting under his skin. He couldn't allow her to do that.

You can seduce her. You are after all the Dark Duke.

Maybe if he had her once it would purge her from his system.

What am I doing?

He ran a hand through his hair. He was actually standing outside a patient's room and contemplating seducing the estranged daughter of his colleague, a physician he truly admired. When had he become so jaded?

But he knew the answer to that.

"Lord Twinsbury seems to have stabilized," Geraldine said, coming out of ICU and disposing of her gown and gloves. "What is your assessment, Mr. Ashwood?"

"I think he should stay in the intensive care unit for now. The last time I thought his condition had stabilized, we prepped him to take him out of the ICU and his stats took a dive. It's better he stay here for now. There's no rush to move him."

Geraldine nodded. "Well, I've done all I can here. I think I'll head back to the practice and assist my father."

"Yes, that's probably for the best. Do you want me to escort you back to Harley Street?"

She smiled at him. "I think I can find my way back there. I managed to get from Holland Park to there."

"Holland Park?"

"I'm staying with my father for the time being, just until I find my own place, but I have to say that I'm enjoying his town house in Holland Park. It's peaceful there. So different from Glasgow."

"Yes, Holland Park is one of my favorite places. I have a flat in Notting Hill, actually. I have a very spacious flat."

"You're not far away, then," she said.

Thomas shrugged. "As you said, Harley Street is not far from Kensington. Twenty some odd minutes on Westway."

"As long as it's not jammed." They chuckled together

over that goofy private joke. A blush tinged her cheeks and she tucked an errant strand of brown hair behind her ear, drawing his attention to her long slender neck. It was in that moment that pink tinged her creamy white skin that he knew he was in serious trouble. She was beautiful.

He had to make his excuses and get out of there. It was best if he kept his distance from her. They were business partners and nothing more. That's all they could be and the fact that he had to keep reminding himself of that was not a good sign.

"Well, I have some other surgical patients to make rounds on. I'll leave you to your work." It was a complete lie. There was no one else to see, but the more he lingered here the harder it was to leave. He found himself enjoying her company.

"I'll see you later. I should head back to the practice." She nodded and walked away from him, doing what he couldn't do. And he watched her walk down the hall toward the elevators.

This was bad.

When had she gone from someone he loathed—someone he planned to put through her paces because he wanted Charles's practice all to himself—to not being able to tear himself away from her? Escorting her to the hospital and admiring the flush of her skin, the red of her lips and wondering what it would be like to take her in his arms and kiss her?

The moment you saw her.

Which was true. He may have been rude to her when she was in the doctors' lounge, but when he'd seen her sitting there, looking around, he couldn't help but be intrigued by her. Why she was there and who she was.

And he knew that he was in big trouble if he didn't tread carefully.

The problem was he wasn't sure if he could stop himself.

* * *

Why did I let my father make an appointment for me?

Geri tried to really listen to what the stylist was saying as she was wandered around Harvey Nichols, but all the dresses blurred together in a great amorphous blob of color. When she'd got back to Harley Street, she'd met some patients and then her father had announced that Jensen was taking her to Knightsbridge to buy a dress for the social gathering she didn't want to attend.

"As my heiress you have to attend."

"I'm not an heiress. I'm just a doctor from Glasgow."

"I'm sorry, Geraldine, but as my only child you are an heiress."

"Why couldn't I be illegitimate?"

"Believe me, your mother isn't the only one who regrets our marriage." Then he gasped. *"I didn't mean it like that. I didn't mean... I'm glad you're here, Geraldine."*

"I know, Father. It's okay."

Geri had chuckled over that. Her mother had often reminded her she'd made a mistake in marrying her father.

"I should've chose the other man. I would've been far better off. Of course, I wasn't keen on his child and told him so."

Her mother wasn't keen on children, period. Something Geri was painfully aware of. Still, she was her father's only child.

There weren't any other relatives either. There was no one but her. She was it and even though she didn't like it, she had to do her duty and mingle with the social elite in London.

She hadn't minded the ride to Knightsbridge. She'd been a bit tired after her long day, and had just not expected the stylist to pounce on her the moment she walked through the doors of the department store.

She'd even tried to fend her off by telling her she'd just

poke around the dresses on her own, but that was a definite faux pas.

Take a deep breath. It'll be over soon. All you have to do is pick one.

"Do you have anything in silver?" she asked. "I like silver."

The stylist gasped. "You need color! It's almost Christmas and this is a big event."

"It is?"

The stylist nodded. "Your father was quite insistent about you picking out something absolutely stunning."

"Yes, but the thing is I don't like to stand out too much."

Which was true.

To avoid her mother's ire she had always remained quiet and retreated into the background. She didn't like being the center of attention, because no good came from it. Then Frederick had spotted her in a crowd of interns and had singled her out.

It had been thrilling, but she hadn't earned his respect. Only disdain and censure when their relationship had ended. No other surgeon had trusted her.

There was no way she wanted to stand out at the Gileses' social event.

The stylist ignored her and was clucking away through the fabric about chiffon or some other such nonsense. Geri groaned and cursed inwardly and as she looked around the department store she caught sight of Mr. Ashwood across the floor.

He was with a young woman who was blonde, stunningly beautiful, lean and tall, but not as tall as him. She was clinging to his arm and they were laughing. A flash of jealousy coursed through her.

She shouldn't be surprised that Thomas had a beautiful significant other. He was incredibly handsome. Dark, intense and sexy as hell.

He was a bad boy wrapped up in a respectable package.
Stop it, Geri!

He bent down and kissed the woman on the forehead.
Geri looked away. She didn't want Thomas to recognize
her.

"I think I've found the perfect dress for you!" the stylist
announced as she took Geri's hand and pulled her toward
the change rooms. "You'll love it."

"I'm sure I will." And hopefully by the time she'd tried
on the dress and bought it, Thomas and his girlfriend
would be gone.

Her father had paid for the dress and the stylist. So all Geri
had to do was wait for it to be wrapped up. It was a lovely
dress, but it was also the most expensive piece of clothing
she'd ever owned. Usually she bought her clothes from
fashionable, chic places that didn't cost an arm and leg.

She'd been a bridesmaid once at her friend's wedding
just after medical school and that dress hadn't cost her
what this dress was costing her father.

If the bridesmaid's dress hadn't been so hideous and
teal, she would've just worn that to the social gathering.

She smiled secretly to herself. Maybe she should just
return this designer gown and dig out that old teal monstrosity of lace and puffed sleeves to wear after all. Except she did really like the dress the stylist had picked out.

It was festive and Geri did so love Christmas.

When she walked out into the street she breathed in
the fresh, crisp December air. It had just begun to snow
softly and the Christmas lights were just starting to come
on along Knightsbridge.

Jensen pulled up in her father's black town car. He got
out and opened the door, but she wasn't quite ready to go
back home to Holland Park just yet. She wanted to take a
long leisurely walk and revel in Christmas.

It was her favorite time of the year, even if her mother wasn't a big celebrator of Christmas. Geri would spend her Christmases curled up on the couch, watching Christmas specials, and those happy families and stories of hope were the family love she'd secretly craved as a child.

Now this new life she found herself in felt overwhelming and she just wanted to take a moment and be by herself, soaking in the first real Christmas snow of December.

She handed Jensen the garment bag and a bag with various other accessories and shoes that went with it. "Can you take this home, Jensen? You can tell my father I've bought a dress and shoes. I'm going to go to his social function, but right now I just want to take a walk."

"Are you sure, my lady?"

"You don't need to call me that, Jensen."

He took the parcels. "I'm afraid I do."

"Then I'm sure. I'll be home later, but I'm thirty years old. I think I can manage a walk about town on my own."

He nodded. "Of course."

Jensen placed the items in the back of the car and drove away. Her father would be annoyed that once again she wasn't allowing Jensen to drive her home at night, but she didn't care. She needed a few moments to clear her mind.

Collect herself. She'd been unable to think straight when she'd been in the store. Actually, it had been a long time since she'd had the chance to really think straight, period. Finding her father and discovering who she was and being offered this partnership had been dizzying. She turned down a side street and wandered aimlessly while people bustled around her, doing their Christmas shopping. She was completely in her own thoughts when she ran smack dab into a muscular wall of a man.

"Whoa, are you quite…? Geraldine?"

Oh, no.

She glanced up to see Thomas Ashwood and his companion standing in front of her. They had just stepped out of a coffee shop and she hadn't been paying any attention and had run smack into the very person she wanted to avoid.

Curse Murphy.

"Mr. Ashwood, I'm surprised to see you here."

"I wouldn't think you would be too shocked as we were both in Harvey Nichols at the same time," he teased.

Heat bloomed in her cheeks as she realized he'd noticed she'd been there. "Were we?"

Thomas grinned. "We were."

Geri's glanced landed on the young woman next to Thomas, who was busy staring at her phone and looking completely bored. "Sorry for ruining your date."

The girl wrinkled her nose and laughed. "Date? Thomas is my elder half brother. And I do mean elder."

Thomas glared at her. "Yes, Zoe, that's quite enough out of you."

Zoe chuckled and then nodded at Geri. "It's a pleasure to meet you."

"Well, at least my half sister has manners." Thomas cleared his throat. "Dr. Geraldine Collins, I would like to introduce you to my half sister Zoe Western."

"I'm also illegitimate." Zoe grinned and Geri couldn't help but chuckle as Thomas rolled his eyes.

"Why do you feel the need to convey that to all my acquaintances?" Thomas groaned.

Zoe shrugged. "Usually they're a bit more shocked. She's not. Means she's worldly. I like that."

"Scamp, and what would you know about the world?" he asked.

Zoe playfully stuck out her tongue while Geri tried not to laugh.

"How much of an age difference is there between you two?" Geri asked.

"A lot," Zoe teased, while Thomas groaned. "I'm seventeen."

"Yes, but she's still not mature enough to take care of herself. Since our father died and her mother is working with Doctors Without Borders in Africa, I am currently Zoe's legal guardian." He smiled down at his younger sister with much tenderness. "We were just doing some Christmas shopping. She wanted to send her mother something nice to try to entice her back to London."

"Yes, so I can spend school holidays away from this tyrant," Zoe teased. "Which reminds me, a group of my friends are meeting over on Brompton Road at the cinema. Can I please go? Jennifer can give me a lift back to the flat."

"I suppose so, but I want you home by eleven."

Zoe rolled her eyes. "Yes, tyrant."

"Scamp." Thomas ruffled her hair.

"Nice to meet you, Dr. Collins." And with that Zoe left them, heading down Sloane Street back to Knightsbridge.

"I have to say I'm relieved she's your sister."

Thomas cocked an eyebrow. "Jealous, are we, Dr. Collins?"

"Hardly."

Liar.

"Then why are you so relieved?" he asked.

"Actually, I was worried that an older man was with a young girl. It looked a bit icky if you ask me."

Thomas laughed out loud. "Icky? Never heard that one before. And you do know many men in your father's circles have second or third wives who are scandalously younger than themselves. I mean, I saw Lord Twinsbury eyeing you up today. Perhaps you can be the next Lady Sainsbury?"

"No, thank you," Geri said. "Well, I won't keep you."

He grabbed her arm, stopping her from leaving. His

hand so strong on her arm, so reassuring it made her feel nervous, because it felt so good.

"You're not keeping me. Where are you off to?"

"I was just taking a leisurely stroll."

He cocked an eyebrow and then took her arm, slipping it through the crook of his arm. "In December at night?"

"Is there some sort of law against that?" she asked.

"No, but I'm thinking about the thousand fits your father is going to have."

"I'm thirty. He shouldn't worry so much."

"Maybe he's trying to make up for lost time?" Thomas suggested tentatively.

"It's hardly your place to say that, Mr. Ashwood," Geri replied icily. But a niggling voice in her head had said the same thing.

"True. Just a suggestion. From one gentleman regarding another gentleman.

Geri smiled. "Yes, you are a gentleman, aren't you? I don't know of another man who would take time out of his night to walk a new business partner down some random street in the snow."

"You're obsessed with winter, it seems."

"No, just Christmas."

"I don't get Christmas."

"What don't you get about Christmas?"

He shrugged. "It was never a big deal when I was growing up. I mean, I guess I didn't have a loving family. Detached was more like it. So Christmas was just another day."

"Same here," she said. "But I loved the idea of it being something more. Which made me just want to love it all the more the older I got."

"Well, it did get considerably better when Zoe came on the scene. It was nice being able to buy toys and dolls when I was young man and celebrating Christmas with her and her mother."

"Were they together long, Zoe's mother and your father?"

Thomas shrugged. "Long enough. But Zoe's mother wouldn't marry my father. She was smart."

"Why?"

"He was… He had a lot of resentment. He never did get over my mother's death."

"I'm sorry."

Thomas shrugged. "Zoe's mother always made me feel like a son. Didn't have much of a mother figure growing up and my father was distant. I lost my mother when I was very young. I don't recall her, but people have told me my father was happy. Though I never saw it."

"I understand. My mother was not the most pleasant. I'm sorry about your mother."

He nodded. "Yes, I was heartbroken. It was a myocardial infarction during a pregnancy that did it. The baby died as well. She wasn't far along when it happened. Crushed my father. He didn't really get over her."

Geri squeezed his arm. "That's nice they loved each other. My parents did *not* love each other. They were two ships that passed in the night."

"You sure about that?" he questioned.

"Of course. Why wouldn't I be?"

"They married."

"So?" Geri shrugged. "Love and marriage don't always go hand in hand."

"Still, there must have been some feelings."

"Whatever feelings they had I don't wish to discuss." She shuddered. "Why are you so adamant they were in love?"

He shrugged. "I heard different."

Geri pulled him to a stop and to one side so they

wouldn't get trampled by the Christmas shoppers on the sidewalk. "What do you know?"

"Nothing, just rumors."

"Tell me."

He opened his mouth to say something but his pager went off, as did hers. Thomas reached his first and pulled it out, frowning when he read the text.

"It's Lord Twinsbury. We have to get back to the hospital."

"I sent Jensen away," Geri fretted.

"Don't worry, my car is down the street." He grabbed her hand. "Let's go. Thankfully the hospital isn't far."

She nodded and let Thomas guide her along the busy road to his car. She still wanted to know what he knew about her parents, but right now Lord Twinsbury was the most important thing. Everything else could wait, because really what difference would it make if her parents had been in love thirty years ago?

It wouldn't change the past and wouldn't shape her future.

CHAPTER FOUR

"SUCTION, PLEASE." THOMAS WORKED over Lord Twinsbury. The graft had thrown a clot and begun to leak. It was the first time in a long time Thomas had performed a coronary artery bypass graft that had failed, but it was one of those things that could happen. There were so many factors that could lead to the graft leaking.

He was annoyed, but as he worked on Lord Twinsbury he could see the tissue was friable and he had a hard time suturing. All he seemed to be doing was macerating the vessels and he couldn't take another one from the groin. He glanced up to see Geri watching from the viewing gallery.

She was biting her lip and pacing, which wasn't helping, but he understood. She was worried about their patient. Her first patient since she'd started working with her father. He had a sneaking suspicion she liked the old coot and, truth be told, he did too.

Come on.

There was a buzz from the gallery.

"Mr. Ashwood, may I suggest something?"

"I'm all ears, Dr. Collins." What she could possibly suggest he didn't know, but if he didn't get the graft to work, if he didn't get the vessels to connect, he would lose Lord Twinsbury and he refused to let the old man go.

"Does the hospital have any donated umbilical vessels

that can be used instead of trying to take another one from the patient?"

"Brilliant, Dr. Collins." He nodded to a surgical fellow who took off to see if that could be found while he continued to work on saving Lord Twinsbury's life. It didn't take long for the fellow to return with an umbilical vein, prepped, stripped and ready to go.

Thomas gently took and placed it just below the faulty graft, praying that this one would be stronger than the one before. He was impressed Geraldine had known to suggest it. It was a trick only a well-read surgeon would know.

"Take him off bypass." Thomas closed his eyes and waited with bated breath. He glanced up at Geri, who had her hands pressed against the glass, worrying her bottom lip as she watched too.

The bypass machine slowed, the whirring sound ending, and the blood was allowed to flow through the heart.

Come on.

He didn't have to wait too long before the heart began to beat on its own again. The new graft was holding and he sent up silent thanks. Geri was clapping and smiling in the gallery and he smiled to himself as he finished the operation.

It was the best part of his job, saving lives, and it reminded him he was healing hearts, so that others didn't have to go through the pain he and his father had gone through when his mother had died. So other families didn't have to be devastated.

He couldn't heal his own heart, but he'd made his peace with that. He wouldn't pass the fear he faced along to children. This would never be their life. After what had happened with his mother and father, he knew he couldn't trust himself to love that deeply, to put his own heart at risk. His existence for the last thirty-odd years had worked and that's how it would stay.

When he'd finished with Lord Twinsbury he left it to his cardiothoracic fellow to take their patient up to the ICU. Tonight he would have his fellow monitor Lord Twinsbury's vitals. Charles wouldn't be happy, but he was tired from pulling an all-nighter just recently and it was Zoe's first day back from boarding school for the Christmas holidays. He wanted to be there for her.

Even if she spent most of her free time with her friends.

At least he would be home for her.

He would be the constant for Zoe, which he'd never had as a child.

Thomas leaned over the sink in the scrub room, rolling his neck. Every part of him was hurting and he couldn't remember the last time he'd felt so bone weary.

"You did amazingly."

He turned to see Geri, in scrubs, standing just outside the scrub room.

"You changed into scrubs to come and tell me I'm amazing? I'm impressed."

Geri shrugged. "I was going to do rounds on a couple of patients of my father's who were admitted for minor issues, so I thought I would come down here and congratulate you on that nice save."

"I should've thought of umbilical veins. It was the farthest thing from my mind as I tried to make the anastomosis with the original vein graft work. Thank you for being my reason back there."

"It's part of my job." She blushed. "Thank you for the acknowledgment."

"You're welcome, but it's not part of your job. It's a surgeon's job," he said. "Why didn't you become a surgeon again?"

"I wanted to be in a clinic instead of an OR. I wasn't cut out to be a surgeon."

She'd said something similar before and he'd believed

her at the time, but now he didn't really believe her; she was being evasive. Something else had made her decide not become a surgeon.

"Are you staying tonight?" she asked, changing the subject.

"No, I want to be home and see if Zoe makes her curfew." He dried his hands. "I'll grab something vile from the cafeteria to eat and then head for my flat."

"Enjoy your vile dinner. I'm going to make my quick rounds and then head back to Holland Park. I'm sure my father is wondering why a dress and shoes made it home but I didn't."

"A dress?"

"Yes, for that social event I'm being forced to go to."

"Ah, I'd completely forgotten about it."

She snorted. "I don't blame you."

And though he shouldn't offer it, he couldn't help himself. "Well, if I'm still here when you've done your rounds I'll give you a ride home."

"Thomas, it's okay, really. You don't have to stick around. You've just done grueling surgery and you need to go home and check on your sister. Make sure she made her curfew."

"Of course."

She nodded. "I'll see you tomorrow at the office."

Thomas watched her walk away from the scrub room, her long delicate hands thrust deep into the pockets of her white lab coat. Her glorious hair was braided and piled under a hideous scrub cap, but she still looked very desirable.

And he hated himself for his weakness when it came to her.

It was well after midnight when the taxi pulled up in front of her father's Holland Park town house. The lights were still on and she had no doubt her father was pacing. It was sweet of him, but he needed his rest. Part of the reason for his retirement was because he had cancer. He was fighting it and he needed to conserve every last ounce of his energy.

It was bad enough he wasn't telling anyone besides her that he was fighting the disease. He even went so far as to go to another hospital on the far side of the city to get his treatment. That way no one would know.

He was stubborn.

Just like her. Or at least that's what her mother had always said. Something she'd clung to as a child when she'd been wondering who her father was.

She had resented him for taking so long to find her and even then only finding her when it was too late almost to form a proper relationship.

"You're here now, Geraldine. That's all that matters."

She paid her cabbie and pulled out her key. There was a thick blanket of snow on St. James's Gardens across the road from her father's townhome and the streetlights gave the snow a warm golden glow.

The steps up to the navy door of her father's home had been meticulously cleared. That had probably been Jensen, who had gone back to his own home, which was not far from her father's. Her father might be of the gentry, but, other than Jensen, Molly, the cleaning lady and cook, he didn't employ servants, whereas Geri knew that Lord Twinsbury did.

Of course, Lord Twinsbury lived in Hampshire and when he came to London stayed at his club.

She didn't even have a chance to get the key in the door when her father swung it open, frowning.

"Where were you?"

"I was at the hospital, doing rounds on two of your patients. I also stayed to make sure that Lord Twinsbury's repair surgery went off smoothly." She pushed past her father into the entranceway and took off her jacket, hanging it on a coat hanger.

"Repair surgery?" Her father asked, concerned. "What happened? Is Lionel okay?"

"The vein graft leaked. The anastomosis from the original coronary artery bypass graft wouldn't hold. His veins were very friable."

And she was glad she'd been in the gallery to suggest the alternative graft. It had been her first surgical triumph as a resident on her first solo coronary artery bypass graft. She'd used an umbilical vein to save a young woman's life when that young woman's veins had also been very friable.

It was her signature move.

Frederick had felt a bit threatened by her at that point. She was sure now it was that surgery that had destroyed their romance a year ago. Still, Lord Twinsbury's life had been saved, even if she hadn't been the one to do the surgery. Even though she hadn't been able to see the full surgery from the gallery, she'd closed her eyes and could see it all step by step in her mind while Thomas had operated. And as she'd watched from the gallery she'd realized how much she missed surgery. Painfully.

She missed holding a heart in her hand, because it was a beautiful thing indeed.

It was comforting and she loved its complexities.

"Blast," he cursed under his breath, shaking her from her thoughts. Her father then ran a hand through his white hair. "Do you want a drink?"

"It's midnight."

"Yes, I know, but I can't sleep anyway. Damn pain." Her father wandered into the sitting room and began to pour himself a drink. She could hear the crackle of a fire.

Geri sighed, sinking down onto the very comfortable couch. "Sure, I'll have a gin and tonic."

"I thought you were a whisky lass," her father teased, pouring her a small glass.

"Usually, but I do have to get up early and go to the hospital first to check on our patients. Do you start chemo tomorrow?"

"Yes." Her father sat down in his leather wing chair. "I do."

"I wish you'd just get treated at St. Thomas Aquinas. Who cares if people know you have cancer?"

"I care." Her father took a sip. "I want to keep it to myself. Private."

She understood his need for privacy. There were things about her life no one knew and didn't need to know. Like she was a disgraced surgical resident, for one thing.

"If you were at the hospital I could check on you."

Her father raised any eyebrow. "Would you, then?"

"Of course." And it was true. As angry as she was at him, she knew none of this was really his fault. He had told her when they'd met that her mother had purposefully obscured the knowledge of her existence, until he'd received a letter from her a month before they'd met, telling him that he had a daughter. Even then, she hadn't formally met her father until the results of the DNA test to prove that they were actually related had been available. Their first meeting in the laboratory after it was confirmed had been awkward, to say the least.

"She called you Geraldine."

"Yes. Your mother...my grandmother, I suppose, had that name?"

"Yes." Her father cleared his throat. "She did. It's my favorite name."

For so long she'd been mad at her father for not coming to find her, but when she'd met him she'd realized the damage and hurt her mother had caused for them both.

Which was another reason she lived with her father.

She wanted to get to know him better, but it was hard. It was hard to trust another parent.

They may be related by blood, but they were both strangers who had been hurt and loath to trust again.

"Geraldine, I don't want you to waste time on me. My oncologist at Meadowgate Hospital is one of the best. Jensen can stay with me. He's already offered, and didn't ask for a wage, though of course I will pay him. Damn fool."

Geri smiled. "Remind me to thank him later."

"He brought in your dress." Her father smiled. "You'll look stunning at the function this weekend."

"You looked?"

"Of course." He grinned. "You'll really turn heads at your unofficial debut."

She winced. "Don't remind me. I'm liable to make a bloody mess of it."

"There's the Scot I know and love." Her father chuckled and winked. Only he didn't know her and she had a hard time believing that he loved her. She wasn't even sure if she loved him. Cared for him, yes. He was a brilliant doctor, but love? That was going a bit too far for her. Besides, how did one love an absent parent? Or even a parent when she hadn't even got love from her mother. She didn't believe in love. Look what had happened with Frederick.

"I really would prefer not to go," she said, hoping he would take pity on her.

"It'll be good for you to go. You can meet eligible, respectable men."

"Are you trying to marry me off already?"

He shrugged. "You're a lady of means. You will attract attention, just make a wise choice."

"I don't need to get married. Doubt I ever will."

Because I always fall for the wrong guys.

Plus she couldn't risk her heart again. Frederick had destroyed every single piece of trust she'd had. Love just hurt and there was no room in her heart for it. The only thing she could rely on was medicine. That was her true love.

"Never say never." Her father winked and she groaned.

"I'm headed for bed. I suggest you are too." She set down the glass on the bar, putting an end to the conversation. This was not a Regency romance. She was not going to make a suitable match. If she ever did decide to get married she was going to do so for love, not connections. She chuckled at that thought as she headed up the stairs to her room. She really doubted her father would go to bed any time soon.

She didn't blame him.

Cancer scared her as well.

She knew the reality of it. As did he.

And she wished it didn't have to be anyone's reality.

CHAPTER FIVE

"YOUR NEXT PATIENT is here to see you, Dr. Collins."

Geri looked up from her work. "Show them in, Ms. Smythe."

Mrs. Smythe nodded and disappeared. Geri was rather enjoying her time in the office. She liked getting to know her new patients. And sitting down to do reports was better than charting while standing up at a nurses' station, but it was the silence in between patients that she found a bit hard. The hustle and bustle of a hospital was far more relaxing to her than the quiet. It was getting to her.

The door opened wider and she was shocked to see Thomas's little sister Zoe enter her office. And she looked extremely nervous. She could tell by the way her green eyes were shifting around the office and she wouldn't meet her gaze.

"Thank you, Ms. Smythe," Geri said, dismissing the receptionist.

When the door was shut Zoe took a seat in front of the desk. "Thank you for seeing me."

"You wanted to see me?" Geri asked, and then she started worrying about all the reasons a seventeen-year-old girl might need to see a doctor she was familiar with.

Zoe nodded. "I chose a day that I knew my brother

wouldn't be here. Your father has been seeing me every time I come home."

Oh. No.

Her mind immediately jumped to the obvious, but then it dawned on her that she'd said she was seeing Charles as a doctor. So it couldn't be that.

She was confused and checked the computer for Zoe Western. "He doesn't have a file on you."

Zoe reached into her bag and handed her a file. "Your father let me keep it because of patient confidentiality and I don't want my brother knowing."

She took the file from Zoe and flipped it open, scanning the pages. "You have an atrial septal defect?"

Zoe nodded. "I was born with it and it went away, but when I was ten the hole opened up again. My mother took me to see your father and he referred me to a surgeon who did the catheterization. Thomas was at school then."

"It didn't work, though? You have a pacemaker?" Geri asked, as she flipped through eight years of medical reports.

"An arrhythmia. Your father has been caring for me since I was ten and I'm hoping you can do the same, under the condition that my brother doesn't know."

Geri shut the folder. "Why don't you want your brother to know?"

"Did he tell you his mother died of a heart attack?" Zoe asked, hedging because it was apparently a sensitive subject.

"Yes. He did."

"When I was first born with the atrial septal defect I was hooked up to a machine to help me breathe. The doctors didn't know if I was going to live or not and…he almost ran off from school he was so worried. Then there was this huge fight with our father…"

Geri held up her hand. She didn't really want to hear this from Zoe. If Thomas wanted her to know, which she seriously doubted, he would tell her himself. Zoe did have a point, though—patient confidentiality—but she was under age.

"Thomas is your legal guardian. He should know."

"My mother is. Thomas is one of my guardians, but if you need to talk to someone you can contact my mother in Malawi."

She sighed. "Okay, I'll take you on."

"Thank you." Zoe grinned. "I'm so relieved. Your father was always so good to me and I knew you'd be as well."

"Because of my father?" Geri asked, confused.

"No, by the way Thomas was going on and on about you and your brilliant suggestion in the operating theater with Lord Twinsbury."

Geri blushed at the idea of Thomas praising her.

Don't think about it.

"So this is a regular visit?" she asked.

Zoe nodded. "Yes. I hope it is."

Geri got up. "You need a checkup on your pacemaker, by the looks of your file."

"Yes."

Zoe followed her into the exam room that was attached to her office and sat down on the exam table, taking off her top. Geri handed her a gown, giving Zoe some privacy while she got ready for the check.

She wheeled over her computer and Zoe lay down flat.

"You're an old pro at this," Geri teased.

Zoe laughed. "Just a bit."

"So I don't have to explain the procedure to you."

"You can if you want."

Geri grinned. "No, I think I'll pass."

"I'm ready."

She attached the electrodes to Zoe's chest and her legs and then pulled out the magnet, placing it over the pacemaker so the computer could read the pacemaker. Geri watched the reading and there was nothing to worry about. Zoe's pacemaker was working fine.

"Your father never mentioned you before," Zoe said. "Well, until last year."

"That's because he didn't know I existed until last year."

Zoe smiled. "Cool, we can form a club."

"Club?"

"Illegitimate debutantes."

Geri chuckled. "I hate to break it to you but my parents were married. They divorced after I was born. I'm not illegitimate."

"Oh," Zoe said with disappointment. "Well, you're no fun. I was hoping you were as well so we could both shock everyone."

"You're quite witty for a seventeen-year-old."

She shrugged. "You have met my brother, haven't you?"

"Very true." The computer finished its reading and Geri took off the electrodes and the magnet. "You're all done."

"Thank you, Dr. Collins, and I appreciate you helping me and not telling my brother."

"It was my pleasure, but, Zoe, I think you should tell him. I mean, it has to come from you."

"I know. Your father has said the same thing to me several times."

It warmed her heart to hear how her father cared for all his patients. Especially pediatric ones. A trait they shared.

"Well, your pacemaker is good to go for another year. You know the drill. If you have arrhythmias or any other strange symptoms, please go to the nearest hospital."

"I know." Zoe pulled on her shirt. "Why is your father retiring? I mean, it just came out of the blue."

"Well, he wants to travel more."

Zoe looked confused. "Really? I thought maybe his cancer had become worse."

"You know about his cancer?"

She nodded. "He told me. We talked a lot."

"Well, then, not travel." Geri shut off the computer. "My father's cancer is worse. Stage four stomach cancer."

Zoe's face fell. "I had a feeling it was something like that. I'm so sorry."

"He starts treatment today. He's in chemo. Across the city because, just like you and your secrecy about health concerns, he doesn't want anyone at his local hospital to know that he's suffering from cancer. He doesn't want any help at all beyond from his chauffeur."

Zoe chuckled. "Poor Jensen."

"Yes, but I don't think Jensen minds too much."

Zoe grabbed her coat and Geri handed her back her file. "Thank you, Dr. Collins. I'll see you around, I'm sure, and definitely next year for my next checkup."

"Yes."

Zoe left the exam room and Geri sighed as she wheeled the computer back to the corner of the room. She couldn't help but think about her father.

He didn't want her there, but maybe she should've forced him to have her there. Jensen was all well and good, but she was his daughter. Even if she didn't totally feel like his daughter yet, she was still that.

She had a sense of duty.

The door in the exam room opened and Thomas peeked in. "Sorry, was that my sister Zoe that I saw leaving here?"

Blast.

"Yes, it was. She was looking for you and you weren't here. You just missed her. She's on the way to do some shopping with some friends." Geri worried her lip and hope that her lie went over with Thomas.

She wasn't the best liar ever and for one moment she saw a flicker of disbelief in Thomas's eyes.

"Oh, well, sorry I missed her. I got tied up with a cauterization and, of course, checking on Lionel." He grinned sardonically.

"I didn't think you were allowed to use his name?" Geri teased.

"I know, but he'll never know, now, will he?" Thomas tapped the side of his nose. "So what are you doing for the rest of the day? I know you don't have any more patients."

She cocked an eyebrow. "How do you know that?"

"I checked with Ms. Smythe."

"Why would you do that?" she asked cautiously, afraid of what his motives were, and then she cursed herself for questioning his motives. When had she become so untrusting?

"I was wondering if you wanted to have a ride over to the hospital where your father is getting his chemotherapy."

"How...how did you know?"

"I have a friend who works in Oncology at Meadowgate Hospital and he mentioned Dr. Collins had checked in. He thought I knew when he accidentally broke confidentiality."

"My father is not going to be happy that you know. He wanted it to be kept secret."

"I won't say a word. My lips are sealed. So, do you want to go?"

Yes. No.

"He didn't want me there. I think I'll honor his wishes. I don't think he'd be particularly happy if he found out that you'd brought me, as well."

"Ah, point taken."

Geri moved out to her office and Thomas followed her. "Don't you have patients to see?"

Thomas glanced at his wrist. "Not for another two hours. Do you want to get some lunch?"

"No." She laughed. Why was he so persistent? Couldn't he take a hint?

"What's so funny?"

"Are you the only surgeon who has such an open schedule? You're so different from the surgeons I knew in Glasgow. They never even had time to have a coffee."

"I serve a very different clientele here than the surgeons in Glasgow, I'm sure."

"I'm sure, Lord Hoity-Toity."

Thomas laughed. "I'm not exclusive to the 'hoity-toity,' as you put it. Anyone who wants my service, if I get the proper referral, can come and see me. Not all the hoity or toity come, though."

"Don't they?" she teased.

He rolled his eyes. "Okay, some do. I am the best."

She rolled her eyes. "I have a lot of work to do."

"Fine, then just turn down the best new café around here and a chance to have lunch with me."

"I'm sure I'll survive." Her phone buzzed and she saw a text from Jensen.

Your father has collapsed. He's not well. Please come.

"What's wrong?" Thomas asked.

"My father. I have to get to Meadowgate Hospital. He's collapsed."

"Come on, I'll take you."

"And what about your patients this afternoon?"

"I'll drop you off. I don't want to upset your father."

Geri nodded and grabbed her coat. Why did Thomas have to be so good to her? He barely knew her, but he'd gone from the standoffish jerk of their first meeting to her first real friend in London.

She didn't deserve that, given that she was rarely, if ever, friendly to him, but right now she'd take it.

Thomas had finished seeing his last patient and the support staff had gone home, but he lingered at the office, hoping that Geraldine would return. Which was foolish, but Geraldine was dedicated to her work. She seemed to retreat into her work a lot.

Of course, he did exactly the same thing.

And as if on cue, he heard the key at the front door of their practice and the security code entered.

"Shouldn't you be home, taking care of your father?" He asked.

Geraldine let out a small scream. "My God, man, you scared me."

Thomas chuckled to himself, hearing the Scottish burr slip out. "Sorry, I didn't mean to scare you."

"And what're you doing here? Shouldn't you be at home?" she asked accusingly, her voice still shaking. The accent was still there and fires of rage burned in her hazel eyes.

"No, no, you need to answer my question first."

Geraldine sighed and peeled off her coat, hanging it up. "I need to finish a couple of my charts. My father is stable and is now an inpatient at Meadowgate. He had a bad reaction to the chemotherapy. He'll be there for a couple of days."

"I'm sorry to hear that." And he was truly sorry. He liked Charles.

She shrugged. "Chemotherapy is hard. So now I've answered your question you can answer mine. Quid pro quo, my friend. Why are you still here?"

"I had some charting to catch up on as well. Surgical reports to send off to general practitioners who referred their patients to me. As well as one for you. I've emailed it to you."

"Really?"

"Of course. Lord Twinsbury. Is he not your patient? I do his surgical procedures, but you're his cardiologist. I've also sent one to his general practitioner."

"You're on the ball."

He shrugged. "I like to get loose ends tied up before the Christmas holiday."

"I thought you weren't a fan of Christmas?" she said.

"Ah, but Zoe is and I don't want her to be alone, with me working endless rounds at the hospital and doing surgeries to get through the holiday. Like I used to do."

She smiled at him, a warm smile that made his heart skip a beat. She rarely bestowed them, it seemed. "Very admirable of you."

"I'm going to order in some dinner, continue working. Would you like me to order something for you?"

She seemed to hesitate but then relaxed. "What're you ordering in?"

"That French café also does deliveries."

"Oh, I would love some French food. Surprise me."

He grinned. "Are you sure about that?"

"Nothing weird like brains. I don't mind snails, but I draw the line at brains."

"Fair enough."

She headed into her office and Thomas went to his to place the order. He ordered a variety of the café's most delectable dishes, all of which could be served with the Cabernet Sauvignon he had in his office.

When the food came, he grabbed the bottle of wine and two glasses and knocked on her office door.

"Your food, my lady."

Geraldine looked up. "It smells very good."

"It is good, I assure you." He set down the take-away

bags after she cleared her desk and then the bottle of wine and the two glasses. She cocked an eyebrow in question, seeing the two wineglasses.

"I don't know many surgeons who keep wine and wine glasses in their office."

"Don't you?" he teased as he popped the cork and poured out the wine. "I always have wine on hand to seduce women after hours."

Geraldine laughed. "Oh, really? And who would you be seducing after hours?"

"Doris, the cleaning lady." He waggled his eyebrows and she laughed as he set out the aluminum containers and plastic utensils. "Sorry, my level of sophistication ends with the wineglasses."

"It's okay. It all smells so wonderful I'm ready to eat it with my hands."

"You should laugh more, instead of showing the austere, reserved facade you're trying to pass off to everyone. It suits you."

A blush crept up her cheeks. "I laugh when something is funny. I'm not a total ice queen."

"People at St. Thomas Aquinas beg to differ on that point."

She groaned. "It's just better to keep things professional."

"Oh, well, I can take the food away…" he teased.

"Don't you dare."

He poured the wine. "Can you guess what I've ordered?"

"Since you're serving a Sauvignon I'm going to assume garlic. That, and I can smell it."

"Yes, Coquilles St. Jacques, *aligot*, crusty bread and madeleines are the menu tonight."

"*Aligot* is a word I'm not familiar with." She leaned over. "Smells good, though."

Thomas pulled it out and opened it. "Mashed potatoes

with garlic and melted cheese essentially. *Aligot* sounds much more sophisticated."

Geraldine took a paper plate and he served her a bit of everything and then dished up his own, sitting across from her. He raised his glass. "To a new partnership."

"Cheers," she said, clinking her glass against his. "I have to say this is the nicest and most delicious work dinner I've ever had. I thought grabbing a pot noodle on rounds was as good as it got."

Thomas wrinkled his nose. "Travesty. Though it usually is. This is a rarity."

She smiled and his blood heated. He liked it when she smiled at him and he couldn't help but wonder what it would be like to kiss those lips, to feel her pulse race under his fingertips and wrap her up in his arms, bringing her to ecstasy.

Whatever he had, he had it badly for Geraldine. Usually, with any other woman, he would pursue her, and date her for a short time, until they realized that he was completely dedicated to his work and they would drop him. As soon as they realized he had no intention of settling down, the brief affair would be over and he wouldn't look back.

That's what living with hypertrophic myocardiopathy afforded him. The devastation his father had carried when his mother had died was something he would never wish on anyone. He'd taken a leap of faith when he'd had a fling with Cassandra, but then she'd broken it off and he'd taken it as a sign.

He was meant to be alone. It was better that way.

Only he couldn't do that with Geraldine. She was his partner, the daughter of a man he admired. There was no way he could seduce her to purge her from his system. So why was he bothering with this silly pursuit? The best idea would be to put distance between them but, try as he may, he gravitated to her.

He was drawn to her. He hadn't realized how lonely he was.

"This is heavenly," she said between mouthfuls. "Good choice."

"Thank you," he said. "I spent some time in France in my youth so I'm a bit of a connoisseur."

"I've never been to France. I would love to go to Paris one day."

"I'm sure you'll go one day. I mean you have the money now," he teased.

"I don't. My father does."

"You're his heiress, are you not?"

She frowned, her face unreadable. "Yes, and what of it?"

"Don't get defensive. I'm not a fortune hunter. I'm just stating a fact that as an heiress who stands to inherit a pretty penny you'll be able to afford to go to Paris one day."

"True, but Paris is the city of romance, is it not? I don't want to go there alone."

"Why not? I think it can be a great place to be alone. To get lost in yourself."

She cocked her head to one side. "Is that what you did?"

"Once or twice. I love France, as well."

She was staring at him with a dreamy expression, one he knew all too well from his past conquests. This was heading in the wrong direction fast. He needed to change the subject.

"So what was your mother like?"

"Unpleasant." Geraldine frowned. "She had moments of tenderness, but really I don't think she cared for me."

"Makes you wonder why she kept you and didn't hand you over to Charles."

Geraldine nodded. "I've thought about that too. I guess she just didn't want to make anyone happy. She didn't get along with her parents, she didn't have many friends. Men friends, yes."

"You do know that my father was the other man."

She almost choked. "What?"

He grinned. "Unfortunately, I was the boy who drove your mother into your father's arms. Enraged my father something fierce. It's why your father and my father hated each other. They were both vying for the same woman."

"Be thankful your father didn't marry my mother. It would've been terrible."

"From what you say, I gather that, but honestly how much worse could she have made it? I was already pretty miserable."

"I'm sorry, Thomas." And she smiled at him warmly.

I'm sorry too. They came from different worlds, but really they were the same.

You need to put some distance between you.

He took that warning to heart and stood up.

"Well," he said, clearing his throat and cleaning up the empty containers, "I have a long day of surgery ahead of me tomorrow. I'll get this mess out of your way so you can get back to work and I'll head back to my flat."

A blush tinged her cheeks and she swept an errant strand of hair behind her ear. "Of course, yes. I have a lot of charting to finish up. I don't want to be here all night."

Thomas nodded. "Good night, Geraldine."

"'Night, Thomas."

He left her office, shutting the door behind him. He lingered briefly in the hall then headed back to his office. There was no way he could purge her from his system. He couldn't pursue a friendship or anything more with Geraldine. Things had to be completely professional.

Or he'd forget himself completely and put his heart at risk.

CHAPTER SIX

GERI WAS PACING and still trying to figure out a way to get out of going. Social functions had never been her forte in the past. She was a bit of a wallflower and the couple of times she'd accompanied Frederick somewhere she'd felt very out of place and unwelcome. And she had a sneaking suspicion that she would be unwelcome at this function as well. She was, after all, Lord Collins's estranged daughter.

"You're worrying for nothing, Geraldine."

She glanced up the stairs. Her father was standing at the mirror on the landing, adjusting his bow tie.

"And how do you know I'm worried?" she asked.

"Easy. You pace, just like me."

Geri smiled and then went up the few steps to the landing to help her father with his bow tie.

"You're hopeless at this. I thought a lord would know better," she teased.

"I have someone dress me usually." He was teasing her back and it was nice. Usually he was so careful, so polite.

"There," she said, smoothing his lapels. "All done. What would you do without me?" Then she blushed when she realized what she'd said and she could see the sadness in her father's eyes. A brief flicker of regret.

And she shared it, as well.

All those wasted years her mother had stolen from them.

She cleared her throat.

"You really shouldn't be going to this social event, Father. You've only been out of the hospital for three days."

Her father walked down the stairs slowly. "Nonsense, you're just trying to get out of it."

"I'm not."

Liar.

She was totally trying to get out of it. At least she didn't have to go to the horse show. She liked horses, she just wasn't really *into* them all that much, and enclosed stadiums full of animals were not her thing.

"You look stunning, by the way," her father said as he adjusted the cuff links on his tuxedo. "Absolutely stunning."

She was pleased by that. The dress was bronze-colored, with a fitted strapless bodice and a full taffeta skirt that was bustled up in a haphazard way. She felt very awkward in it, but she'd always secretly dreamed of wearing a dress like this, though after a certain point she'd stopped dreaming about it because she'd thought it would never happen.

Even at school formals, her mother had got her dresses from charity shops because her mother didn't believe in feeding the consumeristic fashion industry.

Vintage was better.

Only Geri secretly craved fashion and being chic.

That was the only upside to this social function, because she was absolutely dreading everything else. She didn't know anyone there and certainly didn't know how to talk to them. She knew nothing about the International Horse Show.

Once she got there and her father was satisfied that she'd met enough people, she'd retreat to a corner and try to stay unnoticed until her father grew tired enough that he'd leave. And she was sure that, given his bad reaction to the chemotherapy, their jaunt out tonight to this ball would not be long.

Her father was having a hard time coming down a flight of stairs. She doubted he would be able to do much socializing tonight. She wrapped her wrap around her shoulders so she wouldn't freeze in the December weather.

"Shall we?" He held out his arm, smiling at her.

"Of course. Let's get this over with."

"Geraldine, don't be such a Debbie Downer. You'll have fun. Who knows, you might meet an eligible and suitable young man."

"So you keep saying, but I'm not looking. Right now it's my career, as I've told you before."

"I can live in hope."

"You're a romantic? You?"

Her father nodded. "Yes. In spite of the hand love dealt me, I'm still hopeful."

She squeezed his arm. She wished she had his optimism, but when love had dealt her a bad hand she'd known it was better to cut her losses than remain hopeful.

Marriage was not in the cards for her.

Jensen was waiting at the bottom of the stairs for them. He held open the door and Geri slid in first, tucking her skirt in as her father climbed in beside her. There was a pained expression on his face. He winced as he shifted.

"Are you sure you should be going tonight?" she asked again.

"Positive," he snapped. "I'm fine, Geraldine. I've never missed this event and I'm damned if I'll miss it now."

She shook her head. "You'll regret it in the morning."

"I can live with that."

They stopped arguing when Jensen got into the car. They rode in silence to Mayfair, where the Gileses were holding the ball. The street and the drive were jam-packed with luxury cars and limousines.

"I'm sure their neighbors love them," Geri mumbled at the congestion.

"Most of the neighbors are invited." Her father smiled at her and took her hand. "Relax. It'll be fine."

Jensen pulled up and parked. He opened the door and her father got out first, then helped her out. Geri tried not to shake with nervousness as her father led her up to the front door.

She was stunned by the beauty of the home and by all the people dressed to the nines. There was a huge Christmas tree at least fifteen feet tall in the foyer. It was decorated in traditional Victorian ornaments and candles.

It was like nothing she'd ever seen before. It was like something from a magazine.

"You've stopped shaking," her father teased.

"It's beautiful," she whispered.

"Admit it. You're glad you came."

"Only a bit." She smiled at her father and gave him a little side hug. "I do like Christmas trees."

Her father just grinned at her and led her down the stairs through the foyer. Above the tree was a large chandelier, which accentuated the large spiral staircase.

"Are you quite all right?" Her father asked as he handed her a flute of champagne.

"I think so." She took the flute and laughed. "Still nervous, but this is just wonderful."

Her father nodded. "I'm going to say hello to our host and hostess. Will you be okay if I leave you for a moment?"

"Of course." Geraldine had already met the host and hostess and her father knew she was nervous about this event enough to make pleasantries.

She walked slowly around the tree, admiring the decorations and listening to the chatter around. There was a group of woman about her age. Debutantes. They barely spared her a glance, but she didn't care. She just stood there, admiring all the Christmas decorations and taking in the sights of a beautiful London home decked out for Christmas.

"I can't believe they invited Duke Weatherstone and that he actually came. He never comes to these things." The ladies began to chatter loudly.

"I heard that he actually seduced Harriet Poncenby, but since he didn't want to get married ever, she dropped him."

"He's devilishly handsome, though."

Geri chuckled to herself as she listened to the gossip and she couldn't help but wonder who this Duke Weatherstone was because she'd heard so much about him. All she could imagine was a middle-aged Lothario, because even though these socialites thought he was devilishly handsome, she doubted very much that he would live up to expectations.

No one ever did.

"He did, he actually came to this event and he looks so handsome in that tuxedo. Too bad he brought his half sister with him."

Geri whipped around to see who they were talking about and she gasped when she saw that it was Thomas and Zoe who were coming down the stairs.

Thomas? He's the Duke of Weatherstone.

And the women were right, he was devilishly handsome in that designer tuxedo. His dark hair was perfectly groomed and a mischievous, devil-may-care smile flitted about his lips. It made her feel weak in the knees and her pulse race. She'd been attracted to Thomas before, he was very handsome, but seeing him like this made her swoon just a bit.

Zoe looked gorgeous in a dark green velvet dress that accentuated her blond hair, the complete opposite of her dark brother. She also looked uncomfortable, but then her gaze met Geri's and she waved. Geri waved back, stunned.

Thomas turned and looked at her and that smile disappeared, replaced by an expression she couldn't read.

Warmth spread across her cheeks and she knew she was blushing.

Run.

He was heading toward her and there was no escaping now.

Zoe moved away to a group of friends who were waving her over, so by the time Thomas reached her it was just the two of them, but she was sure everyone was staring at them as they stood beside that big tree.

"You look beautiful," Thomas said. He took her hand in his and bent over it, kissing the knuckles. His hot breath fanning against her skin made a shiver of anticipation run down her spine. "Just absolutely stunning."

"Thank you," she whispered, finding her voice again.

"I do believe I've rendered you speechless." He grinned. "Good."

"Good?"

"All right, not exactly good, but I quite like being able to take your breath away."

"Thomas, or should I say the Duke of Weatherstone. You're a duke? So when were you planning to inform me? I am, after all, your business partner. Shouldn't I know these things?"

"That's a lot of questions."

"Well, I'm a bit shocked you're a duke."

"Yes, I'm afraid so." He winked.

"The Dark Duke, that's what they call you? Seducer of debutantes."

"And where did you hear that?" He asked.

"It's the *on dit* here tonight." Geri nodded slightly in the direction of the group of ladies, who sent her pointed stares.

He winced. "Again, guilty."

"I don't think I should be associating with you, Your Grace. You're liable to ruin my reputation," she teased, letting her guard down just slightly because she was enjoying her conversation with him.

Dangerous move.

He was a seducer. This was his game and she suddenly felt like the prey, only she wasn't sure she minded too much at the moment.

There was a twinkle in his eyes as he smiled. "Since when did you care about reputation?"

She froze, worrying that he knew something about Glasgow, about Frederick. "I don't... I don't care about reputation."

"Don't get missish on me. I'm only teasing."

She couldn't help but laugh in relief. "You look very svelte," she said, changing the subject.

"Why, thank you. I am, after all, in the line of succession." He ran a hand over his lapels. "I have to look somewhat dashing. I do have a reputation to uphold since I'm a dark seducer of innocents."

"You're such a rogue."

"I'll take that as a compliment."

And then before she could help herself the words tumbled from her lips. "You should. I have a soft spot for rogues."

Thomas cocked an eyebrow, but his pulse began to race the moment Geri said she had a soft spot for rogues. There was a slight twinkle in her eyes and if she'd been anyone else, he might have taken her up on that.

Except she was completely off-limits. He wouldn't seduce Charles's daughter.

Blast.

He'd known she was going to be here and he'd planned to stay away from the event, because he'd managed to stay away from her the last few days. Zoe had been very insistent on coming because of her friends who were planning to attend.

So he'd steeled his resolve and planned to hide away in the corner, but then she'd been standing there beside the tree, looking breathtakingly beautiful in that gown, her hair swept up, her back bare so he could admire the graceful sweep of her long neck.

Then she looked at him and he was lost and for a moment he forgot why he was staying away from her.

She's your colleague. Not a conquest.

"Is your father here?" he asked, trying to change the subject.

"Yes. He went over to speak to the host and hostess." She nodded in that direction and he saw Charles smiling and laughing, though he looked terrible. Charles's face was so gaunt.

"The chemotherapy is hard on him, I can see." Thomas sighed. "It's a shame."

Geraldine frowned. "Yes. I told him we should just stay home, but he was insistent on coming and was very insistent on me attending."

"Of course. This is your first formal function as his daughter."

"Why didn't you tell me you were a duke?" she asked again.

Thomas shrugged. "It's not something I like to brag about. It's just a title. I'm a surgeon. That I will brag about."

"I don't blame you for that in the least." Then she laughed. "A duke living in a flat in Notting Hill."

"I may have stretched the truth a tad. I'm afraid I live in quite a large house in Notting Hill. Staff quarters, the whole thing."

"A flat is what you said."

Thomas shrugged. "Well, my room is like a flat."

Geraldine rolled her eyes and music began to filter out of the ballroom. Even though he shouldn't, he decided he couldn't resist taking her in his arms, even just for tonight, and having a dance. He took her half-filled champagne flute and set it down. Then he took her hand.

"What're you doing?" she asked.

"We're going to have a dance."

"No, I don't think that's wise," she said, dragging her feet.

"I think it's very wise. Besides, what harm can it do? We're friends, right?"

"No," she said. "We barely know each other."

"Well, coworkers, then. Come on."

"I'm a terrible dancer," she said.

"I'll lead. It's not a problem." He winked at her and gave a tug and she followed after him into the ballroom where people were dancing to the slow music played by the live band. He spun her round and then pulled her flush against him, before leading her out on the dance floor. His hand was on the small of her back as he led the dance.

"You know how to dance?"

"Of course. I'm a duke." He winked at her and she laughed at his joke but turned her head away.

It felt so good, having her in his arms. He was cursing himself inwardly for doing something so unlike him again. He was pursuing the wrong woman. He couldn't have her. Only as they moved across the dance floor in sync, his resolve was weakening, because he did want her.

She was forbidden fruit and he was sorely tempted. Geraldine deserved a man who could give her everything he couldn't. He had money to support her, but he didn't have a heart to give her. He couldn't give her a family, even though that's what he wanted to do.

Geraldine had been through enough pain. Just like him. She deserved more.

"Come on, this dance can't be all that bad, Geraldine."

A pink blush tinged her cheeks. "No, it's not. It's actually my first dance. I was a bit of a wallflower growing up. No one ever asked me to dance."

"No one? They were out of their minds then. You're a fantastic dancer, for the most part because that was my toe you just stepped on."

"Sorry," she said. Then she laughed. "Although you do deserve it for forcing me out here."

He shrugged. "It's quite all right."

"Your sister looks beautiful tonight." Geraldine nodded in the direction of Zoe standing on the edge of the dance floor smiling at him as they moved past.

"Yes, she's a brat of the highest order. She's the one who forced me out here tonight."

"And what does she think of her brother being the notorious Dark Duke?"

He grinned. "She thinks it's funny, if a bit disturbing. She adores me, though, so it doesn't matter what I do as long as I'm up-front with her. We don't hide anything from each other."

A strange expression passed over her face.

"What?" he asked.

"Nothing. Just envious of your sibling relationship. I was an only child." Geraldine smiled. "Zoe is a wonderful young woman. You should be proud."

"I am." He glanced back at his sister. "She's my pride."

And the closest thing he'd have to having a daughter.

The dancing ended and they stood there for a moment at the edge of the dance floor while the other dancers clapped the band. He still held onto her, staring down into those deep green eyes. He was so close he could reach down and just kiss her.

"Come on," he whispered in her ear, drinking in her perfume.

"Where are we going?"

"I'm going to give you a reputation worthy of a lady." He winked at her.

She blushed, but followed him to a curtained alcove by a window. It was dark in there and she was trembling in his arms.

"Thomas," she whispered. "This isn't wise."

"I'm not going to do anything." Though he wanted to. "You should've seen everyone looking at you. Looking at us. I have to keep up the appearance of being something of a rogue, so I can get all those matchmaking mothers off my back. I'm a highly desirable bachelor."

"I guess, with your pedigree, you would be highly desirable." She sighed. "My father is pushing me to find a suitable match. Like I need to be married."

Thomas was intrigued. "You don't want to get married?"

"No. Not particularly."

"Why?"

"Does it matter? Why do I have to get married?"

"So, you wouldn't be against a bit of romance that didn't end in something more?"

Don't. You can't have her. Charles's daughter.

"No, I wouldn't mind," she whispered. "I don't need any promises made to me."

His pulse thundered in his ears and he reached down to touch her cheek, which looked almost like alabaster in the moonlight filtering through the window. She didn't need marriage, didn't want it. Just like he didn't want it. Perhaps he could just indulge once. Just one kiss. He was going to lean down and kiss her, but at that moment a scream rent the air.

They came out of the curtained alcove and looked back toward the dance floor to see what the commotion was about. Geraldine saw it first.

"Zoe!" Geraldine shouted, picking up her skirts and running.

Thomas spun around in time to see his sister crumple to the floor and go into a seizure before her body went rigid. By the time he got to her, she wasn't breathing.

"Call emergency services and get a defibrillator here immediately," he screamed above the din. He was handed one and charged it and was about to place the pads on her chest.

"No, you can't!" Geraldine yelled, throwing herself over Zoe's body.

"What're you doing?" Thomas shouted.

"Zoe has a pacemaker. If you shock her with incorrect placement of the paddles, she'll die."

CHAPTER SEVEN

"PACEMAKER?" THOMAS SAID, dumbfounded, as Geraldine did chest compressions. He was angry at himself for not acting faster. For not knowing about Zoe's pacemaker. For hesitating.

Wake up!

"Yes," she answered. "They need to be an inch away if you're going to shock her."

"I know," Thomas snapped. He adjusted the pads an inch away from where Geraldine indicated the device was implanted. "Clear."

Geraldine moved her hands and he shocked his baby sister. It almost too much to bear, watching her convulse as the electric shock moved through her, trying to start her heart again. It was more than he could bear and he cried out as he watched her. The only real family he had. The only one who'd loved him unconditionally since his mother.

"Let me do that," Charles said gently, taking the paddles from his hands. "You can't, you're family."

Thomas mumbled his thanks and took a step back. Feeling lost and helpless, all he could do was watch. It was agonizing.

Geraldine continued chest compressions. "I think the pacemaker stopped firing."

"When was the last time she had it checked?" Thomas demanded.

"Three days ago. She came to see me, and it was fine," Geraldine said.

Thomas was so angry. Why hadn't anyone told him that Zoe had a pacemaker, and since when? He also wanted to know who had put it in. He was ready to throttle whoever had. He felt like his trust had been violated, and he felt like a complete fool for saying that Zoe and he never hid anything from each other.

She clearly did and for one moment he wasn't sure if he could trust anyone.

No wonder Geraldine had looked so oddly at him, it was because she knew the truth. She knew there was something that Zoe had been hiding from him. He felt betrayed and hurt. There was no one he could trust.

"Clear," Charles shouted.

Geraldine stopped compressions and Thomas turned away, not wanting to watch has they shocked his sister again. This time, though, Zoe gasped for breath as the pacemaker obviously kicked back on.

Thank God.

"Zoe, you're okay," Geraldine whispered. "You're okay. Your pacemaker stopped working and you had a seizure."

Zoe didn't say anything, just nodded and took deep breaths. The paramedics arrived then and Thomas stood back as they loaded his sister onto a stretcher, Geraldine and Charles were telling the paramedics all the important health information.

Geraldine picked up her skirts and began to follow the paramedics out. Thomas raced after them and took Zoe's hand.

"I'm her brother and her guardian. I'm going with her," Thomas stated firmly, not letting his sister's hand go. He wouldn't leave her. He'd take care of her. He hadn't been able to save his mother all those years ago, but he'd save his little sister.

The paramedics nodded.

Zoe clung to her brother. She was shaking as she took deep breaths through the oxygen mask. Geraldine helped push the gurney out to the waiting ambulance. She climbed inside.

"You don't have to come, Geraldine. I have it from here." Thomas didn't want to take her from the party. Zoe was his responsibility. The truth was that he didn't want Geraldine to see him at this vulnerable moment with his sister. She couldn't see him like this. No one did. Only there was also a piece of him that wanted her there.

"I'm coming with you. I'm her doctor."

"No, you're not her doctor. I'm her doctor."

"No. You're her brother. You can't help and you know that. I am coming with you," Geraldine said firmly, but with tenderness that he appreciated.

Thomas nodded and then squeezed Geri's hand in thanks. She was right. He had no choice. He was Zoe's brother, family, and there was no way he could be her doctor right now because doctors couldn't work on their own family members. He had to let Geraldine help him.

"What if she needs surgery? You can't help her then," Thomas said. "I'm the cardiothoracic surgeon."

"No, but I can find someone who can. We'll get her help, don't worry." She squeezed his hand back, her touch reassuring. It felt so good to have that human connection. No one had ever shown him compassion like this before. He didn't know what he'd been missing.

Thomas didn't say anything further.

Still, he felt angry and hurt he hadn't known about Zoe's pacemaker. How could both Charles and Geraldine hide this from him? They were his partners. How could Zoe hide this from him? He felt hurt and he felt betrayed, but there was nothing he could do right now.

Right now his focus had to be on his little sister. And he was angry at himself for not seeing the signs of her condition. He was a cardiothoracic surgeon, for God's sake.

The ride to the hospital was tense and he couldn't stop the feelings of anger, confusion and fear whirling around inside him. He felt like he was going to burst at any moment. They pulled up at the hospital and all he could do was hold his sister's hand as they wheeled her into the accident and emergency department.

They called down a cardiothoracic surgeon and Thomas felt foolish standing outside the pod, not being able to do what he was good at. This was the one time his medical training was useless, because there was nothing he could do to help.

And for the first time in a long time he understood what his patients' families went through. He always had that sense of sympathy and connection with them because of what had happened to his mother, but he forgot what it felt like to feel completely helpless, and he didn't like it one bit.

Geraldine stood back as the cardiothoracic surgeon stepped in and started checking the pacemaker. Scans were being ordered. Geraldine was just a cardiologist. She had hospital privileges, but she wasn't a surgeon; didn't have the training.

She glanced back at Thomas through the glass of the trauma pod and he could see the sympathy in her eyes. He went to the doorway.

"Do you want me to leave?" she asked.

"No. Please stay with her. I know there's not much you can do, but it would make me feel better if you stayed with her. Zoe trusts you. She came to you. Not me."

And it killed him to admit it.

"She didn't want to worry you," Geraldine said, trying to ease his concern, but it didn't work.

"I would've rather known. This is a thousand times worse than not knowing."

She shook her head. "I'm sorry, but I couldn't tell you. Doctor-patient confidentiality."

And of course she was right. Geraldine had been just as stuck as him. In the heat of the moment he had been looking for someone to blame, but Geraldine couldn't have told him even if she'd wanted to.

"Please stay. For me. I need you to stay." His heart was tearing in two, waiting for her answer, and for putting his heart on the line, asking her to stay for him, but he needed her. Which terrified him.

Geraldine nodded. "I will. Of course I will."

Geraldine stood by helplessly while the cardiothoracic surgical registrars did their work in the cath lab, but she'd promised Thomas that she would stay with his sister the whole time. She felt a little bit foolish, standing off to the side in a ball gown, but after a bit she didn't care. She'd reminded herself that she'd done more embarrassing things in her younger days. This was nothing. She was doing this for her colleague.

Possibly her friend?

And she was doing this for her patient above all.

She'd seen the hurt in Thomas's eyes. She knew how much he cared for his sister and it broke her heart that this had had to happen. Zoe was too young to have this kind of thing happen to her, but then again she thought that about all her pediatric heart patients.

They were too young to have broken hearts, as it were. They didn't deserve it, which was why she wanted to become a cardiologist. To save lives.

It was why she'd wanted to become a cardiothoracic

surgeon. Only her foolish dealings with Frederick had ruined all that. She'd allowed her emotions to rule her instead of her head.

And when she and Thomas had been in that alcove together, she'd wanted him to kiss her. She had foolishly allowed her emotions to drive her decisions. And she was mad at herself for that. She was so weak.

She wasn't going to let another man get in the way of her career again.

She was here to be a cardiologist. That was it. There would be no running away this time, because she wasn't going to make the same mistake twice.

Right now while they were doing a heart catheterization to repair the damage to Zoe's pacemaker she wished she had her surgical training so that she could help Zoe, to ease Thomas's worry. She knew how to do this. She was good at heart catheterizations. Zoe was her patient and she should be the one in there.

Only she wasn't. And it was all her own fault.

Thomas was pacing in the hallway. The pain etched on his face was more than Geri could bear. She'd never seen him like this. He'd always had that air of devil-may-care, always joking, always smiling, always a twinkle in his eye. There were also times he was so arrogant it set her teeth on edge, but this was different. She felt bad for him. She felt bad that this was happening to him. Her friend. That's all he was. Her first real friend in London.

Geri took a deep breath and stepped out into the hallway. Thomas came rushing over to her, pain and worry etched into his face.

"Well?" he asked.

"They are doing the heart catheterization right now. The pacemaker was fine when I checked it four days ago. The computer ran a perfect test. She's had that pacemaker since she was ten, there was nothing wrong with it."

Thomas cursed under his breath and ran his fingers through his hair. "Yes, but, like all technology, all machines can be faulty. They're not good enough."

"The heart catheterization will work. They'll repair the faulty wiring in the pacemaker. She won't need to have another one inserted again. She's going to be fine."

"How do you know that?" Thomas asked.

"You should know that. You're a surgeon. A heart surgeon even. She's in good hands."

"Who's doing the catheterization?"

"Dr. Sandler is doing it."

Thomas groaned. "Ugh."

"Is there something wrong with Dr. Sandler performing the procedure?" Geraldine asked.

"No. Nothing wrong. He's a good doctor."

"Then you shouldn't be worried."

"Well, I am worried," Thomas snapped. "Zoe's all I have left. My father is gone, my mother is gone... Zoe is all I have."

"I'm here," Geri said. "I promised you I wouldn't leave her side."

"Why are you doing this?" Thomas asked. "We're just colleagues. You've said so yourself several times."

"Yes, we're colleagues and this is what good colleagues do for one another. We're partners in a practice. I would hope when it came to my father you would do something to help."

Thomas's expression softened. "I wish I could do something, but cancer isn't my forte, unless it was cancer of the heart, but even then he wouldn't let me operate on him."

Geri cocked an eyebrow. "Why is that?"

Thomas chuckled. "Because we're too close. He's been my mentor. He was also my father's worst enemy."

She laughed. "Yes. Rivals who fought over my mother apparently."

"Right. I'm sorry for telling you that."

Geri shrugged. "If it's the truth, don't be sorry. It's too bad that my mother caused such a rift between your father and mine. My mother had a way of ruining so much."

"You don't think very highly of your mother."

"She didn't think very highly of me either. My childhood was very lonely, only I didn't have boarding school to escape to or a half sister to show affection to."

"We're pretty similar," he said quietly.

"How? We grew up in different worlds."

"We both had pretty crappy childhoods."

Geri chuckled. "That we did."

Thomas sighed. "Well, if you must know it wasn't just your mother that caused the rift between our fathers. My father was an Oxford man and your father was a Cambridge man. I believe they both were on the rowing teams and your father's team would often best my father's team. It enraged my father that your father seemed to beat him."

"Your father held a lot of grudges."

"There's a very old rivalry between the two schools."

She cocked an eyebrow. "I think it's more than that."

"I agree, my father was a jerk." Then they both laughed at that. "I'm surprised your father gave me the time of day, but he did. He's a good man, you know."

"I know," said Geri, her voice wobbling ever so slightly.

"He'll beat this. He'll come through," Thomas said.

Geri took his hand in hers and gave it a reassuring squeeze. "And Zoe will be fine."

She stared into his eyes and was completely lost at that moment. Her hand felt so tiny in his strong ones and she wanted to hold him closer. To comfort him.

He's not yours.

Thomas snatched his hand back and cleared his throat. He looked uncomfortable. "Thank you for being there with her."

"It's my pleasure. She's my patient."

"Sorry your night was ruined. It was your first social function and I know how much your father was looking forward to you going. He wanted to show you off."

"It's all right. This is why I became a doctor. This is what I'm passionate about, not dressing up in ball gowns and dancing. Though I wish I could've tried some of those desserts."

Thomas laughed. "They weren't that great."

"Oh, come on, they were traditional Victorian Christmas desserts. I mean the whole theme was Victorian Christmas."

He rolled his eyes, but smiled at her. "You and Christmas."

"You know you're a bit of a Grinch," she teased.

"A what?"

"Don't you remember watching that cartoon as a child?"

Thomas shook his head. "I didn't watch cartoons as a child. Remember, I'm not a big Christmas fanatic like you are."

"You mean you've never seen *How the Grinch Stole Christmas* with Zoe?"

"No," he said. "In her younger days, before Zoe's mother joined Doctors Without Borders, Zoe spent Christmases with her. I've only had her at Christmas for the last three years and she was never really interested in watching cartoons by the time she came to me."

"Well, you're maybe going to have to rectify that. She's going to need a few days of bed rest," Geri said.

"I wouldn't even know where to begin with Christmas specials."

"Well, maybe I'll help with that. I have an extensive collection."

"How extensive?" he asked carefully.

"Quite extensive. I have cartoons, funny movies and those Christmas specials that bring a tear to your eye."

"Ugh," he said dramatically. "That doesn't sound painful at all."

"How can you not like a big fat orange cat bringing Christmas to a grandmother? Or a family whose Christmas goes absolutely and completely wrong in a house full of annoying relatives? Or those old classic movies where the Christmas carols were written? Bing crooning away those familiar tunes."

He smiled and she melted slightly. What was she doing? Why was she still trying to get closer to him? Why couldn't she keep away from him? They were colleagues, partners, and that was it. They could be nothing more. She didn't want to be his friend outside work. She didn't want to be anything other than a medical associate. That's all she was here for. She wasn't here for anything else. And he was definitely not the right man for her.

He was a duke. She was struggling with the idea of being a lady, an heiress. She didn't want any part of that life.

Thomas is more than just his title. Just like you are.

"Well," she said, clearing her throat. "I'd better get back in there and see how it's going. You should get some rest in the doctors' lounge. It might be some time yet."

"No, I can wait it out in the hallway here. I'm not leaving her side. As I said, she's all that I have."

Geri nodded and headed back into the heart catheterization lab. All she had was her father. Her mother was off goodness knew where and doing who knew what, they had never really been close. Though she wasn't close to her father yet. She enjoyed being in his company, he was a brilliant physician and she hated seeing him sick. Yet, if he had been on this table, would she be as worried? Would she feel as hurt?

She wasn't sure. It had been so long since she'd cared about anybody. She wasn't even sure that she could anymore. She wasn't sure that she could open up her heart to anyone ever again.

CHAPTER EIGHT

I'M JUST CHECKING up on my patient, that's all.

Geri took a deep calming breath as she stared up at the impressive frontage of Thomas's Notting Hill home. Thomas had taken a week off three days ago when Zoe had been released from the hospital and she was worried about them both. Worried about Zoe's pacemaker failing again, even though the heart catheterization had been successful, and worried about Thomas too. He'd been so torn up over his sister.

She wanted to make sure they were both all right and, truth be told, she missed seeing Thomas every day. Missed his quips, his cheeky smiles. He'd only been in her life a handful of days and she was already missing his company. The thought scared her and Geri almost turned back.

You're checking on your friends. Nothing more.

She'd made up her mind to check on them on Saturday as the practice was closed, and had decided to bring over some of her favorite Christmas movies to lend to Zoe and Thomas. And as she stared up at his home she saw it looked sadly bereft of any Christmas fanfare. Thomas hadn't been kidding when he'd said he didn't make a big deal out of Christmas.

All around his home, other homes and shops were getting ready to welcome Christmas. All except Thomas's, which looked cold, dark and dreary. Not a single wreath, which was a pretty sad state for a duke.

She pushed the buzzer on the gate.

"Hello?" Thomas's voice sounded tired and a bit annoyed.

"It's me, Geraldine Collins. From the practice."

You idiot. He knows who you are.

"Yes. Geraldine Collins from the practice. How are you?" He was teasing her; she could hear the humor in his voice.

"Can I come in or are we going to conduct our entire conversation at your gate while your neighbors stare at me?"

"That is true. I'm most certain they'll stare at you."

"Thomas, are you going to leave me out here?"

"I might. This is fun."

Infuriating man.

"Fine. I'll leave, you cruel man."

She could hear his deep chuckle. "I love that adorable little accent you take on when you get annoyed."

"Aye, well, you'll be hearing it often, then, you fiend."

"All right, I'll let you in."

Then there was a buzz as the gate was unlocked. She pushed it open and then shut it again to lock it once more. She walked up the cleared flagstone path and Thomas met her at the front door.

He was a wearing jeans and a casual deep blue shirt that was open at the neck. His hands were thrust deep in his pockets. Even though he was casually dressed, it was business casual attire and Geri felt instantly underdressed in her leggings, long oversize sweater, ski vest and clunky boots. Her knit cap was a bit battered and her scarf didn't match it.

She felt positively dowdy in his presence suddenly.

It's not like you're staying. You're here to do a quick check, drop the movies and leave.

"What a pleasure to see you here," he said cordially. He looked her up and down and when his gaze landed on her big clunky boots a small smile twitched on his face. "Going hiking through some snowbanks today?"

"Ha-ha. They're warm." She held out the movies. "I brought Zoe some movies, since you're such a Christmas miser. I thought she'd enjoy these."

He took them. "Well, why don't you come in and say hello to her? She'd love to have a visitor. I have been a bit of a friend miser as well. I don't want her catching a cold or something that would be detrimental, given she's just had a heart catheterization."

"Sure. I would actually like to check on her. Father's been bugging me to swing by. He was worried about her, but he's not up for visiting either." She walked into his house and began to unwind her scarf and pull off her hat, trying to smooth down the static in her hair as Thomas shut the door.

"How is he feeling a week postchemo?" he asked.

"Tired," Geri said. "He goes for another treatment on Monday."

Thomas winced. "Not fun."

"No, it's not."

"Well, come upstairs. The family room is on the upper level, and that's where Lady Zoe is holding court at the moment on the couch."

Geri laughed and kicked off her boots, forgetting that she was wearing particularly ugly warm socks, the kind that separated the toes and were striped in rainbow colors. She'd meant to change them but had completely forgotten as she'd been running out the door.

Thomas cocked an eyebrow. "Interesting choice in socks, Lady Collins."

"Don't talk about eccentricities to me, Your Grace. You're the duke who lives in Notting Hill instead of on an estate, tending to your serfs and vassals."

"I have a Buckinghamshire estate, I just don't like it as much as here."

She followed him up the stairs to the next floor, where a cozy, plush sitting room area was. On the wall on the far side was a huge wide-screen television and facing that was an overstuffed, large couch, where Zoe was propped up surrounded by pillows and snuggled down in a blanket, watching a movie.

"Look who's come to see you, Zoe," Thomas said as they entered the room.

Zoe turned and smiled. "Dr. Collins!"

"I'm glad you're happy to see me. I'm sorry your brother now knows. I swear I didn't violate doctor-patient confidentiality."

She shrugged. "It was my own fault, I guess."

"It wasn't your fault," Thomas said. He handed her the stack of movies. "Geraldine has brought you some Christmas movies because she felt you were a bit deprived, given that I'm such a... What did you call me the other day?"

"Grinch," Geri said.

Zoe laughed. "This is wonderful. Can we watch one now?"

"I guess so," Thomas groaned halfheartedly.

She flicked through the movies. "*White Christmas*! I haven't seen this in so long."

"Good choice," Geri said. She stood up. "Well, I'd better head for home. I'm glad you're doing well, Zoe."

"Stay, Geraldine. If you don't have any plans, maybe we can order in some Chinese takeaways and watch *White Christmas* together." Zoe batted her puppy dog eyes in her direction, trying to play on her sympathies.

Geri glanced at Thomas. "If your brother doesn't mind?"

"No, I don't. And that sounds like a great plan." He smiled at her warmly. "I'll put in the order and you two get comfortable. Can I get you something to drink, Geraldine?"

"Tea would be lovely."

He nodded and then disappeared from the living room.

"I'm so glad you came, Geraldine. Thomas has been hovering over me like an overprotective hen. He carries me to bed at night. It's getting a bit much."

"Well, they did run the catheter up through your femoral artery. That's a main artery and prone to quick blood loss."

Zoe rolled her eye. "I know. My brother is a surgeon and he likes to tell me all that kind of stuff all the time. I think he and my mom both think I should enter the medical profession."

"It's not a bad profession to be in, but, then, I'm biased."

Zoe smiled. "Just like Thomas and my mother. I'm surrounded by physicians. If my father was still alive, he might not be pushing me so much."

"What was your father like?" Geri asked, curious about the previous Duke of Weatherstone. From what Thomas had said, he didn't sound like a nice man, yet had managed to sire two children who were warm and friendly.

Zoe shrugged. "He was okay. A bit distant, but pleasant enough to me. He was always angry that my mother didn't want to marry him."

"Why didn't she?"

"My mother knew his heart belonged to Thomas's mother and she didn't want to live in another woman's shadow. She also wanted to continue her work with Doctors Without Borders. Being the next Duchess of Weatherstone wouldn't have afforded her that luxury. My parents were pleasant to each other and Mom encouraged me to spend time with my father and Thomas."

"At least that's something. My mother didn't encourage any kind of relationship."

"Your father has always been very kind to me and my mother. I'm sorry you didn't have him when you were younger."

Zoe's words cut like a knife and tears stung Geri's eyes. No, she wasn't going to cry here now. She cleared her throat. "Do you mind if I check it? See if it's healed enough and give a second opinion?"

"No, I don't mind." Zoe flicked off the blanket. She was wearing a long flannel nightgown and ugly socks similar to hers.

Geri examined the wound. It was still raw and wasn't healing as fast as she would like, but it would hold.

"I think your brother should still carry you up flights of stairs. It's still healing."

Zoe groaned.

"Glad you see it my way. She didn't believe me," Thomas said, entering the room with a tea set on a tray.

Zoe stuck her tongue out at him.

"Not a good way for a proper lady to act, scamp," Thomas teased.

He poured everyone a cup of tea and then they all settled on the couch to watch *White Christmas*. It was one of Geri's all-time favorite Christmas movies. She loved the songs, the costumes and the dancing. The age difference between Bing and Rosemary was a bit too much May-December for her, but it was so minor it didn't detract from her love of the movie.

It was nice sharing it with Thomas and Zoe.

It was nice sharing this movie with someone, and having Chinese food and watching a movie on a comfortable couch was absolute heaven. This was even better than watching it alone. She was sharing it with friends. Which was what Christmas was all about.

She snuck a quick glance at Thomas. He seemed to be enjoying the movie and as if he knew she was watching him he glanced over and smiled back at her.

What're you doing here?

She didn't know. She shouldn't have stayed, but she also didn't want to leave. It was nice being with someone. She'd been alone for so long and though she'd been fine with that as it was what she was used to, she much preferred this.

When the final number came on Zoe sighed.

"I wish we had a Christmas tree like that," Zoe said.

"That's gigantic and a fire hazard," Thomas argued.

"It's no bigger than the one at the party the other night," Geri said.

Thomas glared at her. "You're not helping."

"All right, then, maybe not that big, but I would love to have a Christmas tree nonetheless. Let's go out and get a Christmas tree," Zoe begged. "Please?"

"You're not going anywhere," Thomas said. "So you're definitely not going out to buy a tree."

"You could," Zoe suggested. "You both could go out and get a tree and some decorations and then we can decorate it tonight."

"You're imposing a lot on Geraldine."

"She won't mind." Zoe winked at her.

Geri knew she should leave, but she was enjoying her time with Thomas and Zoe. It had been a long time since she'd enjoyed herself like this, where she felt a part of a family. Where she wasn't alone. It scared her a bit.

"I'd love to but—"

"No buts," Thomas said, and then he took her hand in his, sending a zing of warmth flooding through her veins at the simplicity of his touch. "We'd love to have you."

* * *

Thomas had known that Geraldine had been going to make an excuse to leave and he should've let her go, but he didn't want her to. He'd never seen *White Christmas* before. It was an okay movie, but it was the time with his sister and Geraldine, the quality time, that's what he cherished. It was nice and he wanted to savor it.

And he didn't want it to end.

He had no problem going out and getting a Christmas tree for Zoe, as long as Geraldine came with him. As long as she stayed and helped decorate it.

"Are you sure?" Geraldine asked.

"Of course he is," Zoe insisted. "Please go out and get a proper tree and decorations and we'll decorate it. It would be wonderful."

"I will on one condition. You rest," Geraldine said to Zoe, tucking the blanket around her.

"Deal."

"Oh, I don't think we should leave her alone, though," Geraldine said. "She's still recovering."

"We have servants. Our housekeeper, Mrs. Brown, would be happy to sit with her." Thomas grinned at her. "There's no getting out of it, Geraldine. You're the one who loves Christmas most out of the three of us and you're the best one to pick out the tree and decorations."

"I guess that's settled."

Thomas nodded. "It is. Portobello Road should have everything we require and it's not that far from here. We can walk. I mean, you do have the proper footwear for it."

Geraldine rolled her eyes. "Let's go, then, before you change your mind."

Thomas left the sitting room and arranged for Mrs. Brown to keep an eye on Zoe while he was out with Geraldine, and by the time he was done Geraldine was waiting in the foyer all bundled up again.

Thomas put on his ski jacket and a knitted cap with flaps. When he turned round Geraldine laughed at him.

"You don't look very stately, Your Grace."

"Neither do you, My Lady, but will that stop you from escorting me out on my errand?" He bowed and added a little flourish.

"Of course not."

They headed out of the house. It was dusk and the Christmas lights were starting to come on. It wasn't snowing, though, which was a shame, because for the first time in a long time he felt a bit excited about the prospect of Christmas.

Like a bit of that Christmas spirit he'd thought was long gone was coming back to life. It was nice. They walked along the street and headed toward Portobello Road, which was bustling and overflowing with street vendors, Christmas paraphernalia and shoppers.

"Where do we get a tree?" Thomas asked as they walked through the crowds.

"The vendor over there looks like he has some good trees." Geraldine paused. "I just thought of something. How are we going to get it back to your place?"

"We'll carry it. Come on, we're two strong and healthy doctors. I'm sure we can carry a tree a couple of blocks."

"Okay, so let's get some decorations and tinsel in the Christmas shop there and then we'll pick up the tree. We can't go shopping for decorations lugging an evergreen all over the place."

"Good plan."

They wandered into the little shop that was overflowing with gifts, confectionary and decorations. It was Christmas overload in there. Thomas felt a little bit overwhelmed and wanted to leave, but Geraldine was in her element.

He never seen her like this. Her green eyes were sparkling and she was grinning as she filled a basket full of gaudy decorations. This wasn't the cold, detached doctor he was used to. This was a totally different person and he liked this side of her. This was the side he'd known was buried under that cold facade. This was the real her that she was so desperately trying to hide, but he couldn't figure out why.

"Can't we keep to a theme?" Thomas asked.

"A theme? If this is your first Christmas tree, the theme should be fun. What were you thinking?" Geraldine asked.

"Simplicity." Thomas stared at a box of twinkle lights. "Just a tree and maybe some ribbon."

She frowned at him and then sang a song, "You're a mean one, Mr. Ashwood…"

He rolled his eyes. "Fine, but no flashing lights. I don't want to have a seizure every time I go into the sitting room."

Geraldine laughed. "Deal."

"And no ornaments that bark or meow Christmas carols."

"How about a singing fish?" she asked, and pointed to the abomination wearing a Santa hat on the wall.

"No. Definitely not." As if on cue, someone else in the store pressed the fish and it began to sing "Jingle Bells" like Elvis.

"Why Elvis?" Geraldine asked in horror. "That is awful."

"We need to get out of here before we find out how that monstrosity sings." Thomas pointed towards the very large reindeer head that was hanging on the wall, also adorned with a Santa hat.

"Agreed."

They purchased their lights and decorations and then headed out to pick out a tree. They found one with ease and the man tied it up for them. Together they hoisted it up and portaged it much like a canoe down Portobello Road back towards his home.

He took the back end, because Geraldine wasn't as tall as him, so he could kind of steer. The problem was a lot of the lower branches blocked her view, so he had to guide her through the streets, making sure she didn't crash into anything.

"I'm getting covered in sap!" Thomas shouted.

"You're not a sap," Geraldine's muffled voice said from under the tree.

"I didn't say that I was, I said I'm getting covered in it."

"Oh, well, that's part of the experience."

Thomas groaned, but chuckled to himself. He could imagine his father's horror if he were still alive to see his heir meandering down the street carrying a tree to decorate. His father hadn't liked tomfoolery or antics much.

And this would definitely be tomfoolery in his books.

They got everything back to his house and hoisted it up the stairs to the sitting room. It was a pain and there were pine needles all over the floor. Poor Mrs. Brown didn't look too pleased that the tree was shedding all over the place.

"It looks wonderful," Zoe said.

Thomas set it upright and Geraldine climbed out from under the tree, out of breath but still smiling. "Yes, it does look good. Do you have a tree stand so we can set it up?"

"A what?" Thomas asked.

Zoe was laughing and Geraldine looked horrified.

"A tree stand—you know, to hold the tree up so we can decorate it."

"We have one in the attic, Your Grace. Shall I get it?" Mrs. Brown asked.

"Yes, please, Mrs. Brown, and thank you."

Mrs. Brown nodded and hurried off to find the stand.

Thomas leaned the tree against the wall, praying that it wouldn't leak sap all over the place.

"You'll have to water the tree," Geraldine said.

"I have to water it?" Thomas asked. "This is becoming more of a nuisance."

"You don't want it to dry out, Thomas," said Zoe. "It could catch fire."

"Catch fire?"

Geraldine and Zoe were both laughing now at his expense and he couldn't help but laugh too.

"Next year I want one of those trees that you pop open like an umbrella and it's all decorated for you and doesn't shed. Low-maintenance tree."

"Where's the fun in that?" Geraldine asked as she began to take the ornaments out of the bag so Zoe could look at them.

"The simple things in life, Geraldine, bring me the greatest pleasure."

She just shook her head at him.

Mrs. Brown returned with the antique tree stand and Thomas went about setting up the tree. That involved some more cursing and more jokes at his expense, but it was worth it to see Zoe really enjoying herself. To see her lit up like he hadn't seen her in a long time.

When he'd almost lost her that night when her pacemaker had stopped working, he had been so terrified. Zoe was the only happiness he had in his life. Cassandra had brought him that joy too, for a short while, but it could never have lasted. And he would never know the loving family he had dreamed of as a kid. He lived with it and didn't mourn what he didn't have. Yet today with Zoe and Geraldine he felt something akin to that and he realized that maybe he'd been too hasty in his decision to never let another person in.

No. You made the right decision. It won't always be like this.

Which was true. Zoe would go back to boarding school and eventually her mother would come home from her time in Malawi. A couple more years and Zoe would be a legal adult and making her own way in the world.

He didn't even know what Geraldine wanted. All he knew about her was that she was completely focused on her career and didn't seem at all interested in pursuing anything with him.

This moment would end, because that's all that it was. Just a moment.

Geraldine began to decorate the tree and he stood off to the side, watching as Zoe handed her different ornaments and gave her suggestions on where to place them. Being around Geraldine like this caused him to let his guard down.

And it scared him that she got through to him so easily.

What was it about her?

He had to get out of there. "I need to make a couple of phone calls. You two carry on."

Zoe frowned. "Now?"

Thomas nodded. "Yes, now, I'm afraid."

"Oh, well, the decorating is done and I should really get back home." Geraldine picked up her coat. "I'll see you at work on Monday. Zoe, enjoy the rest of the movies."

"I will, Geraldine. Thank you."

Geraldine nodded and stopped in front of him. "Thank you for the lovely time."

"My pleasure. I'll see you out."

You're a fool, Thomas Ashwood.

He ignored that other part of him that told him to pull Geraldine into his arms and kiss her, because he couldn't remember the last time he'd had this much fun.

Only he resisted as he opened the door for her. "Would you like me to drive you home?"

She shook her head. "No, I can take the tube back to Holland Park. See you Monday."

Thomas watched her walk down the path and through the gate. He stepped outside so he could see her head down the darkened street, heading toward the Underground station.

A bloody fool.

CHAPTER NINE

"WILL I BE in here over Christmas?" Lord Twinsbury demanded. "I can't be in here over the holidays."

"I'm afraid so," Thomas said as he finished his examination. "You're not healing as quickly as I'd like and you're still not ready to go home. You've had two open heart surgeries in the course of a couple of weeks. You need to stay in the hospital. So I'm afraid you'll be here for Christmas."

"Blast, I didn't want to miss the carols from King's College at Cambridge. It's important I attend."

"Understandable, but you're staying put."

Lord Twinsbury groaned. "You, of course, wouldn't understand. You're an Oxford man."

"Oxford or Cambridge makes no difference. You're recovering from surgery." Thomas leaned over. "Oxford is the far superior university anyway. You should know that."

"Young pup, if I weren't laid up…"

Thomas cocked an eyebrow. "You'd do what? Tan my hide? I think I can outrun you."

Lord Twinsbury huffed grumpily.

There was a knock at the door and Thomas turned to see Geraldine standing there. It had only been a couple of days, but his heart skipped a beat seeing her standing there in her business clothes and her pristine white lab coat.

"Am I interrupting?" she asked.

"Ah, now there's a sight for sore eyes!" Lord Twinsbury exclaimed with delight.

"Lionel, you flatter me," she said sweetly.

"Nonsense, you're a damn sight better than the duke here," Lord Twinsbury grumbled.

"That's Mr. Ashwood, my lord," Thomas corrected him.

"Can I speak with you, Mr. Ashwood, about a case?" Geraldine asked.

"Of course." He was glad to get away from Lord Twinsbury's complaining.

"Please come and see me afterward, my lady. Your visits make my day."

Thomas rolled his eyes.

"I will try, Lionel." Geraldine shut the door when Thomas was in the hall. "I'm sorry for pulling you away from your rounds, but I had a referral from a general practitioner in Aylesbury of a pregnant woman who has suffered a myocardial infarction."

"Your mother is dead, Thomas. So is the baby. They're gone and crying won't bring them back."

His father's harsh words haunted him. It had been at that moment his father had turned his back on him. Resented him for being like her. All Thomas had wanted was the comfort of his father when his mother had died, but he'd been denied it. Instead he'd been sent to boarding school. The day his mother had died had been the day he'd really lost both of his parents.

There had never been a chance for him or his father to make things right between them. The day Zoe had been born with the atrial septal defect and had almost died, his father had tossed him out of the room.

"Haven't you haunted me enough?"

It was almost as if his father had been blaming him for Zoe almost dying at birth. It's why Zoe's mother had walked away from his father and instead had became the surrogate of the parent he'd never had. His father had resented him for that too.

And they'd never had a chance to resolve anything. His father had hated him until the day he'd died, when Zoe had been ten.

At least his father had loved Zoe. That was at least something. Her life wasn't as devoid of love as his had been.

"I'm sorry?" Thomas said. His father's voice had drowned out Geraldine's words. The moment she'd mentioned a pregnant patient who had suffered a myocardial infarction he'd been taken back to that terrible day long ago when his father had told him his mother wasn't coming home.

"How is she?"

"I don't know, other than stable. She's in an ambulance on the way here. She's too far along in her pregnancy to be flown in. She's thirty-one weeks and could be on the verge of pre-eclampsia as well. They're trying to keep the baby in there as long as possible, but I have Obstetrics on standby as well."

"What is their plan?"

"Save the baby and then assess the mother."

Thomas nodded. "I can have my fellow finish rounds on my surgical patients and I'll go down to Accident and Emergency and wait for her arrival."

"Thank you. Hopefully she won't need extensive surgery on her heart."

"She'll need a heart catheterization, that much I know. I need to see the extent of the damage, but I want to be in that operating theater to watch her vitals."

"Yes, that's what the obstetric team is hoping for. As she's my patient now, I insisted on you taking care of her. I hope you don't mind."

"Mind? No, that's why we're in practice together."

"Yes." She glanced down at her pager. "They'll be arriving shortly. Shall we?"

"Let's go."

Thomas led the way down to A and E. The obstetrics team was standing by. They were going to deliver that baby so that Thomas could take over.

Focus.

This situation wasn't as dire as his mother's had been. His mother's heart attack had been fatal and his brother had been too young to survive outside the womb at twenty-one weeks. Even now, with all the technological advances, babies still rarely survived if they were born that early.

At least this patient's baby was thirty weeks. Still premature, still a fight ahead, but the percentages on surviving were far greater than they'd been thirty-odd years ago.

The ambulance pulled up and they went to work. Geraldine met the paramedics and the general practitioner, who had ridden with his patient from Aylesbury. He was explaining the situation to Geraldine, which was good. Then he could focus on taking care of the patient's heart as the obstetrics team dealt with the baby.

"She had another heart attack, minor, but another nonetheless on the way here. Her blood pressure is far too high to have flown her in." Thomas heard the general practitioner say.

"We need to get this baby out of her so I can address her heart," Thomas said above the din.

"Get her to a theater now," Mr Jones, the obstetrician, shouted to a resident. "Have the team prepare for a crash C-section."

Thomas took her blood pressure and it was dangerously high, the heart sounding like it was fighting to pump blood through her body. Even if they had stabilized her, the baby wouldn't survive with the mother's heart struggling so much.

From what he was seeing, she needed open heart surgery and she needed it now. Her heart was failing. It sounded like an enlarged heart. Cardiomyopathy.

Damn.

They rushed her to the operating theater and he set up all his monitors, the crash cart ready and standing by. It wouldn't take long to get the baby out and that was a blessing, especially if he needed to get in there and massage the heart or shock the mother's heart back into rhythm.

This operating theater didn't have a gallery, because no one needed to witness this. This was a possible tragedy in the making, but he wished that Geraldine was beside him. Right now he was a horrible mess of emotions.

Live. Just live.

Instead of his patient on the table, he saw his mother.

"Thomas, I love you." His mother's voice was in his head as he watched his patient. He hadn't heard his mother's voice in so long. He'd thought he'd forgotten it, but it came to him now and he closed his eyes, listening to the heart monitor. Willing his patient to live.

Live.

The jostling from the C-section played merry havoc with the heart monitors, but so far she was not having another heart attack. Which was good. In less than five minutes he heard the tiny wail of a premature boy as he was lifted up and placed into the hands of the waiting pediatric team.

Thomas smiled behind his mask and then whispered to his patient, who was under anesthesia, "It's a boy. You have a boy, you need to pull through."

"How is her heart, Mr. Ashwood?" Mr. Jones asked.

"Stable for now, Mr. Jones."

Mr. Jones nodded and continued his work on their patient. At least the baby was out and had a good fighting chance to survive. Thomas's job was making sure that the mother also had a fighting chance.

He was going to save that baby boy's mother, because he'd been unable to save his own.

Geraldine saw that Thomas was still sitting in the room of Mrs. Rimes, their patient who had been pregnant and who'd suffered two heart attacks.

"How is she doing?"

Thomas looked up. "Stable. She had massive damage to her heart and has severe cardiomyopathy. At least with the delivery of the baby she won't succumb to eclampsia."

"What do you think it was?"

"Arrhythmogenic right ventricular dysplasia."

"You're certain?"

He nodded. "She's at a risk for the rest of her life. When she recovers from her surgery I'll speak to her about her options, in particular implanting a device that will shock her heart should it happen again. And it will happen again."

"Poor woman."

Thomas got up and walked out of her room, shutting the door. "How is the baby?"

"Doing well," Geraldine said.

"Good." He scrubbed a hand over his face.

"Are you okay?"

"No, it hits a little too close to home for me. All I could hear was my father's voice in my head, telling me my mother was dead, when you came to tell me about our patient."

Geraldine reached out and touched his arm. She could see his pain again. Like the pain he'd had when Zoe had been in the heart catheterization lab. She couldn't even begin to comprehend what he was going through.

"I need to get a coffee. Would you care to join me?" Thomas asked.

"Of course." They walked toward the small coffee shop that was located in the hospital. Thomas ordered them a couple of cups of coffee and they sat down at a table. It wasn't busy in the coffee shop and that was fine by her.

"I'm so sorry this situation reminded you of your mother," she said.

"It's why I became a heart surgeon. I think we all have a reason why we become what we become. Why did you become a cardiologist? Was it because of your father?"

"No," Geri said quickly. "No, not at all." She was uncomfortable discussing this. It was hard to step back and not be in the operating theater where she belonged. She felt useless and helpless. Almost worthless.

Thomas cocked his head to one side. "You said that with such conviction."

"Well, I didn't know about him and he didn't know about me until last year. No, my decision to be a cardiologist was because I wanted to save lives. But I'm not cut out for the operating theater."

"I disagree," he said.

"Why?"

"You're stronger than you give yourself credit for."

Geri wished she could believe that. "Well, it wasn't in the cards."

And she hoped that would stop the conversation.

"I'm surprised that you didn't become a surgeon."

I wanted to.

"I wasn't made for surgery."

Liar.

"What makes you think that? You didn't shy away in the operating theater when Lord Twinsbury was having his surgery. You thought quickly with that suggestion about the umbilical vein. I think, given your drive, that you belong in the operating theater, as I've said before. I think you're made for it."

Geri sighed. "Well, it's a little too late for that. I'm a cardiologist and I'm taking over my father's practice."

"It's never too late."

"I'm happy as a cardiologist." She took a sip of her coffee. Then she changed the subject. "How is Zoe doing? Is she enjoying her Christmas tree?"

"She's doing well and, yes, she's enjoying her tree. I'm not, for the record."

Geri chuckled. "Why am I not surprised? How can anyone not enjoy a Christmas tree?"

"It sheds. It's worse than my grandmother's Pomeranian, which shed everywhere."

"How can a tree be worse than a dog?"

"It can." As he winked at her, his pager went off. "Our patient is awake and her husband has been waiting very patiently in the waiting room. I'll counsel them on the next steps."

"I look forward to reading your report so I can continue guidance on the matter as well."

Thomas nodded.

She should head back to the office. There was nothing more she could do here. She wasn't a surgeon. There were times she regretted running away, taking the easy way out, like now, and like what had happened with Zoe. But that was her burden to bear.

No one else's. It was all hers.

Despite what Thomas had said, it was too late for her to continue with her specialization. She would never be a surgeon. It's just the way it was and she was okay with that.

Though she had the feeling that Thomas didn't believe her.

And she didn't know why. It shouldn't matter to him. Why did he want her to become a surgeon anyway? There wasn't room in the practice for two surgeons. Did he want her to be competition?

Geri shook her head and threw her empty coffee cup in the garbage. She'd head back to Harley Street and wait for Thomas's report on their new patient, because when she no longer needed the surgeon that's when Geri had a chance to help save a life.

CHAPTER TEN

THOMAS RANG THE DOORBELL at Charles Collins's Holland Park townhome. He knew that Geraldine wasn't there, but it wasn't Geraldine who had asked him to come by. It had been Charles.

Why, he didn't know, but Charles had been most insistent that Thomas stop by while Geraldine was at work. And he was happy to oblige. He just hoped this wasn't some sort of cry off about his daughter, because there was no reason for that.

Wasn't there?

And the thought caught him off guard.

There was something he just didn't want to admit, but Geraldine had seen him at his most vulnerable lately.

And he desired her.

It was something more than a quick seduction game that he played time and time again, but what it was he didn't know and that thought unnerved him because he couldn't have her. He wouldn't put her through any more pain. She'd been through so much already.

"Thomas, come in." Charles opened the door and Thomas stepped past him into the foyer. Charles took his coat and hung it up. "Won't you join me in the sitting room?"

"Of course," he said as he followed Charles into the sitting room. "I get a lot of flak, you know."

"For what?" Charles asked, confused.

"For living in Notting Hill in a modest-sized home, but what I don't understand is why you don't get any flak for living in a town house?"

Charles chuckled. "Who says I don't? Then again, I'm not a duke. I'm so far down the list of succession that a lot of people would have to die before I even had sight of the throne and I'm glad of that. You, on the other hand, are definitely an eccentric."

"Why, thank you."

"Drink?" Charles asked.

"No, I have to make rounds at the hospital soon." Thomas sat down on the sofa. "I'd much rather have the drink. So if you have a mineral water with a twist of lemon that would be great."

"Of course." Charles poured it and handed Thomas the glass. Thomas noticed Charles's hand shook.

"Thank you. Are you sure you're quite well?"

"I'm sure." Charles sat down, ending that topic. "I heard about the pregnant woman."

"Yes."

Charles knew about his mother, but he didn't want to talk about that right now. "How can I help you, Charles?"

"Geraldine tells me you're aware that I have cancer."

"Yes, Charles. I drove her to the hospital when you collapsed during chemo."

"You haven't told anyone else?" Charles asked carefully. He was hedging.

"Of course not. Why are you so concerned with keeping it a secret from your colleagues, though?"

"Just privacy. I don't need a lot of bleeding hearts telling me that I'm in their prayers or giving me sympathetic looks. I don't need that. I don't deserve that after all my sins of the past."

Thomas chuckled. "My father wouldn't be giving you any."

Charles snorted. "Don't even start with me about your father, who would, by the way, not approve of you living in Notting Hill."

"It's why I live there." Thomas winked.

"You are like him in some respects. Cheeky and arrogant, but that's what makes you a brilliant surgeon."

"Thank you again. Why do I deserve so much flattery this afternoon?"

"Because my cancer has moved from my stomach. And don't say it, don't say you're sorry."

"Where is it?" Thomas asked, but he had an idea.

"The heart. My angiosarcoma is small, but it's there."

"Charles, angiosarcoma is spread from soft-tissue cancer."

"Yes, that's where it spread first. Stomach into the heart. I want you to take out as much of the tumor as you can. I know it's not possible to take it all out and I know it's likely to come back, but I want a fighting chance and you're the most talented surgeon to do it."

Thomas wanted a drink as it all sank in. Charles was dying now. Previously he was battling cancer, but angiosarcomas were almost always fatal. In cases of malignancy the cancerous tissue had to be removed, but with a border of cancer-free tissues with good margins. It was almost impossible to do that with a heart.

And he couldn't operate on Charles because he thought of him as a sort of father figure. He respected him too much. He couldn't do it. Only he had to do it. His survival rates for this kind of surgery were the highest in London.

He wouldn't leave Charles high and dry.

"Does Geraldine know?" Thomas asked quietly.

"That it's spread? No. She doesn't and you're not to tell her. She needs to concentrate on work. I won't burden her with this."

"How are you burdening her? You're her father."

Charles's expression was weary. "Yes. In name, but... too much time was lost between us. I'm just looking for a bit more. You have to do the surgery for me."

"You told me you never wanted me to operate on you." It was a flimsy excuse.

"You're the only one who can. Your success rates are higher than most."

"Charles, they may be a bit higher, but angiosarcoma still ends up the same."

"Death, I know. I'm just asking for some more time. Time to get to know my daughter. I have a bit more living I have to do."

Thomas's heart sank. There was no way he could turn this down. "I'll do it, but I won't keep it secret from Geraldine. She needs to know what's happening."

"You're a thorn in my side, Thomas. You know that?" Charles grumbled.

"I know, but now I'm your surgeon and you have to listen to me. Oh, the power I'll wield."

"Ha-ha." Charles leaned back in his chair. "I'll tell her, but after the country party this weekend. If I tell her now she'll try to get out of it."

"You're not going to that? It's in Buckinghamshire and you're not well enough to travel."

"I know, which is why I'm hoping you'll go in my place."

Thomas shook his head. "No, you know my history with the Ponsonby family. You know that they're Cassandra's in-laws. I will not go there."

"Then I won't tell Geraldine about my angiosarcoma.

Take her to Buckinghamshire to the Ponsonby winter party or I won't breathe a word about my condition."

"That's absolute blackmail."

Charles grinned. "I know. Didn't Zoe want to attend that event?"

Thomas groaned. "All right, all right, I'll escort Geraldine to that event. Zoe can't go because she's still recovering from her own surgery. I won't have her traipsing around a winter garden party and being exposed to germs. Not in her fragile state. She can stay at home."

"Thank you, Thomas. Geraldine has so much to learn about our world."

"I hate to break it to you, old man, but I don't think she particularly cares about it."

"I know, but when I go she'll inherit everything, including my seat in the House of Lords. It's tradition, and I want someone I can trust to show her the ropes."

"I'll try, Charles. I will."

"That's all I ask." Charles sighed. "Actually, that's not all."

"Oh?" Thomas asked.

"You have my blessing. Not sure if you know that."

Thomas was confused. "To perform the surgery? I certainly hope so since you've just asked me."

"No, to date Geraldine." Charles scrubbed his hand over his face. It was apparently hard for him to talk about this.

"We're friends, Charles."

Charles shot him a disbelieving look. "I think it's more than that. You care for her, you're attracted to her, and I want you to know in case anything happens to me that you have my blessing. Just because you're your father's son, it doesn't mean I disapprove of you."

Thomas sighed. "Charles, I appreciate it, but... I have hypertrophic cardiomyopathy."

Charles was shocked. "Has it progressed?"

"No, I mean I'm a carrier."

"Then what is the holdup?" Charles asked, confused. "You're a carrier, but it might not amount to anything."

"Heart conditions are in my family. Look at my mother, father and Zoe. I can't do that to her."

"So you do care for her."

Thomas shook his head and stood. "I have to get back to the hospital. Thank you for the drink."

He couldn't talk about this, because it didn't matter if he did care for Geraldine. Nothing could happen. He wouldn't do that to her. Even with Charles's blessing, he just wouldn't put Geraldine's heart in danger.

Charles sighed. "I'll let you get to your rounds."

"Sounds good. I'll book your preoperative assessment and your surgery. The quicker I get in there the better margins I can get. Angiosarcomas grow very fast."

Charles nodded. "I know. Thank you."

"Of course, Charles. I'll show myself out." Thomas grabbed his jacket and then headed back into the street. He wondered how Geraldine was going to react when she found out and he was annoyed that Charles wasn't going to tell her unless he took her to that ridiculous winter garden party.

Now he felt an inkling of what Geraldine must've felt when she'd been unable to tell him about Zoe and the pacemaker.

He cursed under his breath and scrubbed a hand over his face. Families. They were too bloody complicated.

Charles and Geraldine aren't your family, though.

He really didn't want to go to that garden party in Buckinghamshire. He always avoided that party because he had no wish to see Cassandra ever again.

Not after she'd used him.

She wanted to be connected to an aristocratic family who was just that. Aristocratic. Maybe they had a job like barrister or solicitor, even banker, but she'd made it perfectly clear she didn't want a duke who was a surgeon and absolutely committed to his work.

There had been many times she'd been angry he'd missed some kind of function because a patient had been in need.

"Have someone else do it! You're the Duke of Weatherstone. You promised you'd be there."

"I'm well aware of my title, Cassandra, but first and foremost I'm a surgeon. My patient needed me."

"Is this how it's going to be? You're going to leave me high and dry at social functions because someone needs surgery?"

"Yes. Someone's life is more important than a party. I'm a surgeon first, Cassandra, and a duke second."

That had been the argument that had ended it all, although the relationship had been on its last legs ever since he'd explained that he was at risk of heart problems.

It was his fault. He'd chosen his career over love. And when he had started to date again, he'd soon learned that most women were like Cassandra. No one understood his passion for medicine.

Except Geraldine.

Yes, Geraldine understood it, but he wasn't completely sure how dedicated she was because he knew that she wasn't completely satisfied with being a cardiologist.

Why is it your concern? It's her life.

And he didn't know why he was so concerned about it. Geraldine was nothing more than a work friend.

Is she?

"That's a nasty angiosarcoma." Geraldine didn't mean to sneak up on Thomas, but he'd been so absorbed in the MRI of a nasty-looking cancer of the heart that he hadn't heard her come into his office.

He clicked the image closed on his computer and spun around, looking put out that she'd sneaked up behind him.

"Geraldine, I didn't hear you knock."

"I did knock, but you didn't answer and Mrs. Smythe told me you didn't have a patient so I thought it was safe for me to come in. I can see now why you didn't hear me knock. That was an impressive angiosarcoma."

"Yes," Thomas said evasively. "It doesn't look good."

"Have you told the patient about it?" She asked taking a seat.

"The patient knows, but still wants me to proceed with the surgery." Thomas didn't look her in the eye and she had the distinct feeling he was hiding something from her.

It's not your concern.

"Hopefully you can get good margins but with that kind of tumor—"

"I know," Thomas said, cutting her off. "Is there something I can help you with, Geraldine?"

"Yes, I'm hoping you don't mind crying off this weekend garden party. I just don't want to go. I can spend the day in the office and Father will be none the wiser."

"You're not crying off. If I have to go, you have to go," he said sternly.

"If I don't go, why do you have to go? Father told me you didn't want to go either. I thought you were sympathetic to my plight."

Thomas chuckled. "I am, or usually I would be, but your father will have his spies out and I think it's better we go. It'll make him happy."

Geraldine groaned. "You're right. He'll have his spies. Who has a garden party in the middle of December anyway?"

He smiled. "The *ton* are an eccentric group of party-goers. Any excuse for a function or showing off."

"I'm surprised you don't throw a party to show off."

"My father used to, but they weren't my cup of tea. Of course, he would have functions at the family estate in Buckinghamshire. I live in Notting Hill."

"What happened to the estate?"

"It's still there. I rent it out occasionally, and part of it is open for tours. People tour the home and the gardens."

"Really, one day I would love to see where you grew up."

"Well, we can go tomorrow after we make our perfunctory rounds at the garden party."

Now she was intrigued. "That makes going to this garden party almost worth it."

He leaned across the desk, his hands folded. "And going with me isn't worth it?"

"I think it'll be entertaining," she teased.

"That's it?"

She shrugged. "What more do you want?"

"Touché."

"What time are you going to pick me up?"

"I have to drive?"

"I don't have a car. Remember, I take the Underground regularly."

"Hmm, how convenient." Then he grinned. "I'll pick you up tomorrow at ten in the morning. If we get to the garden party unfashionably early then we can probably make the last tour of my childhood home."

"I don't get a private tour?"

"Oh, you want a private tour?" His voice was husky and she realized she was treading on dangerous ground. She still remembered those women talking at that party about how the Duke of Weatherstone was a womanizer.

"No, I'll just stick with the standard one, thank you very much." She got up. "I'll leave you to your angiosarcoma. If you need any... What am I saying? I can't help you with that."

"You could if you were a surgeon."

It was a barb. "Why are you so obsessed with me becoming a surgeon?"

"Only because I think you'd be brilliant at it."

A warm flush spread across her cheeks. "Well, I'm not. I'll see you tomorrow."

She got out of his office as quickly as she could. She didn't want to discuss her being a surgeon anymore. It wasn't any of his business.

What was done was done. She was happy with her lot in life.

Are you?

And the answer was simple. She wasn't, but she was too scared to change it.

CHAPTER ELEVEN

"YOU CAME WITH the Duke of Weatherstone?"

Geri had been accosted by another group of ladies. It seemed that at the Gileses' party she had been seen with Thomas on the dance floor and slinking off to the alcove. He'd warned her that night he was giving her a reputation and he was right. The groups who had slighted her before suddenly couldn't let her be.

She was the new flavor of the month, it seemed.

"Yes. I did." It seemed like every time she ran into a new group of people at this garden party and they discovered she'd come with Thomas they were in a bit of shock.

"Thomas Ashwood?" another woman asked, that same dumbfounded look on her face.

"Yes. Is there another Duke of Weatherstone?" Geri was secretly enjoying this. She glanced across the room and could see Thomas engaged in a discussion with another group of people. As if he knew she was looking at him, he looked over and smiled, winking mischievously as if he was in on the joke. She wished for a moment that they were alone. She really hated these social gatherings.

"He's a bit of a womanizer," Mrs. Ponsonby, the hostess, said. "A love-them-and-leave-them type. My sister Harriet was his last victim—last winter, I believe. She wanted marriage, though, and he, of course, won't marry. So she moved on to someone more suitable."

"So I've heard, but I assure you there's nothing untoward about our relationship. We work together."

There were a few disbelieving glances exchanged.

"That's what he wants you to think and then the next thing you know he's taking you on a tour of his estate and you're in his bed."

"Oh, yes," another woman sighed. "And what a wonderful place to be."

Geri's stomach knotted and she almost choked on the glass of wine she was taking a drink from. The women she was standing with continued to talk and all she could think about was the fact that after they left here they were going to see his estate.

She refused to end up in his bed, though. She refused to get involved with another coworker. Not after what had happened to her in Glasgow with Frederick.

Only that relationship had played out similarly. Colleagues then friends and then lovers before Frederick had dumped her for another surgeon, whom he'd ultimately ended up marrying.

And she had a sickening sense of familiarity.

Was Thomas doing the same thing?

"He's never been the same since Cassandra," Mrs. Ponsonby said.

"Pardon?" Geri realized that the other ladies in the group had wandered away and it was just her and Mrs. Ponsonby standing there now.

"Thomas and Cassandra Greensby were in a relationship at least seven years ago now. After Cassandra called it off Thomas began his womanizing ways. His father was none too pleased. I think that's what caused the late duke's heart attack."

Geri rolled her eyes. "I believe it was hypertrophic

cardiomyopathy that caused it. It's when the heart tissue thickens."

The other woman gave her a confused stare. "What?"

"Never mind." Geri shook her head. "Why did she break it off?"

Mrs. Ponsonby shrugged her shoulders. "I don't know. I just know that it absolutely crushed him."

Geri felt guilty that she was being made privy to this information, which was none of her business. It was up to Thomas to tell her these things and he hadn't, so clearly he didn't want her to know. Just like she didn't tell him the reason she hadn't pursued becoming a surgeon was because of Frederick. How he'd run the surgical program and she was a coward, not facing her broken heart and not becoming the surgeon she'd always dreamed of being.

Instead, she'd taken the offer of her father.

She never wanted Thomas to know that secret shame of hers and she was sure that he didn't want her to know about this Cassandra Greensby, whoever she was.

"Excuse me, Mrs. Ponsonby. I think I'll take a quick stroll around your lovely conservatory."

"By all means, do. I'm sorry your father couldn't be here. This is where he met your dear mother." Mrs. Ponsonby wandered off. She didn't correct Mrs. Ponsonby over calling her mother "dear." There was nothing dear about her mother.

"Although your mother was a party crasher."

"So I heard." And it was nothing surprising. Her mother had often crashed big formal events. It was embarrassing really.

Geri had no real interest in knowing about how her parents had met, she knew the stories, but the more she lingered at this party the more she wanted to go back to London, back to Holland Park and her bed. Just shut the world out for a couple of hours and lock away all these feelings that were getting stirred up in her today.

The conservatory was quite extensive, overgrown with lush tropical greenery and winding paths. It was like something that should be a tourist attraction. Other people wandered along the paths, drinks in hand, as they soaked up the sun filtering through the glass.

Geri found a quiet bench where she could sit and collect her thoughts and enjoy the rest of her glass of wine in privacy.

"There you are. I despaired of ever finding you in this jungle."

She glanced up to see Thomas standing in front of her. He was grinning from ear to ear.

"Blast, I thought I was better hidden," she teased.

He chuckled. "You sounded quite like Lionel there."

Geri couldn't help but laugh at that. "Well, he's a bit of a bad influence and every time I'm in the hospital he demands to see me. He's also demanding to know when he'll get out."

"I know," Thomas groaned. "And I've told him time and time again it won't be before Christmas, but apparently that's not the answer that he wants to hear."

"I don't blame him. He said he looks forward to the King's College Choir carols every Christmas Eve. He's never missed it."

"He will this year."

"I was thinking about taking him to it," she said offhandedly. "As his physician naturally."

"He's barely out of the intensive care unit and you want to expose him to all the germs and the draughts of King's College Chapel and take him over an hour away from the hospital? I think not."

"Maybe you're right."

"Of course I'm right. I'm always right." Thomas winked.

"I've been getting quite an earful about you," Geri teased.

"Yes. I'm sure that you have," he said. "I saw you were talking to our hostess. She's a busybody."

"She told me that you're going to seduce me when you take me out to your estate."

Thomas's eyes darkened a bit. "Would you like that?"

Yes.

"Not particularly."

"Ouch." He grabbed his chest. "You don't pull any punches, do you?"

"I'm sorry."

"You're completely not, because you're laughing about it."

"I swear I'm not." She took another sip of her wine. "When can we make an exit?"

"Oh, we're not leaving anytime soon. I'm going to drag out this event as long as I can since you're been so cruel to me." His eyes were twinkling and she gave him a little shove with her shoulder.

"Mrs. Ponsonby also mentioned this is the place my parents met."

"You say that with such apathy…"

"How my mother crashed a party. I guess it's good they met or I wouldn't be here."

"And for that I'm thankful."

Geri blushed at his compliment. "It's not like it was a great romance. They had a brief marriage and went their separate ways. I was born and my father never knew about me."

"No, I guess you really don't have much sentimental value placed on where they met, do you?"

"I would if they'd actually had some kind of romantic feelings about each other, but from what I understand from my mother it was just sex that attracted her to my father.

The marriage had been spur-of-the-moment, and the lust wore out eventually, but it resulted in me. That's what she said. I don't think she loved my father much either. No love lost there. And, frankly, thinking about my parents together..." She shuddered for effect and Thomas laughed.

"Yes. I understand. I like to think I was an immaculate conception."

She choked on her wine, trying not to laugh.

"Don't laugh at me," Thomas teased.

"You make it so easy, though." She smiled at him. "I can't remember ever laughing so much in my life."

"Well, at least I'm good for something. Did you ever get your father's side of the story?" Thomas asked.

"No. What does it matter? It's in the past. You can't change the past."

"You certainly can't," Thomas said wistfully. "Only I wish..."

"You wish what?" Geri asked as he trailed off, but he wasn't listening to her. He was staring at the woman and man who had entered the conservatory. The woman was stunningly beautiful, blonde, tall. Like a model.

And she couldn't help but wonder if it was a past conquest or perhaps Cassandra.

"Let's go," Thomas said quickly. He took her hand and pulled her to her feet.

"I'm good with that. I've had my fill."

Thomas didn't say anything but dragged her along the path away from the woman and the man she was with.

"Thomas?"

He stopped and Geri almost slammed into his back. She could hear him cursing under his breath and he turned around. Geri saw the tall blonde walking toward them.

"Cassandra," he said through gritted teeth. "How very nice to see you."

"I doubt that very much, Thomas." She turned to the man who was with her. "My husband, Lord Greensby."

Thomas nodded and then pointed to Cassandra. "May I present Lady Collins."

Cassandra was taken aback. "Lord Collins got married? And to a much younger woman, I see."

"I'm not his wife, I'm his daughter," Geri said. She already didn't like Cassandra on principle for breaking Thomas's heart, but other than her looks she didn't know what Thomas saw in her. She was downright snobbish.

The more she saw of this circle her father belonged to the less she liked it. She resented it, as well. Her father put so much stock in this world and for what? She didn't like the people she met.

Except Thomas.

And he was part of this. If the rumors were to be believed, he'd almost married someone like Cassandra. Was that what Thomas really liked? If so, she needed to put an end to this because she was never going to be like one of these women. She was never going to be so vain and shallow.

Her career came first.

"Oh, yes, I thought I heard something about that," Cassandra said flippantly. "I didn't really pay much attention to it. I am really surprised to see you here, Thomas. I never thought you would be at one of these functions again."

"I'm surprised that I'm here myself, to be honest," Thomas said, sounding completely bored.

"Why are you here?" Cassandra asked, and Geri sensed a faint sense of hope in her tone.

"I promised Lord Collins I would escort Lady Collins here. He's tied up at work."

"Doctors," she said with disgust.

"Do you have an issue with doctors?" Geri asked.

"Not in particular, but it's the weekend."

"So? Life and death don't stop at the weekend," Geri countered.

Cassandra's ice-blue eyes narrowed on her. "You're quite passionate about medicine."

"I'm a doctor as well."

"How droll. I've never heard of an heiress becoming a surgeon."

"Have you been living in a cave?" Geri was about to hit this woman, but Thomas squeezed her hand and she took a deep calming breath.

"If you'll excuse us, Cassandra. I have to take Lady Collins back to London." Thomas didn't wait for any more polite exchanges as he dragged Geri off. She set her empty wineglass on a tray a waiter held and followed Thomas to pick up their coats in the foyer.

Only when they were outside, waiting for Thomas's car to be brought round to the front door, did Thomas finally give a sigh, which sounded like one of relief, and then he chuckled.

"'Have you been living in a cave?' That was priceless. The look on her face." Thomas grinned at her and Geri couldn't help but laugh, as well.

"Well, I mean, honestly. A lot of heiresses have careers. Why does she find it so surprising?"

"Probably because she finds it horrifying," he replied.

"That I do believe."

Thomas's car appeared and he took his keys from the valet. They climbed into the car and Thomas drove away from the Ponsonbys' home.

"How do you know Cassandra Greensby?"

"I'm surprised Mrs. Ponsonby hasn't told you."

"She did," Geri admitted.

Thomas cursed under his breath. "I thought as much."

"Well, you dodged a bullet there."

Thomas didn't respond, but his hands gripped the wheel

tightly as they drove through a small village, whipping round a roundabout before turning down another small road.

"Are you taking me back to London? I do have a lot of work," she said.

"Oh, no, we're still going to my estate, but I promise you I won't act in any untoward fashion." He smiled.

"Good, I would like to see it. Father hasn't taken me to ours, not that it's large, just a manor house in Oxfordshire, but he rents it out."

Thomas nodded. "Yes, I know. I've seen it once and it's nothing too grand. His Holland Park home is much nicer, but as he's a member of the House of Lords he also keeps his estate."

"The House of Lords is sitting next week. I don't think he'll be making it, given his condition."

Thomas's heart skipped a beat and he hoped Charles had finally told Geraldine about the angiosarcoma. "Condition?"

"His chemotherapy. I don't think he's in any shape to attend a House of Lords session."

"Of course." Thomas sighed. For one moment he'd thought she knew about the angiosarcoma. If Charles lived up to his end of the bargain she would know soon enough.

"Are you going to go?"

"Good lord, no." Thomas winked at her and she smiled.

"You're an idiot, you know that?"

"Hardly." And he laughed. "No one has ever called me an idiot before."

"No one?" she asked in disbelief.

"I believe my father often referred to me as a buffoon but that's not the same thing."

"I think you'll find it is."

"I hope you don't mind, but my family estate will be covered in Christmas decorations. I know how you hate that."

Geri rolled her eyes. "Really?"

He shrugged. "I know it was a foolish thing to ask, but I didn't want you to be surprised by the extent of Christmas decorations at my home."

"I'm actually surprised at that," Geraldine said. "I didn't think you liked Christmas too much."

"I don't, but it brings in the tourists and the trust that runs the tours is all about bringing in the tourists. They love it. They've been trying to get me to come to a Christmas event—you know, Christmas luncheon with the Duke and all that. They've been trying for years, but I haven't been very interested."

Geraldine perked up. "That sounds like fun!"

"It's not really that much fun."

She grinned at him. "Well, I think it would be. Why don't you do it this year?"

"Maybe I will…"

The rest of the drive was pretty pleasant. They wound their way through back country roads far off the motorway until they came to a long winding road with signs that pointed to Weatherstone House.

Geri had been expecting something similar to her father's estate, which she had seen photographs of. She was in no way prepared for what she was looking at as they came up the long tree-lined drive, before coming to a clearing and getting a chance to see the house in all its glory.

The house was grand. It looked like something out of a Jane Austen movie. She wasn't expecting anything like this.

"This is your family estate. You told me it was just a small estate home."

"Did I?" Thomas asked, grinning.

"This is huge."

It was definitely bigger than her father's estate. She'd expected Thomas's home to be slightly bigger, she just wasn't expecting it to be *Mr. Darcy* bigger.

"Have I seen this in a television production?" she asked.

He shrugged. "Could be. It was used for filming for some Hollywood movies in the sixties and seventies. Some period pieces, I'm not quite sure what."

Thomas drove down a private driveway that was marked for family only and whipped around to the back of the house. When he parked the car and she got out she could see several cars, and that indeed the building was decked out in Christmas flair.

Dusk was starting to settle and the Christmas lights started to come on, thousands upon thousands of white Christmas twinkle lights. It was almost magical.

"We'll be just in time for the last tour," Thomas quipped cheerfully.

"Isn't this your home? Does it matter if we're in time for the last tour? Don't I get a private one?"

"Good point," he said, grinning. He took her hand. "Come on, then, you wanted to see my house."

"You offered."

"Right. And I promise no hanky-panky."

Geri's cheeks heated as he reminded her that he'd be good, even though she actually didn't want him to be.

She followed him into the back entrance, into the private part of the home.

"This is where I stay when I come here to manage some of the land and deal with the trust that takes care of the public part of the house and operates the tours, but for the most part I'm not here. This part is pretty boring, pretty modern. This is the part my father had redone, because he lived here the whole time there were tours running. He used to attend the events arranged for Christmas—luncheons with the Duke."

From everything that Thomas had said about his father, Geri could believe him doing that. "Did your mother enjoy attending the Christmas lunches with the Duke?"

He grinned and then laughed. "Yes, she did. In fact, it was her idea to start opening up the house for tours."

They walked through a few more doors and suddenly they were in the main foyer, which held a profusion of marble, gilt and had a high ceiling with a crystal chandelier in the very center. It reminded her of the home in Mayfair where they'd attended the Christmas social event the night Zoe's pacemaker had failed.

And like in that foyer, there was a huge tree here. It was bigger than the one in the Mayfair house and it was decked out in gold, reds and greens. It was the brilliant, rich colors that reminded her of Victorian Christmases. It was overwhelming. It was like she'd stepped back in time.

Art adorned the walls, and she could tell from a glance that some of the paintings were by the great masters. The winding staircase was breathtaking, its banister covered in garlands. If she closed her eyes she could imagine a Victorian lady coming down the stairs in a wide ball gown.

"It's not much, but it's sort of home," Thomas said self-deprecatingly.

"Not much? This is amazing."

"Well, they take good care of it. Come on, this way." He led her through double doors to the dining room, which was set out as if they were expecting a Royal visit. Porcelain dishes were laid out on a table that had to be at least forty feet long. It was decorated as if there was going to be a Christmas dinner. There was a lot of holly, ivy, garlands and pine boughs, as well as poinsettias, which Thomas said came from the hothouse.

There was even a Yule log, not burning but in the fireplace.

She craned her neck to look up at the painted ceilings. The walls were papered in a deep red and the frames of the portraits were gilt. Geri wandered over to one of the windows and looked out at the extensive parkland at the back of the house, where there was a large sweeping garden with a canal pond and fountain.

At that moment it felt like she'd been transported to a different world.

"How much land does your family own?"

"Why?" he asked. "Is that important to you?"

"No, of course not. I'm just curious. This place is huge."

He laughed again. "Yes, it's a large estate. Not as big as some, mind you, but quite extensive. There's an arboretum, woods and a sculpture garden. Honestly, I don't know what's back there anymore. I think there are stables, but I'm not sure. I'm not into horseback riding, as my forebears were."

"That's interesting. Men like you usually are."

"Are you?" he asked.

"No. I never had the opportunity to be around horses. Horses were a luxury for a girl growing up in a single income home in Glasgow. I didn't even know who my father was."

"So I can say the same about you. Usually aristocratic women love horseback riding."

"Do you own horses? Maybe you can teach me."

"I own some racehorses, but teach you to ride? I'm afraid I can't do that. Would you care to see more of the house?"

"Of course," she said.

Geri followed him into a library that had a vast collection of old books. Thomas showed her some first editions... Dickens and Austen to name a few. There were books that his family had been collecting since the time of King Henry VIII.

Some books were behind glass because they were so old they couldn't be handled without gloves.

"I'm really thankful for having parts of the house put into the care of the trust and offering tours. They can take care of all this properly."

"It's too bad you can't use this room anymore."

"I can," he said. "There are certain times of the year that the house isn't open to tours. I try not to touch the books, though, especially the very old ones. I don't want to damage them. Again, I'm very thankful the trust takes care of my family's history like this."

Eventually they wandered upstairs.

He opened a door. "This is a representation of what the duchess's room might've looked like at the turn of the last century."

Geri walked into a beautiful room that was Orient themed, which had been the style of that time. There were some clothes laid out and a mother-of-pearl handled hairbrush on a dressing table.

"Was this your mother's room?" she asked.

He shook his head. "No. This is not the Duchess's room. It was a guest room when the house was private. My father kept the actual Duke and Duchess's rooms in the private part of the house, but this room was set up to look like it. This was actually my great-grandmother's room."

"So your great-grandmother used it?"

"Yes. You could call this the Dowager's room. Anyway, the trust decided to set this room up as the Duchess's room for the tours. These are just smaller than the actual rooms they represent." He opened the door. "This is the door that leads to the Duke's room."

"So he could visit the Duchess at night." Then her cheeks heated as she realized what she'd just said.

He smiled at her lazily and took a step toward her. "Why, yes, if they wanted the bloodline to continue, that is."

"I... I suppose so." Geri found it hard to breathe at the moment, standing so close to him. She could reach out and touch him. Her pulse was thundering in her ears and before she could stop what she wanted to happen, Thomas's arm slipped around her and he was pulling her tight up against him, his lips capturing hers in a kiss that sent a zing of heat through her body.

She melted into him, but the moment his hand slipped down her back she knew she had to put a stop to this now before something they both regretted happened.

He broke the kiss off before she did. "I'm terribly sorry, Geraldine. I don't know what came over me."

"It's okay," she whispered, trying to regain her composure. "It's okay."

"No, it's not. I promised you I wouldn't do that."

"Thomas, let's just forget it ever happened." And that's what she wanted to do, before his kiss made her imagine something out of a historical romance novel and Thomas coming through that door on their wedding night.

It was a silly notion, but she understood why he brought women here, and then it completely sobered her that he *had* brought other women here. She refused to fall for another bad boy. She wasn't going to be seduced by someone who was going to break her heart again. She just wouldn't let that happen.

The Duke's room was darker and more masculine than the Duchess's room. She walked around it, trying to put some distance between the two of them. She couldn't help but wonder what the real rooms looked like.

The Duke's room had dark wood paneling, heavy curtains and decor in forest green or burgundy. It was very much a contrast to the Duchess's room.

"Very dark. Is that where you got your nickname?"

"Perhaps, but I didn't have a say over the decor in here. It was the style at the time."

She didn't know what else to say but she knew she had to get out of the rooms before Thomas tried to kiss her again or, worse, she tried to kiss him.

They just stood there, staring at each other, not saying a word.

Suddenly they heard a group of people talking and Thomas dashed across the room and took her hand, leading her out of the room.

"Where are we going?" she asked.

"To another room. The tour is coming and I really don't want to be seen."

"Would they even know who you were?"

He shot her a look. "They know who I am. My portrait hangs in the portrait gallery."

Now she was intrigued. "There's a portrait gallery?"

"Of course. Every good estate has one."

"Can I see it?"

"Yes," he groaned halfheartedly. He took her down the stairs to a long hallway where every Duke and Duchess of Weatherstone's portrait hung, with his own large portrait at the very end.

The portrait was painted to match all the others. In it he was dressed in a naval uniform.

"I didn't know you served in the Navy," she said.

Thomas nodded.

Geri couldn't help but stare up at the portrait. He looked so young in it. So handsome. He still was handsome, but seeing him in that uniform made her feel weak in the knees. Thomas Ashwood had hidden depths.

"Well, it's getting late," Thomas said, interrupting her thoughts. "Perhaps we should get back to London now."

"Right. Of course. Thank you for showing me your home."

"My pleasure."

"Don't forget about our arrangement."

"What arrangement was that again?" he asked.

"That you attend a Christmas function for one of your tours."

He groaned. "I thought you'd forgotten about that."

"No, I didn't forget. I plan to hold you to it."

"Well, as long as you plan to attend my special Christmas appearance. I mean, it wouldn't be a traditional Weatherstone Christmas with just the Duke by himself."

"But I'm not a Duchess," she said, and then she realized what she'd just said and felt completely mortified.

A strange look passed across his face. "No. I guess you're not."

"No, I'm not."

And she never would be.

CHAPTER TWELVE

THOMAS STOOD IN the MRI lab, waiting for Charles's scans to come up. He stood next to Dr. Hunyadi, who was the radiologist at Meadowgate Hospital. Dr. Hunyadi was a bit put out to be called down to assess the scans, but with an angiosarcoma you couldn't always wait.

"Really, Mr. Ashwood, I can look at these later and diagnose it. You don't have to be here."

Thomas shook his head. "There's no need to diagnose it. We know what he has. I just need to see how much it's grown. I need to see these scans now. This patient is very important."

Thomas didn't really have any privileges at Meadowgate Hospital, but Charles was insistent that everything take place here, where he was getting his chemo. He did not want to be recognized and pitied at the hospital where they all worked. Which was silly, and Thomas had told him that.

Dr. Hunyadi just shook his head and Thomas ignored him. He watched Charles in the MRI tube, waiting for the scans of the heart to be produced. He wanted to see how far it had progressed since the last scan, because angiosarcomas of the heart were one of the fastest growing and rarest tumors. He wanted to make sure it hadn't spread into Charles's lungs yet, because if it spread into his lungs it was going to make surgery even more difficult.

The image began to load. Thomas leaned over the technician to watch, holding his breath as if that would have any impact on what was going on in Charles's body.

The angiosarcoma was small, thankfully, and he breathed an inward sigh of relief to see it. It hadn't spread, which made Thomas even happier, but it was still there and it still needed to come out or it would grow until Charles's heart failed.

There was some free fluid buildup around his heart, which would make things trickier. If it hadn't been for the routine scan for his stomach cancer they would never have found this angiosarcoma. Usually they were discovered when it was too late, as angiosarcomas didn't have any obvious symptoms.

When they were found it was sometimes mistaken for congestive heart failure, where symptoms were fluid around the heart and pain like angina. Even before those symptoms set in Charles could've formed an embolism that would've blocked a blood vessel and put him at risk of a stroke or sudden death.

Either way, having this angiosarcoma was dangerous to Charles, and Thomas was going to do everything in his power to save him for Geraldine's sake. To give her a chance to make amends with her father. A chance he himself had never got. A chance he'd never taken and something he regretted.

"That's a nasty angiosarcoma," Dr. Hunyadi said.

"I've seen worse," Thomas said. "Much worse."

"Still," Dr. Hunyadi said, "it's going to be difficult to get clear margins."

Thomas nodded. "I know."

And then and there that he wanted to do the surgery at the hospital where he had privileges. Their hospital. He didn't want to do it here. He wanted his scrub nurse, his tools, his team of surgeons, nurses and anesthesiologists. People he trusted to help him.

He wanted the operating theater he was comfortable in. That way he could do the most effective surgery and save Charles's life for now because even if he could get most of the angiosarcoma out there was no way he could get 100 percent of it out with a really clean border.

It was something they would have to monitor and do several surgeries on until they couldn't any longer.

He was going to have to try to convince Charles to give up his pride and vanity and have the surgery done at the proper place. And he would have to keep Geraldine away or he would have to convince Charles to tell his daughter what was actually going on. She had a right to know.

Just like he'd had the right to know about Zoe.

The tech went and took Charles out of the scanner and took out the IV filled with the contrast fluid that had been pumping through his veins so Thomas could get a look at the angiosarcoma.

"Have them sent to my office," Thomas said, handing Dr. Hunyadi his business card.

Dr. Hunyadi nodded and pocketed the card. "I will. Are you going to be doing the surgery here?"

"Why?" Thomas asked.

"I would like to observe it. I have never seen an angiosarcoma removal done before and I would like to watch."

"If Lord Collins allows you to, which I'm sure he will. He is all for education."

"Lord Collins?" Dr. Hunyadi said. "You mean the Lord Collins who is a cardiologist?"

"Yes," Thomas said.

"He was the cardiologist for my mother. He's an amazing doctor."

Thomas nodded. "He is...or he was. He's not practicing anymore."

"Who's taking over his practice?"

"His daughter." Thomas ended the conversation. He didn't really want to talk about it anymore. He didn't want to talk about Geraldine at this moment because he felt incredibly guilty about her not knowing about her father's condition.

And when he thought about her, he couldn't get that kiss out of his head.

He'd promised her that he wouldn't put any moves on her at his estate. Yes, he had taken other women there for that sole purpose in his younger days, when he'd been foolish. But in recent years he had avoided going there because when he walked through those halls all he could think about was his lonely childhood and the family he would never have.

And then he was reminded of his beloved mother and the brother he was supposed to have had.

He was reminded of his father's bitterness and loneliness, but seeing it through Geraldine's eyes had put it a new light. And he couldn't help but pull her into his arms and kiss her, like he'd always wanted to. He was falling for her. Though he didn't want to.

Don't think about her right now.

He had to put her out of his mind because he was with her father and he was about to discuss her father's cancer with him.

"Well?" Charles asked when Thomas walked into the room.

Thomas shook his head. "It's not good."

Charles sighed. "How much as it grown?"

"Just a little bit. A millimeter, but it's only been a few days since your last scan. So it's growing rapidly. I need to get in there and get it out."

Charles nodded. "Well, I'm ready. I'm sure I can get an operating theater set up here—"

"No," Thomas said, cutting him off. "I can't do the surgery here. I want my team with me."

Charles began to argue, but Thomas cut him off again. "You're not a surgeon, Charles. You're a damn fine cardiologist. You've shown me so much that I won't ever be able to repay you for, but a surgeon needs familiarity when tackling an insurmountable challenge."

"Are you saying my tumor is insurmountable?" Charles teased.

"Well, as you know, it's almost impossible to get every last bit of an angiosarcoma out. There's no way to leave clean margins in a heart."

"I know," Charles said. "I don't even care anymore if other people know at our hospital, it's Geraldine I'm concerned about."

"Why don't you tell her? You promised me if I took her to the garden party you'd tell her."

"Tell her what? That I'm dying? She knows that."

"Tell her about the angiosarcoma. People pull through stomach cancer all the time. That's what she believes. Yes, you have stomach cancer. I could see the tumor in your stomach on the MRI. It's been responding well to the chemotherapy since your last scan. You could beat stomach cancer, but this angiosarcoma... You're in for a lot of surgeries. Chemotherapy is weakening your body. The medication you're on is weakening your body. You could suffer from neutropenia, blood loss, pneumonia. Your body is about to be put through the wringer and you want me to cut open your chest and take apart your heart in a hospital I'm not familiar with. I'm not comfortable doing that, Charles. I need to be where I'm comfortable."

Charles looked sullen, but Thomas knew in that moment that Charles understood. That he had been beaten.

"Well, maybe I'll get someone else to do it."

Thomas saw the twinkle in Charles's eyes and knew

he was teasing him. "And who else are you going to get to do it? Who else is better than me? I'm the top cardio-thoracic surgeon in London. You know how many people I've worked on?"

"I know, I know."

"And who better to do surgery than a duke?" Thomas teased.

Charles groaned and rolled his eyes. "Just as arrogant as your father."

"And don't you love it."

"All right, all right," Charles said. "I'll have the surgery done at our hospital. Today?"

Thomas nodded. "If I can do it today."

"I want it done today. The sooner the better. I don't want Geraldine to know."

"That's up to you, but you're backing out on our deal. You said I could tell her if you didn't," Thomas said. "So if she asks me I'm not hiding anything from her."

"You're my doctor. Doctor-patient confidentiality."

"You're also my friend. I shouldn't even be doing this surgery. You're my mentor and I think of you like a father. You know that, don't you?"

Charles was silent, at a loss for words. "Thank you."

"So are you going to tell Geraldine?"

"If I have to."

"It's not if you have to," Thomas said. "You should. Open up to her, Charles."

"How can I open up to her when she won't open up to me? She hates me."

"I don't think she hates you."

"Maybe not hate, but she's not warm to me. We're not friends. I'm just a housemate."

"What do you expect, Charles? She lived without knowing who her father was for most of her life and then you just show up out of the blue."

"I didn't know she existed until last year. Her mother never told me she was pregnant. Her mother left me. I was brokenhearted. I never for once thought that when she left she was carrying Geraldine. If I had known I was going be a father I would've done something much sooner. I always wanted a child."

"You're telling the wrong person," Thomas said. "Tell Geraldine. Tell her before it's too late."

"Promise me something, Thomas."

His stomach sank, because he knew what Charles was going to ask him and he wasn't sure that he was able to give a promise.

"What do you need, Charles?"

"Take care of Geraldine for me. If I die, please take care of her. She has no one else."

And though he shouldn't, he nodded. "I promise."

Though he wasn't sure he was the right person to do that. How could he promise to take care of someone when his own future was so uncertain?

"You know that Christmas is only a few days away, my dear."

"I do know that, Lord Twinsbury," Geri said. He was trying everything to get her to discharge him. Only she couldn't. Thomas had to.

He *tsked* under his breath. "I told you to call me Lionel. Lord Twinsbury makes me feel ancient."

"You're not ancient," Geri said. "You're pretty spritely for seventy-three."

Lord Twinsbury groaned. "Oh, when you say that, I feel even older."

"My apologies. Now hold still so I can take your blood pressure."

"The nurse has just done that."

"Nonetheless," Geri chastised him as she wrapped the

band around Lord Twinsbury's arm and hit the button. The machine flashed a blood pressure figure that was stable but still not the best.

"How is it?" Lord Twinsbury asked.

"Stable, but you'll be in here over Christmas."

"I have never missed the King's College carols."

"I'm sorry to disappoint you, but this time you will. Your health is important."

"Stuff and nonsense."

Geri shook her head. "Lie back and try to rest. I hear you've been giving the nurses grief."

Lord Twinsbury grinned. "I don't think so."

"Behave—that's a warning." Geri picked up her chart and left his room. When she turned the corner of the intensive care unit she saw that Thomas was waiting at the end of the hall. He didn't smile at her when he saw her.

I knew it. I knew that kiss was going to make things awkward for us.

She approached him, but he still didn't smile at her in the way he usually did, and she had a sinking feeling that something had happened.

"Is it Zoe?" she asked.

"No. Zoe is fine. It's something else."

"Thomas, I thought we agreed not to talk about that kiss again," she said under her breath.

A funny expression crossed his face. "What?"

"I don't want it to affect our business relationship."

Thomas scrubbed his hand over his face. "It's not that."

"What is it, then?"

"Your father."

The blood drained from her face, but she kept her composure. "What about him?"

"He's been admitted here and he's having surgery tomorrow. He would have surgery today, but there isn't an operating theater available."

"Oh, is that all?"

Thomas frowned. "What do you mean, is that all?"

"I take it it's about his stomach cancer. Who is doing the surgery?"

Thomas grabbed her by the shoulders. "It's not the stomach cancer. He's on this floor, at the end of the hall. Go and see him. He'll explain."

Before she could grill him further about it he walked away from her.

Geri shook her head and headed down the hall. Thomas was right, her father was there. A nurse was finishing up his vitals and he was in his pajamas, an IV started already.

"Is everything okay here?" Geri asked, confused.

"Just finishing the preoperative workup, Dr. Collins," the nurse said cheerfully.

"Preoperative workup?"

"Yes, Mr. Ashwood asked for it." The nurse finished up and left the room.

"What was she talking about?" Geri asked finally. "What does she mean, Mr. Ashwood has asked for a pre-operative workup?"

"Just exactly that, Geraldine. I'm going in for surgery tomorrow," Charles said.

"Tomorrow? You're supposed to have chemotherapy tomorrow."

"It's been postponed. Thomas and my oncologist agree that this is the best course of treatment for the moment."

"To cut the stomach cancer out?" She was confused.

"No, my angiosarcoma."

The world began to spin as the words began to sink in. She knew exactly what that was and the thought of the father she just found having it made her angry.

"Geraldine, I know this isn't ideal—"

"Well, of course not. It's serious, but at least you're getting it dealt with." She couldn't deal with this. She'd just found her father and now he might die tomorrow. She had to get out of there. "I'll let you rest. You have a big day tomorrow."

"Geraldine…"

She ignored him and left his room. There were so many emotions going through her. Ones she couldn't even process. She just knew that she had to put distance between herself and her father.

A father who was about to abandon her again.

She grabbed her purse and coat from the doctors' lounge and headed out into the street. It was snowing lightly, but instead of enjoying it, like she usually did, she kept her head down and walked. She had every intention of returning to Harley Street and throwing herself into her work.

When she kept herself busy she didn't have to feel anything.

It numbed unwelcome feelings.

Only she didn't head back to Harley Street. She wandered around Knightsbridge for a few hours and then, instead of heading to Holland Park, she found herself standing in front of Thomas's Notting Hill home. She didn't know if he was home or not, but she tried the buzzer.

"Yes?" Thomas sounded agitated.

"It's me, Geraldine. Can I come in?"

"Yes," he said quickly. He buzzed the gate open and as she walked up the path he met her outside. "I've been looking all over for you."

"Why?" she asked.

"Your father said you were in a daze when he broke the news. I was worried so I went to the office, but Mrs. Smythe said you hadn't been in, and then I went to Holland Park. I was about to go back to the hospital and start over again."

"I just went for a walk. I'm fine."

No. I'm not.

Only she wasn't sure how she was processing this information.

"I don't think you are. Come inside where it's warmer." When she was inside she began to shiver and he helped her out of her coat. "You must be chilled to the bone, walking from the hospital to here. That's a long walk."

"It didn't feel like a long walk until this moment." She kicked off her shoes, her feet feeling like blocks of ice because she'd been wearing a skirt and stockings instead of slacks.

Thomas wrapped an arm around her. His body heat felt good and she snuggled up against him, shivering, while he rubbed her shoulders. Then before she had a moment to protest he scooped her up in his arms and carried her upstairs, but not to the sitting room where they had been the night before.

"Where are we going?"

"My room is the warmest. I have a gas fire going in there. Zoe was in there earlier today, but she's gone over to a friend's house for the night."

A blush crept up her neck. "Why don't we go to the sitting room?"

"Because it's being cleaned. Now, stop fidgeting so I can carry you upstairs properly."

Thomas took her to his bedroom at the top of the stairs. It was a large room and there was a sitting area, where a gas fireplace was giving off heat. He set her down on the couch and tucked a blanket around her. Geri could see he had been working. Spread out on a coffee table were scans and medical journals.

"I was doing some research, brushing up on my surgical skills and hoping I can find something that would benefit your father's surgery tomorrow."

Geri picked up the MRI scan and stared at the angiosarcoma in her father's heart. Like a monster, eating away at him. She set it down quickly.

"I'm sorry for interrupting your work. I just didn't want to be alone right now."

Thomas sat down next to her. "I don't blame you. It's a scary thing."

"It'll be impossible for you get to good margins. When I was doing my residency as a surgeon…" Then she realized what she'd been saying and the floodgates opened. She couldn't hide it anymore. Was tired of hiding it.

She was a surgeon in her heart.

She missed it and because of her training she knew what had to happen to her father and it terrified her.

"You were going to be a surgeon. I knew it."

"Yes."

"Why did you stop?"

Tears stung her eyes. "I fell in love with the wrong man, my teacher, and I thought he loved me, but… I was a fool. So I walked away from surgery and it was then I discovered I had a father and he was offering me a practice far away from Glasgow. Far away from Frederick. I ran away from my problems."

"You're not the only one," Thomas said.

"I'm not?"

"I have hypertrophic cardiomyopathy. Or at least the genetic traits for it. I ran from any form of happiness, because there's no guarantee I won't die prematurely as well."

Geri ran a hand through her hair and leaned back against the couch. "We're a right pair of loons, aren't we?"

Thomas chuckled and then reached out, his hand on her knee. "He'll be okay."

His simple touch felt so good and she recalled the way it had felt to be in his arms. How safe he'd made her feel. How good that kiss had been. She just wanted to forget everything. For once she wanted to not think about every consequence and throw caution to the wind once more.

To taste passion again.

It might not mean anything, because she was too afraid to feel love again, but she wanted to be with Thomas, wanted the Dark Duke to seduce her. She didn't want to feel at the moment, just wanted to taste passion and give in to the temptation.

She leaned over and kissed Thomas on the lips, catching him off guard, but only for a moment, and then he was kissing her back. This was what she wanted. She just wanted to feel this moment with him.

"Geraldine," he said huskily. "I don't want to ruin anything…"

"You won't." She wrapped her hand around his neck. "This doesn't have to mean anything. Please, just stay with me. Be with me."

Thomas gave in with a groan and took her in his arms and carried her over to his large bed across the room. Her pulse was racing with anticipation over what was going to happen, because she wanted this to happen. And she wanted it to be Thomas to erase the memories of Frederick.

To make her not feel anything.

She just wanted to be herself again.

They sank onto the mattress together, kissing. She didn't want any part of them separated. She just wanted to feel him pressed against her. No words were needed, because she knew that at this moment they both wanted the same thing. The kiss ended and they began to undress each other, slowly, kissing in between because they didn't want to break the connection of their lips.

Geri knew if they stopped for too long it might not happen.

And she wanted it to happen.

"I wanted to kiss you the moment I met you," Thomas whispered against her cheek. "I wanted you."

"I wanted you to kiss me too." She was terrified because the last time she had been this vulnerable to somebody, he'd broken her heart. Only she hadn't given her heart to Thomas, so there was no way he could break it.

Are you sure?

She shook that thought out of her head and let herself be vulnerable to him. There was no point in questioning the inevitable. She wanted this. Only under Thomas's smoldering gaze she suddenly felt a bit embarrassed about being naked in front of him. That she was so exposed to him.

"You don't need to hide from me," he said, as if sensing her apprehension.

They lay next to each other, both exposed and naked. She couldn't get enough of touching him, feeling his muscles ripple under her fingertips, running her hands over his skin and through his hair, but the most heady feeling was having his strong hands on her.

"I haven't been with anyone since Frederick," she admitted, embarrassed.

He tipped her chin so she was looking at him. "Don't be embarrassed." He kissed her again, his lips urgent as he pulled her body flush with his.

This was it.

This was the moment. He pressed her against the mattress. His hands entwined with hers, his body so large over hers, she felt safe.

Thomas gave her a kiss that seared her very soul. The warmth spread through her veins and then his lips moved from her mouth down her neck, following the erratic pulse points under her skin.

Geri couldn't ever remember feeling this way before. Not with anyone else. There was something different about this.

"I want you so much," she said, and she was surprised at herself for being so vocal about her desire, her need to have him possess her. She felt free. Her whole life had been about control. It had been the only way to keep the feelings out, to muddle through each day. The only way to cope with a life that had dealt with her harshly.

His body shifted.

"Where are you going?" she asked in a daze.

"To get protection. I didn't get it sooner because I couldn't think clearly with you kissing me like that."

He moved away and got protection. When he came back she trembled in his arms.

"Don't be nervous," he said.

"I'm not." And that was the truth. She wasn't nervous, but she could feel the tremendous amount of emotion welling up inside her.

He stroked her cheek and kissed her gently again. His lips gently nipped at her mouth, his hand on her breast and the other touching her between her legs. Desire coursed through her, was overwhelming. No man had ever made her feel this way before.

Not even Frederick, who she'd thought had been her most passionate love affair, but then Frederick had said she was always cold between the sheets.

"I know you want me," Thomas whispered huskily.

"I do."

He kissed her deeply as he entered her. She cried out in the pleasure of him taking her, because she couldn't ever recall feeling like this before. He was so deep. She wrapped her legs around his legs, urging him to go even deeper. To take all of her.

To completely possess her.

She felt so alive. So free in that moment.

Nothing existed but the two of them locked together in a passionate embrace. She wanted him completely as he thrust in her. It wasn't long before both of them released, close together, in shared pleasure.

When it was over he rolled on his back, holding her tight against him. She could hear his heart racing in time with hers. She'd never expected it to be like this with him. Of course she'd never expected it to be like anything with him, but the more time she'd spent with him the more she'd felt the ice around her heart thawing. The more she felt the control on her emotions slip away, the more alive she felt.

And it frightened her, because she didn't know anything else but heartache and pain.

CHAPTER THIRTEEN

THOMAS COULDN'T BELIEVE what had just happened. When he'd first seen Geraldine he'd been attracted to her, there was no doubt about it, and he'd thought about seducing her. Though he'd grown tired of that game. The chase and seduction. His reputation as the Dark Duke. He'd still wanted Geraldine. He just hadn't had any intention of pursuing it further, because there was no further for him.

Once he'd learned she was Charles's daughter and his new partner she had become off-limits. He'd never thought this day would come. He had been going to make sure this wouldn't happen.

Even with Charles's blessing.

When they'd grown closer, he'd often fantasized about holding her in his arms, just like this, because even though he'd sworn he would never let this happen, he had desired her. The more he'd got to know her, the more he'd enjoyed being in her company, the more he'd wanted her.

Since his father's death and his diagnosis he'd had affair after affair, seducing women and not thinking any more about them afterwards, but he realized now it had never been like this with anyone. Not even Cassandra, who had been his longest relationship.

Usually those seductions had taken place at their place or in a hotel. Even once in a cloakroom closet. This was the first time he'd brought someone into his home, to his room and his bed, and made love to them.

It had been so long since he'd made love to anyone.

This was something different and it scared him.

There were so many emotions churning inside him. Lying here next to Geraldine was something totally different and for one moment he got an inkling of what his father had felt for his mother.

It scared him to think of losing Geraldine because it would crush him.

No. This isn't love. It can't be.

Geraldine didn't love him. She just needed him. She was going through something emotionally overwhelming. This was just about sating the desire they both had for each other. There had been no promises made. She'd made that clear. She just wanted him at this moment and he couldn't let his heart open again. Not even to her.

Why?

He looked down at her against the pillow, her honey-brown hair fanning around her head like a halo, her body relaxed. Everything he'd just told himself seemed just like an excuse, because what he'd thought would only take once to get her out of his system made him realize that he needed more of her.

He wanted more of her. And that scared him.

As if she knew he was looking at her she opened her eyes and smiled up at him. A pink tinge flushed those creamy white cheeks.

"Sorry, I drifted off."

"It's quite all right," he said. "I'm sorry for disturbing you. You must be exhausted."

"Not totally exhausted." She smiled and then sat up. She got out of bed and picked up her clothes, pulling them on.

"What're you doing?" he asked.

"Getting dressed. I should probably get home."

"Don't you want to go to the hospital and see your father?"

She shrugged. "I saw him."

"Do you not care that your father is going to be going through this major surgery tomorrow?"

"You're the surgeon. You'll do a good job."

"Yes, but usually when people's loved ones go through surgeries like this—"

She cut him off. "There's a difference, though. He may be my father biologically but I don't know him well enough to feel the emotion you're expecting from me."

He was shocked by her cold words. "He cares about you."

"He has a funny way of showing it. He's never really gone out of his way to show me that he cares. I mean, was he even going to tell me about this angiosarcoma? He's always so secretive. He went to a hospital across town to have chemotherapy."

"No," he sighed.

"Don't loved ones usually tell their family about surgeries like that?" she asked testily.

"He didn't want you to be upset."

She gave him a disbelieving look and began to pull on her clothing. "This is the way he's always been. When he introduced himself to me last year, he said, 'Hello, my name is Charles Collins and I'm your father.' He's so formal. I don't know what he expects from me. He was never there when I needed him."

"He didn't know that you existed."

"Why are you telling me this, Thomas?" she snapped. "He should be the one telling me this."

"You're absolutely right. He should be the one telling you this. Go to him."

"Would you stop pushing my father on me? I don't need him. Just like every man in my life, he was never there when I needed him. He never supported me, he abandoned me. You should know about abandonment. Look what your father did to you."

It was like a slap across the face, but she was right.

"You're right."

"I think I'd better go," Geraldine whispered.

"Yes. Go and run away from your problems again," he snapped.

What he'd said was like a knife through the heart, when he'd told her that she was running again. Because that's exactly what she was doing, but saying it out loud stung all the more because he knew that she was vulnerable.

She didn't like feeling vulnerable.

When Frederick had made her feel this way, she'd run away from him and given up her dream of being a surgeon.

The one time she'd taken a chance and let a man in when she'd told herself not to she'd been hurt again. Thomas had hurt her.

"You don't know what you're saying," she said. "You haven't been through what I've been through."

He shook his head. "How can you say that? I've told you about my childhood. My father was bitter. He lost my mother and unborn baby brother and that was it for him. He was done. I was just a reminder of the woman he loved. He didn't want me around. At least your mother loved you."

"That's where you're wrong," she said. "My mother didn't love me. I was a nuisance. I cramped her lifestyle. I don't know why she didn't send me off to live with my father, but she never did. She liked to remind me I was a burden, a mistake. I was alone most of my childhood."

"That is no reason to run away from your father now. Make it right."

"You don't know anything," she snapped. "It's my life. I didn't ask you to be a part of it."

His spine stiffened and his face was like thunder. "Is that how it's going to be, then?"

"Yes," she said.

"Fine." He turned his back to her, closing her out, and she knew she'd ruined her chance with him. She knew she'd ruined everything and there was no going back, but Thomas didn't know what he was talking about. He was meddling where he shouldn't.

She couldn't make up with her father. The anger she carried for him was still there, although buried. She'd been alone for so long. She didn't know how to be anything else but alone.

Maybe you didn't realize how lonely you were.

"I'm not the only one running away, you know. You use your father and your heart condition as an excuse to run from any kind of attachment. To push people away. You're no better than me. You just don't want to admit it."

He didn't acknowledge her.

Stubborn.

She let herself out of Thomas's home and wandered down the street towards Holland Park. She only walked for a bit until she decided to take a taxi back to her father's home.

She just had to put it all out of her mind. She shouldn't have slept with Thomas. That had been a huge mistake. They were supposed to be just business partners. That was it, but she'd let him through her barriers. He'd made her feel and having emotions that weren't controlled was a dangerous thing indeed.

As she walked into her father's home it was empty. Strangely empty. Even though there had been times over the past couple of months that her father had been working or out with friends he had always come home.

Her mother would go out sometimes and not return for days.

She'd gotten used to having someone around. She just hadn't realized it until now, in this moment. She'd gotten used to his presence without even knowing it. Wandering into the sitting room, she walked around aimlessly, staring at all the photographs of family members she didn't know and who had been long gone before she'd ever come into the picture. Pictures of her father when he'd been young. Then she saw it. A picture she'd never noticed before.

A picture of him and her mother. Happy.

She picked up the frame and felt something taped to the back. It was a letter that was marked "Return to sender." It was from her father to her mother and was addressed to her mother's home in Glasgow, the home she'd grown up in, but scrawled in red ink on the front of the envelope was, "Moved, no longer lives here."

Which had not been true.

Geri set the letter back down because it was not her business to read it, but she couldn't help herself. She opened the letter and read what the words said. Tears began to stream down her face as she realized the letter had been sent just before she was born.

And her father was begging her mother to come back to him. How much he loved her. How he didn't care that she wasn't part of his social class. He wanted to be with her, only her, and that there would be nobody else.

Which was true. Her father had never remarried. Or had another romance.

Why did her mother send the letter back? If she had just opened this letter...

Geri shook her head. No, her mother had never loved her father. She'd made that clear. She had no interest in him, or Geraldine for that matter.

As she looked in the mirror above the mantel she didn't see much of her mother in herself, but she did see her father. His eyes, the color of his hair back then, his mannerisms, and she realized that he too had shut out emotions.

Lived without feeling.

And she realized that she was throwing away the opportunity to get to know her father. Maybe if she gave him half a chance she would know what it was like to have a parent love her. She decided she was going to go to the hospital and make things right.

She had to make it right with her father.

Thomas was still fuming over his fight with Geraldine, but really what had he expected? He knew better than to dabble in the affairs of the heart.

Perhaps she is hurt too.

He shook that thought out of his head as he marched into the hospital in the middle of the night and headed up to see Charles.

He had to swallow all his emotions at the moment. He couldn't let them interfere right now, because he respected Charles too much to let him know what had just happened. His feelings aside, he had to work with Geraldine in a professional capacity. And he planned to keep it that way.

No matter what his emotions were telling him.

Charles was sitting up in bed. Pensive.

"Charles?" Thomas said, unwinding his scarf as he came into the room.

"An operating theater has become available. I want you to do the surgery. I am prepared for it. I've fasted. I'm ready."

Thomas scrubbed a hand over his face. "Are you certain?"

Charles nodded. "I am. It's growing too fast and I need it out. Or as much as you can get out."

"Have you spoken to Geraldine about this?"

"I tried to call her a moment ago, but there was no answer."

Not surprising.

Geraldine had made it quite clear that she didn't have much affection for her father and he wondered if she had any emotions at all.

"Do you still want to proceed with the surgery or shall we wait until you get hold of Geraldine?"

"No, there is no point of waiting. She'd approve."

"Yes."

Geraldine wouldn't want this surgery not to take place. Detached as she was from her father, she was logical when it came to medicine.

"If you're sure."

Charles looked at him sternly. "Very sure."

Thomas nodded. It would take a couple of hours for him to get his team ready and to call in his favorite scrub nurse, who he had no doubt would come in and assist him in this surgery as she was fond of Charles as well.

He was uneasy about operating on Charles when nothing was settled between him and his daughter, but what choice did he have? Charles was his patient and insisted on having the surgery done.

It was also in Charles's best interests to attend to the angiosarcoma as quickly as possible. He walked into the surgeons' locker room and began to change out of his street clothes. He tried to focus solely on the surgery that was about to take place, like he would do for any other patient. The only difference this time was he couldn't help but think of Geraldine.

The hurt it would cause her if her father died before she had made peace with him. It was something he had to bear daily.

Charles might not survive this surgery. Something the

three of them were all aware of, but they hadn't spoken to each other about. After he was in his scrubs he grabbed Charles's file and went over the angiosarcoma images. He closed his eyes and tried to picture it in the heart, planning where he would cut and how he would he would attack it.

"Mr. Ashwood?"

Thomas turned to see his scrub nurse, Margaret, standing there.

"Yes, Madge?"

"Dr. Collins is in the operating theater and ready."

Thomas nodded. "Thank you, Madge. I'll be there in a moment. Take the scans and make sure they're loaded somewhere I can see them."

"Of course, Mr. Ashwood."

Margaret left and Thomas closed the file. He put on his scrub cap and readied himself to head to the operating theater.

"Where is he?"

Thomas turned around to see Geraldine and even though it had only been a few hours and she had hurt him so much, his heart skipped a beat. She looked done in, apprehensive, by the way she was wringing her hands. He'd never seen her like this before.

"Your father is in the operating theater and being put under at the moment."

Geraldine worried her bottom lip. "You're going to do the surgery now?"

"I am. A theater became available and your father was insistent on it being done now."

She nodded. "He didn't call me."

"He did. You weren't…home."

A flush tinged her cheeks, because only a couple hours ago they'd been together and then the unpleasantness had occurred. The argument that still stung.

"I need to speak with him."

Thomas shook his head. "I wish I could allow that, but you know that's not possible. He's being put under general anesthesia and I can't have you contaminate the sterile field."

"But I—"

"You what?" Thomas snapped.

Tears stung her eyes and she brushed them away quickly. "It can wait."

Of course it could.

He was hoping she was going to show some kind of emotion. Admit that she cared for her father. Cared for something. Even cared for him. But instead she stood there with no expression on her face. Just a few tears.

"I have to go now."

He turned his back on her.

"Thomas?"

He turned around.

"Please. Save him." It was sincere. She was asking for another chance, the chance he'd never got with his father, and his heart melted.

He couldn't help but smile at her and he did something that he'd never done in his entire career as a surgeon. "I promise."

And he hoped that he could keep his promise to her.

He planned to keep that promise to her. He would make sure Charles pulled through this surgery.

As he scrubbed in he couldn't help but think of the chance he hadn't had with his father to say what he'd felt. How he'd hated that he had been isolated as a child after his mother had died. How his father had resented him.

How lonely he'd felt.

How he'd needed his father, but had never had one.

Even Zoe hadn't really had their father, though he'd tolerated her more, but she had been so young when their father had died. She didn't have the same feelings of disconnection or resentment that he had. Instead, he'd stepped up to be the father theirs had never been.

Charles had wanted to be a father, but had been denied that chance and Geraldine wasn't giving it to him. Wasn't allowing him to be a father. So he was damn well going to make sure that Charles pulled through so that there was a chance for them.

When he entered the operating theater he was gowned and gloved. His instruments were ready and Margaret was waiting for him.

Charles was under general and everything was ready to go.

He took a calming breath and closed his eyes. He emptied his mind of everything. Including Geraldine. All he could see was the heart, the organ he knew so well, visualized for him in his mind.

And he thought of where the angiosarcoma lay.

He knew where to begin the point of attack.

"Scalpel."

Margaret handed him the scalpel and he went to work. As he worked he could feel he was being watched and glanced up at the gallery. He didn't think that anyone would be in there because it was the middle of the night, but Geraldine was there. Standing, watching pensively.

He nodded at her in acknowledgment.

And she returned the nod.

Even though she shouldn't be watching her father undergoing this surgery he knew there was no way she was going to budge. Geraldine was here for the long haul.

As was he.

He turned his attention back to Charles and put Geraldine out of his mind. He told himself she wasn't even there, because right now he had to stay focused. He was going to save his friend, his mentor. The man who was a bit of a father figure to him. If he failed in this endeavor he knew all would be lost with Geraldine. Even though she'd hurt him deeply with her words, she'd been right to say them. Just as she'd run from surgery, he too had run from finding any kind of happiness. From allowing any kind of love to enter his heart, using the excuse of his father and a genetic condition to decide his destiny.

They were the same, try as he may to deny it in his own mind. He was in love with Geraldine Collins, because she saw him for who he really was when he couldn't even see it himself.

CHAPTER FOURTEEN

"DR. COLLINS?"

Geraldine woke with a start, her body cramped because she'd been curled up in a chair in the gallery. The last thing she remembered was watching Thomas performing surgery on her father. It had been a long surgery, as most heart surgeries of this nature were. They had been trying to remove a tumor that was growing inside her father's heart.

She'd watched for as long as she could, all the while praying her father would pull through.

Geri had watched as Thomas's hands had worked so diligently to save her father.

To give her a second chance of knowing her father. There was beauty in Thomas's surgical skill, the way he moved. She hoped one day to return to the operating theater herself. She had to stop running. She had to try again.

Thomas had been working so hard to save her father when she had treated him so poorly. And when she'd been standing in her father's home last night, staring at the words he'd written to her mother, she'd realized that she was doing exactly the same thing as her mother had done to her father. She had been pushing him away.

Geri had never thought she was like her mother. She'd striven so hard not to be like her mother, yet she was.

When it came to matters of the heart she was just as cold and emotionless as her mother was.

She'd come to the hospital to make amends and when she'd seen her father wasn't in his room, it had been more than she could bear. And she'd been worried that she'd missed her chance. So she'd begged Thomas to make a promise she knew it was impossible to keep, because one never knew when doing a surgery of this nature. It was a promise surgeons didn't make to patients, yet he'd looked down at her, his expression soft, and he'd made her that promise.

"I promise."

Thomas's words ran through her head during the surgery and she'd closed her eyes, praying that she would be given a chance to right the wrongs she'd done.

She'd blown it with Thomas, but if her father pulled through there was a chance that she could make it right with him. Geri swore she would make it right.

"Dr. Collins, the surgery ended an hour ago."

"What time is it?" Geri asked the nurse who had come to wake her.

"It's seven in the morning. There's a class of medical students coming in and they need the gallery. They're going to view a cholecystectomy."

She got up. "I'm so sorry. I didn't mean to delay the surgery."

The nurse smiled. "It's quite all right. You haven't delayed anything."

"Where is my father?" she asked with some trepidation.

"He's in the intensive care unit."

Relief washed over her. "He survived?"

The nurse smiled. "He did."

Geri got up out of the chair and headed out of the gallery. Her body was stiff and she felt a bit like death warmed over, but she had to go and see her father. She was going to start making things right.

When she got down to the intensive care unit she paused at the door. Thomas was in the chair, charting. Her father was unconscious and pale. As if sensing her presence, Thomas looked up from his charting and stood up.

"Geraldine, are you...? How are you?" he asked. "I was wondering where you were."

"Fine. I was sleeping in the gallery."

He winced. "That sounds uncomfortable."

"It was." She worried her bottom lip. "How is my father?"

Thomas nodded. "He's good. He did very well coming off bypass."

Geraldine nodded. "Good."

"I was able to removed ninety-five percent of the tumor. The five percent that's still there is small and we'll start a very intensive chemotherapy and radiation routine. He'll probably need more surgery, but perhaps we can slow the growth of the angiosarcoma."

Tears stung her eyes. "That's...that's wonderful."

Thomas nodded. "I've finished his charting. I'll...leave you with him."

As he walked past Geraldine grabbed his hand. He glanced over his shoulder at her as she held it tight and whispered, "Thank you."

He didn't say anything, just nodded and then left the room.

Geraldine's knees knocked together and she took the chair that Thomas had just vacated. It was so quiet in the room, except for the sounds of the monitors, but she never really noticed those sounds. Those sounds were comforting to her.

Those sounds meant that her father was still alive. That she would have another chance with him. A chance to make it right and get to know him. She took her father's hand in hers and squeezed it tight.

"I read the letter," she whispered. "The one that's taped behind the picture of you and Mother. I'm sorry, I think I misjudged you."

Her father's eyes opened. Just briefly, then they met hers and lit up with recognition. He tried to open his mouth to say something, but winced.

"Don't try to speak," Geraldine said.

"How?" he croaked out.

"How did it go?"

He nodded very slightly.

"It went well. Thomas got ninety-five percent of the angiosarcoma. You'll need intensive chemotherapy and radiation therapy, but it went well."

Her father smiled and relaxed, squeezing her hand.

"I'm sorry, Father," she whispered.

His eyes opened again, a questioning expression on his face.

"I was cold to you. I was angry with you for not being there all those years."

His expression softened and he opened his mouth, but she shook her head.

"Don't speak. Please, just let me talk. I know you didn't know about me, but that didn't matter to me. I just pushed you away, but I know... I know how Mother hurt you. You tried to reach out to her. You sent her a letter to a Glasgow address, that's where I grew up. We were there. She lied to you and me. I swore I would never be like her, but I was. I was pushing you away when you were just trying to get to know me. I don't know you, but I want to. I want a chance before it's too late. I'm so sorry, Father."

She leaned her head on his arm and let the tears pour out of her. His hand touched the back of her head, stroking her hair, and when she looked up she could see tears in his eyes too.

"I'd like that very much, Geraldine."

Geri clung to her father. She was going to make things right.

She was going to make everything right in her life, no matter how long it took.

Geraldine took a seat in Lord Twinsbury's reserved first-class train compartment. He'd graduated from Cambridge and had a long-reserved standing seat at King's College Chapel for their Festival of Nine Lessons and Carols that was held every Christmas Eve.

She hadn't particularly wanted to leave London and come to Cambridge for this, but her father and Lord Twinsbury had insisted that she attend.

"Not everyone gets a chance to attend," her father had argued. *"Lord Twinsbury is offering you one of his seats. Take the chance and go. It's spectacular."*

Her father was going to be in the hospital over Christmas. She was going to be spending Christmas morning at the hospital with him. And since she was going to be alone on Christmas Eve, she'd decided to take her father's advice and attend the Cambridge event.

Since Jensen had the night off, she was taking the train to Cambridge and planned to stay overnight at a small inn near the university. Jensen had promised to pick her up tomorrow morning because he had plans to visit her father too.

So she sat, watching the world pass outside her train window. People bustling along the platform, carrying brightly colored packages and greeting loved ones. She envied them.

Though she had her father now. And that was something. She was going to make the most of every moment they had.

"Is this seat taken?"

Geri was surprised to see Thomas standing in the doorway of Lord Twinsbury's first-class compartment. He didn't wait for her to answer and shut the door, sitting across from her.

Her heart skipped a beat, seeing him. There was so much she wanted to say to him but she didn't know how to say it. "I don't believe it's taken."

Thomas grinned. "Good."

"I thought you didn't like to come to these things?" she said as he leaned back against the seat. "I mean, this is going to be televised."

"Yes, well, I thought I would make an exception this time."

"Really?"

Thomas nodded. "Yes. It's time to start making a big deal about Christmas, I think."

"I'm very glad to hear about that." She nodded. "It's the one time of year I truly love."

"Yes. I know." He grinned. "You've made amends with your father, I see."

"I have," she said. "And with myself. I'm afraid I'm going to have to find our practice a replacement cardiologist."

"Why?" He frowned.

"I'm going to return to surgery. I'm going to be a surgeon. I only had one year left. I've let fear drive me for so long. I've pushed people out and run away when things got too hard. Just like my mother always did. I suffered for it. I wanted to be a surgeon and I really see no other choice. I want to be a surgeon."

Thomas smiled. "I'm pleased. I knew you wanted to be a surgeon."

"Yes, well, don't look so pleased with yourself."

"I think I will gloat a bit." He grinned.

"You were right about it all and I'm... I'm sorry for the things I said. I was completely wrong about you."

"No, you weren't," he said, and she was confused.

"Of course I was."

"No, because I did the same as you. I pushed you away."

"I think we both pushed each other away," she said.

"I think I pushed the hardest. I was scared of a genetic condition that might not amount to anything. I pushed people away, afraid to suffer loss like I did as a child. I guess I didn't feel worthy enough to have love."

"You have Zoe," she whispered. "You have plenty of love."

Thomas nodded. "I do, but I don't have you."

The words caught her off guard and she wasn't sure that she'd heard him correctly. "Pardon?"

"You, Geraldine. It's you I love. You saw me for more than my title, which was all Cassandra and the women I had brief affairs with saw. My father saw me as a reminder of my mother. Only Zoe could see me for who I really was, but then you came along and you were so unimpressed by everything. All you saw me as was the surgeon. The only thing, except for my sister, I loved and had left in this world. You saw me."

"I didn't see you, Thomas. How could I when I didn't even see myself?" Her voice hitched.

"You did, though. You pushed through the walls I'd built for so long to protect myself. Just as I broke through yours." He took her hand and placed it across his chest. "You are my heart and soul. You made me realize I want to risk it all. I love you."

A tear escaped from her eye and rolled down her cheek, because there was no sense in hiding what she felt. "I was so afraid of love. No one ever loved me. I thought Frederick did, but I was wrong. I didn't know what love was until I met you. You infuriating man. I love you too."

Thomas moved beside her and touched her face gently, wiping away the tears slipping down her cheeks and kissing her in the private compartment, while people buzzed and milled about outside, trying to find their own trains or seats.

Normally this would bother her, people seeing her like this, but she didn't care as she clung to Thomas. She'd thought she'd ruined her chance with him. Her chance at love, because she'd been so afraid to chase after it.

So afraid that what had happened before would happen again.

He was, after all, a notorious seducer of women, but the only thing he seduced at this moment was her heart.

It belonged to him completely and she had to take the chance and let him hold a piece of it, damaged as it was, because she was certain that only his love could mend it, and that she would mend his as well.

"I love you, Lady Collins. I am a bit put out that you're leaving our practice high and dry without a cardiologist and I think Zoe will be most displeased that you won't be her doctor anymore, but she'll understand."

"I am sorry about that, but I'll help you find a suitable replacement. I still have a share in our practice, you know."

He nodded. "I hope you won't be returning to Glasgow to finish your surgical residency."

"No, I have too much in London to leave. I'll be doing my residency at St. Thomas Aquinas."

"Well, don't think you'll be getting any favours from the surgeon you'll be learning from. Even if you are sleeping with him." He winked.

"I wouldn't dream of it." She kissed him again. "Merry Christmas, Your Grace."

"Happy Christmas, Lady Collins."

EPILOGUE

Christmas Eve, one year later

"You're shaking," her father remarked.

Geri turned and took her father's hand as they sat in the back of her father's car on their way to Buckinghamshire, where she was marrying Thomas and becoming the Duchess of Weatherstone.

She'd wanted to spend the night before her wedding in Holland Park with her father, who was doing well, given that he was still undergoing chemotherapy. He'd lost his hair, but Geraldine had told him that it suited him.

He'd been happy to learn that she and Thomas were engaged and getting married, but he'd tried to get out of walking her down the aisle because he hadn't wanted to scare anyone with his looks. Chemotherapy was taking its toll, but he still looked quite debonair in his grey morning suit.

"I look like a billiard ball."

"No, you look like Daddy Warbucks," Thomas had teased.

"I assure you I'm nowhere near as wealthy as Daddy Warbucks," her father had groused.

"You're handsome, Father, and you'll look great walking me down the aisle."

"Are you cold?" Her father asked, concerned. "I think you should've picked a dress that was warmer."

"I think she looks great," Zoe commented from the other side of Geri's father. Zoe had insisted on spending the night before the wedding at Holland Park as well, as she was the bridesmaid.

Her father smiled at her. "You were the one who picked out the wedding gown. Did it really have to show so much skin?"

Geri laughed. "I like the dress too." And she did. It was simple but gorgeous and even though her father said it showed a lot of skin, it was covered with lace. It reminded her of the gown Grace Kelly had worn for her wedding, which had always been her favorite.

A dream dress of hers. She'd never thought she would get the chance to wear a wedding gown, but there she was, sitting in the back of her father's car, which Jensen was driving to Weatherstone House to marry Thomas.

The love of her life.

"I'm nervous, that's all. I just wanted a simple wedding."

Her father patted her hand. "You're marrying the Duke of Weatherstone. A small wedding is out of the question."

It had been a whirlwind year. She'd finished off her residency and was now a surgeon working at St. Thomas Aquinas. Thomas and her father had found a suitable cardiologist to replace her at the practice and she enjoyed working in the hospital, doing surgeries far more often than Thomas, still in the private practice.

The car turned up the long drive and Geri took a deep breath. She was terrified, but she'd never wanted anything more in her life.

She wanted Thomas and wanted to spend the rest of her life with him.

"There's press here!" Zoe exclaimed.

Geri cursed under her breath. "Why is there press here?"

"He's the Duke of Weatherstone," her father reminded her.

"What have I got myself into?" Then she laughed with her father.

"Did your mother respond to your invitation?" he asked.

"No. She won't be coming. She's on a cruise at the moment." Geri may have been able to repair relations with her father, but she doubted whether she and her mother would ever have any kind of relationship. It was clear that her mother didn't want anything more to do with her. It hurt, but Geri had long ago moved on.

Geri wasn't going to live a life like her mother's.

She was happy for the first time in a long time and she intended to keep it that way.

Jensen parked the car in front of the chapel that was in the grounds of Weatherstone. It was a small church, so by society standards their wedding *was* small. Jensen got out and opened the door to help Zoe out in her aubergine-colored bridesmaid's dress.

"Are you ready?" Charles asked.

"Yes." Her voice shook. "More than ready."

He nodded and climbed out the opposite side, waiting for her as Jensen held out his hand. She took it and he helped her out.

"My lady," Jensen said, beaming.

Geri gave him a quick peck on the cheek while Zoe fluffed out her dress. She took her father's hand and he led her up the steps, only now he was the one shaking.

"Are you all right, Father?"

He nodded and placed his top hat on his head. "I've just found you and now I'm giving you away. That town house will be quiet now."

Tears stung her eyes and she kissed her father. "I'm only a short tube ride away in Notting Hill."

Her father groaned. "The tube? Honestly? A duchess riding on the tube?"

"I'm not a duchess yet," she teased.

"You will be in a moment," he said. "Come on, then."

The doors opened and Zoe started down the aisle. Geri took a deep breath and held her father tight as he walked her in. All she could see for the first few moments was a sea of brightly colored hats. Which was overwhelming as everyone stood up. Her father took off his top hat and tucked it under his arm, while she clung to the other one.

Then she focused her attention to the end of the aisle and saw Thomas standing there in his morning suit, his hands clasped behind his back, grinning from ear to ear. When his gaze landed on her, she almost melted.

That twinkle in his eyes, the secret smile was just for her. It was hard to believe that a year ago that same smile and same twinkle had made her want to run in the opposite direction. Now she was running toward him.

She knew the vicar was saying something, but she couldn't quite hear him as her father passed her hand to Thomas and took his seat in the front pew of the church. Thomas just beamed at her and she couldn't believe how lucky she was.

Love was something she hadn't ever believed in after her mother and Frederick had toyed with her heart, but Thomas had made everything right.

The final vows were made and the rings slipped on their fingers.

"You may now kiss the bride," the vicar said.

Thomas leaned in and kissed her on the lips.

"I love you," she said, as he took her hand and led her down the aisle.

"I have a surprise for you." Thomas led her out of the chapel and across the lawn to the house.

"Why are we going in here? We have to have pictures

in the arboretum first," she said as he brought her into the main hall. The house and estate were closed to tourists today, thankfully. Thomas covered her eyes and led her inside.

"Now you can look," he said with excitement.

Geri gasped as "Christmas trees! Two of them."

There were two thirty-foot Christmas trees in the foyer, one on either side of the large staircase. They were covered in twinkling lights and brightly colored baubles that accentuated the deep cherry-red of the wood.

"What do you think?"

"It's gorgeous. You did this?"

He nodded. "Guilty."

"But you don't like Christmas trees."

"I can change my mind."

"Last year you compared them to Pomeranians, wasn't that it?"

Thomas groaned. "I did, but that was last year and this is a gift for the new Duchess."

"Oh, no," she gasped.

Thomas cocked an eyebrow. "What's wrong?"

"I'd just got used to the idea of being Lady Collins and being way down on the list of succession."

"Yes, and…?"

"Now I'm going to be a duchess, and any children we have are going to be further up the list than me."

"Children?"

She laughed. "Yes. I assume you have to continue your line."

"Can we wait a bit on the children, though?"

"Perhaps." She wrapped her arms around him. "I suppose I have to get used to being called Your Grace. No going back now."

He kissed her possessively. "No, there isn't. And just to show you there is no going back I have something else for you." He reached into his pocket and pulled out a flat velvet box.

"What is it?" She took it from him.

"As you're the Duchess of Weatherstone this belongs to you now."

Geri opened the box and gasped at the stunning diamond necklace and earrings that lay against the silk inside the box. "They're beautiful."

"They were my mother's. They're quite old." He reached into the box and pulled out the necklace. He stepped behind her and she felt the weight of the diamonds on her neck and a kiss against her pulse point after he finished clasping it. "They have been worn by every Duchess of Weatherstone since the time of James III."

"It's beautiful," Geri said, touching it. "It makes me nervous to have something so old in my possession."

"Well, if you had accepted Lord Twinsbury's proposal…"

"You're impossible."

"What do you think of your gifts?" Thomas asked as she wrapped his arms around her again.

"I love them."

"Is that all?"

"I love you too, Your Grace."

"And I you. Thank you for bringing me back to life and mending my heart."

"Thank you for mending mine." She grabbed him by the lapels of his morning coat and kissed him before the wedding guests came in to enjoy the wedding brunch.

After the brunch they would head off to Greece, to escape the winter.

"I can't wait to get you to Greece and get away from all of this."

"I thought you were a Christmas convert?" she asked.

"I am, believe me I am, but I'm looking forward to some

sunshine and spending many a hot night with you wrapped up in my arms, until we head back to reality."

"That sounds divine, Your Grace. Absolutely divine."

She'd tell him about the baby later.

* * * * *

LET'S TALK
Romance

For exclusive extracts, competitions
and special offers, find us online:

f facebook.com/millsandboon

🐦 @MillsandBoon

📷 @MillsandBoonUK

Get in touch on 01413 063232

For all the latest titles coming soon, visit
millsandboon.co.uk/nextmonth

JOIN US ON SOCIAL MEDIA!

Stay up to date with our latest releases, author news and gossip, special offers and discounts, and all the behind-the-scenes action from Mills & Boon...

 millsandboon

 millsandboonuk

 millsandboon

It might just be true love...